CHILDREN
OF THE
EARTH

CHILDREN OF THE EARTH

A MOTHMAR NOVEL
BOOK TWO

AMANDA AULER

SPIRELIGHT
PRESS

SPIRELIGHT
PRESS

964 High House Rd #3042 Cary, NC 27513
Copyright © 2023 Amanda Auler
All rights reserved. No portion of this book may be reproduced in any form without permission from the publisher, except as permitted by U.S. copyright law.

For permissions contact: amanda@authoramandaauler.com

www.authoramandaauler.com

Character Illustrations by Nemaiza Rhayne

Map Illustrated by Rebecca Paavo

Chapter Illustrations by Sarah Cools

Edited by Eva Campney
Cover by Fantastical Ink
Type set in Garamond EB

ISBN:

979-8-9865922-3-7 (paperback)
979-8-9865922-4-4 (hardback)
979-8-9865922-5-1 (ebook)

10 9 8 7 6 5 4 3 2 1

Library of Congress Control Number: 2023912146
Printed in United States of America
This book is a work of fiction. Any references to historical events, real people, or real places are used fictitiously. Other names, characters, places, and events are products of the author's imagination, and any resemblance to actual events or places or persons, living or dead, is entirely coincidental.

ALSO BY Amanda Auler

The Mothmar Trilogy
Daughter of the Sun
Children of the Earth
Son of the Stars
Tales of Mothmar: A Short Story Collection

Anthologies
Amidst Fury and Valor by Twenty Hills – "Little Rider"

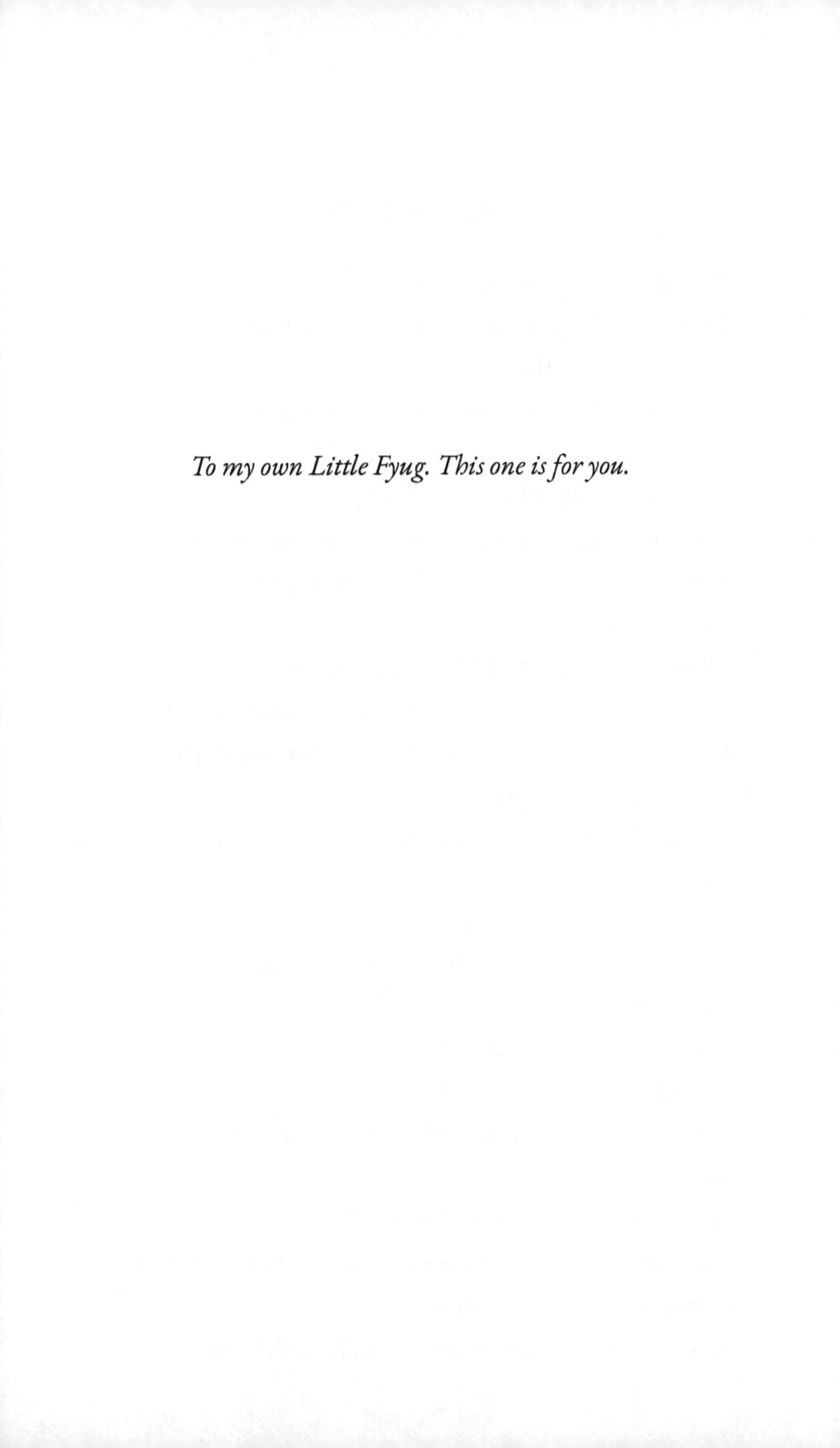

To my own Little Fyug. This one is for you.

GLOSSARY

Austur – The easternmost village

Bardagis – The illegal sport of setting two Gifted people to fight against each other

Cohsta – The basic monetary unit of certain regions of Mothmar

Darlöh – A state of unnatural sleep

Dauda – A Mothmarian ceremony to honor the dead

Eldfall – The tallest mountain bordering the eastern side of the valley

Eldur – Someone with Heitt skilled enough to wield flame

Endirinn – The city at the very northeastern tip of Mothmar

Fera – The Gift, given by the Stars, that allows the Gifted to tether to an inanimate object

Finnevel – A device used to enhance one's Gift over great distances

Häfa/Häfan – A Mothmari curse

Heitt – The Gift, given by the Sun, that allows the Gifted to warm and heal

Hekla – A volcano, also a Mothmari curse

Hytast – The meeting hall

Lóthkol – The advanced school that focuses on Gifts

Mothmar – A country

Rána – Someone born without a Gift

Sháskol – The primer school where students fulfill, at least, their first six years of schooling

Sodur – The southernmost village, Pallah's home

Takanah – A city east of the valley

Taka Reu – Worship of The Mother, the Dark Gifts and those who practice them

Tala – The Gift, given by the Moon, that allows the Gifted to tether to an animal

Thonethren – A city north of the valley

Vestur – The westernmost village, Solyana's home

GIFTS

Acute Fera – The ability to manipulate only one specific type of object

Acute Tala – The ability to manipulate only one specific type of animal

Bein Fera – The ability to manipulate bone

Blou Fera – The ability to manipulate blood

Broad Fera – The ability to manipulate inanimate objects

Broad Tala – The ability to manipulate all animals

Gler Fera – The ability to manipulate glass

Lakimi Fera – The ability to manipulate muscles

Malmur Fera – The ability to manipulate metal

Predatory Tala – The Gifted's aptitude is a predatory creature

Prey Tala – The Gifted's aptitude is a prey creature

Smilodon Tala – The ability to manipulate sabertooth tigers

Stein Fera – The ability to manipulate stone

Vatin Fera – The ability to manipulate water

Vior Fera – The ability to manipulate wood

Falki Tala – The ability to manipulate falcons

Fiskur Tala – The ability to manipulate fish

Fugali Tala – The ability to manipulate birds

Heri Tala – The ability to manipulate hares

Mammut Tala – The ability to manipulate mammoths

Mann Tala – The ability to manipulate man

Ugla Tala – The ability to manipulate owls

Ulfur Tala – The ability to manipulate wolves

OCEAN
KAZAN
MOUNT HEKLA
THONETHREN
THE PINES
HYTAST
SHASKOL
LOTHKOL
VATINO SEA
ELDFA
ELD PLATEAU
OUR HOME
SPRETTA RIVER
VESTUR
TEMPLE CELESTIAL
AUSTUR
SODUR
KANA'IN FOREST
SHADOW WOOD
LEIF'S CABIN
WHITE WOOD
BELJA RIVER
SKRI

MOTHMAR
MOUNT ENDIRINN
ENDIRINN
CAVE OF CRYSTALS
THE CAVE OF RED
TAKANAH
PASS
MOUNTAINS
SEA

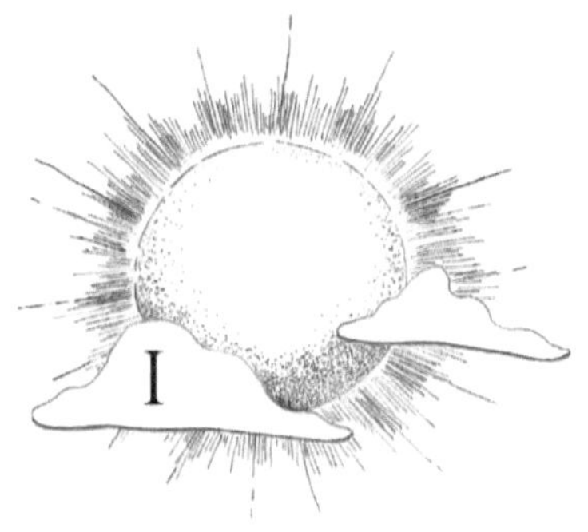

PATH OF PERIL

SOLYANA

RISING FROM THE PEAK, blackened trunks pointed toward an evening sky that churned with color. These trees, burned to husks, surrounded a group of four, hemming them in, shielding them in a circle of melted snow and dirt, safe from the world beyond.

Solyana stared down at her home in the valley below, cookfires flickering to life. Her people, the Mothmarians, would be boiling snow and bones, enough to keep their families from hunger and thirst. Did they know the mountain above had almost broken upon them?

The raging fire consuming the peak must surely have been visible from the three villages of Vestur, Sodur, and Austur. Only by some miracle had the fire not produced an avalanche, as snow had melted and buried the trails, boulders, and wildlife in its wake.

The soft glow of the lantern by her feet extended to Gamaliel's back, his arms wrapped around the boy who broke the mountain.

Or had she broken it?

Lone thought so. She blamed Solyana for the wreckage, for the loss.

Solyana could still hear Lone's angry screams as realization struck; most of their supplies had disappeared and half their sled dogs had been swept away by the storm. Their chances of survival—already slim—were now next to nothing. A wall of tension barricaded the space between Solyana and the older girl, but she set it aside, more concerned with the man on the ground. Gamaliel hadn't uttered a single word since Jonas had collapsed, having given his Gift to Solyana.

The Norlos, the ribbon of color above, began to fade as the sun warmed the heavens. The group would need to continue on. They only had one moon cycle to reach the mountain where a boy waited; the boy who tethered light and angered the Celestials to the point of causing their valley's unending cold.

Solyana turned at the sound of crunching snow. Lone stood in a patch of white somehow untouched by the flames from the previous night. Her hood shadowed her face, her hardened gaze fixed on the valley below.

"We can go back," Solyana whispered, feeling small in the shadow of the mountain. "Jonas should be with Priestess Avi."

Lone stepped beside her, the tip of her pink nose peeking out from the fur of her hood. "Even if we wanted to, we couldn't."

Solyana tucked her braid into her parka and pulled up her hood, shivering against the cold. Heavy in her chest, her labored breathing caught in the frost. They needed to descend. "It would add two—maybe three—days, at most."

"You don't understand." Lone still refused to look at Solyana, even as she spoke to her. "It's impossible." Her arm extended, black parka dusted and smeared with ash, directing Solyana's eyes to the destruction. "Eldfall is impassable behind us. Boulders and trees felled by the storm will have created caverns buried beneath the snow—tombs in waiting. We continue onward, as planned."

"Then I'll try tethering to Jonas with my Heitt. I've been practicing on Vinur. It's not so much a tether but...like I'm cocooning him. Does it feel that way when you tether to bone?"

"You what?" Gamaliel's low rumble came from the ground and the two girls turned as the hunter staggered to his feet. Jonas was wrapped in a blanket, clutched in his arms. "You tethered to Vinur?"

Lone scoffed and shook her head as she walked away, leaving them at the edge.

"What? What's wrong with—"

"You don't tether to another person's beast, Sol." Gamaliel's face held lines and shadows. He looked like he hadn't slept at all. Maybe he hadn't. "It's...violating."

"I'm sorry, Gam. I didn't know." Solyana reached out to him, but he jerked away, so fast she thought she'd burned him. She turned her hands over, but they were empty of flame or light. "*Stars*, I'm sorry. Did I—"

"No." Gamaliel shook his head, holding Jonas close to his chest. "It's fine. Just don't—don't do it again."

Don't touch him again? Don't tether to Vinur again? A sliver of cold wound its way into Solyana's belly and coiled there, waiting.

"I'm not comfortable with you tethering to Jonas, either." Gamaliel laid the boy down by the embers of the fire.

"Why not?" She folded her arms. Her new power sat with burning tension at the back of her skull.

"It's too new." He turned and mirrored her stance. "You don't know how to wield it. And you saw what happens when it's unpracticed. Until we reach a time when the need outweighs the risks, please don't."

Her skin prickled with discomfort at his words, but she was just as unsure.

"And Lone is right," Gamaliel said. "We continue on."

Feeling more enemy than friend, Solyana's throat grew tight. She knew little of Heitt theory, but something had awoken inside of her when she received the power from Jonas. When they had used it together, she had accessed some kind of ancient knowledge, an instinctual understanding which had long lain dormant. Whatever comprehension Jonas had of his Gift had fused to her soul.

"I have *some* understanding. I'm not useless."

Gamaliel eyed her warily.

"Have I lost your trust so quickly? In only a night?"

"He's all I have, Solyana." He walked away from her and Solyana's heart dropped. All he had? What, then, was she?

With a sigh, Solyana stepped close to Jonas; his placid face would have seemed peaceful, if it weren't for the unknown of when he would wake...*if* he would wake.

Just like Rhuth. Too much like her. Solyana's eyes burned at the thought of her sister, and she swallowed the emotion rising in her throat, focusing instead on the boy in front of her.

The unknown dangers of his condition tugged at her. Gamaliel wouldn't have to know if she attempted a latch. She pressed two fingers to the hollow of his neck beneath his jaw, feeling a strong pulse. The steady beat calmed her as she stroked his sandy hair away from his forehead. The brightening light of morning revealed the freckles dusting his pale cheeks.

"What are you doing?" Gamaliel's voice came out urgent and strained, his shadow falling over her as the sun made its presence known over the Hasta Mountains.

"I'm not tethering to him," Solyana assured. "His pulse is strong."

Gamaliel nodded with a grunt before turning back to his work. Solyana wished more than anything he would offer her reassurances, a hug—anything other than wary looks and cold shoulders.

They finished loading the last few items between the two surviving sleds. Jonas's sled had been consumed by flame, and only sixteen dogs remained between them, including Vinur. Solyana scratched him behind the ears before climbing onto Gamaliel's sled. The wolf's tongue lolled out the side of his grinning mouth. At least someone still enjoyed her company.

Their original plan to take the lower pass was out of the question now. After last night's catastrophe, the mountain had become far too dangerous to scale back down. They had to continue from the peak. Eldfall was the first of many mountains in the Hasta Range that rose east into greater Mothmar.

They stood at the precipice of the pass. To continue across the mountain range, they would need to carefully weave their way down through the narrow path that was hardly visible between the peaks on either side. Solyana studied a sketch on a piece of parchment held in her hand. Before gently securing Jonas in Lone's sled, Solyana had checked his pockets for more clues as to why he had erupted into a human torch. She had found several scrolls and pieces of parchment untouched by flame. Many of them seemed to be recent sketches of surrounding terrain. Lone and Gamaliel dismissed them as more of his artwork.

Solyana had other theories.

The wind whipped ice into Solyana's face, and she pulled her scarf up a bit higher. Her parka kept her warm, thanks to her mother's expert craftsmanship. She snuggled deeper into it as Gamaliel surveyed the land beneath.

The sun crept ever higher, drawing the breath from her lungs. Of all the things that had happened, it was this that was most foreign to her. The skies of Mothmar bore a constant blanket of cloud that she, until now, hadn't realized was so debilitating.

Now that she was Heitt, she could feel the rays of the Father of the Day imbue her with energy, as if there were a direct link between them. She glanced at the boy bundled at the base of Lone's sled. How had Jonas gained energy to use his Heitt before? Without a visible sun, she couldn't imagine how he would even have been able to produce flame or even warm a cup of tea.

"I wonder how Avi maintains her power," she said out loud, turning in her seat to face Gamaliel on the skis behind her.

He pulled his hair into a knot on his head, taking a breath. "I've been trying to tell you. There's something off about that woman."

"I'm not saying she's doing anything wrong." Solyana's lips twisted in thought. "I'm just thinking about Heitt. The power itself is directly linked to the sun. I mean...it's in all our history. I never paid enough attention, or had reason to. But it doesn't explain how Priestess Avi is so powerful. She warms all three villages on the coldest nights. She is keeping my sister alive in darlöh. How can she do all of that without a daily connection to the sun?"

"Maybe it has to do with her..." He glanced at Lone, who was still packing a few things into her sled, and lowered his voice. "Taka Reu."

The argument on her tongue died as Solyana turned it over. The priestess had revealed she had been using the Taka Reu as a method of wielding multiple Gifts, to keep everything running smoothly. It wasn't entirely unbelievable.

"I don't trust her," Gamaliel said with a sniff.

Solyana turned away from him. "You've made that clear."

With a shift of the sled, Gamaliel hopped off and joined Lone. He gripped her elbow, drawing her close, and spoke in her ear. Unease wormed its way into Solyana's heart as she watched them. He was probably explaining the plan, but why did he feel the need to leave her out?

She was the least experienced in tracking, hiking, and sledding. But she still couldn't help the pit in her stomach that opened at the sight of them being so close. She remembered what Lone had said to her just before they left: *he's not so much of a hermit now, though, is he?*

Gamaliel and Lone turned, a ghost of a grin on Lone's lips as they approached Solyana.

"You ready for this?" Lone asked, pulling her black hood down to reveal her cropped, near-white hair. She eyed Solyana. "You're not going to combust into flame?"

Solyana ignored her and turned to Gamaliel. "Where exactly are we going?"

Gamaliel crouched beside her, pointing to the mountain peaks. "It gets really steep here. See how it stretches up both sides, leaving only a deep crevice to pass through? The problem is, the path only touches one mountainside, so the other drops into the abyss at the base of these mountains. And let's just say, even with Lone's Bein Fera, after a fall like that, your bones wouldn't have enough substance left for her to fix them up."

"I could try melting a bit of the path, decrease our chances of sliding off the edge," Solyana suggested.

"That would cause slippage in the snow. These mountains will already be prone to avalanches after the fire." Gamaliel crossed to the other sled and laid a hand on Jonas's forehead. "Hang in there, buddy."

"I understand, but perhaps it would make the way a little bit easier?" She wasn't an item packed in a sled; she had power now and wanted to use it. "I could practice on the snow on the way down to the pass and—"

"He said no," Lone interrupted. "It's too dangerous."

Solyana turned away from the girl, not wanting to give her the satisfaction of the hurt she knew was playing across her face. Was Lone the one chosen by the Celestials? What authority did she have to overrule Solyana?

"We've got to make it through this while we still have light." Gamaliel mounted his skis. "Then we'll trace the Norlos tonight, camp, and follow through in the morning. Everyone in agreement?"

Solyana nodded, avoiding both of their gazes, and continued staring down at the pass below.

"Lead the way, Gam," Lone spoke over her shoulder as she sauntered back to her own sled.

Gamaliel clicked his tongue, and they were off, each breath taking them farther away from the valley they called home.

They began at a brisk pace but slowed to a crawl within the hour. Solyana's stomach pitched and rolled as they reached the shallow ledge leading into the pass. The skis of the sled barely fit on the path, and occasionally the edge of one ski would slip over the drop before snow-packed ground climbed up to meet it again, sending her heart into her throat each time.

An eerie silence trailed after them, broken only by the scrape of skis and the pant of dogs. Solyana felt herself holding her breath, leaning toward the mountain in silent panic.

Gamaliel and Lone stood like twin stones, determination etched on their faces, a sheen of sweat on their foreheads.

Solyana peered around Gamaliel to see Jonas's mop of hair bouncing in time with Lone's sled. He would be fine, she assured herself. He had to be fine.

Did worry prickle at the backs of their minds as it did hers? Were they as keenly aware of how much was stacked against them? Pushing it from her mind over and over only layered her worries atop one another, forming a pile teetering on collapse. But she would hold steady, in spite of it all. Between starvation and cold, at least she could combat the latter.

"No! Gamaliel! Help!"

Lone's shrill cry pierced Solyana's thoughts, shocking her after sitting so long in quiet. The noise bounced off both peaks, echoing until it was smothered by snow. Lone's lead dog had stumbled off the cliff's edge, pulling the rest of the dogs and the attached sled behind it.

Gamaliel's hand flew out to the side, latching to the animals with his tether. He mumbled something between blue lips. Solyana watched as the dogs who remained on the cliffside dug in their claws and scrambled back to the side of the cliff's face.

"He's weighing them down!" Lone screeched, uselessly gripping the reins. The dog that dangled off the edge twisted and whined as he was buffeted. The rest of the team were sliding precariously close to the edge, unable to handle the hanging dog's weight.

Gamaliel pulled his sled to a halt, jumped off, and seized the line that held the dog off the edge. Gripping the animal by the scruff of its neck, he hauled it up and over the ledge, tossing it desperately behind him. On his back, Gamaliel panted harder than the dogs surrounding him.

The snow groaned and Solyana's eyes grew wide as the ground shifted around Gamaliel, the entire section of the ledge he was lying on dropping marginally. Reaching out her hand, Solyana gripped Gamaliel's forearm as the ledge beneath him crumbled and fell. Solyana wrapped her free hand around the other side of the sled, bracing her legs against the wooden sides as her team of dogs took off on what was surely Gamaliel's command, pulling their master from a drop to his death. Lone's sled rushed behind them, barely making it over the gap in the ledge, her blue eyes round with panic.

The dogs at a full run, Gamaliel pulled himself up Solyana's arm. She gritted her teeth with pain as he finally got to the skis of his sled. He released her and she flopped back, rubbing at her shoulder.

With a guttural groan, Gamaliel threw his hands out, connecting to the animals with his tether.

The dogs, heeding his call, came to a skittering halt. Solyana grabbed the sides of the sled to keep herself from being flung out headfirst.

Shocked silence clung to them like the frost on Solyana's eyelashes.

Then she heard a rumble.

Turning her head slowly, she and Gamaliel locked eyes.

"We need to move. *Now!*" Lone shouted.

"*Hike!*" Gamaliel commanded, and their sled sprang forward.

The thunderous roar of mountains shifting filled the atmosphere around them, a cadence of their flight through the pass.

Solyana peered out from her sled, catching a glimpse of Lone and Jonas. Behind them, the mountain snow careened down like a waterfall to swallow them up in its mighty wake. She had to do something.

Solyana got to her feet and crouched, one hand gripping the wooden side, the other reaching toward the mountains above. She drew as much energy from the sun as she could without producing flame and directed the heat into the mountain itself.

The avalanche picked up speed.

"What are you doing?" Lone shrieked, snow beginning to interfere with her skis and fishtailing her sled. The dogs ran faster, breaking formation in blind terror.

Solyana released her tether, scanning the scene behind them. The avalanche was barreling straight through the pass. If she could close the pass off, block it from—

Something clicked into place. She stood tall, ignoring Gamaliel's cries that she sit down, his voice fading beneath the roar of mountain.

Shoving her palms before her, she felt the fierce power of the Father of the Day rush through her as she directed all the heat she could muster to the far end of the pass.

High on the right side, there was a shift. Snow began to cascade down the side, subverting the avalanche, redirecting it to fall between one side of the pass and the chasm on the other.

The onslaught of snow slowed behind Lone's sled, and she turned to look. When she turned back to Solyana, she grinned. "Did you do that?"

Solyana nodded and Gamaliel gave her a weak smile. "We're not out of this yet."

Turning around, Solyana spotted his source of worry. The end of the pass didn't quite meet the ground they so desperately needed to reach. Only a steep drop from mountain to snowy earth awaited their arrival.

The dogs came to a halt and Solyana turned back to Gamaliel. "If I push heat beneath us, it may drop us slowly, create a more gradual slide to get us down to the ground."

"You just redirected that avalanche," Gamaliel said softly. "I think you can handle this, if you think you can."

Solyana nodded and turned back, heart in her throat. "Steady on, then." She heated the earth beneath them.

The path began to shift and turn, their sled careening this way and that through uneven snow. The dogs tripped and stumbled, a yelp ringing out into the biting air.

"Stop!" Gamaliel shouted and Solyana closed her palms, but it didn't abate.

Eyes wide, Solyana looked back at Gamaliel. "I can't!"

The snow began to crumble beneath them, attempting to pull them into the bowels of the pass. The dogs scrambled, looking for purchase and safety.

"I can't keep them going! The snow is pulling them down!" Gamaliel's voice held a note of resignation, and Solyana couldn't bear to hear it. "We're too heavy for them. They can't pull us through this." Eyes flicking from the dogs, to the pass, to Lone behind them; her thoughts couldn't keep up with the scale of the catastrophe.

"Let them go!" The words came from Solyana's mouth, but even she couldn't believe them.

"What?"

"If we release them, they can get out of here! And maybe—" She bit her lip, eyes still searching for a way out as the ledge began to crumble away and pull them faster downhill. "Maybe we can slide down without fear of running them over."

Vinur began to whine, and Gamaliel nodded quickly. "Grab Vinur and do it!" He turned back, shouting to Lone. "Release your dogs!"

The pass descended further, crumbling and falling away, the dogs barely keeping the lead.

Solyana reached for the hatchet in its holster. Priestess Avi had entrusted her with this gift for the boy on the mountain, but she could use it in the meantime. She swung it hard, severing the slackened leads. Grabbing Vinur's harness, she pulled him into the sled.

And the dogs, free of their lines, bolted down the disappearing ledge.

Their sled plummeted, escaping the mountain's appetite, only to be consumed by the rumble of the pass below.

THE LAST SUPPER

PALLAH

PALLAH RUMMAGED THROUGH THE broken bits of table and debris in the place that had once been her home. Her fingers searched far better than her eyes could; there was no light in the house, no light on the grounds, the moon still shrouded in cloud.

The weight of her knapsack foretold a long journey away from this valley; she wouldn't be back anytime soon. Fingers brushed against an etched handle. Pallah lifted her hatchet from beneath a board of wood and slipped it through the crude leather holster at her side. She took one last look at her home. Memories from the last sixteen years lurked in the corners of each room, ready to trap her.

Leave this häfan life behind. The voice—no, his name was Erval—spoke to her. Of all the bizarre things that had happened tonight, the voice giving itself a name was the most jarring. Pallah pushed open the door and left.

Only hours before, she had found her mother unconscious, her Heitt having snapped, freezing her from the inside out. Vá-mae had healed her, and Ahren had honorably protected his family. Pallah had joined him, her intentions anything but honorable.

Leather shoes whispered over grass as Pallah remembered her use of the Taka Reu. She was Gifted with Acute Tala, only able to tether to her smilodon. But connecting to the Mother Below had empowered her with bloodlust, violence, and the need to see her father punished.

In due time, Pallah.

She shoved the thoughts aside.

The night sky shifted from pitch black to cobalt blue as she crept her way through Sodur. The people of her village had begun to stir. Though she doubted a search for Pallah Bogson was underway quite yet, she wasn't taking any chances with Chief Olafur and his council. Pallah would not serve the gods Bogdur worshiped. She would not be forced into a life of a Serviseer of the Temple.

They couldn't catch her. She wouldn't let them.

Sprinting into the mercifully thick Shadow Wood, the densest of the forests, where the trees were plentiful and towering, Pallah formulated a checklist.

First, get Tinloh. Her tether to him had severed sometime in the night. He would be frightened, but he would be fine. Secondly, find Freya, her mother's midwife. Phyllir, Pallah's mother, had confessed Bogdur's disdain for Pallah. Freya would know why. Thirdly, find a way to make sure Bogdur never hurt anyone again.

Or you could skip all that nonsense and come to me.

Pallah skittered to a halt and leaned against a tall pine, the sun just now glittering through the trees. "If I talk to you, people are going to think I've lost it."

Who cares what people think?

Lips twisting in thought, Pallah continued her trek forward.

There's only one person's opinion worth caring about.

She blinked, almost unaware of her steps.

Your own.

Pallah stopped again, pride suffusing her, warming her chest. "I have to find Freya. I'll...find you after."

See that you do. I've been waiting too long to meet you in the flesh.

Crunching through the leaf-covered forest, the edge of Shadow Wood came into view. The chill of impending winter wound its way through the trees, blowing Pallah's hair from her shoulders.

A scream pierced the morning air, inhuman and frantic.

All thoughts of Erval vanished as Pallah's feet took over, charging out of the wood and into the clearing that held Leif's home.

It was a field of red. Carnage and bodies littered the grounds surrounding Leif's cabin.

"*Häfa,*" she whispered.

A tiny, raging storm in the shape of Tinloh flew with wild abandon from one helpless rabbit to the next. Even from the tree line, Pallah could tell something was wrong with his behavior, his movements frenetic and jittery. Reaching out with her tether, Pallah attempted a latch.

She gasped and fell back against a tree, her mind whirling. He was already tethered; someone else was latched to him. Karav? Why would she do this?

Panicked and angry, Pallah barreled down the hill to the cabin and the wild beast in front of it. The rabbit, clutched in Tinloh's claws, shrieked again, forcing Pallah to cover her ears. She shot her tether out once more and this time found purchase, the other tether retracting. Pallah felt its residual presence, something dark and ragged. Nausea rocked her, the taste of blood in her mouth, blood she knew coated Tinloh's tongue.

Gagging, Pallah stumbled to the ground, taking in shaky breaths. She sent calm to him, peace. "You don't need it. You're not hungry. Leave it be."

After a few seconds of repeating this mantra, Tinloh calmed. He retracted claws and teeth from his quarry, the rabbit's side fluttering rapidly. Pallah crawled through mud and mire and wrapped a hand around Tinloh's middle. His body went limp, whether from exhaustion or her tether she didn't know, but he flopped into her arms and purred.

The cabin door slammed against the outside wall and Pallah's head snapped up to see a shirtless Leif lurch from the building. "No!" he bellowed as he stumbled about the yard. "You!" He wheeled on her, and the hair on Pallah's arms stood to attention. The man was muscle stacked atop muscle, and he was charging her like an angry boar.

"I didn't know it was happening!" Pallah scrambled backward, her shoulders ramming into the base of the cabin. "I'm so sorry! It wasn't his fault."

Leif's fists shook as his face turned a red that matched his hair, which flew in all directions like wildfire, like the blood that covered the ground. "It's your fault, or it's his." He stabbed a meaty finger in turn. "It can't be neither."

"Someone else was tethered to him!" Pallah's voice quaked.

Eyebrows shooting up, Leif gave a dark laugh. "Someone? You mean Karav?" He folded his arms across his chest, biceps bulging, a subtle reminder of the damage he could deal. "You blame her for this?"

"N-no, I just—"

Leif spun on his heel and stormed away. She kept her eyes on him as he walked about the grounds with morose respect. He sniffed and wiped his eyes before settling down to coax a fire to life.

Seeing this as a sign he had calmed, Pallah stood and made her way to him.

"I am really sorry," she said.

Ignoring her, he approached a line of clay jars at the side of his cabin. He opened one, peered inside, then replaced it. He opened the next, peered within, and brought it with him to the fire. He shoved in a hand and withdrew some red powder, which he tossed into the flames.

In response, the fire's smoke turned from a dull gray to a brilliant red as it made its way skyward. He replaced the jar and dusted his hands before weaving his way through his rabbits, counting on his fingers.

Pallah stood near the crimson pillar, watching him and waiting. For what, she didn't know. Punishment, maybe. But, she reminded herself, she wasn't the one at fault; someone else had been tethered to Tinloh. Though, if not Karav, who else could it have been?

Leif came back to the fire, a white hare in his arms, fur muddled pink with blood. Pallah wasn't sure if it was dead or alive. "Your *cat*"—he spit the word out like poison—"murdered *eight* of my hares."

"I—"

He held up a hand, eyes closed, nostrils flaring. Pallah shut her mouth. "You look like Hekla. Go inside, wash up, and get ready."

"For what?" Pallah's stomach tightened into a hard ball.

"Vil will decide what to do," he said sullenly, his eyes red and brimming. "With the both of you."

The smoke brought the Taka Reu. The troupe of misfits wound their way through the wood and into the clearing, each of them bearing expressions of worry, skepticism, and suspicion as they eyed the bloodstained grass and the cub that rolled in it. Whatever the red smoke had meant, it couldn't have been good.

Leif skinned the final hare and stuck it through with a short cooking spear before fastening it over the fire. The group of Taka Reu were gathered around a long, low table set with plates, they all began talking amongst themselves. Pallah avoided them, keeping to herself, feeling the distance between them.

Finally, Leif gave Vil a nod, who stood, a mug raised in his hand.

"We've been signaled with emergency smoke. Based on Leif and his hares, the bloodstains on the ground, we can assume what's happened. But we'd like to hear both sides of the story." Vil gestured to the red-headed man before sitting back down.

Leif wiped his hands on a blood-stained rag and stood. He was dressed now, his hair in its usual plait. "Pallah commanded her beast to murder my hares—"

"No!" Pallah launched to her feet and Tinloh hurried to her side. "I—"

"Sit down, Pallah," Vil said, though not unkindly. His cornflower blue eyes wrinkled at the corners as he gave her a placating smile.

Pallah sat down, keeping her eyes on Vil.

Leif cleared his throat. "Only when I came out here did she make him stop. Eight are dead."

Vil, brows furrowed, looked through them to Pallah. "Did you do this?"

"No." Pallah hoped her eyes conveyed her innocence. "I—I don't know what happened. I did tether him last night. I know I shouldn't have." She took a breath and surveyed the faces about the table. Issha, Karav, Kristjan, and Rolf all either avoided her gaze or stared at her with contempt. Steadying herself, she continued. "The tether snapped. It wasn't until I came to the cabin that I realized what was happening. And I couldn't stop him right away. Someone else had been tethered to him." Pallah's eyes drifted to Karav and then away just as quickly.

But Vil noticed, raising an eyebrow and glancing at Karav.

"It wasn't me!" Karav lifted her hands with a brittle half laugh. "She must have pushed me off when she latched from the Temple. Sometimes when doing a distance latch, you don't feel the other person; it's sloppy. Which is why you *don't do it*." She pursed her lips. "I took a chance on you. After we found that scroll in your bag, *I* was the one who convinced Vil we could use another Tala in the group. *I* said you would be a good fit. *I* stuck my neck out, for *you*."

"Well, someone tethered him," Pallah said quietly, looking down at her fingers laced through Tinloh's fur. "And if it wasn't me or you…who was it?" She was too tired for this. Had her family really imploded last night? Having been awake over twenty-four hours, she was having trouble focusing. This argument about Leif's rabbits was inconsequential in comparison. She needed to leave and find Freya. When she looked up from Tinloh, the entire group was silent, the only sound that of the crackling fire.

"No one else knows about Tinloh. No one else here is Tala." Karav spoke slowly, carefully, her eyes landing on Issha. "Not that we know of, anyway."

Issha narrowed her eyes at Karav as she bit into the leg of meat on her plate, juice dripping down her chin.

"It wasn't a normal tether," Pallah said, fear making her sweat at the thought of some unknown person latching onto her cat. "It was…dark, ragged, bent on destruction."

Leif sniffed and wiped his eyes before pulling the rabbit from the spit. He motioned to Kristjan and the two of them began stripping meat from the bones and onto a plate; it steamed into the morning air. Each member took a portion as it passed over the table.

"I'm sorry." Pallah emphasized the words with exaggerated effort. "A lot happened last night." She closed her eyes and pinched the bridge of her nose. "Everyone knows by now the beast that attacked the town at the Feast of Haust was a smilodon with a cub. Someone could have figured out that I took the other one."

"The only way someone would have found out is if you slipped up, Pallah." Karav tapped a finger on the table. "Who else knows?"

Pallah opened her mouth to answer but stopped herself. Her mother knew. Pallah had found Tinloh with her just the day before, before her mother had snapped. Could she have told someone within that time?

"Your silence is answer enough." Karav rolled her eyes. "So, any Broad Tala could have tethered him."

"Not just anyone," Vil corrected. "They would have to know he was here, in this very location. Right?"

The group nodded and murmured their agreement.

"Then our location has been compromised," Vil said thoughtfully as he pulled pieces of meat from his plate and chewed. "We need to lay low for a while, part ways while we restructure."

"Actually—" Pallah cleared her throat. "I was already planning on leaving."

The sounds of eating halted. The group stared at her as one.

"Already?" Vil raised an eyebrow. "You were planning on going before this?"

Pallah nodded. "My family got into a fight last night." She took a shaky breath. This wasn't something she'd wanted to discuss with each person at the table, but she felt the situation called for transparency. "My mother is in the infirmary. My father is in the cells. My brother has been sent to a foster family. And my sister and I are to be Temple Serviseers."

"Not Vámae!" Rolf gasped.

Karav rolled her eyes.

"My mother's one request of me was to find her midwife," Pallah continued. "She has information I need to clarify a few things. Her name is Freya."

Issha snapped to attention.

"You know her?" Vil asked her.

Issha rubbed a hand over her shaved head, her shoulders dropping in resignation. "Yes, my mother worked under her for a time. She's northeast of here, on the road to Takanah."

"It's settled then," Vil said, though nothing was remotely settled. "With our location at risk, the council looking for Pallah, and Tinloh's actions, you will leave as quickly as possible."

Although Pallah agreed, she couldn't help the tightening in her chest at Vil's words.

This sounds oddly familiar. He seems quite eager to see you gone, Pallah. Erval's words squashed any hope. *I know what it's like to be shunted aside for the 'greater good.'*

"Issha, do you know where Freya lives?" Vil asked.

"Yes," Issha reluctantly said. "But I'm not—"

"You'll go with Pallah."

"I'm no courier." Issha rose to her feet, her leather cuirass and arm cuffs reflecting the morning light as she stared at Vil from across the table. "You can't command me to—"

"Are you a part of this group, or not?" Vil's blue eyes dipped into something dark and dangerous. "You know the way; you will take her there."

"I don't need her help if—" Pallah started.

"Oh!" Issha barked out a laugh. "You need my help."

"If you have something—"

The table began to rattle. Pallah's eyes shifted from Issha to the spread before her to find each cup vibrating, the water inside roiling and churning. It began softly but steadily grew into a roar before going completely still. The clink and clatter of a meal shared disappeared as the Taka Reu went crypt-silent. All eyes, wide and round, locked on the only Vatin Fera amidst their number.

Vil cleared his throat and removed his palms from the table, wiping them on his tunic. "We have delicate plans that need not be broken by a simple mishap." Vil's eyes locked onto Pallah's and she stared back, afraid to look away. Did he blame her for tethering Tinloh the night before? But then his features softened. "Come here, Pallah." He beckoned to her.

Pallah left Tinloh at her seat and kneeled beside Vil at the low table, grass tickling her ankles. He tucked a strand of hair behind her ear and leaned in so close their noses almost touched. "I care for you, Pallah. Let me protect you as best I can. You go, and when you come back"—he cupped her cheek in his hand—"we'll pick things up where we left off."

A shaky breath escaped her, and she leaned into his touch. Before she knew what she was saying, she opened her mouth. "Come with me." She searched his eyes. "I don't want to make this journey with anyone but you." She could fix this between them, whatever it was.

His hand was warm and strong, and deep in her belly, the butterflies began to dance. She wanted to feel his lips on hers like she did on Eldfall, wholly, desperately. "Please." She laced her fingers through his.

Vil turned her hand over in his own, studying it. He pressed the back of it to his lips, brushing her skin so softly she thought she would melt. "I would go anywhere with you." He gave her hand a squeeze and met her eyes. "But you need to lie low. The council is on your tail. I have plans for that temple of heretics, Pal. But I must be *here* to make them happen." He pulled back from her. "Karav will go with you, too. She can teach you how to tether properly, so you don't have any more *issues*."

The way his lips formed his last word shot doubt through her mind. Did he not believe her when she said there had been another tether? Pallah blinked and dropped his hand. He didn't reach for her again.

The group was clearing dishes and chatting, a flurry of motion that finally caught up to Pallah as she stood to retrieve Tinloh.

"I'll miss you, Issy." Rolf leaned close to Issha. "Or I can come too, keep you safe...and warm." He winked at his brother.

Issha slammed her fist onto a fork, which flipped once and hit the boy in the eye.

"Hey!" He scrambled backwards and stood, mumbling something about emotional women as he grabbed a stack of plates.

"Leave it to me to woo the ladies next time." Kristjan grinned, plates in his hands as well.

Rolf growled, and the two threw a few mild, one-handed punches before Leif stepped between them to wrestle the dishes away.

"These were my great-great grandmother's!" he hissed. Then he spun on his heel and stalked away, braid swinging with each step.

Tinloh in her arms, Pallah watched the group fall into their familiar rhythms. Rhythms that didn't seem to have a place for her, if they ever had.

"Pallah..." Vil grabbed her elbow, pulling her from her spiral. She faced him as the group dispersed in pairs. "Come back to me, okay?" He took her chin in his thumb and knuckle and tipped her head up to meet his own. "Please."

Then he kissed her, long and slow.

Pallah melted.

Within the hour, the three girls had packed what they needed, said their goodbyes, and stood at the tree line, the sun growing bright in the late morning.

"Lead the way," Pallah said, and Issha began a quick pace east that Karav and Pallah strained to match.

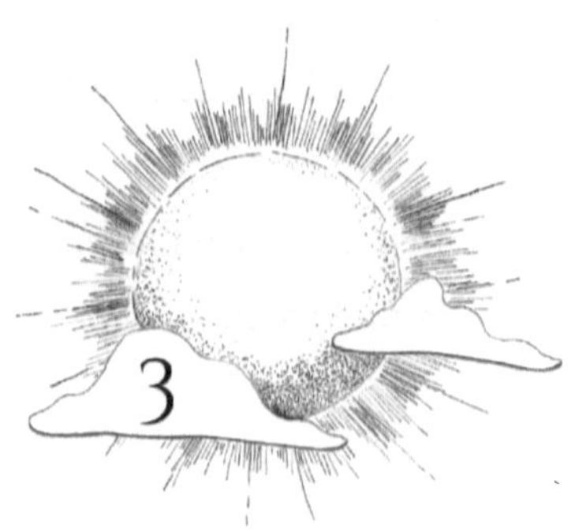

BEAST RIDERS

SOLYANA

WHEN TRAPPED BENEATH SNOW, what is there to do? Once entombed, there is only diminishing oxygen and time. Nothing but the cold, blanketing in its sweet embrace and its darkness, enticing its victims with sleep. The snow, tempting with its taste, serves only to steal body heat, and then—the shakes.

Solyana knew survival tactics better than most of her peers. Born without a Gift, she had nothing to fall back on should things become dire. And she dedicated herself with diligence to ensuring her usefulness to the valley community.

Solyana wanted a new tunic? Mama taught her to sew. She wanted to learn to hunt like the Tala? Papa taught her to shoot a longbow. She craved salmon? She was handed an axe and sent off to the Vatino to cut the ice and fish. Her body showed evidence of each lesson—bloodied knuckles, calloused palms, and shaking knees—she had always hated the ice. Even now, her fingers felt the familiar touch of grappling ice blocks from the waters, clearing space for line and bait.

Solyana tried to gauge her surroundings, but they were all deep blue, and precarious drifts threatened to suffocate her. How long had it been since she'd cut the sled dogs free? Had she doomed them, even as she'd tried to save them? Wherever she was encased, Vinur was no longer with her. She could only pray he had been flung to safety. She smelled the wet iron of the snow.

She wasn't dead yet.

She was buried.

Then she remembered.

She was Heitt.

Solyana almost laughed.

She tugged on the Gift as she pulled off her gloves, spread her fingers, and turned her palms upward. Or the way she hoped was up. Suspended in snowy stasis, she had no way of knowing which way held salvation.

Taking a breath, she channeled the sun upward into flame, burning a hole straight through the snow.

Shouts of alarm rang distantly.

Thank the *stars*.

"Fire! Over there!"

"Gamaliel?" Solyana called out as the snow began rapidly piling around her. She adjusted her aim and continued to warm the area until she could pop her head over the top. What she saw stole her breath.

At quick count, there were ten of them.

People. *Other* people.

Each of them was dressed in furs and fabrics that barely covered their many tattoos and markings, spotting every glimpse of skin. Plates of leather and metal armor layered over their tunics, protecting their chests. Their necks, exposed to the cold, were covered only in patterns of ink beneath the skin. Most of the warriors had shaved the sides of their heads, leaving the very top with long braids that either hung down over their breastplates or wrapped carefully around their shoulders. They carried spears, bows, and long blades, hanging at their sides or resting on their backs. Two of the archers, their bows drawn, aimed at Solyana.

But it wasn't the differences in their appearance or their weaponry that shocked her. Each person sat astride a wild beast. Polar bears, grizzlies, elk, and large mountain cats huffed and stamped the ground before her, each rider staring, steel set in their eyes and their hands.

"State your name and land!" one of the archers shouted into the wind-whipped quiet, the string of his longbow steady.

"Solyana," she whispered, barely keeping the tremble from her voice. Her hands groped in search of her own weapons, lost in the snow. "Solyana of Vestur." She raised her hands in surrender. "My father is Marus, Chief of Mothmar."

The archer turned, giving a look to a foreboding man riding a polar bear. Her heart thundered in her ears and she found it difficult to swallow the fear rising in her throat. The polar bear took a step forward, bringing its rider to the front of the group. The beast was *massive*; even at Solyana's distance, terror flooded the blood in her veins. The only thing stopping her from bolting was the bone-deep cold. The bear's mouth hung open in what appeared to be relaxation, but she wasn't fooled. Her eyes flashed to paws the size of Solyana's head, tipped with thick claws that anchored into the snow—it could rip her to pieces with one swipe.

The man's lip quirked. "Your father is the Chief of the *entirety* of Mothmar?" He was about Papa's age, his accent thick and unrecognizable. Unlike the men back home, he was clean shaven. A facial tattoo ran across his forehead, masking his eyes in black, then running down his nose, over his lips, and down his neck before landing somewhere beneath his leather cuirass. "And I have never heard of this, Vestur. We ask once more," he said, raising a meaty finger. "Once." The polar bear beneath him shifted. "State your land."

Solyana gathered her tether to the creak of bow strings, preparing for their inevitable release. Could she burn up an arrow before it reached her?

Maybe.

"Mothmar," she tried again, but in response, the air resounded with the hum of a bowstring. An arrow embedded itself in the snow a hand's width from Solyana's shoulder. "Beyond the Hasta Pass," she rushed the words out, "on the other side!" She lifted her hands in surrender. "There's a valley, comprised of three villages!" Her eyes searched for Gamaliel, Lone, Jonas, or Vinur, but there was nothing but white in every direction. To her left rose the Hasta Mountain Range. The pass had spit them out on the other side.

The beast-rider narrowed his shadowed eyes, his bald head shining in the light of the sun. "How did you get through the pass?"

"We came from the peak," she stuttered. "From Eldfall." Solyana's hands lowered in time with the archers. An infinitesimal amount of trust, but it bolstered her confidence. "Have you found others?"

"Yes," said a woman astride an elk behind the man. She bore a similar tattoo, though it stopped at her upper lip. The man on the polar bear whipped his head to the side, silencing her.

Relief spread through Solyana, but it was stayed by the glaring knowledge that even if they'd found her friends, it didn't mean they were uninjured.

It didn't mean they were *alive*.

"We will bring you with us, Solyana of Vestur, daughter of the Chief of Mothmar." He gave a low chuckle. "Let's go to my home, and we will see the truth to this tale of yours." The man tugged on the reins of his polar bear, which swung its head and began a slow lumbering walk eastward.

Solyana glanced at the woman who had spoken. Her body was half-obscured by winding antlers, still thick with velvet, but her eyes shone with kindness beneath the dark tattoo crossing her temples. Solyana drew her eyebrows together in a silent plea: were they really safe? The woman gave the smallest of nods, and Solyana released a steady stream of air.

Gloves held tight in the crook of her elbow, Solyana clambered gracelessly out of the hole she'd constructed and stood on the hill before them. Fear and adrenaline simmered in her chest at the thought of going with these people into the unknown.

But she was Heitt now, was she not? She had *power*. They didn't have to know she barely knew how to use it.

"I will not be *brought*." Solyana opened both palms. "But I will *accompany* you, to find my friends." With a shock of heat to her hands, she produced flames in each. The archers immediately raised their weapons once more. The man on the polar bear swung his beast back around, eyebrows raised.

Solyana's scar burned, making a dramatic entrance on her face. The blackened skin, or *aska,* burned anew. She had gained this unnatural scar from the first blizzard which had brought her and her sister, Rhuth, so close to death. Priestess Avi at the Temple Celestial had assured Solyana this scar would ebb and flow. And here it was, flowing to the surface once more.

Though her legs shook, she hoped her display was enough to fool them, and maybe herself too.

The man on the bear raised one eyebrow before bursting into raucous laughter. The entire team joined in, howling and slapping thighs and beasts until Solyana extinguished the flames, her cheeks red.

"I like this one," the man said, wiping his eyes with a meaty thumb. "You are like a little fox. Little arctic fox. Feisty. Cute. Little."

Solyana picked her way down the hill in silence and stood before him. Her face burned, equal parts *aska* and embarrassment. The man's muscular neck cracked as he turned his chin, eyeing the left side of her face. His eyes narrowed to slits.

"A little fox with a little secret, I see." He hocked up a wad of spit, chewed, and shot it into the ground by her feet with a grin. His polar bear swung its massive head around to sniff Solyana's face; her hair blew back with a gust from its nostrils.

The polar bear studied her, and Solyana found herself mesmerized by its eyes. They held depth, as if behind the pools of black lay a soul. When she lifted a hand to touch the bear's nose, its mighty head turned, and all together, the line of beast-riders began their shambling walk to the east.

Separated from her group and with no supplies, Solyana had no choice but to follow. Trudging through the piled snow, she soon realized she would be left behind. The snow was too deep and powdery to walk without snowshoes. Gamaliel came to mind, his feet walking delicately over the snow without shoes to buoy him. She placed a foot gently on the surface, balancing for a moment, before the snow crunched, swallowing her mukluk whole.

Had Gamaliel survived? Lone and Jonas? She sent a prayer to the Celestials, requesting safety and unity once more.

The elk broke off from the trail of animals. It circled Solyana and stopped beside her. The woman riding it extended a hand, her eyes wrinkled in a smile. "You'll freeze before you make it at this rate." Her hand held the long and coiling tattoo of a snake. "Ride with me?"

Relieved but unwilling to admit it, Solyana silently clasped arms with the woman who then lifted her onto the elk and settled Solyana in front of her. Solyana couldn't help but feel like a child, but it was better than trying to walk.

The sun's glow warmed her as it set, lighting the way for the entire party before the Father of the Day disappeared behind the mountain pass. Solyana looked up at the Norlos as it gave the first glimpse of its ribbon flow.

"I am Maral." The woman's breath was warm on Solyana's ear. "I apologize for Orson. He enjoys intimidating; it's a favorite pastime of his."

Solyana stared at the woman's hands held on either side of her, steadying the reins. They were young hands, but the callouses spoke of hard labor. She wondered at Maral's kindness—her existence at all—in this savage land.

"How...how many are there?" Now that she wasn't in immediate danger, Solyana could finally allow facts to seep in. They weren't alone. After an entire life believing Mothmar was singular in its survival, a valley of the last people to endure the cold that had stamped out all other life—Solyana was in the presence of *new* people.

How silly—how *naïve*—she had been.

"How many what?" Maral asked.

"Your people." Solyana pushed past the lump in her throat. They weren't *alone*. She couldn't wrap her mind around it.

"Oh...we are not a large people. Just under two thousand at last count."

Solyana's stomach dropped. Two thousand? Sodur, Vestur, and Austur together barely made up six hundred.

She felt so small. So insignificant.

"How many Rána?"

"Oh, those without Gifts?" Maral asked. "Those are very rare."

Solyana licked her lips, thankful the woman couldn't see her face. She had to remind herself, she wasn't without a Gift anymore. Still, the number of those born without a Gift had only increased in Mothmar...yet none here?

"What is your home called?"

"Our country is Mothmar. My city is Takanah." Maral took a breath. "We are neighbors, I suppose. The Hasta Mountains, the pass"—Solyana could feel the woman nodding toward the range behind them—"they have protected our village for many years. They keep unwanted things out. They are our defenders."

"You don't get blizzards at the full moon?"

Maral chuckled. "Not that I have noticed. You will find our city to be quite comfortable."

Glancing down, Solyana noticed again the snake tattoo on Maral's forearm. She wasn't wearing a heavy parka. She squinted at the line of people astride beasts, a dark river in the night, as the moon and the Norlos grew steadily brighter. None of them wore heavy gear. Instead of parkas, they donned different furs, much like Gamaliel's preferred method of dress. How could they possibly hunt for avalanche survivors in such minimal gear?

"Your people," Maral ventured. "Have they been dealing with these blizzards long?"

Solyana felt like she had already given too much away. Could she trust anyone outside of Mothmar?

No, she corrected herself, that was the name of an entire country.

What could she call her valley now? Suddenly her home felt lost to her, as if it was never hers to begin with.

She had only ever trusted those she'd known in the valley, those she'd grown up beside, an extended family forged, not by blood, but by communal living and shared faith.

"For generations," she said with a sniff, her eyes on the lights silently guiding their way from above.

"And yet you still do not know how to behave in a mountain pass? You caused this avalanche, no?"

Solyana clenched her teeth in irritation. "No one has ever made it through that pass. I think we did better than most."

"That is not true," Maral stated.

Solyana turned to look at Maral, but the woman was altogether too close to her, their bodies swaying in step with the elk. "What do you mean?"

"Others *have* come through." Maral cleared her throat. "It's been some time since the last one, but you are the first to cause an avalanche."

Solyana's eyes widened. "Others? Who?"

"The last was over a decade ago. He always talks about going back for his son, but it's impossible to get back over the mountain. It's strange really...we have not figured out why people can come through but cannot return."

"What is his name?" Solyana's mind rifled through the possibilities. Who had left their village ten years ago? She would have been six years old at the time, but she might recognize a name.

"Reynir," Maral said.

Solyana shook her head. "I don't know him."

"Ah, well. We're almost there. Just beyond this hill. I'm sure I can introduce you."

The elk plodded steadily onward, cresting the mound of snow. But just before they reached the top, Solyana heard it, the beat and lilt of a city. Cresting over the horizon, ears perked and eyes ready, her mouth fell open in awe.

FORTIFIED BEAST

PALLAH

PALLAH, ISSHA, AND KARAV hiked until dusk the first night, traveling eastward to cross Belja River that ran from the Vatino to Skrim Sea. Once through, they began angling north as the last of the golden light painted the tops of the trees. By the second day, Pallah was irritable, hungry, and running on fumes. Tinloh was beginning to adopt some of her attitude, and she snatched him up before he could swipe at Issha's ankle again. Tucked cozily between the base of her neck and her over-filled knapsack, Tinloh purred and fell asleep. Bringing her winter gear had seemed important at the time, but now it was heavy, and her snowshoes clicked annoyingly against her thigh.

"This place is as good as any," Issha mumbled as they found a dry clearing within a copse of birch trees. Pallah let her knapsack slide off her, Tinloh landing nimbly on his feet. He stretched, his haunches peaking. He yawned, saberteeth clicking together, before he pounced on some invisible bug.

The three got to work. Karav disappeared to find dinner and Issha set to making a fire with the wood Pallah retrieved from the forest. They worked silently, the stress of their trip melting beneath menial tasks, becoming replaced by exhaustion. Bellies full, eyes drooping, Pallah hadn't realized she had fallen asleep until someone toed her in the gut.

"Wha—" She sat up to find Issha standing above her, lit by the glow of embers. "I fell asleep."

"Clearly," Issha said, her knee popping as she sat beside Pallah. "I'm getting old." A soft snore came from across the fire and Pallah spotted Karav bundled in a blanket, her face serene.

"How old *are* you?"

"Nineteen." Issha prodded at the fire with a stick; it flared. "Why are we going to Freya?"

Pallah rubbed the sleep from her eyes. "She was my mother's midwife. She knows the reason my father—" Pallah stopped, the title newly banished from her tongue. "She knows why Bogdur hates me." Saying the words out loud, at least to someone other than Vil, speared a lance of anxiety through her gut. But after travelling together, a measure of trust had blossomed between them. Perhaps Issha was softer than she seemed.

"At least he stayed."

"Bogdur?"

"Yeah." Issha leaned her chin on her folded hands.

"I'm sorry," Pallah whispered into the midnight dark.

"Don't be." Issha flashed a rare smile. "It's what brought my mother to Freya. I grew up in Takanah, north of her cottage. With Mama's aptitude, she was an asset for the deliveries."

"Deliveries?"

"The babies."

"Oh, right."

Crickets sang a sonata, the fire crackled back to life, and Issha cleared her throat. "Sorry I woke you. It's your turn to keep watch, I'm just not tired yet."

Pallah tucked her cloak tighter around herself and laid a blanket on her lap.

Silence hung in the air, tangible and expectant. Pallah had been waiting to ask Issha about her Gift, and they were alone now.

"What's your Gift? Vil says even he doesn't know."

Issha opened her mouth to answer when a crack echoed in the distance. She was on her feet in an instant, eyes searching the shadowed clearing. "Where's your cat?"

The blanket slid to the ground as Pallah stood and cupped her hands around her mouth. "Tinloh!" she whispered, tugging on the tether with her mind. But it wasn't there. It had snapped. "Why does that keep happening?"

"What?" Issha asked over her shoulder, eyes still on the tree line. No other sounds emanated from the forest as Pallah crept around the fire, careful not to wake Karav.

"When my tether snapped two nights ago, I had assumed it was a combination of distance and...well, emotion. My guard was down, and my emotions were high. But I don't feel that way now."

"Would he try to go back to Sodur?"

Pallah hadn't thought of that. "Tinloh!" she called again as she shoved a branch into the embers, the top of it lit. She walked forward with her makeshift torch and picked her way through the high grass.

The moon, a sliver in the darkness, offered little help as her eyes wandered across the wood. The trees rustled and creaked, swaying lazily in the night.

A low growl rolled in from her left, and she turned so fast the wind snuffed out her light. "*Häfa*, Tinloh." She gritted her teeth, reaching out with her tether once more in the direction of the noise. "Come on, boy. What are you doing?" Her tether flapped around the suspected area but came up short.

Her search had taken her to the line of woods across the clearing; she hadn't noticed she'd gone so far until she looked up. The stars blinked between the tops of the pines as they rocked and swayed in the wind.

"Tinloh?" Her voice was low now, something in her gut telling her to draw her hatchet. But there was nothing in these woods, or Karav would've felt it. She always checked for other animals, making sure they were out of any predator's territory. Karav's tether hadn't found a thing.

For the first time since making camp, Pallah recognized the oddness of that fact. Nothing? In a wood that should have teemed with creatures?

The shadows shifted before her and, like a dark sheet slipping free, a beast lumbered into the moonlight.

It was not Tinloh.

Pallah backpedaled, heart hammering in her ribcage. A grizzly bear snorted and stood to its full height, twice the size of Pallah.

"Issha!" she cried, unsure if the girl could hear her from all the way back at the fire. The fire! She needed to get back. The fire would scare it away. But where was Tinloh?

Mind racing, a flash of memory from her classes at Lóthkol told her not to run, to back away slowly, avoid eye contact. Too late for that, but she averted her eyes anyway, hoping her silhouette was enough to keep the grizzly from seeing her face. The bear huffed and stepped forward, head down, sniffing the earth. It kept pace with her as she crept backward. Sweat broke out on her chest and back.

The tether that had lain dormant in her mind suddenly jerked to attention, and before Pallah could do anything about it, a tiny furball burst into sight, tearing between Pallah and the grizzly.

"Tinloh, no!" she screamed, but stood helpless as the cat gave a tiny roar and swiped air with a clawed paw. The bear shifted, dark and wild eyes falling from Pallah to the beast at its feet. A growl rumbled from its chest and its muscles bunched, preparing to strike. One hit from its paw would obliterate Tinloh, and Pallah would be next.

Thinking of nothing but the life of her cub, Pallah dove for Tinloh, rolling to the side as the bear swiped at the space the cat had just occupied. Pallah took off. Feet scrambling for purchase in leather shoes, she charged through the grass and weeds to an empty fire. Where were Issha and Karav? She whirled back around to face the bear, tossing Tinloh behind her, and yanked her hatchet out of its holster.

Karav appeared on her right, palms facing the earth, fingers holding her up as she crouched low, eyes on the bear. "Get behind me!" she screamed, braids brushing the ground. Pallah ducked behind Karav, hatchet clutched in two clammy fists.

Karav shook from head to toe. With a groan, her body tensed and the bear halted in its charge, stumbling and falling to its side. "I can't keep it down!" she shrieked, the bear regaining its footing. "There's something blocking it!"

Tinloh leapt toward the bear again, and Pallah sent a fierce warning through her tether. He obeyed, but reluctance pulled at their connection. "Like Tinloh's mother?"

"Yes!" Karav wailed and dropped to one knee. "I can't hold it! My tether keeps slipping off!"

"Together, then!" Issha's voice came from the other side of the animal. She must have crept around back.

The bear rose to its full height once more, unimpeded by the girls' feeble attempts to keep it grounded. It released a deafening roar that rattled Pallah's bones.

"You're Tala?" Karav barked, falling to both knees.

Issha gave no answer. In the breaking light of dawn, Pallah watched the girl connect to the Mother, the Taka Reu. "It's like the bear's mind is a maze," Issha said, calm and measured. "We need to solve the maze to tether the beast!"

Then both girls went quiet, leaving Pallah to scramble on her own as the bear dropped to all fours and began making its way once more. They needed more time. She could see it in their stances, their fingers digging into the dirt, knees locked to the earth.

Pallah, you need to connect to the Mother.

"What?" Uncaring if the other two heard her, Pallah kept her eyes on her hatchet. "Why?"

Connect to your cat through the Mother. His fury could take down the beast. Though he may not survive...

"Never!" Pallah's heart stuttered at the thought. "I won't do that!"

Then you should leave. You're useless here.

"They'll figure out the maze." Pallah nodded, ignoring Erval.

Use the Taka Reu, Pallah. If not with your beast, then with your fury. That hatchet is for more than just making kindling.

Perhaps there was something to that. Pallah jumped to her feet and mimicked the stance of her peers, crouching and pressing her fingers to the earth below. Squeezing her eyes shut, she called upon the Mother beneath her. There was an immediate response, as if the deity herself had been anxiously awaiting Pallah's plea.

Power suffused her body as she straightened and walked boldly to the bear, hatchet held to the side. She blinked, every part of her consumed with dark terror, echoing the night with her family, when she had first called on the Mother. She breathed it in, then smiled.

"Pallah?" Karav whimpered.

But Pallah held no fear, not anymore. She lunged forward with her hatchet, twirling it once in her hand before uppercutting the bear with a grunt held back between teeth. The bear's massive maw jerked upward, head knocked back as blood spurted from the wound.

It roared, then rounded on Pallah, charging her with new-found ferocity.

Pallah laughed.

That's my girl.

Diving out of the way, Pallah slashed out with the hatchet just as the bear brushed past her. Her blade caught behind its front shoulder, tugging Pallah off her feet. She stumbled to the ground, pulling the hatchet free and twisting to catch its back foot between axe and earth.

The bear roared, turning so fast—too fast. The animal spun on her, front paws landing on either side of her face. Pallah screamed.

"I got it!" Issha yelled from across the clearing.

And then all Pallah saw was red: vision-swimming, nose-filling, mouth-choking red.

She was drowning, suffocating, dying.

Dead.

SUBTERFUGE

ERVAL

IGH ABOVE THE CITY of Thonethren, clouds gathered in thick clumps around a waxing moon. It was the perfect night for subterfuge. But Erval Mikkaelson, son of King Mikkael Vargonson the Benevolent, First of his Name, was no spy. He was a prince. And the lecture he would receive would be stern and full of metaphor if he were to be found outside the castle grounds at this hour.

Erval sped down cobblestone streets, pulling his cap down over his ears. If even one person recognized him, *holy Hekla*, he would be stuck assisting Halldora with lessons for the next month.

Thinking of his sister now, he hoped she hadn't grown weary of waiting up for him. If she had fallen asleep or locked the window, he would be done for. It was her room which sat atop the vine-covered turret made for climbing, made for escape; something they both agreed to keep from Shahann.

He ducked down an alleyway, the stench of the city hitting him in full force—rotten vegetables, refuse, and *something* darker he could never name but was always there. He splashed through a murky puddle and was rewarded with that same pungent odor. The viscous liquid sucked his leather shoe off with a loud *schloop*. Erval stumbled forward and fell to the grimy stones.

"*Häfa!*" He scooped his shoe out from what he hoped was only mud, but knew it wasn't. A long line of a black and sticky substance stretched from shoe to puddle, the smell triggering his gag reflex. Hopping on one foot, he tore off his other shoe and continued barefoot. The vine-covered wall, his last hurdle before the castle grounds, was close, and he would need his feet bare anyway.

Thonethren was vast, but no longer grand. In the last century, this same sticky material had overtaken the city. Buildings, streets and wildlife were rife with the stuff. Ridding their city of it had become more work than it was worth. Now, more often than not, the people left it to fester.

Erval made a habit of escaping the castle at least once a week. He relished the anonymity, mingling with the common people, betting on bardagis. These people—Erval could hear them now, singing their tavern songs—were impoverished. The wealthy lived on the northern end of town, keeping their distance from the rabble. There was no in-between, no middle. One was either slumming it at a bardagi or enjoying volcanic mud baths with the elite. Any middle class that had dwelled in Thonethren in times past were long gone.

He knew these things because it was his *job* to know. He had spent his life learning. He could not be privy to the sights and smells of the city while stuck within the confines of his ancestral home. He grinned, thinking of the forty cohstas he made at tonight's match, tucked into the pockets of his cloak. He would have to keep that from Shahann, too.

He pushed aside the crates he had used to cover the missing bricks in the wall and crawled through, replacing them once he was on the other side. Safe in the narrow gap between brick and stone wall covered in a few aging vines, he shoved his leather shoes into his cloak. The soggy leather bled through to his skin, making him shiver.

Veins appeared on his arms as he scaled the vines, his cloak drifting backward, gravity threatening to return him to the waiting ground. But Erval had always been a good climber. He made it to the top of the wall in less than two minutes, swung a leg over, and stopped to survey his kingdom.

Well, it wasn't *his* kingdom, not yet. But it would be by this time next year. He'd been groomed since he was a child to succeed his father. Though it would surely be a day of sorrow, he easily bore the thought of his father's passing with the one fact that overshadowed all others: he would be king. Thonethren boasted over forty thousand people, and they would all fall under Erval's rule. He would decide whether there was a curfew, what holidays should be celebrated, whether a good old bardagi was legal or not. He patted the pocket that held his cohstas with a contented sigh. People needed an outlet to showcase their strength. What better way than pitting them against each other in a match of Tala versus Tala, Fera versus Fera, Heitt versus Heitt? Though he could never compete himself, he did have a talent for choosing the right man and usually came away victorious.

The wind pushed through his cloak, pulling his cap from his wavy, dark hair. He caught it in midair, wishing for a moment Halldora had been there to see him do it. The cold season was upon them and, judging by the clouds that rolled across the night sky, the snows were not far off.

He swung his other leg over the wall, knees jutting out like skinny gargoyles. He would have to jump down, sneak toward the turret where his sister's quarters were, and scale the stone structure before sliding in through the window. He sighed. The things he did for erudition.

Stuffing his cap in yet another pocket in his cloak, he readied himself for the drop. A muffled voice wafted toward him. His eyes grew wide and he crouched low, making himself small on the narrow wall. Who would be out at this hour? His gaze roved over the grounds, stone buildings and gardens blocking his view. Finally, coming out of the maze of shrubs and tailored trees, came two figures. Their faces alternated in light and shadow as a pair of flames rotated in the palm of one man's hand. King Mikkael and Priest Henrik. The priest always preferred a few dancing flames to one large one; it was his tell.

"If we do this, Henrik, they will cast me from my throne. A king getting into bed with the Temple? My legacy would not stand for it."

"Oh, mighty King, no!" Priest Henrik was young, and whether his voice shook from cold or fear, Erval didn't know. "The people will praise you! The Celestials are full of grace, and they will forgive past hurts against them. The people will see the benefits, in time."

"And by the Celestials, we speak of the paths of the sky?"

"Excuse me, sire?"

"My grandfather, King Johan, once taught me of the..." The king shook his head. "Pathways? Connections?"

"You will have *connections* to the Father of the Day, Mother of the Night, and Children of the Sky, yes my King."

King Mikkael was silent for a beat. "And what of Erval?"

Erval crouched lower, afraid the mention of his name would somehow draw the men's eyes up to his spot on the wall.

"He will understand. He's a bright boy. Caring." Priest Henrik spoke as if he knew Erval. Erval narrowed his eyes; the man had never said more than two words to him. "Halldora will fulfill the role according to the natural order of the Celestials. The Blue Moon determines succession, not gender or order of birth."

"Yes, yes. So you've said." The king sighed. "It won't go over well. The children..." Erval's father took a weighty breath. "They're competitive in all things, and Erval has been studying to reign his entire life."

"Then he will make a fine advisor to his sister." The priest's fire began to wink out as they rounded the door to the castle. "Thren Temple welcomes you into its chambers, my king. May you find peace for your soul among its saints."

The last of his fire disappeared as the men stepped into the castle. Erval waited, his mind roaring. After a moment, the priest stepped back out again, his hands encased in his cavernous sleeves, and shuffled across the front yard, flanked by two castle guards. They disappeared beneath Erval and through to the other side, where the guards would deliver the priest to Thren Temple before returning to their station.

Erval jumped, falling into a roll on his right shoulder before springing up and using his momentum to carry him through the gardens and to the base of the turret. He climbed, his mind consumed with the implications of what he'd just heard.

His father was converting, that much was certain. Thren Temple was his great-grandfather's doing; King Johan had worshiped the Celestials before his son Vargon ascended the throne. But Vargon had disliked the idea of distant gods and practiced his Gifts through the Taka Reu. The city had taken it on as their own, disregarding all love for Celestials and choosing instead the Mother Below.

But now, Erval was to be pushed aside? And for what? A change in *religion*? A simple prayer to a different god was to alter his entire path? Halldora would be queen? Rage boiled inside of him—not against his sister, but against his father. Halldora wouldn't *want* to lead; she hadn't been trained for it. She would abdicate...yes.

Or he would make her.

Sweat trickled down his chest and over the back of his neck as he climbed the last of the vines. Sliding over the stone parapet, he was ready for his bed, though sleep would not come easily tonight.

The window remained unlatched, and Erval slipped into his sister's room, his leather shoes still in his cloak, his bare feet silent on the stone floor. Halldora was asleep, the room dark, the curtains drawn around her four-poster bed. He hadn't stayed out *that* late, had he?

He took a moment to catch his breath. Should he wake Halldora and tell her of what he had overheard? Or go to sleep and wait for his father's announcement in the morning? Perhaps she would be pleased at being told such a secret before it was made known; she was always jealous he was made privy to the workings of the castle before her. Now was the time to get her on his side.

He made his way toward her bed, his hand outstretched.

A sound outside the door made him freeze. He collapsed to his belly and shimmied underneath the bed, using his cloak as cover.

The door to his sister's chambers squeaked open, revealing the silhouette of Shahann. He was a spidery man, his pale skin stretched over the points of his bones. Usually garbed in ministerial robes, he now wore something akin to a nightgown, complete with a lopsided cap. He had never seen the eunuch so underdressed. Shahann carried a single guttering candle in danger of winking out, victimized by shaky breath and scurrying feet.

"Halldora," he rasped as he whipped a curtain to the side. "Halldora, wake up! *Stars*, child, why is it so cold in here?"

"Shahann?" Halldora's voice rose groggily.

"Your window is open." Shahann's feet, Erval could see now, were donned in soft woolen slippers. He shuffled to the window and pulled it shut. "Is there something wrong with your window? No matter, you won't be in this room much longer."

"Oh!" Halldora squeaked, and Erval knew she was thinking he was still out there, waiting to come in. "I...I like my window open, Shahann. Can you—"

"My apologies, Princess, but there is no time. Quick, please come with me."

"It's the middle of the night..." Halldora trailed off and Erval somehow knew, even from under the bed, that his sister was scrutinizing their advisor's choice of clothing. "Shahann...what are you wearing?" Erval grinned. He *did* know his sister well. Probably better than anyone. He would make a good advisor.

No, he scowled. He was to be king.

"Where is Erval?" Shahann asked. "He's not in his rooms."

"What?" Halldora's voice pitched with attempted nonchalance, Erval rolled his eyes.

"Where is he?"

"Perhaps he went to the kitchens."

Erval's stomach growled.

"You ought not be covering for him, Halldora. You're smarter than that. Now, answer truthfully. Did he sneak out?"

Halldora hesitated. "No."

"Halldora."

"I don't know where he is!"

"I will never understand you children." Shahann sighed. "Now, hop to it."

His sister's bare feet came down to block his view of the room. She wrapped one around the other to scratch the back of her ankle, then rested them side by side. "Where are we going?"

"I'll explain on the way. Change is afoot, and it reeks of betrayal."

Erval furrowed his brow. Betrayal? Shahann couldn't yet know what Erval was turning over in his mind, for even Erval hadn't fully arranged those thoughts. And besides, was it betrayal if his decisions were rooted in saving his beloved sister from a lifetime of harrowing rulership? No, it wasn't betrayal. It was *love*.

Halldora scurried around the room, collecting her things, but Shahann cleared his throat. "Not now, Dora. Rumors spread like plague here." The spidery man ushered Halldora quickly out the door, one candle between them.

As soon as the door closed behind them and he decided no one was returning, Erval scrambled out from under the bed. He stretched his arms out behind him, his shoulders releasing pent-up tension.

He would have to follow them…he would have to win Halldora before they tried to fill her mind with hope she would be queen. For she would not. Being king had always been the only certainty in his life, the only thing that had made all the lessons and discipline worth it. To rule. To reign.

The steps of his sister and advisor were long gone; silence wrapped the room. It would take Erval several minutes to catch up to them in the castle's expansive corridors. He reached down inside himself and felt the tether, waiting, biding its time. He didn't often let it out; he couldn't.

He was permitted practice of his Tala only in the presence of his father. And even then, used only just enough to learn to wield it safely. It was to be reserved solely for times of war; never for daily use, never for politics. Certainly never at a bardagis match, or to find someone in a large, slumbering castle. Truthfully, he had been using his aptitude for years, but never enough to get caught. Only enough to win when he wanted to. When he needed to.

And now, Erval needed to win.

He released his tether, eager and at the ready. It sped through the halls of the castle. He closed his eyes, picturing it careening swiftly through rooms and frigid floors.

Ah, there she was.

A shiver of pleasure trilled deep inside Erval as his tether latched onto the soul of his sister, anchored and sure. Had she noticed? Surely not. He grinned and meandered out of her room, sauntering down the hall. He could return to his own quarters.

She would come to him.

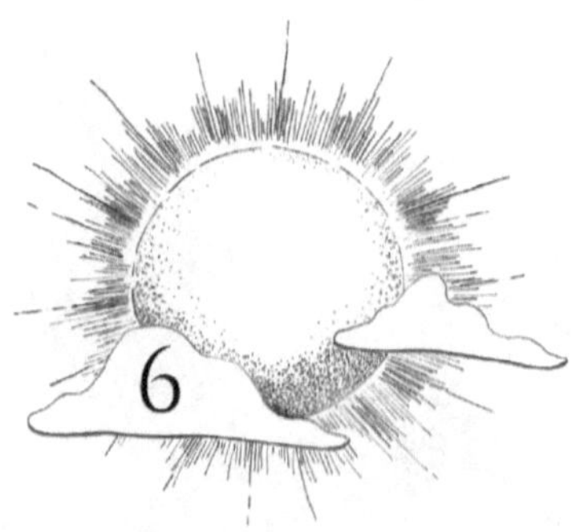

TAKANAH

SOLYANA

SOLYANA UNDERSTOOD NOW WHY the Beast Riders had been wearing nothing but tunics and furs. Warmth emanated from the city as they approached the high stone walls, wooden gates flung open in welcome. Cookfires, laughter, music, and lantern lights brought a smile to Solyana's face as they passed beneath the balustrade and bridge holding guards who pulled the gate shut behind them. The city, though open to the moon high above, held little semblance of the night, so lit as it was by brazier and torch.

Maral kept her elk moving, winding their way over cobblestoned streets, hedged in by buildings stretching tall and wide before them. Solyana could do nothing but gape at the amount of people before her, dancing and embracing, buying and selling. They did not seem to be starving here, as Solyana's people were back home. No, they thrived.

The elk plodded along the main thoroughfare, where rows upon rows of booths made Solyana's courtyard back home look like paltry child's play. Vendors shouted cheerily from their stalls, meat swung from pegs, and hands cupped warm drinks, steam rushing toward the sky. A few buskers played drums while others plucked stringed instruments Solyana had never seen before. Fingers flew over strings and hands pounded animal hide as a group of villagers danced and stomped around them.

Solyana stripped off her parka and tucked it into her lap. She felt her scar fade, replaced by a smile. Animals milled in the streets, docile and tame. Solyana was aware she was riding atop an elk, but the idea of animals wandering the village was a thrilling concept, if not nerve-wracking.

"This is..." She shook her head, unable to articulate the combination of awe and disillusionment clutching at her throat.

"Takanah," Maral said with a smile.

All this time, there had been more people. Having lived her entire life in the valley, Solyana had believed they were the sole survivors of the Age of Ice. Their Gifts diminishing, the erratic uptick of deadly blizzards—all of it seemed to be relegated solely to their valley. Here was a city, thriving and full of blessings from the Celestials, just beyond their reach.

"Amazing," Solyana whispered. They passed a butcher, his cleaver descending with a thwack into a rack of ribs. "Why is everyone so active at night? Is there a feast?

Maral chuckled. "No feast. The people of Takanah have simply grown to appreciate nightfall. Most sleep during the day."

Solyana thought on this, but she had too many other questions. "How is it so warm here?"

"Your people do not have Heitt?"

"We have—" Solyana fell silent, feeling self-conscious of her people's plight. "Do you have many?" she asked instead.

"Of course," Maral said. "It's how we keep the temperature constant."

Solyana needed to talk to Jonas about this, but the thought of his name dispelled any warmth. Was he still asleep? Was he going to be okay?

"Are you taking me to my friends?" Her question held more bite than intended. Maral pulled back on the reins, the elk halting with a snort.

"Yes." Maral swung her leg behind her and slid off the side of the animal. "They're here." Solyana turned to look down at the woman's kind, round face. She extended her arms up to help Solyana down, but she waved her off.

"I've got it." She slid off the side.

"Suit yourself," Maral said with a shrug. "It's easy to mother everyone else when you're a mother yourself." Maral's green eyes found Solyana's and searched her face. "How old are you, Solyana?"

"Sixteen," Solyana said, standing a little taller, wrapping her parka tight around her arms.

"Sixteen..." Maral trailed off, shaking her head. "So young to be traveling alone."

"I'm not alone. I have my friends."

Maral nodded sagely. "You'll find them through here."

Solyana stepped forward and grasped the metal handle. The house was in immaculate condition, nothing like the small huts they had back home. She peered up at it. Was it two stories? She turned back to Maral, who had gathered her reins and mounted her elk once more.

"There's an inn, if Healer Kora won't allow you to stay here with your friends. It's toward the main square. But if they don't have room…" Maral threaded the reins through her fingers. "You can come stay with me. It's just me and my kids, now that my husband is no longer with us. We're in the Eastern District, near the apothecary and the saddle maker—big, yellow house. You can't miss it." She grinned at her hands, then at Solyana; her face lost years in the smile. "You will be safe under my roof."

Maral extended her arm to Solyana who stepped forward and gripped the woman's forearm. They shook once, a measure of trust passing between them.

With a click of tongue in cheek, Maral rode away, leaving Solyana to push open the Healer's door.

"Solyana!" The smell of cedar and cave smoke enveloped her senses as Gamaliel pulled her face into his chest. She gripped him hard, her fingers digging into the curve of his back, tears springing to her eyes. Part of her thought she had lost him—lost all of them—and the caravan of Beast Riders had just been dragging her along, waiting to impart the news once she was within the walls of their city.

"I thought…I thought…" Her tears descended into sobs as she pushed deeper into him, and he tucked his face into the hollow of her neck, his stubble scratching her ear. The smell of him brought back the Mothmar she knew, and an ache formed in her chest.

"I know. It's okay," he whispered, his breath warm in her ear. "I did, too. We're all okay."

"Are we?" Solyana pulled back from him, eyes roving across his face, looking for any signs of distress.

"Jonas and Lone are fine." He tilted his head toward a bed in the corner of the room which held a small, prone figure wrapped in blankets. Lone sat at the foot of it facing away from the two near the door, her feet propped up on the side of the fireplace. Something in Solyana relaxed at the sight of them, but when she turned back to Gamaliel, she spotted a brokenness shooting across his face. "A few of the dogs were found and brought to the kennels, but we lost the rest of them." He sniffed. "They served us well."

"And Vinur?" A cold, wet nose pried its way beneath her palm and relief flooded her. She bent down, burying her face in the black and white fur of the wolf she'd grown to love. "Hi, boy."

"He's fine," Gamaliel said, crouching with her. "I had to restrain him here. He kept trying to get out. I think he wanted to find you."

Solyana smiled, but as her eyes found Lone again, her mouth became a thin line. The girl was picking something out from under her nail with a knife, her eyes on her work. Lone had made it clear she was displeased with Solyana at the peak of Eldfall.

Would she blame Solyana here, too?

The blankets beside Lone rose and fell in a steady rhythm as the boy beneath them breathed in sleep. Solyana went to him, thankful he was still here, thankful this unnatural sleep hadn't taken him under, not yet.

She knelt beside the bed, dropping her parka and gloves beside her as she went to feel his forehead. His eyes fluttered. "Jonas?" She looked up at Lone. "Is he—has he woken up?"

"Not yet," the girl answered coolly.

Gamaliel stood at the head of the bed. "But he's getting close. This is the Healer's house. She's been rousing him. She said it would take a few hours, but she's confident she can draw him out of darlöh."

"That's possible?" Solyana's mind began racing faster than she could keep up with it. Could they bring this Healer back to her valley? Could she draw Rhuth out of her sleep? Since being trapped in the blizzard together only a few weeks ago, Rhuth had yet to wake. "Maybe we could bring her back. She could teach Priestess Avi! This could save so many people! Rhuth could be healed."

"I didn't even think of that." Gamaliel's brow furrowed, and he looked across to Lone. "She's teaching you, right?"

"Yes, in case it happens again."

Then Solyana remembered Maral's words to her as they had trekked back to Takanah. No one was able to cross into the valley. Something unknown kept Solyana's people sequestered and untouched. If what she said was true, they couldn't go back. Not until Solyana fulfilled her duty and turned their world of white to green. "Maral told me no one has ever made it back over the pass."

"Maral?" Gamaliel's eyes grew wide. "And what do you mean 'made it back?' Someone has come here before?"

"The woman who brought me here said the last person to come through the pass was a decade ago."

Gamaliel went quiet, his eyes studying the bedspread before him.

"So, what's the plan?" Lone asked, still avoiding Solyana's gaze. "We're in this new city, with these new people. We need supplies but have nothing to trade. Who knows how long it will take Jonas to come out of this. And you"—she finally looked at Solyana and pointed her knife in her direction—"need to figure out what you're doing with Jonas's Gift. Nothing good has come from you stealing it from him, and your inexperience has led to this."

"Stealing?" Solyana's mouth dropped open. "He begged me to take it on Eldfall. He was burning everything down! And in case you haven't been informed, the whole purpose of this trip is for me to acquire all three Gifts! If you're not okay with this *stealing* happening two more times, maybe you should stay here. I'm not sure why you volunteered in the first place."

Lone's blonde lashes lowered over narrowed eyes as she brought her legs down from the windowsill. "Trust me, it wasn't my idea. My parents..." Lone's gaze went to the ceiling as she rubbed a hand over her cropped white-blonde hair. "They're devout. And saw this as the best thing I could do for the Celestials." She leaned forward, her blue eyes searching Solyana's. "I'm not your enemy, Solyana. But Jonas had one thing to protect himself. And now? He has nothing. You should have saved this Gifting business for someone we don't all love or care for." She stood, looking down at the boy in the bed. "Just something to think about before pushing someone else to the brink of death."

Lone walked to the door and turned back with her fingers gripping the handle. "I'm tired and I'm hungry. I'm going to get us some food."

"Lone," Gamaliel ventured, but Solyana placed her hand on his arm, quieting him.

"I'm hungry, too. Thanks, Lone."

Lone stepped out the door. It clicked shut behind her.

"I don't like us being split up," Gamaliel said. "We don't know this place and they don't know us."

"Hey." Solyana squeezed his arm before taking Lone's seat by the fire. Gamaliel pulled up a chair beside her. "She'll be fine. And she's not wrong. Maybe I did take something away from Jonas he was meant to keep." She shrugged with a shake of her head. "But my friend was in danger, so I helped him. Our people are in danger, so..." She peered at Gamaliel, his eyes reflecting the flames. "I'll help them, too. And doing that is going to involve taking two more Gifts. If Lone isn't okay with that, better to discuss it now than later."

"You're right." Gamaliel nudged her knee with his own. "I'll feel better about all this once Jonas is up and running around again. I miss him."

"Me, too."

"So, Takanah." Gamaliel spread his arms wide. "What do we know?"

"First of all, Mothmar as a country is more than just our valley. This city is proof that much lies beyond our three villages back home. In the past, some have successfully left, but they seem unable to return."

"Do you think your father knows about this?" Gamaliel raised an eyebrow.

"No way." Solyana shook her head. "Priestess Avi?" She began to braid her hair, the familiar motion calming her.

"Oh, she definitely knows." Gamaliel huffed as he got to his feet and paced the slats of the wooden floor. "She knows much more than she's letting on."

"We don't know that for sure, Gam." Solyana's mistrust of the woman had grown since Gamaliel voiced his opinions about Priestess Avi using the Taka Reu. But she couldn't believe the woman had any malicious intent. Not now, with Rhuth still in the Priestess's care, not after having come so far from home on her instruction.

"Second." Gamaliel furrowed his brow. "It's significantly warmer here than back home. Why?"

"It's their Heitt," Solyana said. "Maral told me."

Gamaliel tapped at this chin. "They would have to have hundreds! What else did this Maral say?"

"Maybe they do." Finishing the braid, she laid it on her shoulder. "She said the people do most of their business after dark."

"That explains the activity."

Solyana nodded. "And she welcomed us to stay the night with her if the inn was full."

"There's an inn?" Gamaliel shook his head slowly. "Which means people travel here…"

Solyana's eyes grew wide. "*Other* people. There's even *more*."

Gamaliel nodded sagely. "Do you think they get monthly blizzards here, too?"

"Maral said they didn't." Solyana shook her head. "This is all too much. I have so many questions."

"Me, too." Gamaliel admitted before his stomach let out a gurgling growl. "Yes, yes, I know," he said as he patted his belly.

Solyana grinned.

The door opened and Lone backed in, a smile spread over her face, arms full of small, brown packages. "I brought fiflas!"

"Perfect timing. I don't know what fiflas are but"—he sniffed the air—"they smell amazing!"

"It's a hand pie, filled with fish." Lone handed each of them a package before unwrapping her own and producing a small pie.

"They use these small, round pieces of gold for trade; the woman called them 'coins.'" Lone took a bite, and steam rose from the pie. "She let me take these for free, though; said it was common courtesy to help newcomers."

Solyana took a bite from her own, grateful for Lone's change of attitude. The atmosphere shifted in the room as they ate together, as if each of them remembered their reasons for being here. As if, in some way, they were able to come to terms with their situation—though they knew so little about it.

The door opened again and an old woman tottered in, her kindly, wrinkled face smiling softly. "I see you found yourself some food." She held up a bowl of something steaming. "This is for the boy."

"Healer Kora," Lone began. "Would we be able to stay here for the night? Or should we find lodging at the inn?"

"Oh, you're welcome to stay here. I have no other patients. But the night is still young." Healer Kora knelt beside Jonas and deftly pulled him into a seated position. Solyana's heart jumped to her throat as she watched the woman work. Jonas's eyes fluttered open, his body shifting of its own accord. "Besides, the chief has requested to see you."

"Now?" Gamaliel asked with a yawn.

"Our chief likes to do his work under the moon," the old woman said, spooning broth into Jonas's mouth. "I will stay with the boy." She looked up and found Lone. "You stay too, so I can finish our lessons."

"We need supplies and more sled dogs," Solyana said, looking from Lone to Gamaliel, who both nodded in turn.

Vinur's head poked up from beside the fire. "Stay with Lone," Gamaliel said. The wolf let out a *hmph*. "Let's go talk to the chief."

The Healer had spouted off directions and assured them Jonas would wake up soon.

Hope held in her heart, Solyana prayed it was true—he would wake.

The cobblestone streets of Takanah held an air of anticipation. The excitement of some place new kept a fire beneath Solyana's feet, nipping at her heels as they stepped into the night that didn't feel like night, as she made her way to the Chief's Hall. Night came early in Vestur; it was sometimes completely dark when Solyana and her family sat for their evening meal. And once completed, the day was done. But here in Takanah, it did not seem to be so.

The streets in her valley were hardly streets, but rather paths. As snow continually poured down, Vatin Fera moved it as quickly as possible, but it was never enough to keep them truly clear. But here in Takanah, her mukluks easily found purchase on dry ground. The ease of her steps, an unfamiliar relief.

She and Gamaliel passed rows of homes. Some were around the same size as the Healer's, but most were smaller one-story buildings. Guttering lanterns and torches spotted the walls of every building, casting long shadows beneath eaves and down alleys. Perhaps the people of Takanah didn't need to sleep in this city of magic and light.

They reached a courtyard even larger than the one Solyana had gone through on the back of Maral's elk. The space was cluttered with booths of people selling finer things. Solyana spotted a tailor and a tea shop serving lavender tea and cakes. The smells made her eyes widen and her mouth water. The fifla had barely touched the hunger that still rumbled through her belly. Gold coins passed between patrons and vendors; the city burst with life.

"Wow," Solyana whispered.

Gamaliel grinned.

Music floated in from somewhere, fast and free, painting the night as something to revel in. Solyana's foot started tapping and she couldn't help but laugh. "This place..." She shook her head. "It can't be real."

Gamaliel let out a whoop and grabbed Solyana, twirling her to the beat, his hair flowing behind him. Solyana laughed loudly and a few spectators clapped along.

"Did you just *dance* with me?" she asked, panting.

"No." Gamaliel straightened himself with a grin and tied his long hair up into a knot. "No, of course not."

"Ah, there you are."

Solyana turned to see Maral approaching from further in the maze of booths.

"Maral!" Solyana motioned to the woman. "Gamaliel, meet Maral. Maral, Gamaliel."

Maral dipped her head in a graceful greeting. She had exchanged her warrior's gear for a simple leather vest. A single pelt sat clasped around her left shoulder, tied with a leather strap. Her blonde hair was set in several intricate braids on one half of her head, though it hung loose in waves on the other side. A dark, smoky powder still covered her eyes, stretching from one temple to the other. Up close, Solyana realized it was paint, not a tattoo like Orson's had been.

"Chief Orson sent me to find you," Maral said. "He thought you might have gotten lost."

"Orson is the chief?" Solyana's mind went to the big man atop the polar bear. Fear dropped like a knife in her belly.

"Yes." Maral motioned for them to follow and began to walk, then stopped and looked over her shoulder. "He requested only you." She pointed to Solyana.

"We stay together," Gamaliel said firmly, coming beside her.

Maral shrugged and motioned them to follow.

Weaving their way through the heart of Takanah, their parkas and other outer layers back at the Healer's house, Solyana could almost fool herself into thinking it had happened—the long-awaited spring. She shifted her gaze to take in the rows of different foods surrounding them. Where did it all come from? With her own village slowly losing its herds, the greenhouses struggling, and fish disappearing, she never thought she would ever see such abundance—not like this.

As the music continued to draw them into this new place, Solyana couldn't help but feel an underlying current of something she could not name. Something deep and roiling, pulling at her from the inside.

"I'll leave you here." Maral tipped her head.

"Thank you," Gamaliel said as he and Solyana began to ascend the steps of the hall.

But before getting too far, Maral reached out and grabbed Solyana's arm. "Be careful," she said with a quick look at the door and back to her.

Solyana narrowed her eyes, unease turning in her gut. Maral gave her another curt nod before disappearing into the crowd of people in the market.

The base of the Chief's Hall held a row of steps leading to a double door, a large emblem emblazoned on the front like a brand. It was circular, stark and bold, with lines crisscrossing the edges. To the left of the door was a large metal cage containing several people who appeared to be sleeping. The bars were wide, wider than the people themselves, and the gate sat open. Guarding the door was a black wolf, almost as tall as the cage itself. The unnatural beast's eyes followed them, sending a chill down Solyana's spine.

Gamaliel's mouth hung agape. "It's a direwolf," he whispered. "I didn't think they were real. Legend has it, they're extremely loyal. Whoever his master is, they have a firm hold. He's not even blinking." Then Gamaliel glanced past her to the pen, studying the lethargic people inside. Some of them appeared to be totally asleep, while others still had their eyes partially open and moving marginally beneath lazy lids.

The two made their way up the stairs, keeping a wide berth from the direwolf. Gamaliel grabbed Solyana's hand. "I'm sure Chief Orson has an explanation."

Two broad men flanked the double wooden doors. Black tattoos covered their eyes, which narrowed in assessment. Finding them sufficient, the guards nodded them onward.

Solyana looked up to the sky. Amidst the lights of the city, the Norlos was difficult to see. The faint ribbon streaming so delicately above them, Solyana thought how easy it would be to forget their intended goal. How wonderful a life in Takanah would be, what a welcome distraction in which to settle herself.

Without a word, the soldiers opened the double doors before them, and Solyana and Gamaliel stepped through.

SISTERS?

PALLAH

A BONE-CRUSHING WEIGHT PRESSED Pallah into the soft earth, pushing the air from her lungs. The blood that had tried to drown her sloshed around her body as she wriggled her way out from underneath the bear. Finally free, Pallah stood, coughing, heaving, and sputtering. Blood poured from her nose and mouth, and sweet air rushed back in.

"You okay?" Issha's voice held concern.

Pallah peered up at her, wiping her mouth. "Not really."

"You look like you just murdered someone." Karav chuckled, as if Pallah hadn't almost been killed herself.

Pallah straightened, fruitlessly wiping her face with a dry piece of her cloak. "What happened?"

"You gave me a good opening," Issha said. "You're pretty good with that hatchet."

"You're not Tala, though." Karav leaned to the side, her hip jutting out. "You're Blou Fera, aren't you?"

Pallah's head snapped up, staring at Issha. Blou Fera was the aptitude for blood. Issha's face hardened with resolution. "Yes."

"I didn't know there were any Blou Fera left," Pallah said.

"There aren't many. Maybe no one, other than myself. Since the eradication of it a few generations ago, my mother was sure to teach me how to hide, and how to fight if I needed to." Issha's eyebrows came together as she looked Pallah from head to toe. "I'm sorry about almost drowning you. I haven't been able to practice much since joining the Taka Reu. Gaining energy from the earth is a lot faster, and a lot stronger than when you connect with the Celestials. I lost control." She wiped her hands on her trousers, leaving streaks of dirt and blood. "There's a creek south of the clearing. Let's go and get cleaned up."

The trio left the bear to Tinloh, who was already happily digging in. "Don't make yourself sick," Pallah told him. He tore a large swath of hide away, burying his face in lieu of response.

"What did you do exactly?" Pallah asked, peeling off her sodden layers of clothing to wash up.

"The only thing I know how to do. I used those cuts you made with your hatchet and tethered to its blood. I meant to clot it, to be honest, but that obviously didn't happen."

"It's not your fault. Who knows what the council would do if they found out you have Blou Fera," Karav said.

Issha's features hardened. "It's how my grandmother died."

Pallah shivered in the freezing water. "Does anyone else know about you?"

"Just you two."

"I won't say anything," Karav offered quickly.

Pallah nodded her agreement.

Freshly cleaned and dressed, they packed up to continue their final day of travel. They walked in companionable silence. The attack the night before bonded them in the way danger and trauma draws people together. Maybe now they would forget about the incident at Leif's cabin. They were her friends, or something that resembled friends. Pallah smiled to herself as they trekked farther east.

Pallah had never traveled outside the valley, save for the occasional trip to the ocean. It was odd knowing her mother had grown up somewhere outside of Sodur. Takanah was through the Hasta Pass, east of their valley. Other than the occasional Leirman selling wares, her own mother, and now Issha, Pallah had never met any outsiders before.

Her mother had lived a whole life before Pallah was born. She knew, even as she traveled for hours on aching feet, the answers to what she sought lay in a bed back in Sodur. Yet here she was, traveling farther than she had ever gone, simply because a wall had been erected between her and her mother. It hadn't always been there, surely. Something had driven it between them. No, not something. Someone. Bogdur was the reason for the walls each member of their family hid behind like shields. He alone was to blame.

In some ways, this journey east was a way to make amends with the mother Pallah never felt she'd had. By revealing the truth about her past, Pallah could bridge the rift that had yawned wider and wider between her and her mother over the years. She could come to understand and reconnect in a relationship that was no longer plagued by Bogdur and his abuse.

As they exited the wood and made their way across a rocky outcropping, Karav and Issha taught Pallah more about wielding the Taka Reu. She had connected to the Mother twice now, and it had seemed easier the second time. Even if it did come with its own rush of questions.

"Does the Taka Reu make your Gift stronger?" Pallah asked, nimbly navigating over the rocks.

"Yeah!" Karav said. "Our connection to the Mother Below is physically closer than the connection to the Celestials above." She hopped from one boulder to the next like a rabbit. "And the power is immediate. So, where you're always trying to grow your power with the Celestials, with the Taka Reu, you're usually having to hold it back. Some have been known to become more confident, faster, and more powerful while using it."

"That's exactly how it felt," Pallah admitted. "I didn't know it amplified more than my Gift, but me as a person, as well. Am I given access to other Gifts, too?"

"No," Issha said from the front. "You can still only use the Gift you've been given. That fact is a big reason why Vil wants access to all the ancient Taka Reu scrolls." Issha shaded her eyes, searching the tree line. "He claims there's a way to obtain more than one Gift. Something about the meaning of Taka Reu, why it's called 'The Taking.'"

Pallah pondered this, allowing it to bury deep and take up residence.

"I see smoke!" Karav said as she leapt from the final boulder.

Like Issha, Pallah stood, one hand over her eyes to watch the trail of smoke far in the distance, weaving its way into the sky.

"That would be Freya." Issha popped her waterskin open and took a long pull. "We'll get there by dusk." She handed it to Pallah, who drank. "I had a lot of questions when I joined the group, too."

"Yeah, like why The Cove is all woodsy," Karav chirped.

Issha nodded. "That one was weird."

"Well, why is it?" Pallah remembered the daisy she'd pulled from the wall of the cave that led to The Cove. She had been in awe of the lush meadow floor, walls of grass, and trees covered in fruit.

Karav tossed her braids over her shoulder. "I think it's because the Taka Reu is good for the environment."

"That's a theory," Issha offered with a grin.

"But it's true!" Karav flung her arms wide. "Whenever you use the Taka Reu in one place for a while, it makes the area grow."

Pallah remembered the group saying they would be found out simply by someone else walking in there, and she hadn't understood what they'd meant at the time. It made sense now.

"There's not a lot known about the Taka Reu," Issha reminded them. "Whenever it crops up, the priests or priestesses squash any discussion of it and turn the people back to Celestial worship. There was a priest long ago who pioneered the Taka Reu. He claimed the truest source is the core of the earth. Some scrolls refer to this power as coming from mountains of fire, or what we think are volcanos." She shrugged. "But the scrolls are in ancient Mothmari, and none of us are fluent."

"Hekla." Pallah said quietly. "It's north of Sodur, right?"

"Yeah, Vil said he would take us there." Karav swung her arms at her side, her belt of weapons and tools clinking against one another. "I think it would feel like going home."

"Regardless of what happened when you connected to the Mother," Issha continued, "it will be extremely difficult for you to connect to the Celestials again, if not impossible."

Pallah had heard that before. Unease pricked at her mind.

"She won't go back," Karav said with mischief in her voice. "The Reu will have her in a chokehold soon enough."

"It doesn't matter," Pallah said as she continued toward the line of smoke. "There's something comforting about being separated from Bogdur's gods."

Neither of them said anything to that.

"So," Pallah said, afraid to ask her next question. "I have to connect to Tinloh in this way then?"

"You're not tethered to him now?" Karav asked.

"No." If Pallah was honest, since using the Taka Reu in her house, she struggled to tether to Tinloh. Perhaps that had been the real reason he had slaughtered Leif's hares.

"Go ahead and try, Pal," Karav suggested.

Pallah pulled the cat from her shoulders. He growled sleepily, then sprung up, hackles rising. "Hey, 'Loh," she soothed and knelt on the ground. Spreading her fingers wide over the earth, she focused on Tinloh.

Be gentle now, Erval reminded her. *It requires a delicate touch.*

Pallah heeded him, knowing she could easily slip and hurt Tinloh. Pondering tender thoughts, she tethered to him, like a butterfly landing on a flower petal.

"Wow." Karav let out a breath. "That was so clean."

"She's latched?" Issha's eyes were wide, glancing between Karav, Pallah, and the sabertoothed cat. "You're latched?"

"Yes," Pallah said, focused on her charge. "It's so powerful...I can feel every single emotion. Even more than that, I feel like I could get him to do anything I want."

"That's because you probably could," Karav agreed. "He's young and hasn't been hardened by Tala use. And you seem to be a natural."

"More than a natural," Issha said. Pallah smiled satisfyingly to herself.

Freya's small cottage sat nestled in a large clearing, the entire yard littered with lawn ornaments of every type of material. From wooden animals to metal caricatures of humans, the ornaments greeted them with eyes that seemed to follow their trek to the front door.

There were two other buildings on the property, spread amongst the weeds and waving grasses that came up to their knees. If not for the smoke rising from the chimney of the cottage, Pallah would have assumed the place to be an abandoned commune. The buildings were dilapidated and hollow, boards losing their hold and windows frosted over with grime.

"I haven't been here in years." Issha stood still, the wind pulling at her clothes. "Freya was old then; she must be ancient now."

They approached the door and Pallah's mind suddenly kicked into action, as if she had forgotten the entire reason she had come was to talk to Freya. What was she going to say? Tinloh was perched on her shoulders again, and she tightened her connection to him before concealing him in her cloak.

Issha rapped on the door. Pallah took another look at the grounds behind her, the last of the sunlight touching each lawn creature for a brief, shining moment. The breeze jostled a few wind chimes near Pallah's head, and she jumped just as the door swung open, assaulting Pallah with the smell of sage, smoke, and sweat.

"Greetings, weary travelers." A small woman, her wiry gray hair smashed flat beneath a knitted cap, popped her head out of the door. "Who—ah! You!" Her tiny body scuttled outside, wrapping the three girls in one giant hug. "Isshoo!"

"Issha." Issha corrected. "It's been a while, Freya."

"I would say!" Freya stepped back, releasing the three of them. "My, you've grown! Look at you!" She turned to Pallah. "Look at her!"

"I see her," Pallah mumbled, but Freya was already circling Issha with an inquisitive and appraising eye.

"So sleek." She motioned to Issha's lack of hair. "And such strong muscles." The woman poked Issha's bicep. "Have you found yourself a man yet?"

"Freya." Issha rolled her eyes.

"Who are these two? This one a bodyguard? She looks intense." Freya was so close to Pallah, she could have sworn the woman was smelling her. A hoot resounded overhead and Pallah jumped again, only to spot a row of owls peeking out from the eaves. Their bright yellow eyes momentarily disappeared as they blinked.

The woman giggled. "Can't be a bodyguard; she's scared of my owls!" The woman turned her bright brown eyes on Karav and did the same sniffing motion close to her face. "This one has nice bone structure."

"Freya, please. We've traveled a long way. May we come in?" Issha's jaw tensed.

"You were never one for small talk, even when you were"—Freya lowered a hand close to the ground—"small-sized." She snorted derisively. "Fine. Come in. I was just making tea anyway."

The three girls ducked under multiple wind chimes to follow her into a heavily decorated kitchen that boasted two chairs, a wooden table, a tiny stove, and countless jars and bottles that lined the walls. Another two owls stared at them curiously from their perch in a corner. A kettle bubbled as they entered, and Freya bustled to the stove, removing the kettle and serving prepared cups of steaming tea, as if she had known they were coming. Or perhaps she had made tea for someone else. Pallah peered around the tiny kitchen, wondering if they were truly alone.

Nursing their tea, the three girls eyed Freya as she scoured her shelves for ingredients. "A bit of cranberry? No, too much. How about dill weed to liven him up, or maybe..." The woman talked to herself, unaware or simply uncaring the three girls were now crowded around her tiny kitchen table.

Pallah looked at Karav and Issha, both nodding in unison, urging her to talk to Freya. Pallah silently gestured toward the woman, feeling helpless and foolish. Tinloh was growing restless, pressed against her side beneath the folds of fabric, she pulled her tether taut and he stilled.

"Freya," Pallah began, but Freya continued her puttering. "I'm Pallah Bogson. My mother was recently in an accident, and she told me there were some answers I could find...with you." Pallah raised an eyebrow as Freya slowly came to a halt, a bundle of dried twigs in her hand, her back to Pallah. "My father, you see... I need to know why...why he—"

"What is your mother's name, child?" Freya's whimsical manner evaporated and was replaced by the hardened midwife Pallah had expected.

"Phyllir Hildeson."

Freya turned so slowly, Pallah was able to count five breaths until Freya's eyes met her own.

"Now that is a name I have not heard in some time," Freya said flatly.

"You remember her?" Pallah's chest released some tension, their endeavor proving to be more than a wild goose chase. "She had twins, me and my sister, Vámae...then Ahren, a few years later. Do you really remember her?"

"Sweetie..." Freya's shoulders slumped, her arms drooping to her sides. "I could never forget your mother. She was, and still is, the only pregnancy I have ever witnessed where implantation occurred twice in the same cycle." Freya's face turned dream-like as she spoke, her eyes seeing past Pallah, remembering a different time.

Pallah glanced at her friends; Issha's eyes were wide, but Karav only shrugged. She looked back at Freya who was now staring directly at her. "Twice in the same cycle?" Pallah repeated uneasily.

"She never told you?" Freya's eyes grew wide. She began making quick, twitchy movements with her fingers.

"Told me what?" The tension returned and Pallah found it difficult to breathe.

"You still favor him. Hmm...I thought perhaps we were wrong. But it was obvious, from the day you were born."

"Please explain, I have no idea what you're talking about." Tin-loh rolled at Pallah's side. She pulled tight on her tether and he let out a small yip that Pallah covered with a cough.

"I'm referring to... You shouldn't be hearing this from me, but..." She covered her mouth with a tiny, weathered hand, her large eyes meeting Pallah's, mirrored by the two owls behind her. "It means you and Vámae were conceived by two different fathers." Freya held up two fingers. "Two implantations," she dropped one finger away. "One cycle. Pallah Bogson, you are Vámae's twin, yes...but even more precise, you and Vámae are half-sisters."

Pallah blinked. Her hand gripping the mug began to shake. Tea speckled the table. "What?"

"She wasn't perfect, but you know your father." Freya's eyes softened. "He's not an easy man to be with, or so Phyllir told me. Settle in, I'll warm your mug. We have much to discuss."

DEFECTION

ERVAL

AN HOUR AFTER ERVAL had tethered to his sister, his door creaked open to reveal a flickering candle in the hall.

"Erval," his sister whispered through the dark, hand carefully cupped around the flame.

"Halldora?" He rubbed his eyes to sell the lie he had been asleep. "What are you—"

"You're a fool."

He blinked, not exactly the emotion he was expecting from her. In fact, he couldn't feel much emotion from his tether at all. Odd.

"Good evening to you as well." He kept his tone light, sarcastic even. It was better this way with Halldora. "Pray tell, what are you doing in my rooms?" People were better led when they believed they were the ones calling the shots.

"How did you get back inside?"

"Snuck in through the window, dear sister. Right before our *häfan* advisor burst into the room in his nightgown." He flung back his covers and stretched his arms high with a sideways glance at Halldora. "You should really dust under your bed."

"Stop jesting, brother." There was a wariness in her voice that Erval didn't like, something that fought for freedom from his hold. He was tethered, wasn't he? "Shahann brought important news. Life changing news."

So, the spider had already told her.

"Halldora." Erval's rage flared quickly and quietly.

"Erval, I think you should know what he said—"

"I know what he said." He tightened the tether between them, but Halldora simply narrowed her eyes.

"How can you know already?"

"I am the heir." He stepped close, tilting his head. "Aren't I?" He cupped her chin. "I'm *always* the first to know." The waxing moon cast a sliver of light on his sister's face, the shadows beneath her eyes lengthening as her prideful gaze slid to the floor. "Don't worry, Dora. I won't let this burden pass to you. I'm to secure my coronation in but one full moon cycle. Father will not discard me at the cusp of my reign."

"Brother..." Halldora stepped from his grasp and sat primly on the side of his bed. "The Blue Moon demands—"

"Demands? It demands..." Erval paced before her. He squeezed the tether, digging it in deeper. What if he made her...hurt? He never *wanted* to hurt Halldora; he loved her. In fact, anytime he tethered a human, it sparked a love for them, an intimacy that made him fiercely protective. It's what won him so many bardagis.

During the times he had inflicted pain on someone using his Gift, it felt like his own skin was peeling away, flayed open and raw.

It was maddening.

"What are you doing?" She stood from the bed abruptly, clutching her chest. "Are you...did you..." Her mouth dropped open in realization. "You tethered me?"

"No, of course not." He waved her away, releasing his tether completely.

"Why did—"

"Halldora, we must fight this absurd violation together!" He grasped her hands in his own, pressing the bones just hard enough to be both earnest and painful. "Our ancestors fought for freedom of religion, and now we are to be marched right back into Thren Temple?" He scoffed. "I think not."

"Is it truly freedom if we have been cut off from the Temple for so long? I don't know, brother." Halldora pulled her hands away and lifted her chin. "They say I am to be queen."

Erval clutched his chest and injected fear into his voice. "You would tear me from my throne? After all we've been through?" He kept his eyes wide, bright blue pools that sparkled with hurt.

She said nothing.

"Wait." He released her and snapped his fingers. "I see your scheme! Become queen in a month's time, only to turn your back on Priest Henrik! I love it. Then I'll be reinstated and—"

"Erval..."

"Don't."

A groan of floorboards drew Erval's attention to the door. "Where were you?" Shahann extended one of his spindly arms, a torch held at the end.

"Get out of here, Shahann." Erval wheeled away. "You'll get my sheets all smoky."

Halldora rose from the bed and shuffled to Shahann's side, casting Erval a pitying glance over her shoulder.

And with that simple act, Erval knew he had no other choice. She had chosen her side. How quickly and easily her mind had been poisoned. If she were to betray him, better now than later.

"Were you gambling?" Shahann asked, oblivious to anything that mattered.

"I don't see why my whereabouts are too important anymore, do you?" He narrowed his eyes at the man, a silent implication.

Shahann blustered a moment and straightened his night-cap. "Well, you're home now. Please do not leave the grounds again." He motioned Halldora to the door. "Let's get back, Halldora."

"That's it?" Erval spread his arms wide. "No, slap on the wrist? No further interrogation? Why, Shahann, how lax you've become!"

The man at the door stiffened, frozen for only a moment before marching close to Erval. "Fine." Shahann bent down and sniffed Erval's hair.

In the hour between his escape from Halldora's room and their conversation here, Erval had only enough time to change his clothes, but not to bathe.

Häfa, he cursed to himself.

Shahann wrinkled his nose. "You smell of the bardagis."

"What?" Erval made a show of sniffing under his arms. "That's just the stench of a man, Shahann! I understand how you wouldn't recognize it."

Shahann's face grew red. "Your father will hear of this." Then he guided Halldora out of the room, leaving Erval in the dark.

Sleep eluded Erval, and by the time his servants threw open the curtains, his eyes were bloodshot and his head pounded. The servants only woke him like this when his father wanted him at breakfast.

He rubbed his eyes, then plodded over to the scalding tub of water left in his chambers. One thing he loved about Thonethren: the luxury of hot water and steam, provided by the sheer good fortune that his great city lay at the base of a dormant volcano.

The door to his chambers opened and three servants filed in, each holding an article of clothing.

Erval raised an eyebrow. "It's *this* kind of breakfast, is it?" He eyed the formal suit, all tails and cuffs and uncomfortable stuffiness. "Does it even still fit?" He hadn't worn his formals in ages.

"We took your measurements last week, sir," Jethro said. Gray-haired and loyal, the valet had been with the family all Erval's life. The man leaned close to begin removing Erval's linen pants. He let them undress, bathe, and redress him.

As they worked, Erval thought. The hour, the dress, all of it, pointed to an important conversation King Mikkael was hoping to have with his son. Erval was ready for it. He had spent most of the night mulling it over. There was no way he would not be king; it simply wasn't an option.

Erval's speech was ready. He would deliver it to his father, and the servants would do what they did best: gossip their little hearts out.

He was counting on it.

Erval strode down the corridor, his dress shoes clopping on the sanded stone like a royal show horse. He whistled a tune he'd heard while passing a tavern the night before, and when he burst through the double doors of the dining hall, all eyes turned to him. His father sat at the head of the table, his sister to his left, and Erval took his rightful seat at his father's right hand. Erval grinned at the king.

King Mikkael smiled sadly at his son, and something cold poured into Erval.

So, his father was set on it.

No matter; he would convince him. And if not him, then the servants...and they would sway his people.

There was no talk as the three of them ate, only clinks and scrapes of cutlery on plates and the occasional delicate cough from one of the servants lining the room. Shahann was nowhere to be seen, which Erval thought odd; he wouldn't voluntarily miss Erval's supposed fall from grace. And though the absence gave him cause for concern, it didn't stop him from shoveling eggs, sausage, and stewed beans into his mouth.

Erval glanced up between bites to see his father and sister sipping from teacups.

He hadn't been given any tea.

"Some tea!" he commanded, ringing the small bell near his plate.

His father stood abruptly.

Erval looked at him, then at Halldora. She was biting her lower lip as she slowly lowered her cup to the table, eyes on her plate.

"Erval," his father began. Erval leaned back in his chair, keeping the front two legs off the ground. "Can you sit still for a moment?"

He plopped the chair back in place, the thump echoing around the room. "What's on your mind, Father?"

"There has been a change in the night. A change that affects you greatly." King Mikkael's eyes were soft, but his mouth held a hard line.

"Did you sack Shahann?" Erval asked innocently, standing to his feet, hands clasped behind his back as he began to stride around the table. "Personally, I thought he was a gem. Oh, or Jethro? Now *him,* I would truly miss." He snapped his fingers and turned on his heel, facing his father once more. "Oh, I know! New curtains in the hall!"

That's when he heard it: the roar of thousands of voices coming through the southern double doors of the dining hall, massive frames hewn from aspen, which led to a courtyard below. Shahann and a servant swept into the room, pushing the doors open together.

A heavy hand landed on Erval's shoulder, and he glanced at his father. He matched the man in height now, though not quite in bulk.

"Erval, I wish we had more time." King Mikkael sighed and rubbed a hand over his salt and pepper hair. "I know you will do me proud, son. You will act with wisdom, with piety, and with grace. You are wise beyond your years, and more mature than you pretend to be."

Erval didn't know what to say. His father had never been one for compliments. Did he truly believe that of him? Could he accept being plucked from his place to stand at his sister's side? Erval's habits were no real secret, least of all to his father; his gallivanting through the streets of Thonethren, his foolish use of his power, his allowance spent on bets and debts time and time again. Emotions like guilt and embarrassment were of no use to a prince, but now, standing in his father's gaze, Erval felt nothing but shame for all those momentary pleasures.

He wanted to tell his father not to do it, to stop him from going out there, to have a moment, a word, an appeal. He could abdicate to Halldora, possibly, but couldn't his father talk to him first? All he wanted was honesty.

But the people demanded their king.

"Mikkael! Mikkael!" His name rose from the grounds like a cresting wave and his father stepped forward. King Mikkael secured two golden cuffs that covered his wrists and forearms as he reached the edge of the balcony.

The chanting continued, each iteration chipping at the grip Erval held on his panic. It was happening too quickly. Surely, the king wouldn't pronounce such a thing before properly—

"Mikkael! Mikkael! Mikkael!"

King Mikkael crossed his cuffed arms and held them up until the sun glinted off them. The people roared their response. He brought his arms down and the crowd fell silent.

In the pause, a pulse of violence surged through Erval. He needed to stop his father. He could push him from the balcony, make it look like the king stumbled. It would be too easy. But as soon as the thought entered his mind, nausea rolled in his stomach. No...he corrected himself. He could never.

"People of Thonethren," King Mikkael addressed the gathered assembly. "For years, we have followed my forefather's decrees of worship. Giving you access to the earth, the Mother, the Taka Reu. Although this has brought prosperity to our people, we have seen a darkness within our kingdom that ought not be."

Shahann appeared to Erval's right, his bony hand giving Erval a gentle push. He stepped closer to his father, Halldora a mirror image on his other side. Below, the people stood much as Erval expected them to. The myriad of wealthy at the far end of the courtyard, and the lower classes craning their necks from the front.

"Under the guidance of Priest Henrik"—the king waved a hand toward his left and the priest stepped beside Erval, giving a modest wave to the people—"I am decreeing Thonethren to be a Celestial worshiping people."

The people went silent, caught off guard.

"Thren Temple is our place of worship, and the Celestials, our gods. No longer are we to hold to the Mother below our feet, but we are to look to the Father of the Day." King Mikkael motioned to the sun, its warmth welcome in the chilly morning air. "If anyone is caught worshiping the Taka Reu, swift action will be taken. Together we will worship the Father of the Day, the Mother of the Night, and Children of the Sky!"

A collective gasp threaded through the people and murmurs rippled across the courtyard.

"In accordance with the Celestials and the Temple, we will follow the succession they demand—"

Erval struck out with his tether, bold and seething, aimed directly at his father. He would stop him here, declare himself king, and denounce this foolish endeavor. His tether latched, but just as it had with Halldora the night before, no emotions were brought to him. His father's mind remained untouched.

King Mikkael halted and turned to look at him, his eyes creased in blatant disgust. Never in his eighteen years had Erval seen his father look at him with such disdain. From his peripheral, Erval watched the guards take a step forward.

"Father…" he pleaded, fear constricting his throat. "Please, can we speak about this?"

"Did you just attempt to tether me, son?" Fury poured from Mikkael's face like smoke.

"Please," Erval pleaded. "*Talk* to me."

The guards continued to close in on him, quiet but determined. King Mikkael held up a hand and the guards stopped. "Answer me, son."

Erval worked his jaw. If his father had already felt it, what was the point of lying? "Yes. But it didn't work!"

The king's face hardened still more. Erval's stomach dropped.

"Guards," the king said. He signaled with his hand.

In an instant, the guards were on Erval, grappling with his arms and legs, pulling him back from the balcony, away from the king, his father.

"What was I supposed to do?" Erval screamed at him, uncaring of the crowd below. He threw his tether out in several directions but was blocked at every turn. What was this? He didn't understand. It was as if they were all guarded against his Gift.

"Keep strong, sire." Shahann's unwelcome voice wavered over the balcony. "The tea will protect you."

The tea. At breakfast. Erval had been the only one without a cup.

It didn't stop him from trying to tether again and again as the guards wrenched him away from the balcony, away from his family. Fighting against them, Erval cried out to his father who had turned his back, unable or unwilling to look at his son. Then he felt it: a nudge at the center of his chest. He wrenched himself sideways to survey the group.

Someone here hadn't drunk the tea. Someone just through the dining hall and down the servant's stairwell.

He shot his tether backwards at the unsuspecting servant girl and latched onto her instantly. Erval laughed from the core of his belly, so full and discomfiting, it gave the guards pause.

They redoubled their efforts, dragging him into the dining hall. Erval gave the girl a tug and, like a dog to heel, she walked out from the stairwell. Her mind, simple enough, wouldn't even remember what he would make her do; a mercy.

Erval slumped to throw the guards off-balance, and they were pulled down with the shift of his weight. The servant girl slid a knife from the table.

With singular purpose, she marched toward Erval and lifted the knife high overhead. One of the guards had time to release his grip but didn't get his hands up before the knife came down, punching into the exposed flesh between his helmet and his chest plate.

Erval smiled, relief washing through him, as she moved on to the next guard. Blood splashing them both as she stabbed and stabbed. The third guard tackled the girl, and the fourth joined him. Erval scrambled to his feet and watched as they yanked her by the hair, a dagger of their own poised to snuff out the deadly threat so close to the royal family. He released his tether, not wanting to feel the blade himself.

"Halt!" King Mikkael stormed in from the balcony, his hand outstretched, and the guard stayed his killing blow. The servant girl began to wail. Mikkael looked at his son. "Are you mad, boy? Stop this foolishness!"

"You would choose the Celestials over your family?" Erval asked, panting from the use of his Gift. He took a step backward. "Over me?"

The king opened his mouth to speak but held his tongue, shaking his head, the lines in his face brought on by age growing deeper.

Shahann spoke from the corner, where he and Halldora cowered. "How could you lead with the Gift you have? It would always end this way."

The truth of the words, though they would sink deeper still, struck him through the heart like a dagger. Yes. How had he not realized sooner? A king with the Gift of Mann Tala could never be trusted; his motives and intentions would forever be doubted. And those that served him, always at risk. Had it all been a farce? The years of training? His entire childhood? He hadn't the time to consider it now.

"Erval." King Mikkael stepped forward, a hand raised. "You've proven you do not have the disposition or temperament to support your sister as she ascends to her divinely ordained station. You leave me no choice." He lowered his hand.

Three guards lunged in his direction, but Erval slipped away, pedaling backward instead of running through the dining hall.

Then he turned on his heel, barreling straight for the corner of the balcony and the drop to the courtyard below.

A murmur of surprise rippled through the crowd as Erval leapt. Tucking himself into a ball, he cleared the parapet, and finally extended his arms, barely grasping the corner of the balcony adjacent. His shoulders screamed in agony, but he gritted his teeth and forced himself to flash a smile for the onlookers. His momentum carrying his legs forward, he kicked off the stone side of the castle and released his grip, completing a backflip that pushed him to the balcony below. He landed hard, his ankle giving way beneath him. He tottered for a moment before standing to the chant of his name. He ran to the edge and gave a bow, ignoring the pain clawing up his leg. He grinned, basking in their adulation.

"Erval! Erval! Erval!"

The love of the people—he could use that. But for now, he needed to get out of his *häfan* castle. He needed to *run*. He jumped onto the stone ledge, planning to work his way down to ground level. There were many caves burrowed in the side of Mount Hekla; the volcanic mountain would hide him well.

He looked up at his home for what would be the last time, at least for now, but not forever.

Halldora looked down at him, so small now from his vantage point, her hair whipping in the wind. He winked, then launched himself away from the castle and into the undulating crowd below.

FEAST OF DARKNESS

SOLYANA

"MY LITTLE ARCTIC FOX! Here she comes!" The chief's voice echoed down the cavernous hall crafted of intricately cut alder wood. Illustrious and gleaming, its pillars were shaped and hewn so smoothly, they seemed to defy all human engineering. Solyana had only seen this kind of handiwork replicated in stone at the Temple Celestial, and that had taken *generations* of Stein Fera to craft and perfect.

Fire hung from the ceiling, crackling in large iron braziers high above their heads. Solyana's gaze followed them down until she saw a long wooden table set with plates and cups. Beyond the table at the far end of the hall sat the chief on his throne, his clean-shaven face grinning.

But this man was no chief.

He was a king.

"Did I not tell you?" Orson said to the men and women lining the wall behind him. "She is just tiny—feisty, too! Her fire is strong! Strong for being so small." He chuckled, his expansive chest lifting and falling like mighty bellows. He wore only a shoulder-strapped fur pelt and pants, every inch of his chest and stomach corded with muscle.

Murmurs of agreement came from behind the throne. Solyana recognized them as the Beast Riders who had found her in the snow.

"Come closer, little fox," Orson's voice rumbled as he beckoned Solyana forward. She reached for Gamaliel's hand and grasped it firmly as the two of them stepped together. Her hackles rose the closer she got to the throne, realization hitting her in the chest.

It was made of bones.

Whitewashed and melded together, the throne glowed in the moonlight that pierced into the room from windows set high on the walls.

Orson's eyes, bright and hungry behind his black tattoo, roved over her. He turned to Gamaliel. "This is the boy we pulled from the snow? I asked only for the fox, not the wolf."

One of the Beast Riders leaned forward and whispered something to him.

"Oh!" The chief's smile returned. "I called you a wolf, and here you are. Ulfur Tala, yes?" He chuckled.

"I tether to wolves, yes, but I'm Broad Tala," Gamaliel clarified. "I can tether to most predators."

"Good...good." Without any preamble or warning, Orson bounded from his throne of bones and walked past them. "Where are my manners? Sit! Feast with me!"

Solyana and Gamaliel turned to find a flurry of servants decorating the table with the foods they'd passed at the market: roasted elk, wood-fired beets, seeded pumpkin bread, and chalices full of something sharp and acidic-smelling that when Solyana lifted it to her nose, made it wrinkle. Chief Orson clapped his meaty hands to their shoulders and led them to the table, seating Solyana on one side and Gamaliel on the other, before sitting himself at the head.

The man ate with his hands. Juices from elk ribs dripped from his mouth, making a trail down his ink-laden face. With every bite, Solyana's eyes flicked back to his throne. She took a sip of the drink set before her and, though it was cold, it burned the back of her throat and made her head swim. She set it to the side.

"Go on, eat. Eat!" He waved them on, wiping his face with the back of his forearm.

Solyana and Gamaliel did as they were told. They hadn't eaten a true meal since leaving the valley, and Solyana's stomach grumbled as she piled her plate. She took a bite of the warm pumpkin bread and her whole body relaxed.

"I'm sorry about the misunderstanding before," Chief Orson stated between smacks of his lips. "We heard the avalanche and went to investigate. We didn't expect to find people in the snow." He wiped his mouth with a chuckle. "And when you say you are Solyana of Vestur? Your father, Chief of Mothmar? It felt a bit like you were trying to deceive us. I have never heard of this Vestur, and there is no chief over all Mothmar."

Solyana looked up from her meal, swallowing the last of the bread, unsure of the answer he was looking for.

Orson's eyes drifted over her as he took a long swallow of his drink. "Are there more villages where you are from?"

"Yes," Solyana said. "The others are Austur and Sodur." She exchanged a glance with Gamaliel. They needed supplies, and a lot of them, if they were going to continue on their journey. Getting on Orson's good side was imperative, whether she enjoyed playing diplomat or not.

"Austur..." Chief Orson set his meat down and licked his fingers in turn. "Yes, I've heard of that one." He turned in his seat, scanning the faces of the Beast Riders still standing at attention behind his throne. He snorted and turned back to his meal. "Now, onto the real reason you're here." His eyes caught Solyana's, nostrils flaring.

"Yes, thank you for your kindness. My friend Jonas is improving quickly under your Healer's care."

Orson waved away her thanks with a soft smile. "Yes, yes, of course. But I am referring to your dangerous journey, far from your home. You are the first in a decade to come through the Hasta Pass and survive. But several have come before, and the ones who have lived are usually looking for the same thing."

"And what's that?" Gamaliel asked.

The chief glanced at him, his eyelids lowering and mouth curling with distaste. "I am not speaking to you, wolf boy."

Gamaliel stiffened.

Solyana's stomach turned and she set down her fork.

Orson turned back to her, his features darkening even as his eyes smiled. "Prophecy." The word came out gravelly and slow, and the room stayed quiet under its weight. "Some have come through the pass looking for other things: adventure...fame...people gone before. Of those, I do not mind having guests. But prophecy I do not abide. Prophecy has no place here, in my city. Have you come to seek what I forbid, fox?"

Solyana looked up into the eyes of the man.

She would tell him the truth.

Her voice came out small at first. "I've heard tales of long ago, when all children were born with a Gift." Solyana stood, beginning a slow walk around the perimeter of the table. "When feasts were plentiful, and people were nourished and fat. When blizzards came only at the full moon—a reminder of our need for the Celestials." She stopped her walk, now closer to the chief. His eyes were locked on hers, a rivulet of grease running down his chin. "But my valley is not so, Chief Orson. Many of my people are born without Gifts, unable to withstand the cold or provide for themselves. The blizzards, which came at the full moon, have become erratic, as if the Celestials themselves have turned from us. We have no food, we have no comfort, and my people perish. So, yes, Chief. I am here because of a prophecy." The chief broke eye contact and took a large pull from his chalice. Solyana continued undeterred. "I have no qualm with you, or with your people. I am simply asking for aid, and we will be on our way."

The chief set down his drink and studied her behind his dark tattoos. "And what prophecy would this be, little fox?"

"I am the one who is destined to turn our world from white to green. You know of what I speak."

Orson's chair groaned and creaked as he shifted, crossing his arms.

"Yes." He sighed. "But it is a fallacy."

Solyana blinked once, then twice. "I would agree the timeline could possibly be wrong; it isn't specific. But as my valley holds the

Temple Celestial, it stands at the precipice of eternal winter. And the Celestials have given us evidence." Heat rose into her face. "And it's me." She thanked the Celestials for their impeccable timing. Someone near the throne gasped as the crescent scar revealed itself.

"I was born without a Gift. Yet I stand before you now with Heitt—an Eldur, able to wield flame." She opened her palm and produced a small fire that rippled and grew; she quickly closed her fist, snuffing it out. "I carry the mark that heralds the new age fast approaching." Solyana stepped closer to the chief. "I will follow the Norlos before it disappears at the end of this lunar cycle. I will find the boy at its end, the boy who tethers the light itself. He will return with me, and we will bring the green."

The room was silent, interrupted by a long creak as one side of the double doors swung inward. The chief kept his eyes on Solyana. In her peripheral vision, she saw someone slink into the room, their shoulders hunched.

"Pretty words, from a pretty fox," Orson said with a slow smile. He stood from the table, crossed to her in two strides, and placed an arm over her shoulders. "But you see, Solyana of Vestur, you are not the first to come through Takanah in search of this particular prophecy."

Solyana tried to step away from him, but his arm stayed clamped, trapping her. She shot a look at Gamaliel who was poised in his seat, fork and knife held fast in his fists.

"There have been others?" Solyana relaxed her shoulders and the chief's arm slid off as he stepped away.

"Why, of course!" He let out a bark of laughter. "Did you think you were the first?"

Solyana's insides crumpled as if she had been punched. Other people had gone before? "Then they must have failed. And that is something I will not do. I will bring the green!"

"Well," the chief asked quietly, "do you wish to know *how* the others failed?"

A bitter chill slithered down Solyana's spine and she felt Gamaliel's gaze burn into her. "How?" Solyana asked. But there was no answer. She looked up to find Chief Orson turned toward a thin man that ambled toward their table. Gamaliel's mouth hung open, stuttering, his eyes wide and brimming with disbelief.

"Gamaliel?" The sound of the name from another's voice froze Solyana in place. He was a crooked question mark of a man, a collection of skin and bones hunched over itself, his hands cradling his stomach, long black hair hanging down to his waist. "Is it...is it truly you?"

Gamaliel stood, his chair screeching across the wooden floor. "Father?" he whispered.

"Reynir, I was wondering where you—" The chief's rebuke went unheard as Gamaliel hurried to his father. Though when he reached to embrace him, Reynir flinched, his arms wrapping tighter around himself, a defense against his own son.

"I-I-I'm so s-s-sorry," Reynir choked between sobs, curling over his knees until he was a heap on the floor.

"Father!" Gamaliel dropped to his knees and cradled his father in his arms, stroking his hair and tears away from his face. The group of Beast Riders lining the walls turned away, and as Solyana lowered her eyes, she noticed Chief Orson did not extend the same courtesy.

A lump rose in Solyana's throat as she furtively watched their reunion, thinking of her own father. What was he doing right now? Had another blizzard struck since she'd left? Were the Rána still trying to get them to move from the valley and resettle closer to Kana Ocean?

"I thought you were dead." Gamaliel's face held nothing but shock. "You've been gone for so long..."

"Oh, son." Reynir sniffed, sitting cross-legged on the floor. He pressed a hand to Gamaliel's cheek and gave a withered smile across cracked lips. "I tried to come back. But that pass...it's as if it disappeared the moment I came through it." His eyes darted over his son as if memorizing every part of him. He made to stand with Gamaliel's help, wavering on spindly legs. "Just look at you...how you've grown." Reynir pulled at his son's tunic and all of Gamaliel tensed.

"Why did you leave in the first place?" he asked, his tone sharp.

A grimace replaced the smile. "Perhaps we should step out, go talk somewhere more private."

"Reynir, when I saw this boy, I knew he must be yours." Chief Orson said with a grin.

"Yes, Chief Orson." Reynir cowered under Orson's gaze, his eyes darting to his feet.

"And now I return him to you!" The chief threw his arms wide.

"Praise the Mother Below!" Reynir lifted his hands and bowed his head, his entire body trembling in submission.

Wheels spun in Solyana's mind, the cogs of understanding clicking together as she heard the phrase she had read in scrolls, the name of the deity of something dark, spoken from the lips of a priestess. Reynir was praising not the Mother of the Night, but Mother Earth.

The Mother Below.

"Ha!" Orson's heavy hands clapped onto the shoulders of the father and son; Reynir almost crumpled to the ground once more. "Much rejoicing! What a time of celebration! You must stay, both of you. Little fox and wolf boy! Enjoy our city! Perhaps..." He lifted his hands and made two enormous fists. "You will join the Beast Riders, like your father." He wrapped a muscled arm around Gamaliel's shoulders, dwarfing him in his grip.

Solyana stared at Gamaliel, willing him to look at her, every second passing a lost opportunity to run from the hall. But his eyes were on his father. He gave a placating laugh and stepped out from beneath the chief's arm.

"I insist," Orson said, gripping his shoulder again. His hand squeezed so tightly Gamaliel winced. "You will stay."

"How did the other's fail?" Solyana asked again, though she was unsure if she wanted to know the answer.

The chief turned, floorboards creaking underfoot as he relinquished his hold on father and son and came close to Solyana, his hot breath warming her hair. Solyana couldn't stop herself from shaking as Orson's finger rose to trail the moon-shaped scar on her face.

"Hey!" Gamaliel finally saw past his reunion and took two quick steps forward, but Orson raised a hand to stop him.

"Another prophet, another green-seeker." He breathed in deeply, and something in the atmosphere shifted. "I have offered all those before you the same." He swung a hand back, and a few of his Beast Riders stepped forward.

Solyana's eyes widened, and she pulled her hands to her sides. Preparing for what, she didn't know. But she wasn't staying here.

"*They* were smart enough to accept my offer. What say you?"

Solyana's gray-blue eyes caught on Chief Orson's, hidden within his dark tattoo. "I respectfully decline."

Chief Orson rubbed at his chin as he nodded slowly. "Well, this presents a problem, little fox. You cannot bring the green, for the Celestials have no place here. Or anywhere. If they did, my power would be lost to me. And I cannot allow that."

Chief Orson's brow lowered, and a horrible groan fell from his lips. It boiled over into a guttural chuckle. When the chief's eyes shot open, only inky blackness stared back at her, blending with the tattoos imprinted across his face. He laughed, a ghostly roll sending horror slicing through her.

Her mind could scream only one word.

Run.

The chief staggered back. Tendrils of smoke, black as pitch, came pouring up from the wooden floor. They surrounded the chief, shooting into his nose and eyes, into his ears and mouth, and he drank them up with a pleasure that made Solyana's stomach twist. The flames in the room flickered, and the Beast Riders who had lined the walls began pacing back and forth like caged animals. Some fell to their knees, but all of them opened their palms to the black substance as it wove its way in and around them.

"Gamaliel…" Solyana turned to him to find her terror mirrored on his face.

Gamaliel turned to his father, but Reynir was on the floor, shaking, convulsing, spittle dribbling from his mouth.

"Father!" Gamaliel dropped beside him, his hands fluttering uselessly. "What's wrong? *Häfan* it all! No! I just found you!"

"Don't let him turn you, Gam. Don't take his offer. You'll never leave! Ga-Gam-garrrrrr!" Gamaliel's name became a growl as Reynir's body transformed from man to massive beast. Fur sprouted from beneath his clothing; it ripped away, shedding to the floor.

Solyana scrambled backwards, ice slicing through her veins, as she watched Reynir's face extend gruesomely into an elongated snout lined with razor-sharp teeth. Ears sprouted from his head, tufted and twitching.

The direwolf.

The room erupted.

Every Beast Rider took off in different directions; half convulsed on the ground, while the others retrieved leather leads and found their beasts as they returned. One came for Reynir, a leather halter in hand. He flashed a wicked grin at Solyana, his solid-black eyes the same as the chief's. He slipped the lead over Reynir's head and mounted his back, yanking the reins hard.

The direwolf crouched and growled with throaty menace, lips peeling back to reveal his fangs.

The wooden double doors launched inward, cracking against the wall. A woman stumbled to the floor, mid-transformation. Portions of her body were covered in white fur. She screamed in what could only be agonizing torture until she stood to her full height, having shifted into a polar bear.

The chief, still chuckling, walked to the bear's side. One of his beast riders secured a lead to the polar bear's massive maw. The chief took two mighty steps before jumping, arms swinging as his momentum carried him off the ground and onto the bear with a grunt. The bear's roar shook the rafters.

"Your ill-fated journey ends here!" Orson declared, wrapping the reins around his hand. The Beast Rider scuttled back to Orson's side, hefting a cleaver the size of an ale barrel up to him. The chief took it and twirled it once. His grin dropped. "Be still and I'll make it quick."

"Let us go! Release my father!" Gamaliel shoved Solyana behind him and drew the staff from his back in one fluid motion.

Chief Orson bellowed a laugh. "You show more spine than your father, boy!" His tone descended. "It will be more satisfying to break."

Orson leaned forward, raising his weapon, and the bear-woman bellowed beneath him.

Solyana stepped out from behind Gamaliel and shoved her palms forward, calling on her Heitt for a burst of flame. But her hands merely glowed. She tried again, but only flickers sputtered over her palms.

Too late.

The chief attacked, cleaver descending on the two just as Gamaliel knocked into Solyana, taking them both to the ground. The weapon buried itself into the floor, splintering the wood.

"To the door!" Gamaliel screamed as beast and human alike brayed and roared throughout the room. But as they clambered around toward the exit, Reynir and his rider leapt into their path, a low growl erupting from his throat, yellow teeth bared, cupped in bulging black gums.

The floor groaned as Chief Orson extricated his cleaver and circled them slowly, a lecherous grin on his face. The riders urged their beasts forward, closing the gap between them and their prey. Solyana spun, her mind reeling, her hands grasping for the fire that continued to elude her.

The polar bear lunged for them, maw open, as Orson's cleaver descended, well-muscled fury behind it. Solyana flung her arms above her head and screamed as Gamaliel spun, raising his staff with two hands to meet the cleaver. He deflected it, but the impact loosened his grip. Orson's cleaver slid along the length of the staff until it found purchase in the wood, severing it in two with a *crack*.

Mouth open, panic begged to free itself from Solyana. She pressed her shaking palms together, reaching deep inside, holding the presence of the Father of the Day in her mind. Then with a cry of exasperation, she again forced her hands outward.

The fire answered, bright and brilliant—but wild.

It whipped out of her, scorching the bear and chief alike. Orson bellowed from somewhere in its midst. He shielded himself with his cleaver, blocking the fire as it tore around and behind him. Solyana brought her hands down, completely forgetting Gamaliel lying before her.

He screamed and rolled away.

Sweat snaking down her back, Solyana squeezed her palms shut as fast as she could, but the fire would not abate. It wove its way up her arms as though to consume her, but her skin remained unharmed. She thought of Jonas, immune to the expression of his Heitt, even as it burned all it touched around him.

Solyana may have been safe from her own flame, but everyone around her was not. She sobbed and slapped her palms against her thighs. "STOP!" she begged with a guttural scream, and the fire finally heeded her, winking out as if it had never been.

Somewhere, Orson was laughing, his bear prowling around its prey. Solyana rushed to Gamaliel, smothering any remaining flames. His breath was hitching, his hair charred on one side, his face a tangle of untamed fear and, thankfully, only a little burnt flesh. Everything in Solyana sought to renounce Heitt, to bury the Gift somewhere deep, where it could never come out again.

But that wasn't an option now.

Solyana's eyes became affixed to the claws gouging scores along the wooden floor with each step as the direwolf loped closer, the man atop shouting something Solyana couldn't understand over the rushing of blood in her ears.

Keeping one arm wrapped around Gamaliel, heart in her throat, Solyana aimed at Reynir's rider and shot fire at his chest.

The rider dropped the reins, arms rising far too late to protect his face. The fire rippled over his skin, latching on and burning, indifferent to his screams. He slumped to the side, legs still holding him in place on the back of Reynir. The fire rolled down the direwolf's fur. He lunged forward, chaotic and feral, eyes bathed in panic until another Beast Rider helped douse the flame.

Chief Orson stared through the flames with his ink-black eyes, sheer disgust marring his features. When he raised his cleaver into the air, the entire room stood to attention. Nothing but the sounds of panting breaths and growing fire remained.

Solyana reached to her belt for the hatchet Priestess Avi had given her, white-knuckled and desperate. Gamaliel shook as his hands felt for the long hair that was no longer on a portion of his head, having taken the brunt of Solyana's burning.

She wished they had died in the snow, entombed by the cold and peacefully swept in sleep, rather than this charred and grisly end, delivered by people consumed and warped by Dark Gifts.

This was the Taka Reu.

And it had ravaged these people.

The hall was burning. The flame from Solyana's own hand had caught and taken hold, licking at the people surrounding them.

"No more games, Solyana of Vestur! You don't appear to be aching for death, and I am in need of a few new beasts for my riders." Orson lowered the cleaver, pointing its edge. "Take them."

They descended on them, beast and rider alike, shrieking and chanting as they charged.

Above the din, but only just, a familiar screech resounded like a warning bell. Solyana lowered her hatchet, her eyes searching for the noise and finding the open door.

A shadow burst through like a fletched arrow, whipping its talons into the closest Beast Rider, sharp points finding purchase in the man's eyes. He screamed as the falcon buffeted his face; its talons sinking deep in his eye sockets. It released him before moving onto the next. Claws tore through a woman's neck like a knife through a loaf of fresh bread before the bird swooped up in a brief arc and dove at the next rider.

Solyana clutched Gamaliel's charred tunic and together they crawled beneath the feasting table. A lynx and rider lunged at her, and Solyana flung her palm out, shooting a burst of fire into the cat's face. Its swipe missed her by a handspan. The falcon went at the rider, going for his shoulder, flapping wildly in his face as the man shouted and batted at the bird.

"What, in all Hekla, is that thing?" Gamaliel's eyes searched her own, his face an angry pink, his hair sticking up and tumbling out of its knot.

"*That*," she said, pointing at the falcon as it dodged and rolled, "is my little sister."

From their hiding spot, Solyana covered her ears to mute the din of dying men. Halina, the falcon tethered by Rhuth, defended them from one air strike to the next. Amid the commotion, Solyana recognized a screech of distress and without hesitation scrambled out, leaving Gamaliel under the table.

"Rhuth!" Halina barely escaped the snapping jaws of the polar bear who turned her monstrous head in Solyana's direction. She fell back against the table as the horror of what her fire had done was revealed. The polar bear—the woman who had taken the form of a polar bear—had been blinded. Blood streamed from her boiled eyes, turning her white fur pink. Chief Orson, now surrounded by the wild flame, manically swung with his cleaver at the screeching falcon.

"We need to go!" Solyana pulled Gamaliel from under the table, and he hauled himself to his feet. They took off in the direction of the door, dodging weapons and weaving around the flames that licked and latched their way across the room.

"Where's my father?" he called out to her. Solyana sensed him slowing.

"There's no time! We have to leave now!"

"I won't lose him again!"

Solyana whipped her head around to find Gamaliel stopped completely. The lynx crouched behind him, waiting.

"Gamaliel!" Solyana raised her palms to call upon her Heitt, but something large shot out from beside her. A giant cat knocked into Gamaliel on its way toward slamming into the lynx mid-pounce, hurling it backward. Gamaliel skid across the floor and Solyana ran to him, her eyes narrow as smoke stole breathable air. While she retained an immunity to the flame she produced, the danger of the smoke was another matter entirely.

Coughing, eyes watering, Solyana helped Gamaliel to his feet. They ran for the door, but the lynx had recovered and slid into their path. The other large cat followed, striking the lynx as the two rolled to the ground and out of Solyana's way. Blinking past the smoke, she only just made out what it was—a smilodon.

Paralyzed by the connections forming in her brain, Solyana could only think of one place she had ever seen a smilodon—Priestess Avi's room, stuffed and poised in the corner.

The resemblance between the preserved creature and the one pawing toward them was uncanny.

Time was running out. Hand in hand, Solyana and Gamaliel stumbled from the hall to find chaos descending on the people of Takanah.

RARE GIFTS

PALLAH

PALLAH DID NOT BELONG.

It all made sense, really.

Her mouth felt full of cotton as she took a shaky sip of her tea. It went down like pond water. Karav sat frozen, her cup to her lips. Issha stared out the window, tea entirely forgotten beside her on the floor.

The midwife, Freya, had just revealed that Pallah and her twin were born from two different fathers. Disbelief gripped Pallah and refused to relent.

Freya placed the kettle back on the stove and turned, her eyebrows knit so closely they looked like one. "Your mother, she had a life here."

"Here," Pallah repeated.

"Yes." The old woman leaned against her countertop, tea to her lips. "You shouldn't be hearing this from me, but if Phyllir sent you here, I suppose I'll pay her the courtesy and tell you the tale of your mother." Her eyes flicked over Pallah's shoulder. "Why don't you girls go scrounge up something for supper."

Karav gave an audible sigh and Pallah heard the two of them rise to their feet.

"Take Mayflower with you," Freya said, pulling on a thick glove that went up to her elbow. "She knows where to go." A large barn owl came from its roost atop the kitchen cabinets and glided to Freya's arm with a flurry of feathers.

Issha stepped forward and offered her leather gilded wrist. Mayflower transferred over and the two girls stepped out into the evening's deepening dark.

Pallah was thankful they wouldn't be hearing such an intimate tale, but their absence left a hollowness in the air between her and Freya. The owls watched them in wide-eyed silence. Tinloh's breaths grew deeper from her lap, reminding her she wasn't quite alone. She adjusted her cloak to be sure he was completely hidden from sight.

"Phyllir Hildeson grew up in Takanah. Her family was close with the Thadson family. Dahvid Thadson was their only son, a boy that grew up loving Phyllir, and Phyllir loved him." Freya's voice was methodical, listing off facts and findings as a midwife would. Pallah sat motionless, grappling with the history she didn't know she had. "But one year, on the Centennial Celebration at the Temple Celestial, Phyllir's father made the journey from Takanah to Sodur and met the Staldson family. They had four sons; the youngest was named Bogdur and he was the same age as Phyllir.

"The Staldsons were dedicated to the Temple and in good standing with the priest at the time. This was appealing to Phyllir's father, and the two families arranged a marriage. Phyllir and Bogdur were wed in Sodur; Dahvid stayed in Takanah."

Pallah held up a hand, pausing the midwife with her mouth still open. "How do *you* know all of this?"

"People tell me things, dear. Your mother had plenty of time with me, and Dahvid, too. But I'm getting to that." Freya's owl-like eyes blinked reproachfully at Pallah who fidgeted in her seat. "Now, I knew Phyllir because I was *her* mother's midwife. Takanah does have its own midwives, but there are quite a few who prefer a quieter, country birth." Freya held her chin up high. "I also keep to more traditional medicines, so I am often called in to Takanah itself."

Pallah nodded.

"Now, after a few years, I find Phyllir coming up over my hill, telling me she and Bogdur were struggling to have children. He had begun screaming at her by that time, nothing worse than that. I told her she could stay with me for as long as she needed to, and he needn't come to fetch her either.

"But things weren't so simple. Phy had convinced herself she loved Bogdur, even with his bluster and his threats. Fool girl. She was determined to go back to him with a remedy to help her conceive. We began a strict regimen of my tinctures, proven to prime the body for bearing. We used all my supply, so I sent her to gather more, and guess who she ran into?"

"Dahvid," Pallah said, attention rapt.

"Yes." Freya nodded. "And before I knew it, he was showing up with firewood for my stove, fresh flowers for my remedies, and different game he'd killed and skinned for dinner. Phyllir opened up to him about the hardships in her marriage, and he was a pleasant distraction for her as she finished up her regimen." She took a deep breath and rubbed a hand down her face. "But their friendship blossomed further than I'd thought, and after only a few short weeks, she told me she was pregnant."

Though she'd known it was coming, Pallah still gasped.

The old midwife nodded sagely, enjoying her captive audience. "I doubted her, at first. 'You can't know that early,' I told her. But Phyllir didn't want to take any chances. She went back to Bogdur to do the deed before he would be the wiser. For if he knew that baby wasn't his own, there was no telling what he would do.

"Seven months later, up she comes over that hill, riding on a wagon, fully with child. And I knew—I knew just by looking at her—she had two in there. She stayed with me for one month, Dahvid tending to her the whole time, before you and your sister were born. One came out, hair like midnight, eyes like the sea, just like Dahvid. The other?" She leaned forward and poked a bony finger into Pallah's forearm. "Scrawny and squealing! Blonde and gray-eyed. We chalked it up to fraternal twins and went on, assuming you had also come from Dahvid."

"But you said we were from two different fathers," Pallah clarified.

"I'm getting to that!" The old woman tutted. "That fact only came to light later. So, your mama returned home to Bogdur with two screaming babies, and she was the happiest I'd ever seen her. Dahvid, though?" She sighed and adjusted a few of the jars. "He kept coming back here, finding excuses to return, asking if I needed anything from the Temple. I knew he was missing your mother, missing his children. But I told him it was over, that he needed to move on. The man didn't have anything for him in Takanah. He had squandered his years pining after Phyllir, and when he finally had her and two baby girls, his love went back to Bogdur."

"Wait." Pallah held up a hand again, thinking of her conversation with her mother only a few days before. "He was Tala, right?"

"Yes," Freya said. "His aptitude quite rare, too."

"What happened between—" Pallah began.

"Hold on, this is the interesting part." Freya clasped her hands together. "Your mother came back, and the verbal abuse had escalated to physical. Now, no one beats on *my* babies. *No one.*" She gritted her teeth and shook her head. "You and your sister were barely over a year old, but Bogdur wanted a boy, you see. They were having trouble again, and he wasn't satisfied with the two girls he'd got." Freya chuffed. "So, she was back for more help, you and your sister in tow. You two loved the owls."

Pallah blinked up at her. She didn't know she had been to this place before, besides the day of her birth. It was strange, to be known by someone she had no recollection of meeting. She looked around at the home once more, wondering if anything would spark a memory.

"Anyway." Freya's voice pulled Pallah back. "I kept you two while your mama went to town for some supplies. She came back at the end of the day with an empty basket. Unbeknownst to me, she had gone to find Dahvid, but he had married." An owl let out a hoot. "Oh hush, Ingrid," she said over her shoulder.

"Well, marriage didn't stop her before," Pallah said numbly. Her mother's past was nothing like she'd imagined it would be.

"Well, Phyllir found him happy and didn't want to make a mess of his life more than she already had. She came back here, started a round of my remedies and—I warned her they could take months, but she wanted to do it anyway. I think she was just trying to get a break from Bogdur. She didn't have marks on her face, but that was only because Bogdur was clever. I saw them on her back, her collarbone, on her upper arms. But you girls loved it here. It took you a few days to warm up, but soon enough, you were running around like you owned the place."

"How long did we stay?" Pallah asked in disbelief.

"You were here for a year or so. Bogdur traveled out once a month to try for a boy before returning home. She became pregnant after only a few tries. I sent word by Mayflower she would stay for the whole pregnancy. Not because she needed to, but because Phy didn't want to go home to her husband. And nine months later, Ahren was born looking just like your sister."

"Vámae," Pallah whispered. Freya's words hacked at the bond she and her brother—*half-brother*—shared.

"I remember catching him and handing him to your mama. The differences between you and them were too great to ignore. We were both concerned, and rightly so." Freya stopped puttering for a moment and came to sit down across from Pallah.

"Phyllir told me Bogdur suspected infidelity. He saw how much you looked like him, and how much Vámae did not. Phyllir knew, if she brought back another one with dark hair and sea-blue eyes, he would know for sure they hadn't come from him. Your mama had that dark hair, true, but she has gray eyes. That blue is stark; it can't be excused away."

"So, my mother *had* slept with Dahvid again."

"Yes. I didn't even know it had been happening. But she had gone to Takanah a few times, leaving you girls with me. It would take her two days to bring back supplies. I didn't know why, at the time." Freya grew somber. "She told me her plan. She couldn't go back to Bogdur, not with two babies looking like the wrong father. Dahvid broke things off with his wife, and both he and Phyllir formed a plan to run away together. Go northwest, up toward Thonethren, raise the family."

Pallah's ears pricked at the city's name.

Sounds like a nice place, Erval rumbled in her mind. Pallah felt oddly calmed by his voice. It made her wonder how she could have ever been so unsettled by it.

"She made plans and kept sending Bogdur notes, telling him there were complications; that she was fine, but the baby needed to stay another month or two. She stalled and stalled. When they were finally fixing to leave, guess who showed up without a single word of warning, but Bogdur. He was in a flying rage: throwing things, ripping through my gardens, making all sorts of demands and accusations. He was a mess. He and Dahvid got into a fight. They both started using their Gifts, one wielding wood like a weapon, the other commanding his beast. Bogdur got the upper hand and killed Dahvid's beast, the poor thing. And Bogdur would have killed him too, if Phyllir hadn't run to her husband and kissed him. It broke my heart, watching her throw her future away to protect the people she loved."

"And, after all that...she just left with him?"

"What other choice did she have? Bogdur would have killed Dahvid and hunted her, hunted all of you, if she hadn't." Freya shook her head. "Never put herself first, that girl. And when she tried to, it all went to Hekla." Freya stood slowly, her old bones creaking. "She told Bogdur she loved him, said they should get home and raise their family, and 'look, she'd had a boy, and didn't he look like her?' And he believed it, for a while.

"I sent owls to make sure she was ok. She wouldn't talk about how he was treating her, but always implored me to take you, Pallah." Freya's eyes landed on Pallah's once more. They froze in time together. "She always sent the same message: 'Take Pallah. She's the one that looks like him, and he can't stand anyone figuring out the only thing he could make was a plain Rána. I'm afraid he'll kill her.' I mean no offense." She put her palms out in penance. "His words, not mine. You see, he was only mildly concerned folks would figure out his wife had been dallying. He was more afraid people would connect the only dud—again, no offense, dear—with his seed."

The silence that followed roared in Pallah's ears, the true depths of Bodgur's depravity finally made clear. Compounded with the fact she was his only true child, that half of her could never escape him, it slammed into her mind like a hammer onto a nail. How he'd favored Vámae and Ahren, not because they were his, but because they weren't. Because they were everything she was not: beautiful, talented, Gifted, and he could claim them as his own. But there would always be doubts and whispered questions by anyone with eyes. Pallah's mere existence threatened his pride, and for that, he hated her.

She was crying as she turned her face up to meet the small woman before her. "Why didn't you take me?"

"Excuse me?" Freya's voice pitched like she was being accused of something.

"She begged you to take me...why didn't you?"

"I..." Freya stood and balanced from one foot to the other. "I wasn't in any state to keep a child here! Besides, every child is best fit to be with their mother."

Pallah choked out a laugh. "With my mother? My mother silenced herself as the man she forced us to live with, the man she was protecting us from, stripped her of all dignity and power, until he finally almost killed her. I promise you, *she* was not my best option." She got up so quickly the chair clattered to the floor. "No one is my best option." Tinloh leapt from Pallah's cloak and was on the kitchen table, crouching and baring his teeth in a readiness that both frightened her and sent a lust for violence coursing through her veins.

Freya's entire body tensed. "Where did you get that?" her question not a question at all, but a hanging statement.

"He's mine." Cold metal kissed her fingertips, and she realized her hand was resting on the head of her hatchet. "He's my Tala aptitude." Pallah scooped the cat up as a second growl escaped him. "I have him under control."

"That you do." Freya's eyes were wide, tipping from fear to wonder as the woman talked to herself. "He said someone else took control, complete control. Perhaps she *is* his. How can she not be with this aptitude? But you can't deny her face."

Freya's eyes snapped to Pallah's, and Pallah could see the woman working through equations in her mind.

"What are you talking about?" Pallah whispered, the hairs on her arms and neck raised.

"This changes everything," the old woman said quietly before holding up a finger. "One moment." Freya shuffled out the back doorway of the kitchen and down a small hallway.

Pallah picked up Tinloh, calming him with her tether, calming herself in equal measure.

There was mumbling, as if Freya was speaking to someone. Pallah's heart jumped into her throat. There was someone else here? She hadn't even checked.

She counted to twenty.

Investigate, Pallah.

Placing Tinloh on the ground beside her, he padded quietly as they followed the short hall. The voices wafted back to her on waves of tension.

"...perhaps you did give her the twins. Both, I mean. She has your Gift! It's simply too rare to overlook—"

Pallah rounded the corner and stepped through the doorway. Tinloh jumped in, a bit too enthusiastically, grunting as he slipped and fell on the wooden floor.

Freya knelt beside a high-backed chair covered in various cushions and blankets, her hands grasping something just in front of her. Pallah's eyes followed them upward, mouth falling open as the smell of urine, sweat, and medicinal alcohol invaded her senses.

The woman held the hands of a man sitting awkwardly in the chair. His back uncomfortably straight, he leaned unnaturally against the pillows. His ocean-blue eyes stared directly ahead out of a face drawn and gaunt. A mop of unevenly chopped hair lined his forehead, and his beard was unkempt in much the same way. The man turned to Pallah, though not entirely. His sea-blue eyes did not move, only his neck rotated until his eyes finally found purchase on her own.

"Pallah," Freya whispered. "This is Dahvid."

The man who'd loved Pallah's mother, the father of Pallah's siblings, was a thinly covered skeleton. Dahvid wore a loose, wrinkled tunic and linen pants, his feet cocooned in knitted brown socks.

"What is this?" Pallah asked, bile rising in her throat. "My mother told me Dahvid was gone. This"—she motioned to the man—"is not gone."

"Oh." Freya stood, something distant in her eyes. "But he is, dear." Freya picked up a cloth and dabbed at a bit of drool coming from the corner of Dahvid's mouth. "You see...Dahvid has been through a lot. He's not...he's not fully able to function."

Pallah couldn't reconcile the emotions that warred inside her. She longed to talk to her mother, to understand the full scope of everything she'd just been told.

Pallah licked her lips and swallowed. "You say I have his Gift." She leaned down and picked up Tinloh by the scruff of his neck. She wouldn't be able to do that much longer; he was growing heavy.

Freya squeezed the old cloth in her hand, her eyes betraying her excitement as she studied the placid cat hanging in the air. It took everything inside of Pallah not to turn and run.

Let him go, Erval prompted, though Pallah was going to do it anyway. Her grip still firm on his scruff, she released her tether, breaking it with a resounding snap in her mind.

Tinloh thrashed, clawed, and bit at the air in an overhaul of release that bordered on what looked like a seizure. Then, as suddenly as he'd begun, he stopped. Pallah's eyes darted to Dahvid who tipped forward, Freya gasped and gripped his shoulders, keeping him from falling to the ground. Dahvid's eyes focused on the small beast that dangled between them. Pallah didn't know how it was possible, but she could feel Dahvid's tether; strong, weighty...ragged.

So, she wasn't the only one.

THE FINNEVEL

ERVAL

THE SCOPE'S GEARS WHIRRED as Erval cranked it one final time. He took a step back from the device and rubbed at his eyes. Eleven long years of waiting, amassing support, and honing his Mann Tala deep within Hekla, was finally reaching fruition. Now if he could just get this *häfan* piece of junk to work. Phineas had explained it was modeled after a tool the sea peoples used—a sextant, he'd called it. This tool was much the same, though larger; angled lines of gilded metal came together in a scope with an eyepiece fit for Erval himself.

"Phineas," Erval crooned wearily. "Please tell me why the"—he waved a hand at the machine before him—"*thing*, isn't working properly?"

Phineas was a man of small stature and even smaller eyes that were hemmed in by doughy cheeks. He lowered his spectacles to the tip of his nose and bustled to the device in question.

"It's called a finnevel," Phineas said. With a throaty cough under Erval's phlegmatic gaze, he added, "M'lord." Phineas tinkered with the machine, twirling a few cogs and twisting a knob on the side. "I see nothing wrong with it, sir."

Erval tugged at his linen vest, fiddling with one of the brass buttons as he paced slowly about the room. "Then why do the subjects I find keep dying?"

Phineas stopped tinkering, his face turning a ghostly white. "M'lord?"

"They keep doing themselves in, one way or another." Erval brought himself close to Phineas. "It's *annoying*."

"Th-that has nothing to do with the device, m'lord."

"Is that so?" Erval mused, tugging at his chin. "Well, that remains to be seen. Off with you, Phineas."

But Phineas stayed put.

Erval turned, eyebrows raised. Phineas wasn't normally so insubordinate. "Something on your mind, Phineas?"

"It's just..." His advisor's bespectacled face shone with sweat. He pushed his glasses higher up his nose. "Every person you have targeted with the finnevel has killed themselves?"

"Correct. Something's wrong with your device, some fault I suggest you find and rectify."

"Have you ever considered, m'lord, perhaps..." Phineas's dry, podgy hands rasped over each other as he wrung them in nervous succession. "The problem does not lie in the device?"

Erval clasped his hands behind him, the audacity of the implication looming in a stretch of silence Erval made sure was long enough to be uncomfortable.

"Phineas," Erval said. "What kind of a ruler do you think I am?"

Phineas dropped to his knees, hands flying up in surrender. "Generous! Benevolent! Full of compassion and grace!"

Erval nodded in agreement.

"You are the rightful heir, the true King of Thonethren!"

"Ah-ah-ah…" Erval wagged a finger in Phineas's direction before placing a hand on the man's head, slick with sweat. Erval patted his damp head three times, then wiped his palm on the man's robes. "Not just Thonethren, my friend. Mothmar." Erval smiled to himself. "All of Mothmar."

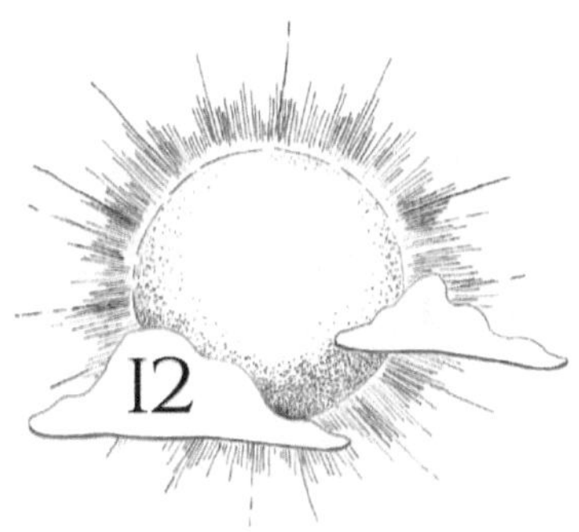

CHANGE STARTS HERE

SOLYANA

TAKANAH WAS BURNING.

Solyana thought the damage had been confined to the Chief's Hall, but the events there were merely sparks that had ignited something long buried. Half the city was aflame, so hot the buildings ablaze had already begun to crumble into ash. The loose animals, which had so placidly meandered the streets, now trampled the townsfolk in frenzied panic, rushing the people, taking them down, leaving their victims mangled and torn. Solyana's mind reeled at the thought of them possibly being people, not animals. She didn't know what to believe anymore.

Coughing and sputtering, Solyana and Gamaliel stumbled down the steps of the Hall, smoke pouring from the building behind them. The beasts and their riders had turned against their own. But why? Solyana couldn't fathom it. The only clear course was to find Lone, Jonas, and Vinur and leave as quickly as possible.

An icy chill seeped into her when she thought of her friends—they were with Maral, a Beast Rider. "Gamaliel! We need to get to Jonas!"

A loud snort drew their attention, close enough to pierce the sounds of the city in riot. They turned to find a massive boar charging straight toward them, its head bobbing low and tusks gleaming.

Solyana stepped in front of Gamaliel, her palms outstretched, but just as she started to call the flame, a spear lodged itself into the side of the animal. Sharp metal *thunked* into soft flesh followed by a wheeze and a groan. The boar toppled over and convulsed, its body twisting and turning, shrinking back into the man it was. He cried pitifully, his blood spreading over the ground.

Bile rose up Solyana's throat, and she searched for who had thrown the spear, but no savior from the warring throng emerged. Gamaliel tugged on her arm and he pointed toward a darkened stall in the courtyard; inside it was Lone, readying another spear. Her chest heaved as she pushed a shock of white hair out of her eyes. Vinur sat beside her, panting, his ears turning every which way.

Gripping Gamaliel's hand, Solyana dashed through the frenzied crowd to the stall. Safe beneath its awning, the four cowered in darkness to scan the battle raging in the courtyard. Villagers fought off the animals and Beast Riders with pitchforks and hoes. Some had bows and broadswords, but though all had mounted a noble defense, they were rapidly losing ground.

The double doors of the Chief's Hall burst open, and the lynx was tossed down the steps. The smilodon sauntered out in its wake, stalking carefully from the building, picking its way down the steps, ensuring the lynx was dead.

Then the smilodon locked eyes with Solyana.

Dread flooded her, twisting her stomach into a knot she couldn't unbind. The gargantuan cat's nocturnal eyes pierced the shade of the stall. Surely, this couldn't be who she thought it was. But if this city—which practiced the Taka Reu—had the ability to transform into beasts, why couldn't someone else she knew?

Solyana nodded slowly, an act of recognition, of thanks.

The smilodon gave a slow nod back, unmistakably human.

Terror filled Solyana as a scramble of dark fur and fury launched from the Chief's Hall. The direwolf was riderless and out of control. The smilodon turned too late as the wolf clamped his jaws on her neck. Solyana cried out.

The smilodon swiped wildly at its assailant, but the direwolf only shook its mighty head, the cat flopping in its maw like a flag in the wind.

"Help her!" she screamed, yanking Gamaliel's arm, motioning to the smilodon and direwolf in turn. Gamaliel was the only person she had confided in, the only person she had told of Priestess Avi's dual wielding of both Light and Dark Gifts. Could he understand as she did?

"Help who?" Gamaliel's eyes scanned the area wildly, a picture of pure pandemonium.

"Stop your father!" Solyana cried out as the direwolf began to drag the smilodon down the stairs.

Gamaliel's eyes went cold, his finger shaking as he pointed. "I am not tethering to—to whatever *that* is."

"But it—" Solyana was cut off by the scream of the falcon as it shot out of the double doors. "Halina!"

The smilodon twisted suddenly, and the direwolf loosened its hold. Though only free for a moment, it was enough time for the big cat to swipe her claws across the wolf's face before bounding away, chasing after Halina as she climbed into the night sky.

"We need to get out of here!" Lone yelled over the chaos. "This way!"

The group dodged and wove through the fray and the fires—had Solyana done this? How many people would die tonight because of her? Because of this *Gift*?

Flames flared from their left, and the group ducked and scurried around it. Gamaliel released Solyana's hand, scooped Vinur into his arms, and laid him over his shoulders, holding the wolf's paws tight below his neck. Solyana scrambled over the cobblestones, desperate to leave, regretting every step she'd made since leaving Vestur.

Over the crackle of flames, pounding of feet, and fading shouts of the dying, Solyana heard Gamaliel.

"He's awake?" Gamaliel shouted.

"Yes," Lone said. "The medicine woman taught me how to rouse him."

"And you left him? With one of them?" Solyana accused.

"*Häfa!* You'd be decorating boar tusks right now if I hadn't!"

"*No one* can be trusted here!" Gamaliel spat. Solyana knew he was thinking of his father.

They ran down an empty street in a section of housing. It was quiet in this district; the fighting seemed to be confined to the courtyard. Only the fire had spread. The buildings grew higher and wider as Solyana and her friends passed a rotund building with a sign above the door depicting a tincture in a bottle.

Remembering Maral's words of welcome, Solyana scanned the line of houses until her eyes landed on what was once a yellow home, though now it was a roaring tower of flame. The silhouette of a child pounded on one of the upper windows.

"Lone!" Solyana screamed but the older girl didn't turn, her legs taking her ever farther, Gamaliel on her heels. "Lone!" Solyana tried again, and this time Lone stopped and whirled around. "There's someone trapped inside!"

Lone ran back to Solyana, hands outstretched toward the window where Solyana pointed. The Bein Fera gasped, "I feel them! They're injured!"

"It's Maral's house!"

A scream tumbled over into sobs, its shrill panic cutting through the thunder of the fire. Solyana whipped her head back in the direction of the yellow house and launched herself through the open front door.

"Solyana!" Gamaliel shouted after her, but she hardly heard him over the roar of the fire and the groan of the wood. She could feel the heat, thick and unyielding, but it wouldn't catch her. This was *her* fire which was winding and finding purchase throughout the city. She was its master, and it would yield to her, if she could be strong enough.

Closing her eyes to the terror, Solyana forced herself to focus on the Father of the Day, remembering his goodness and his mercy. The flame resisted at first, flickering and flaring in defiance. Concentrating harder, she pressed into the Celestials, and the flame began to relent, eddying around her palms, whipping itself into a torrent before disappearing back inside her.

It was like trying to stop the sun itself, and a breathless vertigo began to take her. Solyana opened her eyes, righting herself. The stairs were accessible now, and the wood of the home groaned with relief.

Lone scrambled into the doorway behind her, and Solyana caught a glimpse of her panicked eyes. "Upstairs!" Solyana hissed. Her palms glowed a bright red and the flame grew around her once more. "I can't hold any more! Quick!" She dashed to the stairs, Lone on her heels.

Halfway up to the second floor, Solyana heard a beam crack. She looked down to see Gamaliel pulling Vinur back as a crossbeam fell, the ceiling it once supported collapsing with it. Embers and sparks scattered across the floor making the two recoil and leave. Back outside, Gamaliel shouted for the girls to return.

Ignoring him, Solyana and Lone crested the stairs to find a small room yet to be overcome by flame. They quickly halted at the sight of a feral fox growling and pacing before a small whimpering child.

Lone stepped forward, raising a hand. The fox glared back, panting and snarling, its red fur dark and matted with blood.

"Don't move," Lone whispered, blue eyes trained on the growling fox. With pain in her eyes, Solyana watched as Lone slowly approached, raising her hands, her fingers splayed wide. Lone's fingers bent in succession, each appendage popping slightly as the fox shrieked. Solyana's eyes, wide as the full moon, refused to take in what she was seeing. Never before had she witnessed Bein Fera being used for anything but healing.

"No!" The little girl lunged from the floor, wrapping her arms around the shrieking creature as it flickered in shape from fox to human. "You leave my brother alone!" Lone's hands flew to her horrified face and Solyana gaped as the fox transformed fully into a boy.

Rushing to the children, flames wrapping the room, Solyana assessed them as quickly as possible. "Lone, I need you to grab the boy!"

No sound came but the crackle of flame.

"Lone!" Solyana whipped her head back to find the older girl kneeling in the room, her lips trembling and soot-streaked face wet with tears.

Solyana crawled back to her, her face inches from Lone's. "You had no way of knowing. This isn't your fault. Let's get them to safety."

Lone nodded, squeezing her eyes shut before staggering to her feet. The two of them each cradled a child, the boy slumped in Lone's arms, the girl crying in Solyana's arms. She was heavier than Solyana expected as the four of them stumbled down the stairs, floorboards giving way in their wake.

Shifting the young girl to one side, Solyana extended a hand toward the flame. Concentrating on the Father of the Day, she kept the fire at bay as they clambered over the beam-littered floor and out the front door into the fresh night air.

Gamaliel rushed to them, taking the girl from Solyana's arms as the group huddled at the other side of the cobblestone street. "Who are they?"

"Maral's children," Solyana said, sitting down on the cool ground. "I think."

"They're human beings that needed saving," Lone said in a shaky voice as she laid the boy on the ground.

"What's your name?" Solyana asked the girl, eyes scanning for injury.

"Kat," the girl said with a cough, extricating herself from Gamaliel's grasp. She had tightly-coiled black hair, and her olive skin appeared even darker with a layer of ash and dust. "That's my brother, Darmond. Where's my Mama?"

"She will be outside of the east gate waiting for us. Or at least that's what she told me before we got separated," said Lone. "And it's nice to meet you, Kat. May I see your arm?"

Kat eyed Lone warily, keeping her arm clutched tight to her chest.

"I know that was really scary," Solyana said. She fought to keep her expression calm and kind, even as a wave of nausea attempted to quiet her. "But you did such a good job staying calm. How old are you, Kat?"

"Six," said Kat, her features softening.

"Wow, that's pretty old." Solyana smiled warmly, but it turned to a grimace as a wave of heat washed through her insides. "My friend is going to take care of you, okay? She's a Healer."

"But she hurt Darmond."

"She was trying to protect you from a fox. She didn't know it was your brother. I promise, no more harm will come to either of you."

Kat let out a soft hiss as she offered up her arm. Chewed flesh revealed crimson-stained bones breaching the skin. "He didn't mean it," she whispered, glancing at her brother, who was mercifully asleep.

"No, I don't think he did." Lone said as she got to work on the girl. "Solyana, I'm going to need your help. Can you use your Heitt to—"

But the nausea that had been rolling through Solyana overtook her, and she stumbled away from the group. She vomited, knees hitting the street, everything in her begging for release. The cold sweat worsened, and Solyana's fingers dug into the cobblestones, finding the grooves between the cool rocks. But before she could enjoy the sensation, her hands exploded with flame.

She screamed, though not from pain, but relief, as the flames shot out toward the already crumbling buildings across the street. Finally, it abated, leaving her panting on the ground.

A hand landed on her shoulder, and she turned to find Gamaliel, his face still pink from the incident in the Chief's Hall, his eyes wide. "Are you okay?"

"I'm...I don't know. I feel much better now, though." Solyana righted herself and came back to Kat's side. The small girl's eyes were squeezed shut.

"What happened?" Kat asked, her voice shaking.

"Our friend Solyana is an Eldur," Lone said. "And sometimes Eldurs get firesickness if they take in too much flame." She looked at Solyana. "No more eating fire, okay?"

"I didn't eat it," Solyana argued, taking a deep breath. "But you're right. I'm not doing that again."

Lone shook her head and motioned to the children. "Let's figure out how to help."

Solyana checked Darmond first, using her Heitt to pinpoint where pain was coming from. "The boy has a broken leg and a few cuts and scrapes."

"Well, it's a clean break." Lone took a breath, guilt etched on her face. "But that just means it will be easier to fix." With the boy still unconscious, Lone was able to tether to him, her eyes focused in concentration. They heard a soft *pop* and the group let out a collective breath.

"Now Kat, I need you to stay very still, okay?" Lone asked her, motioning for Solyana to tether to the girl. Solyana blanketed her with Heitt.

"Kathda! Darmond!"

Solyana's head snapped up to see Maral rushing towards them, her face wiped clean of the black powder she had used to match the other Beast Riders. Lone's eyes jerked to the side, but she kept at her work.

"I'm almost done," she said through gritted teeth. Kat's whole face trembled as the bone in her forearm shifted deeper still. Solyana, using her Heitt, pushed healing into the girl, the ancient knowledge coming to her once again, keeping Kat from feeling much pain at all.

"I've done all I can do," Lone said sitting back on her heels.

"Mama!" Kat said, now untethered.

Maral dropped to her knees, hand fluttering over her children and kissing their faces. Solyana looked around. Where was Jonas? Unease dropped like a stone in Solyana's stomach.

"I should have never left them in the house. Oh, Kat! I am so sorry. How is Darmond?" Maral cried as Kat scrambled up to sit in her mother's lap.

Lone relayed the events of the last hour to Maral, holding steady even through admitting to hurting Darmond when he was in fox form. At the mention of the fox, Maral's face went slack and she began to cry. "This is why I left their father." She wiped her eyes. "He was so steeped in the darkness of this city. He started bringing Darmond to meetings, taught him to shift into his aptitude. He's only twelve, for *stars'* sake!" And Maral held Kat close, the mother and daughter finding some semblance of comfort together.

The clash and chaos of battle rang through the air, reminding them their safety was only relative.

Maral turned to them with a sniff and a lift of her chin. "This is my fault." She stood and lifted her injured son in her arms. "I should have left long ago. Come, we need to get out of here."

Maral began a pointed march eastward, surprising Solyana with her speed and strength as she carried her son in her arms. Kat followed close behind. Solyana and her friends kept pace, but she couldn't help but feel they were going in the wrong direction. "Maral," she ventured between breaths. "Where is Jonas?"

"He's waiting for us," Maral said with a glance in Solyana's direction. "When I realized we would have to make a move tonight, I secured your way out, first. Don't worry, Solyana. I stand with you."

Solyana nodded. "Thank you, Maral."

"What *is* happening here?" Gamaliel voiced the question Solyana herself was wondering. "Why are your people at war with each other?"

Maral sighed and hoisted her son up higher. "The city has been on the edge of self-destruction for many moons now. Although we all use the Taka Reu, there are many beneath Orson who have crossed over into complete darkness. The people of Takanah refuse to follow such a path. But Orson applies his position and strength, pressing people into becoming beasts and Beast Riders; my husband and I were two such people."

They ran quickly and quietly through the streets, passing both those running from the fray and those charging into it. No one paid much mind to the six people and their dog-sized wolf.

Maral continued, "My husband began acting more beast than human, and I realized too late how it was overtaking him. The more you transform, the more you lose your humanity. And then he started involving my son." Maral shook her head. "I couldn't stand it, but I didn't know how to leave. I began to see the Taka Reu for what it is: the antithesis of light, of good. But I've had to stay ingrained in the community to keep us safe. I've kept my position as a Beast Rider with the intention of bringing a force together large enough to take down Orson himself."

They went down a small alleyway, whipping around the tight corners and emerging into a courtyard devoid of people. A fountain stood bubbling in the center. Solyana recalled how, just yesterday, similar places in the city had been bursting with what had appeared to be harmony. To hear the violence and come upon the barren, joyless arrangement of stone... Sorrow hung about her shoulders, weighing down her steps.

"If you truly are the one chosen to bring the green, you are our best hope of healing this land," Maral said with conviction. "This night is just the start of something long awaited, and my people are ready. We will rise above and defeat Orson and his followers."

The air had cleared. Glancing around, Solyana realized most of the fire had petered out as they ran close to the city's edge. Only vestiges of smoke now trailed in the air. The city wall rose before them, the opposite side from which they'd entered.

"Halt!" Two guards stepped from either side of the barred city gate, each wearing animal pelts overlayed with leather breastplates. One guard held a spear, and the other stood as a living perch, upon whose shoulder sat the largest bird Solyana had ever seen.

"Please, just let me get my children to safety!" Maral cried out. Vinur whimpered while his master grasped for a missing staff that was either burnt up or lying broken somewhere in the Chief's Hall.

"By decree of Chief Orson, none are permitted leave of this city!"

But Maral simply laid Darmond down on the ground. "Stay with your brother," she whispered to Kat. She stepped forward, palms open in plea. "Please, I can't keep my children here in this city! It's burning!"

The guards stepped forward. The bird on the man's shoulder opened its beak, and the other guard lowered his spear. "Maral?" the one with the spear asked.

"Is that you, Paldin? Jondar?" Maral addressed each in turn and the guards stopped short.

"Maral?" Paldin lowered his spear and squinted at her in the flickering light of the torches hanging from the walls. "Where is your tattoo?"

Maral stepped closer. Extending her hands, she said nothing. Paldin walked forward and clasped her arms in his own, the traditional Mothmari greeting. "Let us pass, Paldin."

The man looked back at Jondar, whose bird was preening on his shoulder. "It's Maral."

"If that's the Maral I know," Jondar said with a sneer, "she would be fighting, not running." Then he addressed Maral directly. "Bardone told me you kicked him out. Were you ever with us?"

"Jondar, the Taka Reu is killing us. Can't you see that?"

"She's defected! Take her, Paldin!"

Maral cried out, and Gamaliel, Lone, and Solyana stepped forward as one. Vinur rushed to Gamaliel's side, growling. Lone's fingers were curled, hands directed toward Paldin. Solyana brought her own hands forward, a flame in one, the other glowing faintly.

The guard's eyes flicked from Maral to the group just beyond her, their bodies tense.

"Let us through," Gamaliel said. "There is no need for bloodshed."

Paldin glanced over his shoulder at Jondar whose face held nothing but disgust. "We are Beast Riders, you unweaned whelp."

Lone raised a hand toward Jondar's shoulder. The large bird stiffened and then tumbled from its perch, landing with a thump on the ground.

Jondar's eyes widened. "What did you do?" he cried.

"She's Bein Fera," Gamaliel continued. "And that was a warning."

"You're going to let us pass," Lone said. "The only question is how many bones it will take." Her hand shifted from the bird to the guard, her fingers ever-so-slowly curling. Jondar's entire body tensed until he shook. He gave a stiff nod to Paldin who released Maral.

Lone folded her arms across her chest, and both man and bird showed palpable relief.

"This is more than just infighting," Maral said to Paldin, placing a hand on his arm. "I hope you choose the right side."

The man shifted uncomfortably. "Open the gate."

With a creaking that could wake the dead, the wrought iron gate opened just enough to admit the group outside the walls. It slammed back to the ground as soon as they were out. Solyana turned to Maral who held Darmond again, Kat at her side.

"How will you get back in?"

"We have a meeting place outside the city. I'll keep the children there. Getting back in alone," she winked. "That's easy."

Solyana nodded, satisfied this brave family would be in no further danger, at least because of her presence.

It was a bitter cold outside of the walls. Only dressed in her tunic and linen pants, she longed for the gear her mother had tailored for her. Above them hung the Mother of the Night, faithful and true. The Norlos wove its way across the sky.

Maral led them to a large outcropping of boulders before spreading a fur pelt on the ground and lying Darmond on top of it. She let out a high, quick whistle. In response, a monstrous silhouette rounded the largest of the boulders. It lumbered forward, a swaying figure atop it. Solyana's exhausted mind reeled as she prepared to conjure flame, hoping her body wasn't too spent. She would protect her people, no matter the cost.

"Hi, guys! Look what I found!" A small voice rang out from the massive shadow as it slowly came to light.

"Well, I didn't think anything else could surprise me today. But I was wrong," Lone said flatly.

"Jonas!" Gamaliel was running, Vinur at his heels. Two mammoths, with wiry fur and sloping tusks, came to a halt before the group. Jonas straddled the larger of the two. Solyana blinked up at the massive creatures in front of her, mouth curving into a grin.

"Come here!" Gamaliel called out, holding his arms out for Jonas. The boy slid off with a giggle, knocking Gamaliel to the ground. He wasted no time in picking Jonas up, awkwardly swaddling him in a prolonged hug.

"You can let me go now," Jonas croaked.

"Never."

"I'm fine!"

"Still not letting go."

"I want to see Solyana!"

"No."

"She smells better than you."

Gamaliel dropped him.

Jonas spun and launched himself at Solyana, almost toppling her over. She laughed and hugged him hard. "I missed you, too," she said, pulling away and tousling his hair.

"I would say the same, but honestly, I've been having the time of my life."

"What?" Solyana laughed harder, and it blended with tears of relief. "Do tell."

"I had the best dreams! Like, at one point, we were all sledding down this huge hill, and we were going so fast!"

"*That* was not a dream," Lone said dryly. "And we almost died."

"Well, I thought it was fun." Jonas gave a toothy smile.

"Come here," Lone said with a smirk, drawing the boy into her arms.

"It won't be long until they find those men." Maral jolted them back to the present. "Chief Orson will come looking for me, and these mammoths."

"You could come with us," Lone suggested. Solyana looked at her in surprise.

Maral shook her head. "Someone needs to stand up to Orson. I need to see this through."

"My father," Gamaliel said, his face haggard and dirty. "Is there any way he can be freed?"

"To be honest, I'm not sure how much of your father is left." Maral rubbed at her red-rimmed eyes. "But I'll see what I can do."

"Maral found me lots of scrolls!" Jonas said excitedly, pointing to the back of one of the mammoths.

"We've packed the supplies you'll need, but Jonas wouldn't stop asking about our archives." She gave the boy a soft smile. "I was able to get you a few scrolls that might lend some insight into what you're trying to do."

"And Odie is coming with us!" Jonas chimed in again.

Maral glanced around. "Ah, yes. He's a bit of a curmudgeon, but he has a good heart. And those mammoths will follow him anywhere. Isn't that right, Odie?"

A stocky, middle-aged man trundled out from behind the boulder, a pack on his back, his arms bearing saddle bags. A significant underbite allowed two teeth to be visible from the depths of his brown beard.

"Eyup," Odie greeted. He dropped his items and removed the hat from his head, revealing mats of dark hair. He gave a small bow to each member of the party. "My name is longer than Odie, but Odie is easier to say." His speech came out with a lisp and his cheeks resembled shiny fruit as he grinned. "I am Mammut Tala, and these are my beasties. I haven't traveled far from Takanah, but if you give me a direction, I can keep these two going." He gave the smaller mammoth a pat.

"We greatly appreciate your expertise." Solyana returned his bow, thankful for one more Tala who could take some of the burden from Gamaliel. "Is that our gear?" The bags at Odie's feet burst with cloth. He nodded and pulled out the heavy parkas they had left at the Healer's home.

"What's your real name?" Jonas grinned as Solyana, Gamaliel, and Lone donned their heavy parkas.

Odie eyed Jonas with a sideways smile. "Odesopholos." Jonas giggled behind his hand. Then he directed his gaze at Solyana. "The honor is all mine." He dipped his head once more before stuffing his hat back on and over his ears.

"This is no normal journey," Lone warned, glancing between Solyana and Odie. "We can't guarantee your return."

"I know." He grinned and hefted his bags more securely. "But if I can help rid the world of this cold, I'll do it. Eyup!" Then in a surprising show of spryness for his age, he climbed up the side of the larger of the two mammoths.

"He is an odd one." Maral stared after the man, and a hint of a smile touched her lips. "But he is steadfast, and loyal." The wind whipped through the fur on their parkas, and Solyana glanced past the mammoths to see the beginnings of a new day peeking over the snowy hills of Mothmar beyond.

Darmond made a sound and Maral hurried to him, kneeling beside him as he stirred. She looked up at Solyana. "Heal our land, Solyana of Mothmar. Your eyes be downward." And she held out her hand.

Solyana grasped Maral's forearm, shaking once before saying, "Upward, Maral. The change starts here." She pointed at Maral's heart and then her eyes. "Your eyes be upward."

"And be filled with light." Lone, Gamaliel and Jonas responded in unison.

Maral nodded, biting her lip, tears springing anew. "Yes." She smiled the barest of smiles and held her children close. "And be filled with light."

CRACKED LIKE STONE

PALLAH

THE BREEZE WAS COLDER here. It whistled its way between trees and over hills to reach her, pulling the heat from her skin as it flirted with her hair. Pallah tucked her chin deeper into her knit cloak and pulled the sleeves of her tunic down around her fists. She surveyed Freya's grounds with new eyes. The landscape witnessed the stories of her past, places of Pallah's late arrival to the truth.

The facts about her mother, about her family, about herself, they swirled inside of Pallah with no place to land; free-floating knowledge with no application. Pallah looked back toward the small hut in the woods.

Phyllir had loved the broken man inside. Pallah could see his former self, if only a glimpse of it. He'd been young and strong once. Did her mother know Dahvid still lived? Surely, she wouldn't have left him to suffer alone all of these years. Surely, she believed him to be dead. Thinking of her mother was a mistake. It dredged up millstones of grief and uncertainty in Pallah's mind. She had left her mother in the hands of Healers, but from what she had overheard, they did not hold much hope for recovery.

Pallah craved a reunion with her mother before she died, but the risks of going back were too dire to ignore. If she were to return now, Chief Olafur and the council would lock her away. She would be shackled as a Temple Serviseer for years before she was old enough to leave. And what then? She had a new life now, filled with new people, a different kind of family, and skill with the Taka Reu she could claim as her own.

Although, Pallah considered, what if she were to surrender herself to Temple service; to help her friends from the inside? Hundreds of scrolls remained inside the Temple Celestial, far more than the meager few they'd managed to gather the night of the smilodon attack. As a Serviseer, she'd have unfettered access to all those records. But the thought of acting the part lit a fire inside. There was no way she could serve the gods that Bogdur served.

If you don't kill him, I will.

Pallah took a deep pull of air at the thrill threading through her belly. "I won't let you take that from me."

That's my girl.

"Have you made up your mind?" Issha had approached silently, as was her way. Pallah didn't turn to look at her, instead watching an owl as it made its way down from a tall pine, soaring over their heads to Freya's home behind them.

"About what?"

"Are you staying here or coming back with us?"

Pallah sighed as she faced Issha, who was dressed in woolen pants and a cloak much like Pallah's. It was light violet, a new color for Issha who usually preferred earthen hues.

"You look nice." Pallah smirked.

"Oh, this?" Issha pulled it away from her body to examine it. "Freya had it. It was my mother's."

"Violet is your color."

"Come on." Issha brushed off the kind sentiment. "Karav nabbed breakfast."

When they returned, Karav was crouched near a cookfire. With a small degree of difficulty, she pierced a rabbit through with a sharpened stick. "I miss Leif." She grimaced as blood spurted, barely missing her pants. "His hares are so much easier to handle; they practically throw themselves onto the coals." She rested the spit over the cookfire and coaxed the flames higher.

"Where's Freya?" Pallah asked; she hadn't seen the woman all morning.

"She left in the night," Issha said.

"How do you know that?" Karav asked, sitting back on her heels.

"Someone has to pay attention." Issha smiled. "Besides, my mother apprenticed under Freya. I know when there's a twilight birth."

"So, she's in Takanah?" Pallah asked. When no one answered, she nodded. "She's in Takanah."

The three of them leaned into the silence, the smell of roasting meat making Pallah's mouth water. Her eyes fell on the door of the cottage, and she thought of Tinloh, still sleeping inside. She should check on him soon.

"So...that guy is your dad?" Karav inquired, eyes on the hare.

Pallah glanced at her sideways. "No." She rubbed a hand down her face, still trying to come to terms with the conversation from the night before. "He's my brother and sister's dad...apparently. My lineage still hails from the great Bogdur himself." Pallah rolled her eyes. "Though, I can't help but wonder how he got to where he is. How did he end up squirreled away in a room at Freya's house? If my mother truly loved him, and he is the father of my siblings, there has to be more information. Ahren and Vámae deserve to know, but I can't go to them with only half the story. Plus, we both have smilodon Tala." Pallah shrugged. "It would be nice to learn from someone who has the same aptitude."

"Well," began Karav, who had heard a revised version of the story from Pallah the night before, "We'll go straight to the infirmary when we get back. Check on your mom."

Pallah gave Karav a conciliatory smile, "Thanks, 'Rav." She tucked her knees up under her chin. Had her mother kept any personal scrolls, perhaps of her life before? It would probably be too risky, with how meticulous Bogdur was...but what about Dahvid? Pallah looked quickly at Freya's cottage.

"I wonder if Dahvid ever wrote anything down."

"Like a record?" Issha asked.

"Yeah."

"Can he, um, write?" Karav said.

"I mean from before. Is it a stupid idea to search his room?"

"Maybe wait until Freya gets home," suggested Karav. "She seems to be able to communicate with him."

Pallah said nothing.

"You don't want her to know," Issha assumed.

"Something tells me she wouldn't be pleased with the idea," admitted Pallah.

Karav rotated the rabbit. "Would *he* tell on you?"

"Even if Freya talks to him"—Pallah shrugged—"it's not like he can talk back." Guilt threatened to stop her.

"It's kind of an invasion of privacy," Karav said before smiling wickedly. "So, naturally, I'm all in."

"Karav!" Issha reprimanded.

Pallah ignored them both, eyes on the cottage. A breeze blew over the grounds, wind chimes and lawn decorations waving this way and that, emitting a discordant clatter.

"When are we leaving?" she asked.

"In an hour, at the latest. The sun is almost completely up," Issha said.

"Stand watch?" Pallah asked, and Issha nodded in return.

"Don't be long. Breakfast is almost ready," Karav said as Pallah broke away from the fire, her stomach rumbling in protest.

The door creaked as she opened it, and an owl turned its attention from the rafters above. She shuddered, unsettled by their silently swiveling heads and large lantern-like eyes. She entered Freya's cottage, made warmer by the morning light.

Pallah made her way down the hall to Dahvid's room. She would have to be efficient. She pushed open the door to find Dahvid in his chair, the fire burning to embers in front of him. Was he asleep? Should she say something, or just sneak around quietly? Before she could decide, he moved his head in jagged bursts until his eyes met her own, his face the blank slate it had been the night before.

"H-Hi, Dahvid," she stammered, unnerved.

He didn't move.

"Can I get you anything?" A stupid question to ask someone non-verbal, but it felt like the decent thing to do before snooping through his things. Nothing indicated he understood her, but nothing indicated he didn't, so she continued. "I'd like to know more about you and my mother. My siblings would like to know you more, too. It would be nice to return with news like this, about a father that's not..." Pallah's words trailed off and she bit the inside of her cheek. "Not Bogdur. I was hoping if you had—"

Her tether suddenly stretched, like someone had hooked the middle of it. The tension increased, pulling sideways, as though to dislodge her hold on Tinloh. She gasped and fortified it, falling to one knee as she concentrated her efforts on keeping it strong. The cat still slept in the other room, and Pallah guarded him through one breath, then two, but the third breath shuddered. The hook released, and Pallah looked up at the man as she knelt before him, her hands shaking.

"You...did you do that?" she asked, though she already knew the answer. "You want me to release my tether?"

Dahvid stared at her.

"So you can tether him instead?"

Dahvid remained unchanged, but deep in Pallah's mind, the hook crept forward again, waiting patiently to strike. The sharpness and strength of it made her tether look like a fragile thread of silk. Pressure increased as the ragged edges of his Tala encroached on her mind. She closed her eyes, concentrating, and blocked it again. Her mind closed him out, and his neck twitched almost imperceptibly.

"No!" she commanded with a strength she didn't feel. "You don't get to come in uninvited." The irony of her statement rolled away as she studied the room. She needed to be quick.

Desperate for answers and uncaring how her presence affected him, Pallah began to scour the room. Opening drawers, sliding her hand beneath the unkempt bed and its frame, shuffling through boxes and pieces of parchment, Pallah searched.

Dropping to her knees, her hands fiddled with the bedside table, searching for unseen cracks or hinges. Scooting forward, her knee pressed down on a floorboard near his bed. It wobbled.

Eyes wide, Pallah dug her nails into the side of it until she got the board just above the lip of the floor. She peered inside. Nestled in the dark hallow were a few sheets of loose parchment, a piece of auburn cloth, and a thick and sturdy scroll.

The sound of the cottage door opening and closing stayed Pallah's hand. She replaced the floorboard, stood, and turned around, her hands folded before her.

Freya's head poked into the room where her eyes jumped from Dahvid to Pallah. "Oh! What are you doing in here?" She stepped into the room, a snowy owl bobbing on her shoulder.

"I was just talking with Dahvid about his Tala." Pallah swallowed. "Since we have the same aptitude and all."

Freya narrowed her eyes. "Well, I need to change his underclothes. Why don't you go on back to your friends?"

Pallah scurried from the room, hoping Dahvid's tether wouldn't follow.

So, when are we going to steal it? Erval crooned. *Tonight?*

"I'll have to try," she said, picking her way across the littered lawn.

Subterfuge, how fun!

Her lips curved to a smile as she made her way back to the cookfire. "Thanks for the heads up," Pallah said sarcastically. "I had no idea Freya was back until she was almost on top of me."

"What were we supposed to do?" Karav asked, handing over a plate. "That woman moves faster than Leif's hares at dinner time."

"Did you find anything?" Issha asked.

Pallah nodded. "I found a scroll, but I couldn't take it from the room. And if I have the chance to find out more about my mother's past, then I'm not going anywhere."

"Not to mention the council cracking down on you if you returned home," Issha said.

"Yeah." Pallah took a bite. "Vil made it pretty clear; he wants me to lie low."

The door to the cottage swung open and Freya trundled out. Grabbing a particularly long walking stick from against the door frame, she wove her way over the hill to sit at the fire. Ingrid, the snowy owl, landed beside Pallah, beak open, yellow eyes scanning.

"Got enough breakfast for an old woman and her bird?"

Issha handed her own plate over without complaint and wiped her mouth before asking, "How was the birth?"

"Mother's fine, baby was a tenner," Freya said between bites.

"A tenner?" Karav asked.

"A baby ten pounds or more," Issha said, sitting back down and stoking the fire with a stick.

"You sure you don't want to stay here and apprentice like your mama?" Freya grinned. "I could use a Fera of your skill again."

"Thank you, Freya, but no. I need to get back."

"To whom?" Freya asked in surprise. "So, there *is* a man waiting for you back in that valley!"

"I simply have a life in Austur." Issha deflected and gave Freya a smile.

"Suit yourself." Freya licked grease from her fingers. "You're all leaving then?"

Issha and Karav looked at Pallah in unison, causing Freya to turn to her, too.

"I'd like to stay a bit longer, if you'll have me." Pallah kept her eyes on the fire, praying the woman had believed her story about chatting with Dahvid. "I'll keep to myself, help with the cooking, and make trips to Takanah if you need me to."

Freya's voice came out harder than expected. "I don't need an extra mouth to feed."

"I'll pull my weight." Pallah finally found Freya's eyes. "I'd like to get to know Dahvid more, if you'll help me."

"He's not who he once was, dear."

"Yes, but my mother cared for him. I owe it to my family to know, especially now that my mother...now that she's unwell."

Freya softly *hmphed*, stood up with the aid of her walking stick, and gave a long stretch. Ingrid took to the sky. "I need sleep. Issha, send word when you're ready to have your own babies, you hear?"

Issha stared at the fire. Pallah thought she was blushing.

"Moody, like her mother." Freya gave a wink and Karav laughed. "Well, if you're gone before I wake, travel safe. Watch out for any of those fortified beasties."

Karav arched an eyebrow. "Fortified?"

Freya gave a chuckle, hand waving above her head as she hobbled back over the hill and through the door. A clang of notes rang out as she knocked wind chimes askew.

Karav turned back to the two. "I forgot to tell you two, but this rabbit, it had a similar pattern as to what we felt in the mind of that bear. Like there was a wall, then almost a maze?" She glanced at Issha and shrugged. "I don't know how to explain it, even as a Tala."

Pallah mulled it over. "I wonder if that's what Freya meant by 'fortified.'"

Karav shrugged. "We'll send for you when things calm down." And she pulled Pallah in for a hug. Pallah returned the embrace fiercely, suddenly aware she would soon be left alone with this quirky old woman and the mysterious man she kept in her home.

When Karav stepped to the side, Issha replaced her, pulling her in tight. "Keep working on your connection to the Taka Reu," Issha whispered before they separated. "I'll tell Vil and the others how proficient you are already, but you need to keep practicing."

Pallah nodded, the mention of Vil filling her with a surge of emotion. "Your eyes be downward."

"And be filled with life," Issha and Karav answered in unison.

The two disappeared over the horizon, cresting the hill that led to the forest. Pallah watched them as Tinloh dashed about the yard, free from all tethers. What would his life have looked like had his mother never descended to Pallah's valley? Where would he have been in this moment? Perhaps roving the forests to hunt or wrestling with his brother? Extending her tether to him, she tried to latch on, but something about the connection fought her. She tried again, the second time more successful.

There were two buildings on Freya's property that Pallah had yet to explore. The long grass was thin and high, and she let the tops of the plants tickle her fingers as she wove her way toward the first: a cylindrical stone tower that rose much higher than the other building. It had two windows at the top on opposite sides, small though they were. She unlatched the door and let herself into an owlery.

There would have been room for thirty owls or more, but a large portion of the nesting boxes had been boarded up, leaving only ten filled with owls of all different shapes and sizes. Pallah hadn't inquired into Freya's Gift or aptitude, but it was quite clear she was Ugla Tala.

Most of the birds slept, but a few peered down at her, annoyed she had disturbed their haven. A scratch at the door signaled Tinloh's arrival, but Pallah quickly pulled her tether taut, encouraging him to back away. He could not gain access to the owlery, not if Pallah wanted Freya's goodwill.

The second building appeared newer, made from wood in a nearly perfect square. Pallah went to the door, but it was locked, the padlock a thing of solid, heavy iron, the kind she had only seen on the cells beneath the Temple Celestial. Her father sat in one of those cells right now.

There was a window on the side. She made her way over to peer into it.

A forge lay dormant within, the anvil near it cold and silent. Several large metal tools lined the walls, hanging on pegs worn smooth from use—a smithy. They had one back in the Valley, near the livestock barns, used often by the Malmur Fera that mined the mountain of silver, gold, and iron. It was nowhere near as well-equipped as this one.

Several weapons appeared to be new, hanging from chains on the wall, glittering in the waning light. Pallah quickly found the axe heads, much like her own weapon of choice. One in particular caught her eye. The haft was cast in silver, smooth and long, a large and menacing axe head protruding from each end, facing opposite directions. Perhaps Freya would allow her to practice with it.

Pallah turned from the smithy to see a deer standing a few paces away. They stared at each other for a moment, the animal's tail twitching as it spotted Tinloh, who crouched beside Pallah. Her sabertooth wouldn't be hungry; he had feasted on a bear only the day before. She reminded Tinloh of the fact, encouraging peace. Pallah wondered if this was one of the fortified animals Freya had mentioned.

We could find out.

"I can't tether it," Pallah whispered. "I only have Smilodon Tala."

I could tether it...through you.

Pallah blinked, fear and thrill mixing in her chest.

But only if you let me.

"Do it." And before the words fully crossed the threshold of her lips, Erval's tether coursed through her and hit the animal. The world spun and Pallah fell to her knees.

The tether hit a wall, bounced off, and struck out again.

This is exciting! I rarely see anything new anymore, but this, THIS. Yes! Let's get in here.

Nausea roiled like a worm within Pallah as he tried again, this time slamming through the defenses and dropping his tether into something akin to a maze.

Pallah wished he would stop, but her mind could do nothing but cower and shake.

Like a runaway elk, Erval's tether galloped through hallways and reared at dead ends.

Interesting. So interesting.

He broke through more walls, more avenues, until finally, Erval released his hold, his voice chuckling in her mind.

Take it, kitty. I've got work to do.

Tinloh strained against Pallah's tether until she relinquished her hold and the cat shot after the deer. White tail high in alert, eyes round with fear, the deer bounded into the woods, Tinloh hot on its heels.

Pallah stood, forcing herself to take deep breaths. "Erval?"

She was answered with silence, the only sounds the rustle of leaves and the desperate pounding of hooves as the deer ran for its life.

"Erval?" A tear slipped down her cheek. Whatever he had done to her, through her, it left her hollow. She sniffed and marched back to the cottage while Tinloh hunted, her mind still whirling and raw. The trust she had begun to build between her and the voice in her mind had cracked like stone beneath a hammer. He hadn't listened to her, hadn't been gentle. But when had anyone in her life offered her such courtesy?

Pallah wasn't meant for a gentle life. And apparently, her mother hadn't been either. But unlike her mother, Pallah would not bow to the whims of others. No, she would rise to challenge and face the naked truth head on. Research was her only path forward now. And Pallah had a scroll to steal.

THE GIRL WHO DIDN'T BREAK

ERVAL

H E HAD BEEN TOO long alone on this side of the mountain. Well, Erval wasn't *alone*; he had Phineas. Dull as he was, the man did bring a smile to his lips. Oh, Phineas. He really did care for his advisor, but his wasn't the kind of company Erval was longing for.

It wasn't romantic entanglements, either. He'd had plenty of those in his youth; women drawn to his appearance, to power, or to his name and the scandal it brought—the notoriety.

What he truly wanted was something deeper than needy bodies or fear-filled grovelers. What he needed was a partner. Someone who could truly understand him, a single individual he could regard with respect; someone who knew his capabilities, marveled at them, and maybe even matched them, too.

He had spent years honing his tether to reach across great dis-tances. The people brought under his influence, simple means to a glorious end. Their use was required by his greater good. If he was to fix his country, he would first need to coax it into submission; a nation on its knees was a nation committed.

He had just passed his thirty-fourth birthday and, with his age, grown wiser. It was in this new wisdom he recognized he couldn't keep tethering to those old enough to reject him. They had lived long enough to know the control they'd lost and seek to sever his reach however they could.

Erval had never held any affection for children; they simply had no place in his life. But as he turned the gear of the finnevel with a languid finger, he thought of them. The children.

There was a village far south, far enough the finnevel might struggle amplifying his Mann Tala to reach it, but...he couldn't keep using it so close to Thonethren. Halldora was beginning to recognize his handiwork. She had scouts everywhere—or Shahann did, if the old coot was still alive—and they hadn't stopped looking for him. His time on the mountain was running out. The haphazard trail of broken bodies was beginning to gain notice. Inconvenient, as he was not yet fully prepared to reveal his hand. Not until his army grew strong enough that he could confidently deploy them and take back the throne.

Erval stood, ice clinking in his half-empty glass as he placed it on the corner table beside the device. He usually called Phineas to adjust the locale of the finnevel, but he decided he'd watched the process enough times. And the soft-hearted man might not agree with his plans. Erval had no desire to entertain the man's contradictory sniveling.

Gears adjusted and dials spun to the coordinates his men had provided. The finnevel should be aligned to a tiny southern village, a hardly notable spit of valley with a hardly notable population. Sodur was its name. Erval's scouts had assured him that this particular village was the perfect place to find someone. Sodur, along with its neighbors, Vestur and Austur, stood alone in their piety. They were steady in their worship of the Celestials, and they would be unsympathetic to Erval's future decrees. It was the perfect spot to raise a disciple, a puppet to be stuffed with his own ideals. And later, if said disciple proved worthy, perhaps they could become a confidant.

He pulled the finnevel close and placed the cup over his eye as he stared out into greater Mothmar. At first, it acted as a simple spyglass, an open window into rolling terrain. But as he released his tether through the Taka Reu, and then through the finnevel, the land folded onto itself and became simple color and light. He felt at one with his tether, as if it had its own tangible presence, and he, its mighty wielder. He liked to call this view 'Kjarn's Eye,' though he hadn't shared that fact with Phineas. If Erval was being honest, he thought Phineas might explain Kjarn's Eye away with his science talk, and Erval preferred to view it as his own magical world. A place of in-between. Yes, Phineas was brighter than Erval gave him credit for. Genius, really; he probably should give the man a raise.

"Now, which one, which one..." He searched for someone who held an open mind, someone who questioned. Children were good at that.

"Let's see..." Erval mumbled, eye flush to the cup. "Someone who holds mistrust. Yes..."

Within Kjarn's Eye, he spotted her, only about six or seven years of age. He prodded her with his tether, finding mistrust and...a heart already stained with darkness. "Excellent." Erval braced himself against the machine, gathering his focus and strength.

Now was the true test. He latched onto the girl's consciousness with the full weight of his tether. Three heartbeats went by, four, five, pounding in his ears.

The girl didn't break.

She gave no inclination of discomfort whatsoever.

Erval blinked and, with a wave of bliss, could see through her eyes as if they were his own.

"Yes!" Erval cried, almost jostling himself from the contraption.

The girl was looking down at her hands, splotched with new tears. Erval suddenly realized he was wholly unprepared for what he would say to this girl. *Hello, I'm a man inside your head*, lacked regality, finesse. Perhaps he could simply nudge her in the right direction, sway her heart deftly toward the Taka Reu, cultivate doubt towards the gods her people served.

Erval planted those thoughts within her and let them carefully bloom: thoughts of rebellion, of dissolution, and whispers of doubt. The girl stopped crying. She appeared to be...surprised. Oh dear, perhaps he had pushed too much or too hard. No matter, he would simply speak to her.

"You don't belong, do you?" He asked the question without malice, but she stood abruptly, searching for the source of his voice. Erval would be lying if he said he didn't feel sympathy for her—he always did, no matter upon whom he practiced his Tala—but he was equally thrilled. She'd heard him!

The girl ran inside, blubbering and shrieking. Erval grinned and began to unlatch his tether, he didn't want to overdo it. But just before he did, he heard the girl's father speak her name. It seared into his mind, the name that would become his singular purpose.

Pallah.

"MY MAMMOTH AND ME"

SOLYANA

"**H**IGH UPON THE ARCH of her hips I ride abreast, I carry no switch! With the barest of touches she does what I ask, the love of a mammoth is sure to last!" Odie's gravelly voice carried over the empty tundra, his pitch and lisp rising and falling like the wind.

"I could give him lock-jaw," Lone suggested, pulling her hood tight around her head.

Solyana rolled her eyes.

It was late in the afternoon of the third day heading northeast, away from Takanah. They marched over hardened ice plains and wove through pine groves, trees spaced barely far enough apart for the mammoths to plod through. In that time, Solyana had discovered something she'd believed to be mythical—a human who annoyed Lone more than Solyana herself.

"Jonas is loving it," Gamaliel said over his shoulder. He sat at the front of the mammoth, Solyana and Lone behind him. Jonas rode the other mammoth, sitting before Odie, clapping his mittened hands in time to the driver's song. Vinur curled up behind them, ears flat against his head. "Kind of a weird song, isn't it?"

"Is he talking about the mammoth's...hips?" Lone shook her head and tucked it behind Solyana. "Just tell me when it's over."

"Stalwart and sure," Odie belted out into the quiet cold, "they plod along, always in time with my song!"

Jonas keeled over in bubbly laughter. Odie had to catch him before he fell like a baby bird tumbling from its nest.

"Careful there, boy. You'll break something from this height." Chuckling, Odie pulled him up before calling over to Solyana's team. "We should give these two a rest!"

"How about that cluster of trees?" Gamaliel pointed over the top of his mammoth's head just as Halina descended into their line of vision. The bird circled once before diving for the bit of woods Gamaliel had spotted. "Halina has the right idea. It looks like it's large enough to hold wildlife. We'll stop for the night, maybe hunt."

Solyana didn't know what to think of the bird's appearance in Takanah, and her uncertainty grew as the falcon seemed intent on accompanying the team on their journey.

"How far can a Tala tether reach?" Solyana asked Gamaliel's back, his shoulders rocking with the mammoth beneath them.

"Depends on a few factors: skill, for one...experience, and relationship with their aptitude." Gamaliel turned his head so he could see her out of the corner of his eye, the hair on that side frayed where it had burned. "You're wondering about Halina, aren't you?"

"Yes," Solyana admitted. "Is it even possible for Rhuth to be tethered this far from home?"

"If it is, I've never heard of it." Gamaliel shrugged, turning forward once more. "But then again, there seems to be much to learn about Tala through the Taka Reu."

Solyana blinked, taken aback. "But Rhuth isn't using the Taka Reu, Gam."

"I know." He was silent for a beat. "But it's weird, tethering at all while in darlöh."

"What if it's something we have yet to discover?" The wind buffeted at her parka, and Solyana huddled closer behind Gamaliel's back. "Something forgotten in ancient scrolls?"

"What are you talking about?" Lone asked, head poking around Solyana's shoulder.

Solyana hesitated, debating how much to tell her. Things had improved between them since Takanah, but was it enough to confess all that had happened with Rhuth and Priestess Avi? The former tethering while in a sleep she may never wake from, the latter having admitted to Solyana she used the Taka Reu herself.

But as Solyana opened her mouth to answer, Odie began his song once more as they entered the tree line. Lone groaned and pulled her hood back over her head. They set a quick camp in a clearing. Maral had sent them off with enough food for a few days and the supplies necessary for a comfortable night's sleep. But as she watched Gamaliel whistle for Vinur and stalk into the woods, Solyana knew that keeping up with their need for food was going to be no small feat.

The mammoths contentedly munched on some brush before settling down, creating a convenient and furry defense from the elements. The fire crackled, and Solyana leaned into the warmth. Colors on the horizon descended from orange to deep purple, and the Norlos began its luminescent wave across the sky.

Halina fluttered into view, something small and white clutched in her talons. Solyana stared as the bird perched on a branch, tucking into her meal. Surely, it couldn't be Rhuth...surely, the bird had just grown attached to them.

Solyana's eyes swept the woods again—the fourth time in the last hour—her chest growing tighter each minute Gamaliel was away.

Odie shuffled back and forth between the mammoths like a mother hen. "Goodnight, Curry," he said to the smaller of the two, one hand on a tusk. "Stay spicy." He clumped over to the larger one and gave its trunk a few pats. "Goodnight, Björg, my strong boy. I'll keep watch first. You rest."

"Did he just tell Curry to 'stay spicy?'" Solyana asked Jonas as he wriggled in beside her with a blanket. Odie's speech impediment made him difficult to understand, though Jonas didn't seem to have any issues at all.

"She really is though." Jonas's eyes were wide, a grin on his face. A pang of sadness came over Solyana as she saw the beginnings of new teeth filling the gaps that had once been there. Had time passed so quickly?

"So..." she began tentatively, unsure how to start the conversation she knew was necessary. "Do you remember what happened on Eldfall?"

"What do you mean?" Jonas's bright eyes flickered over her, questioning.

"Dinner's here!" Gamaliel strode from the wood with Vinur panting at his side, a pair of hares swinging from his fist.

Relief flooded Solyana as Gamaliel lowered his hood, revealing his uneven, charred tufts where long locks had once been. He had kept it down since leaving Takanah since all of it now couldn't quite make it into his usual top knot. Thankfully, his skin had barely been affected.

"Where is everyone?" Gamaliel glanced around.

Lone and Odie each poked their heads out from each of the mammoths lying around the fire. Odie grinned. "A mammoth is the comfiest bed you will ever sleep in."

"He's not wrong." Lone snuggled deeper into Curry's wiry fur. "You sure she's okay with this?"

"Eyup." Odie nodded. "Curry is loving it." The two grinned at each other, and Solyana's heart lightened at the levity. She latched onto the feeling, allowing it to suffuse her spirit.

Gamaliel began skinning the hares, pulling their hides away after a series of precise cuts. "I'm glad you're all so warm and comfortable, while I've been freezing my fingers off out there." Another hare lost its pelt. "Sol." He looked up at her, wiping a speck of blood from his cheek. "Are you able to warm the area?"

Fear sliced through Solyana and she stole a glance at Jonas, images of the night at Eldfall's peak flashing through her mind. Jonas blinked, his mind appearing to work through Gamaliel's request.

"Warm the area?" He looked down at his hands and Solyana watched him as the memory unfurled. "I'm Heitt," he whispered, then shook his head. "No..." His palms closed into fists. "I used to be."

Solyana wrapped an arm around his shoulders, pulling him close. "Do you remember all that work you put into studying if someone could give their Gift to someone else?"

Jonas nodded, eyes growing even wider.

"Well, you figured it out, buddy. And you did it! You gave me your Gift."

Jonas's eyes filled with tears. Solyana squeezed him tight to comfort him; she, of all people, knew what it was like to be without a Gift. But where Solyana had been born ordinary and had been made extraordinary, Jonas had incurred a loss; his act of giving, while generous, was sacrificial.

"Thank you." Jonas wiped his eyes, laughing and crying all at once.

Solyana pulled away, searching his face.

"Jonas?" Gamaliel's brows furrowed.

"The last thing I remember was kneeling at the peak of Eldfall, and the fire just wouldn't stop. It kept burning and burning. But you, Solyana?"

She wiped a tear from his face.

"You stopped it!"

"We did, Jonas. We did it together."

Jonas opened his arms wide, and Solyana drew him in, the two of them holding each other by the crackling fire. Solyana caught him up on everything that had happened, leaving out the scary parts.

"Can you do it? Use your Heitt?" Jonas asked, his eyes searching her hands.

She opened her fist and reluctantly commanded a soft glow to her palm.

"That's amazing!" He laughed. "Now, warm up this whole area so we aren't so *häfan* cold!"

"Jonas!" Gamaliel's hands stuttered in turning the hares over the fire. "Watch your mouth!"

Solyana laughed but grew somber as she thought of the fire that ravaged Takanah. "It's been difficult to get right. I haven't had the time to practice or hone any skills."

"I can teach you!" Jonas grinned, his eyes still on her hands. "Just do what you did before, but less."

Solyana's eyes wandered to Gamaliel, thinking of how he had almost been burned so badly by her hand.

"Sol, it's okay. We were in survival mode in Takanah," Gamaliel soothed. "I think you'll be able to handle it now."

"I don't really remember using it much, but all the scrolls say it's like tethering the top portion of the earth," Jonas babbled, ignorant of her discomfort. "But it's not so much a tether as it is like a covering. Does that make sense?"

Solyana shrank into herself, all her prior confidence in the darkened city of Takanah evaporating with the close intimacy of friends.

"Leave her be." Lone's voice wafted from Curry, the girl unseen, entirely ensconced in brown fur. "She needs to conserve her strength, just like the rest of us."

Solyana's heart swelled, her body relaxing into the boy next to her. "Thanks, Lone."

"The fire is warm"—Gamaliel pointed a stick at the flames—"our mammoths are warm"—he swung the stick again—"and there's food." He sat down in front of his rabbits. "We have what we need."

The smell of roasting meat lured Lone and Odie from their wooly beds. It was nice to see them getting along as they talked and ate before collapsing back into the mammoths. Jonas ate with drooping eyelids and fell asleep, curled up between Gamaliel and Solyana.

They exchanged a look, trapped beneath the boy they both loved, and smiled.

Solyana breathed in the peace of the moment: the fire's low burn and a distant howling that kept Vinur's ears alert. Now alone, she turned to Gamaliel, questions from the day escaping past cold lips. "What did you make of Takanah? The Taka Reu?"

Gamaliel's deep brown eyes locked on her own, and he puffed out his cheeks. "Maral has a job to do, that's for sure. It just goes to show what happens when you meddle with darkness." He raised an eyebrow.

"Gam," Solyana whispered, knowing exactly what he was insinuating. "Priestess Avi has to use it. Maybe it's different when it's a necessity."

"Is it?" He shrugged and poked at the fire with a stick. "So, if Priestess Avi shifted into something, that would be okay?"

Having forgotten all about the smilodon, Solyana's mouth dropped open before snapping shut, mind reeling. "She's just tethered to it. She wouldn't transform."

"Just because we admire people"—Gamaliel's gaze lowered, his shoulders sagging—"or even love them, it doesn't mean they won't disappoint us."

Solyana laid a gloved hand on his, knowing he spoke of his father. "We'll get him back. Maral will find him."

Avoiding her gaze, Gamaliel made a clicking noise in the back of his throat. Vinur slinked away from Curry and trotted to Gamaliel's side. He curled up and laid his head next to Jonas. "If he isn't too far gone. Did you see how everyone transformed? What was that black stuff that came up from the floor?"

"*Aska*." A cold chill spread through Solyana's body at the thought of it. "Priestess Avi told me about it before we left. It's a manifestation of the Taka Reu." She pointed to her scarred cheek. "Apparently it's also in here."

When Solyana looked up, Gamaliel was studying the scar with intent, his dark eyes tracing its lines. At first, shame reddened her cheeks; the scar that marred her was still such a mystery. Having received it after the first rogue blizzard in their valley, Solyana had found little else about its formation other than having a direct link to the prophecy.

Gamaliel's eyes followed the line of the scar down to her lips, following the arch of one, then the other. Slowly, their eyes met. In his gaze, Solyana saw unabashed desire. She inhaled with anticipation.

"Orson said you weren't the first." Gamaliel pulled away slightly. "There were others who had claimed to be the one chosen to fulfill the Green Prophecy."

"Wouldn't we have heard of people going before?" Solyana asked. "Of gaining the scar and accruing three Gifts? He must have lied."

Gamaliel shrugged, falling quiet.

"What's wrong?"

"You wouldn't do it, right?" he whispered. "Not after what we've seen."

"Do what?" Solyana sought to meet his eyes, but he kept them from her.

"If things don't go the way we want..." He turned his face to the moon. "If you are given the choice between sacrificing something important or using the Taka Reu..."

Her eyes dropped to Jonas, then over to the mammoths. They hadn't discussed any of Priestess Avi's ideas with the rest of the group; the potential of using Dark Gifts to achieve the goals of their journey. Jonas survived the transfer of the Gift, which would make it easier to convince someone else to do the same. But would anyone be willing? Who else was out there?

"I—I don't know, Gam."

"You should know," Gamaliel pleaded. "It's wrong."

"But if it brings back the green? If it saves Rhuth?"

"Doing something wrong, even for good reason? No." He shook his head tersely. "It isn't right."

The heat of affection she'd felt turned to frustration, a hot flash over her skin. How dare he? He couldn't understand the weight laid on her shoulders, the responsibilities, the decisions. He had no idea what it was like to be her. "Don't tell me what's right, Gamaliel. You're in no place to make that distinction."

"I'm not?" He turned on her. "I'm here, aren't I? I'm here to help you make exactly those kinds of decisions." His fingertips carefully plied the raw skin of his cheek, a victim of her fire. "To bear them with you, Solyana. I'm with you. And I know—I have to believe—you won't allow the darkness in. You won't be like my father. You won't be like..." He trailed off, but Solyana knew whose name was on the tip of his tongue.

Priestess Avi had admitted to using the Taka Reu along with her Gifts, somehow tangibly communing with both the Celestials and the Mother. She had sworn Solyana to secrecy, but Solyana hadn't been able to bear the burden of such information alone; she'd broken her promise and told Gamaliel. He disapproved of the priestess ever since, calling her untrustworthy, even dark. But Solyana couldn't agree. What kind of monster would it make her if she had left her baby sister in the hands of someone so evil?

No. The priestess had found a way to do both, to find balance in it. And though the idea terrified her, Solyana would do the same if it meant saving her people.

If it meant saving Rhuth, she would do anything.

"I would still be me, Gamaliel." She stared at him from inside her hood, her hair tickling her face as a soft wind blew through their camp.

His smile was laced with sorrow. He reached across and touched Solyana's scar, warm fingers caressing her face. Then his eyes flashed with something unrecognizable, and he retracted his hand. "Sleep, Solyana. I'll keep first watch."

"The Taka Reu?" Jonas's eyes widened and, in naming the Dark Gifts, his voice dropped to a low pitch. "You want to know more about The Taking? Why?"

Jonas and Solyana sat cross-legged on Björg's back. Odie sat in front of them, grinning and humming into the crisp morning air.

"Takanah seemed to be built upon it, instead of the worship of the Celestials, as it is in our valley," Solyana said. Talking about her home brought a depth of longing so heavy, she felt sluggish under its weight. "I want to understand it more thoroughly before we meet more people who are potentially involved with it, spot the signs before we find ourselves in harm's way yet again."

Jonas shuffled through his bag of scrolls, books, and maps. He breathed a quick, frustrated sigh, shook off his mittens, and returned to digging.

"Ah-ha!" Jonas lifted a book from the bag and flipped through the pages before pressing a finger to a line coupled with something mumbled in ancient Mothmari. Finally, a translation stumbled out. "Early signs of its use are often the hardest to perceive. As the hold of Taka Reu develops in three stages, the first almost always goes unnoticed. The second stage's signs are more notable, and the third stage is unmistakable." He looked up quickly, his freckles scrunching as he twisted his lips to the side. "Is this what you're looking for?"

"Yes, perfect. Keep reading."

Jonas nodded. Finding his place, he started again. "The first stage is new growth, and it's exactly as it sounds: lush grasses, trees, all kinds of vegetables, fruits and flowers, growing with wild abandon. This stage fools everyone into thinking what is happening is good and natural, though it is anything but. The growth is fast and concerned with spread more than with depth. Underneath this growth lies the *aska*, the ruin and rot. It lies in wait until the second stage, which is *aska*—"

"Some desire their tusks! Some desire their furs! But me? I desire nothing else than their love, sure and pure!"

Startled, Jonas dropped the book, which Solyana caught just in time, almost losing her seat. She handed it back to him.

"Odie!" Jonas whined. "I'm trying to read."

"And I'm trying to steer," Odie said, though his hands held no reins. "I need to concentrate." He narrowed his eyes over the scene beyond. "It's precarious."

He wasn't wrong. Soon after departing from the wood, they found themselves upon more treacherous ground. The hard-packed snow had transitioned into a roving sea of blue ice whose thickness was anyone's guess. With each lumbering step the mammoths took, moans and cracks groaned and shuddered beneath them. There was no telling if the next step would be the one to break. The sounds dredged up a deep and visceral fear of ice Solyana had always harbored. She dug her gloved hands deeper into the wiry fur of the mammoth beneath her, looking up to distract herself from the surface over which the weighty beasts trod. They kept the mammoths side by side, so if one group began to fall through the ice, the other could aid more quickly. The impending danger kept Odie hyper-focused on Björg's feet.

Harrowing caves, like pock marks of deep indigo, bore stalagmites at their mouths, a warning to all who dared enter. Halina soared high above them. Whether my falcon was bird or girl, Solyana was comforted by her presence.

Jonas swayed, the mammoth moving beneath them, as he read. "*Aska* appears in subtle ways: underneath the surface, sticking to the earth, puffing away like dust. It can be an oily glue or a powdery smoke. While the makeup of the substance is unknown, some scholars believe it is the darkness showing itself, giving a herald. It is the rot coming to fruition, followed closely by the third stage.

"Desolation." Jonas paused, scanning ahead in the text before he continued. "We see this in reckless use of the Taka Reu, although all use of the Taka Reu is inherently reckless. But there are ways by which extended use of the Taka Reu will come to destroy, including fire, darkness, cold, heat, and light. The Taka Reu takes that which is inherently good and amplifies it to excess. It is crucial to identify embedded use of the Dark Gifts before it comes to this third and final stage, for by then, it is a way of life; by then, cultures and kingdoms have been built upon it; entire peoples are beguiled and crushed beneath its weight. May the Celestials have mercy for such busy hands, wayward hearts, and slackened minds. May they not leave us all to rot in a cesspool of our own making."

"So..." Solyana furrowed her brow, thinking. "Takanah is in the second stage?"

"Bordering on three," Odie interrupted without turning to them.

Solyana and Jonas fell quiet, waiting on the older man to speak, but he offered nothing more.

"What about"—Solyana lowered her voice—"humans becoming animals?" She glanced over at Gamaliel, who was sitting with Lone and Vinur astride Curry. Oblivious to the topic at hand, they were laughing about something together. It reminded her of the night before, how close she and Gamaliel had been. The intensity with which he'd studied her face...her lips. Had she imagined it? She turned back to Jonas. "Does your book say anything about that?"

Jonas shook his head. "Maybe there's something about it in the scrolls Maral gave me."

Solyana craned her neck skyward, finding the dark silhouette of Halina against the harsh light of the sun as she rose and fell on streams of wind. If her sister was somehow in the falcon, she needed to know how.

"Well, if there is, I would like to know if someone with Tala can tether to an animal so tightly, they bind to its essence. If they can become *one*."

"Okay, but why?"

Solyana watched the falcon ride the wind and the image of a smilodon breached her thoughts. She bit back mentioning Priestess Avi and her use of the Taka Reu. Instead, she turned to Jonas and grinned. "I want to know about Rhuth."

THE WAY IT WAS MEANT TO BE

PALLAH

TINLOH HOPPED ONTO PALLAH's bed, almost knocking her over.

"Hey, 'Loh." She pushed at him playfully, and he nipped at her hair. "Ah! Get off." She pulled his paw, almost the size of her own palm, off the scroll in her lap. He rubbed his head into her, purring deeply before curling up to sleep. Once small enough to fit in her arms, he now took up half the bed. Her fingers wove into his fur. Had it really been so long?

A week after Issha and Karav had left, and with Erval's encouragement, Pallah had finally been able to pilfer the scroll. Dahvid and Freya had been asleep in their beds, Tinloh quietly waiting at the door, ready for the journey back to Sodur and the Taka Reu. Her knapsack packed, snowshoes clicking at her side, Pallah had begun her way at dawn, when a singular hare had bounced over the hill. Attached to its back was a note.

Pallah didn't have to pull the scrap of parchment out from its hole in the side of her mattress. She knew the contents by heart.

Your mother is partially restored under the care of the Temple Celestial Serviseers, though she remains quite weak and has yet to be able to use her Heitt.

Your father's trial is set to take place after the new moon.

Your sister is a Temple Celestial Serviseer now, and we have initiated contact with her. We hope she will provide us ample opportunity to access Taka Reu scrolls.

Your brother remains with his host family. He asks about you whenever he sees one of us. The council is very concerned with your location, as well. Best to stay put for a while longer. I'll send another letter when it's safe to return.

Ps. The hare is a gift for Tinloh.

No sign off, no name. That part hurt the most.

No other letters had come. Nothing for three full weeks. And now that it had been a month, she had begun to think they had given up on her. Vil had made it clear from the very beginning: he had accepted her into the group for her skills as a thief. And now that she'd finally stolen something—she ran her fingers down the scroll in her lap—he wasn't even there to see it. So, what purpose did she serve? They still needed to build their numbers, she supposed. Vil only ever spoke about stealing scrolls and educating the people. Would he ever rise up against the Temple, or simply whittle away time with passionate speeches?

Rolling to her stomach, Pallah continued her reading.

I have never been one to dabble in dark places; I find that to be for lesser men. However, perhaps now I am lower than most. My mind descends into depths of mire when I think of Bogdur and what he has done. I intend to do what I must to protect Phyllir and to shelter the children. She will not confess they are mine, but they are. All of them.

Pallah rubbed her eyes. Dahvid believed she was his daughter.

If only it were true.

Pallah refused to entirely snuff the glowing speck of possibility. She read on.

I bought a charm off a Leirman traveling from the eastern coastlands. He claims it has the power to protect her. Though it has its dangers, as all charms do, it's worth it if she's safe. 'Stasis' is its name. And I have the ancient words to wield it:

Biddu med mer, eda et brotna.

The Lierman was adamant I only use it if she trusts me fully, irrevocably.

Trust me? She loves me. And that is deeper than trust. I will help her escape, and we will be together forever.

The words to the charm lodged deep in her mind. She had never heard of charms and was curious as to how they worked. Vil would be pleased to have this information. It was taking her too long to make it through the scroll, but over the course of three weeks with Freya, the woman had kept Pallah busy.

Hunting with Tinloh, cleaning the owlery, stocking the cellar, and preparing tinctures for Dahvid; all had become daily tasks placed upon Pallah's shoulders. And any spare moments she had, she attempted connection to the Mother. But things weren't going as well as she'd hoped, and Tinloh was beginning to grow obstinate. Sometimes, when she had gone to tether to him, she had found Dahvid's ragged tether slithering away.

A sinking feeling found greater purchase in her gut as the days went by, the intentions of the man unknowable. She had been open to him teaching her, but it seemed he only wanted to tether when she was unaware. She wanted to leave, if only to put distance between his prying tether and Tinloh. But where could she go? She had considered Takanah. But the people there knew Freya, and the woman had undoubtedly told them all about the girl that wouldn't leave her cottage. Instead, Pallah worked her way through the scroll as if her life depended on it, furiously reading until she fell asleep every night with it unfurled over her chest.

Unwelcome as Dahvid's tethering was, Pallah found her heart softening toward the man the more she read. He had pined after her mother for so long, only to be left alone and incapacitated.

Shaking her thoughts away, Pallah rolled from Tinloh and padded to the kitchen for something to eat. Freya had been out all night again and headed straight to bed upon her early return. Pallah was used to the scattered routine; she had learned quickly it was simply the way of a midwife.

Casting around for something to eat, Pallah found the kitchen empty. She pulled on her cloak, shoved her feet into leather slippers, and tromped outside into the cold. It hit her like a slap in the face, the wind stealing the breath from her lungs. Clutching her cloak tighter, she ran to the cellar. The wooden doors were heavy, and she fought gravity to open them, the hinges screaming the whole way as the door opened and fell to the ground. Pallah descended the stairs.

There was one apple, two potatoes, and an onion. She sighed. How had Freya survived before Pallah's arrival? She would need to hunt later. She gathered the items from the dirt floor, tucked them into her cloak, and ran back to the cottage. Chimes hanging on the eaves clanged as she pushed open the door, and the wind hastened her inside. A thud rattled the frame just as she got it closed, and Pallah jumped, dropping the food in her arms.

"What in the..." She cracked the door open to see Ingrid, Freya's snowy owl, righting herself and fluffing her feathers. "Oh!"

The bird hissed at her and ran inside, talons clicking over the wood floor.

"*Häfan* bird." Pallah closed the door again and turned to find Freya looking disheveled in the kitchen. "Good morning, Freya."

The old woman grumbled something as she bent down to retrieve Ingrid. The owl snuggled close to Freya's bosom and gave a disparaging *hoo* in Pallah's direction. Freya pulled a piece of parchment from the bird's leg and read it silently.

Pallah bit into the apple, watching her host. "What does it say?"

"Kahlee is in labor."

Pallah's heart constricted. She had gotten to know Freya's patients through the midwife's constant stream of chatter. "She's not due for another month."

"Babies wait for no one," Freya said as she gathered items about the room. Tiny bottles of tincture, tools, and towels were stowed into a basket, though with less care than usual. "You will come with me for this one."

"What?" Pallah shook her head. "I don't do births, and I can't leave Tinloh for—"

"Pack a bag," Freya said, ignoring Pallah's excuses. "And wear good shoes."

"I really don't think—"

Freya's knobby hands gripped Pallah by the shoulders. "You're right. It's far too early for Kahlee. But there is a chance we could save this baby; a small one, but only with you by my side. If there is no one there to help me, there's no point in going at all."

Something about the woman's tone echoed Bogdur and his commands, and before Pallah knew it, she nodded.

"Good." Freya released her. "Hurry. We leave now."

"Let me grab Tin—"

"Your cat has no place there," Freya said in a rush. "Dahvid can tether him and keep him close."

Pallah stumbled into her room, stuffing a few things in her knapsack, and debating whether she should wake Tinloh before she left. There wasn't a reason to risk it, as her tether to him had grown strained over the last few weeks. She would waste precious time simply calming him down.

Slipping out her door she peered through to Dahvid's room, finding him propped before the fire in his usual position. His head slowly turned, and his eyes met her own—they were Ahren's eyes, sea-blue and vast.

"Dahvid." She cleared her throat, which was suddenly dry. "Please take care of Tinloh for me. I have to go with Freya."

The man turned back to the fire.

Pallah and Freya fled the home, owls of all different kinds screeching to herald their departure. The wind was relentless, their cloaks flapping as they left Freya's compound in the distance. The journey to Takanah took most of the day by foot. The old woman used her walking stick like a lifeline as she hiked her way across the grasses, brown and bent low by wildlife and wind.

They arrived hours later, exhausted and cold. Takanah was far larger than Pallah had anticipated. They approached the large stone wall, passing through the entrance with a wave from Freya.

The soldiers flanking the entrance offered a bored dismissal. Pallah scuttled along after the midwife, immediately warming as the walls kept the wind at bay. She was enraptured by the sights and sounds: the buildings, so colorful, and the wide streets, teeming with people.

It was bordering dusk, the sun dusting the sky with broad strokes of orange, pink, and yellow. Freya easily wound her way through streets until arriving at a two-story house, dark but for a flickering light seen through a high window.

"You stay here," Freya said, and something in her tone didn't sit right. "I'll see what's going on."

"You brought me along to help, didn't you?" Though Pallah wanted nothing to do with the birth of a baby, she felt vulnerable standing alone in this unusual place.

"Um, well...yes." The midwife leaned her staff against the doorframe and held out a hand to keep Pallah at bay. "But she doesn't know you. Let me check on her first."

Pallah sat down on the step, looking up and down the busy street. It was time for the evening meal, and Pallah watched as people of all kinds made their way back to their homes after a day of work.

With nothing else to do, she pulled the scroll from her bag and rolled it to the spot she'd left off.

Aside from my hope for a life with Phy and the children, I have also been working hard on my experiments. Since I only have access to Smilodon Tala, I have leaned heavily on Freya during this time. I have taught her how to erect a wall inside the minds of the animals surrounding our home. This keeps other Tala out, though not as securely as I'd hoped. My research remains inconclusive, as it's still far too easy to break through the Wall with a strong tether.

Karav had described the bear's mind having a wall wrapped around a maze. Pallah's eyebrows drew together as she continued reading.

I need something stronger. Something more than a simple wall. Walls crumble over time; they need constant reinforcement and repair. A puzzle, perhaps...challenging to navigate, troublesome to crack open and solve.

A rush of fear rolled over her skin, causing sweat to break out over Pallah's back.

I've formulated a maze. Of course, the only way to test it is releasing the animals upon populated areas. But it has been a joy to hear the reports from Freya, the results of how long it takes them to subdue the creature, if at all. It's a daily work, surely, a lifetime of progress to be had. I am giddy just thinking on it.

Her fingers shook as she scrolled further, eyes searching the page.

Now that the Maze and the Wall are in working order, I am anxious to try yet another experiment, untouched by mankind.

It began with a question: Could I successfully contain the Tala behind the tether? A lofty endeavor, I know, and not one to be tampered with lightly. Freya will have to step aside for this one. If only I could find another smilodon. It has been far too long since I have had access to my own aptitude. Once I find one, the next stage can commence.

Memories flashed before her: the long winding cave in Eldfall that led to Tinloh and his brother; Karav's account of the mother, her mind having been altered, blocked; the bear in the woods near Freya's home and the 'maze' Issha and Karav found within. Pallah's panicked eyes read on.

But first, it is time to use Stasis. I know, I have waited too long. Perhaps Phy does not love me as she once did...but she promised to wait for me. Her children are older now; there will be no reason for her to stay behind. They don't need her; she has said as much herself.

She will come to me tomorrow. Everything is set. I will lock her away and then join her myself. Forever together.

Phy and Dahvid, Dahvid and Phy.

The way it was meant to be.

The scroll came to a halt, the parchment curling back upon itself to meet its bulk. Pallah set it down slowly, a low keening in her mind. She rose to find Freya.

Nothing but dust greeted her when she entered the home.

There were no cries for relief or new life.

The house was empty.

Stairs in the back corner caught her attention, and Pallah was up them in less than a minute, panting hard.

Freya was there, huddled with Ingrid, the two of them eating something, hunched like animals. Two pairs of eyes turned on her, and Pallah couldn't tell whose were wider.

"What's going on?" Her voice sounded dangerous, even to her own ears. "Where's Kahlee?"

Freya licked each one of her fingers as she sat against the wall. "I'm sorry." She swallowed. "He made me do it."

"Made you do what?" Pallah thought she knew, her mind working hard to piece things together, but all she saw was red. Seething red. "What's going on?"

"He made me bring you here. Kahlee's not in labor. This isn't even her house." Freya released a manic chuckle that forced Pallah's hand to the hatchet on her hip.

"Dahvid told you to bring me here?"

"Yes."

"What does he want?"

Freya rolled her eyes, a grin lighting her cheeks. "That boy wants the moon, child. He's never stopped dreaming. Not even paralysis could take that from him, not even that *tik* of a woman you call mother."

Chills rolled up Pallah's arms at Freya's words. "My-my mother?"

"Yes," Freya stood, lips curling around crooked teeth, head tilting sideways as she stepped toward Pallah. "Your *mother.*" She spat the word with fresh vehemence. "If she had just trusted Dahvid completely, he would never have lost the use of his body! He tried to *help* her, even after she abandoned him. He still tried to save her from that twisted excuse of a husband!" Freya's eyes were wide, bloodshot, her voice growing frantic as she stepped closer, Ingrid clutching her shoulder. "But the charm demands a price, if the one it's performed upon doesn't possess the trust the charm requires. There is *always* a cost with the Taka Reu."

Pallah's mind ran through the times her mother had left them when they were younger. Dahvid had mentioned he'd intended to perform the Stasis charm when Phyllir's children were grown. When had she—Pallah remembered. Only a few years ago, her mother had sought to take a trip to another temple; Bogdur had agreed. Pallah remembered that week alone with him being one of the worst weeks of her life. Phyllir must have been with Dahvid then. That's when he must have attempted to put her in Stasis...and failed. So Phyllir knew about Dahvid's condition. And she had done nothing but left him to rot.

Breathing hard, Pallah stuttered over her next question, afraid to ask it. Afraid she was already too late. "And the fortified animals? That's all part of his plan? So he can find a smilodon..."

Freya's eyes glittered as Pallah's words trailed away, a wide smile splitting her dry and wrinkled face. "His life's work."

"And you brought me here so he could..."

"He's waited so long!"

Dahvid was stealing Tinloh. A month of tethering him when Pallah wasn't aware would be enough time to establish a structure in the cat's mind. Her Tala use with the smilodon growing more difficult had been no coincidence. It was a symptom of Dahvid's tinkering. His sabotage.

"You snake!" Pallah hissed and bolted down the stairs.

Freya cackled in her wake.

Pallah's lungs burned as she crested the hill behind the moonlit cottage. She attempted a tether on Tinloh and located him quickly. He was in Dahvid's room, but her tether crumbled as it rammed into a wall.

"*Häfa!*" He had done it. He had already done it, the bastard! She charged ahead, bounding across the lawn before she burst through the wooden door, scroll in hand. Her long strides took her directly into Dahvid's room. She was greeted by silence, the only sounds: her own ragged breath and her heart pounding in her ears. Dahvid sat in his usual chair by the hearth, Tinloh at his feet, the both of them unnaturally still. "Let go of him!" she demanded.

Dahvid's head made the arduous turn toward her, slow and measured.

"I know about the Wall, I know about the Maze. I'm not going to let you take Tinloh from me!"

Pallah took a step closer, but Tinloh immediately crouched, eyes trained on her as if she was a stranger. A low growl rumbled through his chest.

Dahvid remained still.

Closing her eyes, Pallah attempted a tether once more, fingers to the floor, as she and Karav had done in the woods as the bear had charged straight at them. Her tether flew out with practiced accuracy and broke through the Wall that had begun forming around Tinloh's mind. Her eyes flew open, and she saw a single crease form between Dahvid's brows.

An expression of worry? Good.

Through the Wall, the tether landed in the Maze, and it made Pallah physically gasp. How could he do such a thing to her beast, her aptitude, without her knowing? The bond between Tala and beast was something sacred, something respected. But not to Dahvid. How could she have felt any semblance of compassion toward this man?

Her tether wove and wound its way through the Maze's long corridors, empty spaces, and finally a dead end. Whatever this Maze was, it was formidable, and it was impossible for Pallah to figure out on her own.

Erval's voice fell into the forefront of her mind. *I'm not sure why you're wasting time on this when you have that hatchet on your hip, Pallah.*

Her hand twitched toward her weapon. Would she be fast enough to kill Dahvid before he sent Tinloh on her? Could she stomach it? She had never killed a person.

Dahvid noticed her hesitation, the right side of his mouth twitching upward.

Häfan bastard! Pallah crouched to the ground, bringing up any and all power she had access to, attempting connection straight to the core of the Earth itself. She screamed, long and loud as her tether broke through the Wall once more and dove back into the Maze. This time, with such a connection to the Taka Reu, her tether smashed through wall after wall, ignoring all twists and turns to simply demolish the work Dahvid had created. Pallah laughed between gritted teeth, power pulsing through her veins.

Something slammed into her tether, something ragged and dark. Dahvid! How was his tether alongside her own? She kept going, ignoring his connection. Where was the exit? How could she—

Dahvid's tether slammed into her again, so hard her body dropped to the ground. There was a tug, a snap, and everything plunged into darkness.

THE TAKING

ERVAL

THE HEELS OF ERVAL'S boots clacked along the hewn-stone corridor, a sound he'd never thought he'd hear again—but here it was. His dark velvet cape caressed his legs with each step, his hands clasped behind him, heavy with the weight of the rings that adorned each finger. From above the first button of his fitted vest bloomed a crimson ascot, displayed prominently beneath his chin. His head, wreathed with a diadem, glittered with any sliver of light that dared touch it. He should have felt something more than lackluster emptiness.

But alas.

After twenty years of living deep within the mountain, amassing support, and creating his rag-tag army, he had marched on Thonethren. His father had finally died, and Halldora ascending to Queen had spurred both his wits and his patience before he'd ventured to procure the kingdom for himself.

"Procure" was a gentle way of putting it. The streets had wept red. Men, women and children had fallen on both sides, and Halldora had fled like the coward she'd become. But now, a year into Erval's kingship, he found himself aching for change.

His goal had been total authoritative control of Mothmar. But once he'd secured control of Thonethren, he found himself growing weary. What had become of his vision, his vigor? Lost to the monotony of kingship, he supposed.

He climbed the ancient marble steps to the pedestal where his father's throne had sat. Erval had replaced it with a standing desk, a globe, the finnevel, and his telescope. His footsteps echoed in the empty hall.

The citizens of Thonethren had been entirely engrossed in the worship of the Celestials by the time Erval had arrived. So fickle. He'd made quick work of it, chucking the priest out by the nape of his neck, tail between his legs. The fool had bounced on the last two steps of Thren Temple before sprawling face down in the mud. Those gathered understood then, as their temple went up in flames, Erval was back. And so was the Taka Reu.

The grounds of Thonethren were beginning to look again as he remembered them, the dark powder he had come to know as *aska* drifting through the streets like cookfire smoke. Unlatching the window, he leaned out and breathed it in.

"Good morning, Thonethren!" he called to the air. A crow cawed in response. The people still hid, afraid. "You only fear what you do not know," he said, more to himself than anyone outside.

"They fear you, sire." Phineas's nasal voice peeped from the entrance of the throne room.

"Oh, please, Phineas." Erval leaned against the sill, his eyes still trained on the city below. "Do elaborate."

"W-well," the pudgy man stammered. "You did take a few of them, and did that thing you do…" He waved a dimpled hand, the other resting on his rotund middle.

Erval spun around, eyebrow raised at his steward. "And what would that be?"

"Well, performing a…Taking."

Lips turned down, fingers tapping the sill behind him, Erval noted how bold Phineas had become. "I've only done it to three of them."

"But they died."

Erval waved the statement away. "Semantics."

"Not—not quite," Phineas said, scratching a spot beneath his belly. "Not quite semantics. They are dead."

Rolling his eyes, Erval plodded over to the globe and gave it a spin with a languid finger. Peering over the rotating ball, he couldn't help but compare his steward's middle to the diameter of the sphere. His eyes crawled up to Phineas's face which held a sheen of sweat. "Something else on your mind, Phin?"

His steward stammered a moment before clasping his hands together, his slippered feet rocking back and forth from heel to toe. "I only wonder at your goals, m'lord. You once told me you wished to take over all Mothmar. Yet now, you fritter away your time with your new…Gifts."

Erval frowned in thought. "Acquiring all of Tala, Fera, and Heitt is not 'frittering.' And they are not Gifts, as things bestowed—more like an inheritance, a right, that is mine to take. The years they have given me are but a benefit."

"Yes, but—"

"Oh, stop your moaning. The people upon which I performed the Taking were criminals. They lost their right to choose when they decided to rebel." The sphere slowed to a stop, the map it displayed only half-finished. He could only see so far with the finnevel, and without a Seer to help him, his cartography skills were lacking.

Erval blinked and stared at his steward once more. Phineas had grown weak. And Erval would not stand for it.

"Phineas, come with me." Erval hopped down the stairs, a pep to his step once more. "We're going on a walk."

"But I'm only wearing my slippers," Phineas squeaked.

They exited the castle in their cramped litter, flanked by guards, to wind their way through the desolate streets of Thonethren.

Pulling back the curtain, Erval watched his subjects scatter before him. He wasn't blind to the fact that any glimpse of his retinue struck fear into their hearts. It wasn't exactly the response he had wanted from them when he had taken control, but what could be done? It was merely a misunderstanding; in time, they would see. The lower castes lauded him as hero, and for now, he could champion them. It was a start.

A group of street rats, dressed in dirty rags and dirtier feet, clambered along the sides of the roads, hands held out for coin.

Erval lowered the window a fraction and thumbed one in their direction. It clinked on the cobblestones and the children scrabbled for the rare treasure, tearing at each other like rabid dogs. Cries of pain trailed the litter as his guards hoisted him onward, toward the prison.

Exiting the litter, they stood at the prison gate as his guards pushed it open. Phineas wrung his fleshy hands, his persistent fidgeting grating Erval's last nerve. The warden snorted phlegm into his throat as Erval crossed the threshold. Choking on it, the man swallowed before standing to attention.

"King Erval." The man, a living collection of dirt, grime, and stringy white hair, bowed low to the ground. "I was not told you was coming. Please forgive the state of the place." The warden finally brought himself upright with a hand to his lower back.

"No need for concern, Raud. We need only...borrow one of the guilty." Erval waved his bejeweled hand.

Raud's face blanched for a moment before regaining his composure. "Yes, yes, of course, my king. The lower floors are full of degenerates to choose from. In fact, we brought in a man just last night. Found him with his hand in the coffers, we did."

Erval blinked, musing a moment. As their judge, he had only selected prisoners who had committed the most heinous of acts. Stealing a few cohstas wasn't quite enough for him to condemn a man to death. "Let's take a look at our options."

Keys jangling, Raud led the two men down a dank hallway lined with torches leading to a narrow, spiraling stairwell. The crooked keeper pulled the nearest torch from the wall and held it out for Phineas, who took it in a white-knuckled grip. They descended into the block of cells below.

Pulling his ascot high over his nose, Erval squinted against the palpable smells and sounds that assaulted him as they passed cell after cell. Arms shot through the bars, grasping for freedom, as moans emanated from gaping mouths.

"Is this all you have?" Erval spun to face the other two men.

Raud blinked wide eyes in dim light. "There are several hundred men here, my king."

"Ah, yes." Erval turned a slow circle. "That is the issue. I was hoping for someone a bit *softer*. It's Phineas's first time." He winked.

The torch in Phineas's hand began to quake.

"Softer, sire?" Raud's eyebrows scrunched together.

Erval tilted his head toward the low ceiling, and his ascot fell off his nose. "*Häfa* to Hekla, I don't know how you stand—a *woman*, Raud." He covered his face again, filtering the smell.

A few eavesdropping prisoners whistled and cat-called.

"Ah. Right this way, sire."

Raud led them further into the darkness, all vestiges of natural light forgotten. Finally, at the end of the hall stood a solid metal door, different from the barred gates holding the other cell blocks.

"What did she do?" Phineas whispered.

"She's a tea smuggler." Raud shoved a skeleton key into the hole in the door. "And a heretic."

Heat rushed down Erval's back and coursed fury into his thoughts. He had banned all Gift-blocking tea from Thonethren, but it seemed his people hadn't harkened his command. She deserved this fate.

The door swung open.

Phineas began to blubber. "M'lord, I—"

Erval held out his hand for the torch, a quick shake of his head quieting his steward. Phineas passed it over and the two stepped into the damp cell. The light revealed a shivering form in the corner. She was skin and bones, her tattered shift hardly covering her as she curled up into herself, eyes squeezed shut. She was so very young; if not for her foolhardy smuggling, she would have had many years before her. Now, Erval's advisor would take the years for his own. Lucky Phineas.

"You've seen me do this three times now, Phin," Erval crooned. "Each person from whom you Take, you glean their life. Every day they would have spent on this earth, given to you. And their Gift—their inheritance—will be yours."

Phineas sucked in a breath and released it with a shaky moan. "I don't want—"

Erval whirled, torch held high, casting his old steward in shadow. "Do you defy me?"

Double chin quivering, tongue wetting dry lips, Phineas shook his head and wrapped his cloak more tightly around his middle.

"Good." Erval smiled. "You're up."

Raud turned away, but Erval watched with bated breath.

Phineas padded forward, his slippers caked in grime, and crouched beside the girl who was quaking like a leaf at autumn's turn. Erval couldn't see Phineas's face, but he could hear the catch in his throat as he spoke the ancient words into the chilly air. Erval passed the dagger forward, tapping it lightly on Phineas's shoulder. When the advisor turned, his eyes were wet, face as white as Raud's.

But Phineas was an obedient steward; of that, Erval was sure. The man's fingers closed around the hilt. Erval thought he heard him whispering apologies to the girl and had to keep from rolling his eyes. She was a rebel, a wretched derelict that dared to defy him. She had made her choice.

Steel pierced skin with a wet punch, a guttural drowning noise coupled the two of them sliding to the floor. Then the smoke came: powdery, lithe, and more than it appeared. It slid from girl to man, climbing him slowly before charging like an arrow into the orifices of his face.

Phineas gasped and his back arched, hands raised as the dagger clattered to the stone below. Then, as quickly as the smoke had come, it vanished. Erval's steward slumped to the floor, lying in a pool of the blood he'd drawn.

Erval grinned. "Feel better?"

"No," his steward mumbled.

"You will," Erval promised as he glimpsed Phineas's eyes, black as the night. He turned to leave the room. "Trust me, Phin. With this? We will live many lives, together."

LIGHT & DARK

SOLYANA

J ONAS FOUND THREE SPECIFIC records on strange Tala cases, none of which helped Solyana feel any better. The first, a record of animals found with some kind of man-made barrier within them, something that made them impenetrable against other Tala. With those barriers in place, whoever mastered them maintained complete control over their beasts. The animals could not be stopped; all instruction given to them by their master was done wholly, unspeakably, even until death.

The second wasn't as horrible. A man in darlöh, much like Rhuth, had tethered to a bison. The animal would visit the man's family, often helping with daily chores: pulling carts, pushing boulders, and keeping an eye on the children. The family documented these occurrences and were convinced it was the man himself, his essence joined wholly with that of the animal. Their theory was supported as the man did not recover, and when he died, whatever connection had been held was severed. And the bison was gone the next day.

The third was only three lines, mentioned in the very back of a journal, written by an unnamed explorer. It read:

"You must kill your beast to truly take them. But once you have its blood on your hands, and their body at your disposal, they are yours for a time. While impermanent and painful, the transformation does not sully the mind as other methods do."

Beneath it was a drawn symbol, circular but with lines intersecting at the edges. She had seen that symbol before, cast into the doors of Chief Orson's Hall.

Halina gripped the leather strap of the bags affixed to Björg's back, wobbling as the mammoth rocked them in time. If Rhuth was tethered to Halina so far from their valley, why did she stay? She wanted to ask Gamaliel to tether to her; perhaps if he did, they could communicate with Rhuth. But after what they saw in Takanah, and the implications from the scroll before her, she knew Gamaliel would never agree. The hunter hardly latched to Vinur if he didn't have to. He would never risk tethering to a human, if such a thing were even possible. Solyana wouldn't ask it of him—not after everything.

She considered the three scenarios as they related to Rhuth's power. The second option seemed the most likely. The thought that Rhuth could be tethered *in*—rather than *to*—Halina was both comforting and not. Speaking of her essence being anywhere but in herself made it seem like she would never wake, like she instead was already halfway to the Celestials themselves.

They had been traveling for four days on the backs of the mammoths. What would have been a month-long journey from their valley had quickly transformed into a trip that would take half the time, so long as conditions remained favorable.

Odie was quick to remind them, however, that goings would be slow as they continued this trek over the ice plains. Precariously navigating for two days, they'd started listing quiet complaints of hunger and exhaustion. They possessed no fishing gear, so Gamaliel tried to tether to the fish, but being that they were somewhere between prey and predator, he hadn't been able to find one.

"I'll give it a shot," Odie said the second evening, surprising all of them.

Gamaliel's eyebrows rose. "You're Broad Tala, Odie?"

"Yes," the older man said. "I don't like tethering to the other creatures much, but I can try." He closed his eyes and wandered around the icy plain at a shuffle. After about ten minutes, he returned with a shrug. "Didn't feel anything. It's been a while, though. It may be my fault."

They survived off the remains of the hare Gamaliel had found and Maral's provisions, hoping the mammoths had enough fat stores to keep them going. Coming upon hard-packed snows once more, the group let out a collective sigh of relief to be off the ice.

Odie cleared his throat and Solyana prepared herself for another rendition of "My Mammoth and Me," but the driver spoke instead.

"You shouldn't be researching that stuff," he said. "It leads to nothing but death."

Jonas turned crimson and began rolling up his scrolls. Putting a hand on his arm, Solyana shook her head with a soft smile. "We do it to save the land, Odie. Surely, you've overheard enough to know our plans?"

"Yes." Odie nodded slowly. "But I still think you kids should let it lie. I've lived my whole life in Takanah. I've watched it descend into darkness. All because of the Taka Reu."

Solyana considered what exactly to tell the man that wasn't a lie. Odie and Jonas couldn't know she had been considering practicing the Dark Gifts, not unless it became absolutely necessary. "The more I know what's happening in the land, the better I can help."

"Help?" Odie harrumphed and cracked his neck from side to side, his hat flopping back and forth. "I suppose it's easy to help when you were born with something so powerful."

"But I wasn't, Odie."

"You have Heitt."

"I was born Rána."

Odie jumped a bit and turned in his seat. He looked at her, perhaps truly *seeing* her for the first time. His bright blue eyes reminded her of Papa's, and something about the wrinkles around them made Solyana feel at home.

"Rána, eh?" He smiled, his snaggle teeth sticking up from his lower jaw. "My daughter was Rána."

"I didn't know you had a daughter," Solyana said.

Odie was quiet.

"What happened to her?" Jonas asked.

Solyana gave Jonas a look before smiling at Odie sympathetically. "I'm sorry, Odie. You don't have to tell us."

"Ah, no. I love talking about my Lena. Hand me that roll." Odie pointed to a blanket, which Jonas handed over. Odie stuffed it behind his lower back and settled in, riding Björg backward, ankles crossed. He pursed his lips, squinting up at the sky. "Steady on, Björg."

Odie dove into the story of his family. It was a story of love and of loss, of Gifts and grief. Lena had died; a result of mixing with zealots of the Taka Reu during its early stages in Takanah. Ashamed of being Rána, Lena had sought them out to learn how to obtain a Gift for herself.

Deep in the forest, one of the zealots had tethered to a grizzly bear and couldn't regain control after it began to rampage. Only two of the group had survived, and Lena hadn't been one of them.

"The Taka Reu has nothing redeemable about it," Odie said with a sigh. "Keep very far away from it. Very far away."

"You don't have to worry about us, Odie," Jonas said. "We would never touch the Taka Reu. It's evil. No one should ever use it. The Celestials have a plan, and they will make a way."

Heat flushed up Solyana's neck. Was she wrong for trusting Priestess Avi's beliefs? Surely, practicing the Taka Reu to fill any gaps was better than going ill-equipped into the situation.

"Well, I'm here to talk, if anyone were to have any questions..." Odie trailed off, causing Solyana to look into his water-blue eyes. He was staring straight into her, like he could read the duplicity of her thoughts.

"Thanks Odie!" Jonas scooted farther down the mammoth. "I'm going to do some more research," he told Solyana, tugging his knapsack along behind him.

Odie stretched and sat up, his eyes unmoving. Did he know? He couldn't...unless Gamaliel had spoken to him about the priestess. And even then, Odie would have had to put two and two together. Besides, Solyana still had time. If they arrived early to the mountain, perhaps there would be another city filled with people, much like Takanah. Hopefully not *quite* like Takanah. Considering the importance of the prophecy, surely they would be able to find two people willing to give her their Tala and Fera.

Odie's expression twisted into a wry grin. "Sorry, I'm staring." He blushed and pulled his cap off his head, wringing it in his hands. "That scar; I hadn't seen it until now. What Maral said is really true, then?"

"Oh." Solyana blinked in surprise; she hadn't felt it form on her face. "Yes, it's true." Even as she nodded, doubt prodded her heart. How could something that heralded their salvation hold both light *and* dark? It didn't sit right. "I need two more Gifts."

"Hmm," he mused. "How old are you?"

"I'll be seventeen, soon."

Odie let out a soft whistle between his snaggle teeth and upper lip before replacing his cap. "Too young to be so weighed down by the world." He gave her a kind smile. "We'll get you where you need to go, kid."

"Thanks, Odie."

The driver turned with an "Eyup," prompting Björg to trundle along a little faster. But suddenly the mammoth emitted a low rumble, his forward movement halted, feet stepping side to side. "Björg?" Odie soothed.

"Do you hear that?" Though Gamaliel's mammoth walked only a few paces behind, the wind of the tundra made his voice small.

"Björg!" Odie exclaimed as the big animal gave a curt trumpet and began backing up. "It's okay, friend. Be calm. We are safe."

Solyana searched the area, seeing nothing but hills of snow, the expanse so white, her vision seemed to lose its sense of depth.

Looking back at Gamaliel, she asked, "What did you hear? I don't—"

She heard it.

A noise, like the keening buzz of thousands of honeybees, both far ahead and...beneath them. Beneath?

Squinting at the ground, Solyana followed a crack in the compacted snow. It cut and branched until it disappeared, as if it followed a path unknown to the group sitting so high on their charges.

"Stop the mammoths!" she cried. "Björg is trying to warn us!"

Odie complied, his brows coming together in a line as he looked between his mammoths.

"Solyana, what's going—" Lone's voice was cut short as Solyana ripped off her seal-skin gloves. Gripping them in her teeth, she took a handful of wiry fur into each hand as she scooted off the back of the mammoth. Still quite a distance from the ground, she lost her grip and fell the rest of the way, mercifully rolling into a softer pile of snow. A high-pitched *kuk-kuk* came from above, and, getting to her feet, Solyana braced herself as Halina landed on her shoulder, her talons sinking into the thick leather of her parka.

"Solyana, wait up!" The fear in Gamaliel's voice slowed her, reminding her of their rush into the burning building a few nights before. They traversed the grounds together, Solyana keeping her body low, her stomach dropping the closer she got to where the crack had disappeared.

"Wait, is this..." Gamaliel trailed off, and Solyana grabbed his hand as they approached the drop-off that sat before them. The ice plains had been so vast, the colors blending and melding together;

Solyana had failed to see it. Every nerve in Solyana's body flagged as the buzz grew into a roar.

"*Holy Hekla*," Gamaliel whispered.

The ledge before them hung over a steep drop that overlooked an expansive plain. Forests stippled the far-off perimeter, then leveled out into great expanses of white and blue. Directly below the ledge, like a gargantuan writhing snake, coiled a sea of people. Their voices rose and fell with the wind that gusted over the side of the icy cliff. Almost as one, their eyes turned to watch Solyana and Gamaliel, perched above them like ruffled flightless owls.

Halina fluffed her feathers and Gamaliel swallowed. "Let's hope they're a bit more welcoming than Takanah."

THE MAZE

PALLAH

IT WAS THE ABSENCE of noise that woke her. Where the usual hoot of an owl, pop of crackling fire, or whistle of her host would have invaded her room, there was naught but hollow anticipation. Pallah shook her head, or tried to; her head didn't move. Panic wrenched her eyes open, but they were heavy, dragged down with unnatural weight. A scream rolled through her chest but came up short, nothing exiting her throat but gasping wind.

Nothing. She saw nothing.

She wondered if she was asleep. She tried to sit up, but again, as if something heavy was sitting on her chest, her arms, each individual finger, no muscle moved at her call.

Straining with everything in her, she tried once more. Her muscles struggled to obey, and it cost her. The weightiness of moving muscle, the strength it took, was too formidable. It was as if the life had been sucked from the room. All energy, all light—perhaps her very soul—had been lost.

Excruciating though it was, she lifted a hand, groping blindly for something, anything, nearby. Her palm grazed a surface cold and slick. She pushed against it, and it resisted the force, like a wall.

Movement was becoming slightly easier. Her limbs felt less like stones and more akin to sacks of grain. She brought one knee up and the other to join it, hand on the wall. It occurred to her then that she was completely naked. But it didn't matter; it was so dark. Darker than any cave she had ever entered, or Shadow Wood on a moonless night. A darkness that swallowed her whole and would never open its maw again.

She was accosted by her memories.

Dahvid.

Tinloh.

The Maze.

Häfa to Hekla, this was no nightmare.

She pushed herself to run, tripping and falling on her face as the weight of her body overcame her. She hauled herself up, again and again, one hand on the wall to feel her way in the dark. It stopped and turned, then stopped and turned again; the corners repeatedly spinning her one way or another. Pallah followed in the darkness until any sense of direction was entirely lost.

Her hands shook, reaching out to discover walls on every side: a dead end. One, she was sure, of many.

This was the Maze, and Pallah was trapped inside it.

FORBIDDEN SCROLL

ERVAL

A RUSH OF WIND ruffled Erval's dark hair as he undid the latch on the window and swung the shutters outward. Yet another decade had passed, though you would never know it by the look of him. Consumed by the hard-fought overthrow of his beloved sister, and then the work at dispelling the rebels in his own kingdom, he had all but forgotten about the young girl, the one who hadn't perished at the sound of his voice.

Pallah of Sodur.

He had begun tethering to her more frequently, but she was proving unsympathetic to his manipulations, and it was beginning to rankle him.

He cracked his neck from side to side.

Though using the finnevel taxed him a bit, it was no longer as much as it had been in the past. Having Taken numerous times, his body now held endless energy, as if all those stored-up lives produced the gumption of ten grown men. What was a decade to someone who would live hundreds of them? Thousands? The reality of the Taking had only begun to dawn on him, the possibilities endless.

He almost called for Phineas, the rotund tinkerer always more skilled at using his inventions, but the man hadn't quite been the same since Taking from that tea-smuggling traitor of a girl. Erval had thought it would've opened his mind, helped him see why Erval's passion for more land had waned. He hadn't foreseen his most trusted steward collapsing in on himself. He had even begun to lose some weight. The last thing Erval needed was for the man to turn useless, even if the costs to clothe him decreased; he'd already found one pet and had no need for another.

Spinning the gears with soft clicks, he wheeled the finnevel to the window. Perched atop a rolling stand, it slid easily about the room, in spite of its weight. *Like Phineas,* Erval chuckled to himself. Overseeing Thonethren, he positioned it just so before pressing his eye to the cup. Erval viewed the world through Kjarn's Eye, all color and shape, hapless lines and pulsing feeling. He found her quick enough.

Tethering was quick and sure, his Mann Tala forming a secure attachment. The finnevel amplified his Tala with enough power that his voice rode into her very mind, no longer her own.

He looked through her eyes and surveyed the room as she saw it. A teacher, at the front of what looked like a classroom, droned on, but Erval was attuned to Pallah's gaze, fixed on a tattered scroll on a shelf. He recognized the look of that scroll.

"It's yours, if you want it," he encouraged her, and her pulse quickened, her leg beginning to bounce. A few classmates looked at her, mouths quirking in jest, eyes full of mean intent. Erval hated them for her, with her, stoking that flame.

"You're better than them, Pallah," Erval spoke directly into her mind.

Her eyes cast down to her lap, hands clasped together.

She counted to ten.

Erval counted with her.

THE GIVING

SOLYANA

FTERNOON TURNED TO DUSK as Solyana and her party navigated down an icy slope to a lower pass, and finally the plain. Cookfires popped and crackled with the smell of roasting game, the people below settling in for their evening meal, thousands of bodies huddling together, speckling the powdered snow as they watched the newcomers approach.

Odie settled the mammoths, blocking the cookfire closest to them from the bone-chilling wind. The people nodded in thanks with shallow bows, welcoming Solyana and her friends to sit with them. After living off the remnants of hard cheese, stale bread, and brush for the last few days, Solyana's stomach rumbled as she welcomed the bowl kindly handed to her.

They remained silent as they ate, this group of strangers around their fire. All had the same look about them: hooked noses, wind-chapped cheeks, and blue eyes that glittered above wild blonde hair they wrapped around their necks like scarves. Perhaps they were a family.

Solyana took a long drink from her waterskin beneath the light of the Norlos, green and blue shimmering in dancing celestial waves, a reminder of her task. She passed the waterskin to Gamaliel, who took it with a nod, his eyes darting to the silent people around them.

"Where are you all from?" Gamaliel asked, wiping his chin.

The girl sitting closest to them blinked at him a few times before taking another bite of her food.

Solyana and Gamaliel exchanged a look.

"We are grateful to share your fire," Gamaliel started again. "And for sharing your meal with us."

The girl looked up once more, then elbowed the boy next to her hard. He gave a low growl and looked up from his food, narrowed eyes studying the newcomers.

"Fonteu ramanah. Oshskahl tonteuei," he said, wiping his mouth with his scarf of wiry hair.

"Ancient Mothmari!" Jonas squeaked like he'd stumbled upon treasure. "They speak ancient Mothmari!"

"What did he say?" Lone asked.

"I thought it was a dead language," Gamaliel added.

"Jonas, why don't you sit here and translate for us?" Solyana tilted her chin toward the space between the two groups.

Jonas scuttled forward, finding a seat between them. He cleared his throat and in a pitchy voice said, "Preleu sharah forundi?"

There was a beat of silence before the entire family, and a few of their neighbors, burst into raucous laughter. Even in the firelight, Solyana could see Jonas's face going as red as the fire before them.

Still wiping at her eyes, the girl said, "Storondi praleu shafanah."

"Oh." Jonas looked sheepishly back at his party. "I was trying to say 'What are your names?' and instead, I think I said 'When did you last poop?'"

Lone choked on her food.

Gamaliel grinned.

Solyana squeezed Jonas's arm. "It's okay. Try again and maybe ask what they're doing out here."

Nodding to her, Jonas cleared his throat and tried again in the ancient tongue.

The girl spoke, her hand gesturing toward the sky. "Viddon fylgum lisonum a hvrah ari Skaer Sky a Endirinn." Then she pointed to herself and then the boy beside her. "Pahlak a brodur minn Rorhan."

"Jonas," Jonas said with a grin and then over his shoulder, "They're brother and sister, and they're following the lights to the great city called Endirinn, where they will witness Skaer Sky."

"Endirinn? Is that where the mountain is?" Solyana asked. "Where the lights end?"

Jonas spoke a few stilted words and Pahlak nodded with a grunt.

Jonas pulled out a piece of parchment and the charcoal pencil he always seemed to have on hand. "Endirinn," he said to himself slowly as he wrote. "I guess we know where we're headed, now."

"And what's this 'Skaer Sky?'" Lone spoke from the fire.

"Oh, I know this one!" Jonas said, still scribbling on his parchment. "It's the last night the Norlos is visible for the year. It's said to be the most brilliant and beautiful." He shrugged shyly. "I read it in a scroll."

Rorhan pursed his lips from the other side of the fire. "Fonteu ramanah. Oshskahl tonteuei?" His ice blue eyes bored into Gamaliel's earthy brown ones.

"He wants to know what we will give them, in return for their hospitality," Jonas said, turning to look at his group.

Lone shrugged, her mouth turning down. "We have nothing. We're barely surviving as it is. What kind of hospitality—"

She quieted as Gamaliel placed a hand on her arm.

"Osha feradahn mammut toragahn." Rorhan lifted his hand, palm to the sky, and pivoted it side to side. The rest of the family repeated the gesture, then stared at Jonas in expectation.

"Y-you can't. They're—" Jonas shook his head. "Vrontohn per shranah. Mammut srel corudohn."

The eyes of the family turned cold, and Rorhan shook his head once in finality.

"Jonas, what's happening?" Solyana leaned forward.

"They want one of the mammoths."

"WHAT?" Odie, who had kept to himself while cushioned against Curry's side, sat up, eyes blazing.

"I don't think a whole mammoth is worth a bowl of—" Lone began.

"Everyone, drop your food!" Odie was already moving, gathering items. "We're leaving. Now."

Gamaliel discarded the last of his elk, though it had been halfway to his mouth.

"Tell them they can't have a mammoth. They're not ours to give." Solyana watched the family's greedy eyes as Jonas translated.

Odie continued his frantic packing, readying the animals for travel.

"Can you handle him?" Solyana asked Gamaliel with a look over her shoulder at Odie. "Perhaps we can negotiate, and they'll accept information instead."

Gamaliel narrowed his eyes. "You're not going to tell them about you."

"I am," she tugged her gloves back on. "Let's pray it's sufficient."

"Solyana." Gamaliel gripped her elbow, drawing her close. "Takanah was proof that there are those out there who don't want to see the prophecy fulfilled." His words came out in puffs of steam, warming the sting of cold on her cheeks. "What if these people feel the same way?" Rolling his eyes, he motioned to her face. "Great timing!"

She felt for the scar she knew was there. A piece of skin flecked off onto her glove, the white of deadness mottled with remnants of black.

"We don't know these people," Gamaliel continued. "We don't even know their language. Do *not* give yourself away."

"They're not going to hurt me."

"No matter how confident you might be, I'm not willing to take the risk." His eyes said more than his lips, and Solyana's neck warmed beneath his gaze.

"Uh, guys?" Jonas's voice came with a shake, snapping Solyana's attention back to the matter at hand.

The tribe was standing, their hands clutching staves, their colorful cloaks wrapped for action. A shift in the air trapped the breath in her lungs, unease twisted her insides.

"What's happening?" Gamaliel stood, gripping the stick that had replaced his staff from over his shoulder. He stepped in front of Solyana.

"Ah nah pettan en gjof. Petta ekki sem skuldar."

"It's not a *gift*; it's what we *owe*," Jonas translated, confusion in his eyes as he stood, too. And then they were all on their feet. The group surrounded them on all sides, all bearing weapons, eyes trained, knees bent at the ready. Odie was separated from the group, having already climbed atop Björg. Would he leave them to fend for themselves? Would the tribe overtake him?

Of the thousands of people, only a small portion knew what was happening with Solyana and her team. They had moments only before news traveled to every ear in the pass, condemning the group once they officially refused to relinquish their mammoth. Solyana scanned the eyes of the people and was met with violent glares. She had only one option.

She stepped forward and lowered her hood.

Pahlak and Rorhan saw her face first, and their eyes lit up with recognition. Pahlak dropped her staff, turned to Rorhan and spoke rapidly. His features hardened. A ripple of murmurs stretched far and wide, chased by the crack of the fires and snorts of the mammoths.

"Oku merki shorondah, da prenelahn." She spoke so feverishly, it made Solyana take a step back. "Oku merki shorondah, da prenalahn!" she repeated.

The entire family rushed Solyana. Gamaliel raised his freshly hewn staff to block them, but he was easily overrun. The tribe examined her as if she were cattle—gripping her jaw, scrutinizing her face, lifting her eyelids, and peering into her ears.

Gamaliel paced behind the circle, his eyes darting to Solyana's, waiting for permission to step in. But though their hands were rough, and they smelled of sweat and something sour, Solyana graciously withstood their scrutiny. They had to believe she was the one who would save them from the ceaseless cold.

"Taralashan!" a gruff voice barked over the crowd, and the circle that had formed around Solyana snapped apart without a moment of hesitation. Like a wave, the people bowed in succession from farthest to nearest as a man who appeared as old as the prophecy itself hobbled his way forward.

His white hair was woven into his beard; Solyana couldn't tell where one stopped and the other began. It reached his knees, made easily possible by the hunch of his back, which swayed with every step he took, aided by his staff. The people remained silent as he passed, their heads bowed, eyes trained on the snow.

A burst of light from the popping fire showed the old man's eyes, milky and blind. He raised his chin, standing as straight as he was able before clearing his throat.

"You," he began. Solyana blinked in surprise; he spoke the Mothmari she did. "You are the One Chosen? The One to whom this land will turn? The One for whom we pray?"

Such weighty questions required answers, but any utterance Solyana could give felt as insubstantial as the snowflakes piled at her feet. "I think—"

"She is." Jonas stepped forward with determination. Solyana turned to him with a grateful smile.

The old man shuffled the last few steps and groped the air with a shaking hand. Solyana took it in her own and pressed it to her cheek. His calloused fingers crawled gently to the scar, feeling the flesh with great care. Solyana studied the old man's face so close to her own. His milk-white eyes held tears pooling at the brim.

"You have Gifts?" he questioned quietly.

"I have one," Solyana whispered for his ears alone.

"The other two?"

Solyana was silent, her heart beating like a tumbling boulder, gaining momentum, picking up speed.

The wizened chief nodded before lifting a single hand into the air, his palm upturned, just as Rorhan had done before. Without a word, three figures robed in white, their faces obscured by veils, wove their way to the front of the crowd. Solyana was struck by how similar their robes were to her parka, the white blending into the landscape at day, though in the night, stark as the full moon.

People of all ages backed away from the small fire where Solyana and her friends sat, leaving only the chief, the brother and sister who had spoken to them, and the three newcomers. The Mother of the Night watched through the Norlos as the figures filed in front of Solyana and knelt before her, their palms upward as if offering something unseen.

"Each have a Gift, ready to give." The old man cocked his head to the side. "What remains to be received?"

"Tala," she said. "And Fera."

"Sun Daughter," he mumbled reverently. With another flick of his hand, one of the veiled figures peeled away, leaving two kneeling before her.

The scar on her face pulsed and grew warm, as if it knew what would soon take place. The devotion of these people filled her with awe as every hair on her skin stood to attention. How had she gone her entire life ignorant of the presence of others? These people lived their faith so fully, they were willing to give their Gifts at a moment's notice. Solyana's own people hadn't offered even one.

"I, Rahgah Voh, forgive you your debt, if you would only give us this honor." The old man blinked slowly.

Gamaliel shifted and cleared his throat. His eyes darted her way, then back to the two veiled figures kneeling on the ground.

"Begin, Sun Daughter." The old chief bowed his head respectfully.

Utter silence fell over the tribe as they watched her like children awaiting a fireside story.

Solyana stepped forward, mind and heart churning with anticipation. A spray of sparks from the fire announced the start of the ceremony.

The two before her held their hands open, palms soft and pale, to the sky. Reality struck her like an ice pick to the skull: she would have to cut those palms, just as she had Jonas's on the peak of Eldfall.

Rorhan stepped forward, ornate knife in hand. He pressed it into the palm of one, drawing a line of red with care. Solyana exhaled with relief. At least she didn't have to harm them. Sweat prickled Solyana's lower back as she reminded herself this was all part of it. She had done it once before; she could do it again.

The two were still kneeling on the ground and Solyana mirrored their stance, meeting them on her knees. She looked from one to the other, wanting to speak to them, to introduce herself, or even hold their eyes with her own. But beneath the expectant silence of the tribe and the scrutiny of their elder, Solyana only lowered her gaze.

Blood dripped to the snow; the constant pattern a reminder she had a decision to make.

Wind rippling the figures' veils, Solyana centered herself in front of the smaller of the two. Delicately, she cupped the bleeding hand in her own before pressing it to the left side of her face. She was answered with a flash of heat and then a steady thrum blooming in the back of her skull.

It suddenly occurred to her she didn't know which kind of Tala or Fera she'd acquire. The speed at which she'd been pushed to make these choices, it took everything in her to keep her knees planted, the bloody hand of a stranger on her face. Tears leaked from her eyes, and she squeezed them shut.

"Please," she whispered, focusing on the Mother Above, who stared down at her with calm consistence. "Please, save my people." She only realized the hand at her cheek had been shaking when it stopped, slackened.

Solyana opened her eyes.

The figure before her tipped forward, crashing into her. Someone screamed as the two of them crumpled to the ground in a heap of tangled limbs.

THE CENTER

PALLAH

PALLAH TOOK STOCK OF her senses. She could feel the icy slickness of the walls and the fading warmth of her own body. Any internal heat she built during her trekking and mapping was sucked away by dry and frigid air; she ceaselessly shivered. She could smell and taste, but the only smell was something that reminded her of the smithy back home, and the only taste she experienced was the salt of sweat. She could hear: her breathing, the scraping of her palms along the walls, and words whispered to herself that resembled a fluxing symphony as they bounced between endless corridors.

She lacked sight, though surely, that was by design. A maze is easier to solve if the person trapped in it can see. In some ways, this bolstered her, kept her trying. If Dahvid was still making efforts to hinder her, then she still had a chance to succeed.

She lacked the need to eat, drink, or relieve herself. Freya must be caring for her body, as she did Dahvid. Pouring liquids down her throat, cleaning her up like a baby. A midwife and the surrogate infant of her own treachery. Pallah shuddered at the thought.

For she knew the body that moved through this place was not physical, or at least, not entirely. Her true body was lying somewhere in Freya's cabin. Whether in Tinloh's mind or her own, she didn't know, but she was locked in a Maze of a madman's making.

When she wasn't mapping the Maze, she was thinking. Always thinking. What would she do if she escaped? What had become of her mother, of Ahren and Vámae? Was her family even safe against Freya's grudge with Tinloh under Dahvid's control? Could she possibly get a word out? A warning?

She thought often of Erval. She tried talking to him, again and again, yet there was never a response. Perhaps he found no worth in her anymore.

Now here she was, mapping the Maze as she did every waking moment. She was close to the center, or so she thought, trying to make her way to the other side. Left, straight, right, left, left, straight, straight, right, left, right—she smacked her face on the wall as she turned.

"*Häfa!*" Pallah rubbed her forehead and stretched out her other hand. Had that wall been there before? Hand on it, she back-tracked and found herself in a small square. There was only room enough for maybe two spans of her shoulders in all directions, a perfect cube. Was this the center? She had been trying to find a way out this entire time, not trap herself in some too-small box.

Pallah would have felt frustration, if she had any feeling left in her. But there was nothing inside anymore. Her inner self was as dark as the space around her, unfeeling and cold. The only sparks of joy she ever relished in this darkness were her fantasies of killing Dahvid—short flares of happiness that she lingered on sparingly.

But this center? It was new, and it was unusual. It represented finality to something she had started to believe was unending.

She heard a muffled sound, undeniably Freya's voice.

Garbled and low as it was, hope filled Pallah so thoroughly her limbs seemed to lighten. She looked around frantically in the dark, the closeness of the walls reminding her of Eldfall, of the tunnel she'd scaled with only cool wind to guide her.

She had tried to climb the walls before, of course, but they had been too slick. However, this tiny room—its walls crushingly close—gave her the one feature she'd been lacking: counterpressure. Shakily, she planted her feet on one side, pressing her back to the other. Then slowly, painstakingly, she began to shimmy her way up.

The sound broadened and the words clarified as she went. The walls were much higher than she'd anticipated, and panic began to grip her. Sweat sprang from the bottoms of her feet, from the palms of her hands. If she fell from this height, would the injuries reflect on her body in Freya's care? Could she die in here?

Her arms and legs shook, tempting gravity, tempting fate. But Pallah pressed on.

After a few more excruciating steps, her toes found purchase on a ridge. She gasped and reached back over her shoulder, finding a second ledge beneath her hand.

Pallah kept her back against the wall and moved her feet up enough to crest the edge across from her. Then she pushed carefully, her thighs shaking with every breath. Groaning with pain, her back scraped over the ledge behind her. She turned, kicking her feet into the open air, and scrambled on top of the Maze.

When she was finally able to slow her breathing, she heard Freya's voice again, clearly this time.

"It's been too long, Dahvid. I thought I saw someone from the west last night. I sent the animals to ward them off, but they're still searching for her. You would think they would've given up after all this time."

A loaded pause stilled the air.

Freya spoke again. "You told me you could figure out how to get her up and walking. It's been months since you claimed she would be mobile, Dahvid!"

Pallah crouched at the top of the ledge, her heart leaping into her throat. Months? Someone was searching for her? Maybe it was Vil. Something fluttery happened in her stomach and she clung to the feeling like a lifeline.

"We need to cut our losses and get rid of her. You have what you wanted, don't you? That *häfan* cat?"

Tinloh. Tears came to her eyes. She had cried a lot at first, but it had been a long time since she had allowed herself the luxury of it. As she wiped her face, her balance shifted, foot slipping off the ledge. Gasping for breath, she flung out hand and foot, gripping the ledge and hugging the wall with every limb. The chill of the surface seeped into her chest, her panic ebbing away.

"Fine. One more week. But if she's not up and moving around by then, we're done. I can give her a draft and she'll be gone in minutes, bury her in the woods. Or maybe your new feline friend can make the remains disapp—No!" Pallah whipped her head around at the exclamation, half expecting some unseen hand to grab her in the dark. "I told you! A week. You know I love you like a son, Dahvid, but I can't do it anymore. It's been two *häfan* years. I am done."

Two years. Pallah blinked, uncomprehending.

Two years.

Then she let herself fall backward, tumbling from the top of the Maze, uncaring if she lived or died.

UNTIL THE VERY END

SOLYANA

SOLYANA SAT LIKE A block of ice on rocky water, untethered and bobbing in the wind. The eruption of noise that had followed the Gifting of Tala to Solyana dimmed to muffled rises and falls. The girl—for she was but a girl—lay still in the snow, stripped of vitality. Her veil had fallen askew, revealing a face still full with the fat of youth, the light in her eyes departed.

Solyana bent over the girl and took in the sight of her, pushing down a surge of nausea, refusing to be sick. She would not add more offenses to this day, or more shame to the records of her memory. Fingers shaking, she traced the girl's face, growing colder in frost and in death.

"I didn't know," Solyana whispered, her tears turning to sobs that racked her chest and made her back ache. Jonas had lived, even stripped of his Gift. What had changed? What was different?

Pressure of a hand on her shoulder brought her up for air. Gamaliel's deep brown eyes were pools of empathy, sorrow, and a flash of anger. "This isn't your fault," he said, though it sounded like he was reassuring himself. "We knew this was a possibility. Back home, we talked about what the legend said: 'When a Gift leaves the soul, the soul leaves with it.'"

Solyana shook her head. She wanted to be left alone, to grieve this girl that lay before her, to grieve the girl Solyana herself used to be and was no longer. Not after this.

"We must continue." Rahgah Voh's voice snapped her into clarity. "The Gifting of Fera awaits."

Gamaliel's voice came hard and fast, his anger clearly for this man. "Have you not heard a single thing we've been—"

"Quiet, boy," the chief rebuked. "This is much more than you, or her." He pointed to the girl on the ground, veil and clothing fluttering over the lifeless form they covered. "The Celestials receive what is owed. They have made their choice. The Chosen must take what is needed. What is given."

Another pair of legs stepped before Solyana and as she peered up. Lone stood, a guard against the tribe. "Solyana is done." The words fell with icy finality. Three more figures blocked her from the chief: Odie, Jonas, and Vinur with a growl in his throat.

"We have prayed for generations. Our people are chosen and prepare from birth for such an honor!" Rahgah Voh's voice boomed over the entire sea of people who sat silent as their chief spoke. "You will take this final Gift and bring the green!"

A keening wail ripped from Solyana's throat and her scar flared as her palms erupted into twin flames at her sides. Eyes squeezed shut, she saw and heard nothing but the roar of fire in her ears. A small, familiar hand pressed to her face. The flames stuttered, and blinking, she opened her blurry eyes to find Jonas.

"Take a breath," he reassured in his small voice. "You can control it, Solyana. Don't let it take you."

All flame winked out, and the reality of this child comforting her when it was her job to protect him broke the last vestiges of her anger. She wrapped her arms around him and sobbed into his shoulder.

"Have you not studied the texts?" Rahgah Voh would not abate. "Known of the Seers who lost their Gifts and died in the night? When a Gift leaves the soul, the soul leaves with it."

Solyana blinked, pulling away from the boy who had defied that very adage. She gestured to him, hands still shaking. "*He* did," she said weakly. "He survived when he gave me his Heitt."

The ancient chief snapped his mouth shut, white eyebrows shooting upward. "Impossible."

"I witnessed it," Gamaliel said.

"As did I." Lone stepped beside him.

Chief Rahgah Voh took several steps to where Jonas sat beside Solyana. He lowered himself unsteadily to the ground, keeping hold of his staff the entire way. Jonas began to scoot away, but Solyana grabbed his hand and shook her head.

The entire plain was silent but for the wind buffeting the people huddled on the ground. The chief crossed his legs before Jonas who sat in the same way. "Boy," Rahgah Voh uttered just loud enough for Solyana to hear. "They speak the truth?"

"Y-yes," Jonas stammered, eyes flicking from Solyana and back to the chief again and again.

"And you have never been given a Gift before?"

Jonas shook his head and Solyana squeezed his hand. "Oh, no, Chief." Pink touched his cheeks.

The chief let out a low hum, his milky eyes scanning as if some invisible scroll lay before him.

"You may yet hold a Gift inside of you, boy," the old man said, hands on his knees. "Brotnur will know for sure."

Jonas caught Solyana's eyes again and she shrugged.

"Who is Brotnur?" he asked.

"A man who lives by the Celestials' silence. He resides in Endirinn."

Before Jonas could ask any more questions, Rahgah Voh turned his sightless eyes to address Solyana. "Sun Daughter." He shakily stood. "Knowing the paths the Celestials have bestowed, grace us with your acceptance of Fera."

Solyana glanced at the last person hidden beneath a veil, ready to sacrifice themselves for the good of their country. Solyana could understand that willingness, but doing it to someone else was a thing she could not bear.

"I do not accept," she said boldly.

The shoulders of the chief fell as he turned away from her. "Then you are no Chosen One of ours," he spoke clearly, loudly, and it echoed across the plain until it dissipated in the wind. "You have needlessly taken and will fail the Celestials. You have condemned this generation to more years of hardship and have spurned our people." Rahgah Voh held up his palm and sliced it in the air. At the signal, his tribe stood, a wave riding the snow. "Begone from this place! You are no longer welcome here!"

They began to chant, ominous and building. Gamaliel grabbed Solyana's hand, and Lone ushered Jonas away. Odie hoisted Vinur atop his shoulders to climb the seated mammoth.

Solyana only chanced a glance back at them once she was atop Curry with Gamaliel. Her eyes found Pahlak and Rorhan, and she was surprised to find guilt there—unease.

The mammoths got to their feet laboriously, the entire crew holding on tight as they were rocked back and forth.

"Eyup!" Odie rang out and they lumbered away in the night, chased by the dissonant chants of the tribe beneath the moon.

Spent and stripped of title, Solyana curled up behind Gamaliel, gloved hands tucked beneath her arms. Exhaustion washed over her as her tears returned. In her last waking moments, her thoughts were on the Mother Below, the Taka Reu, and the boy on the mountain who had done this to them. Bitterness steamed to a boil in her gut, unruly and bubbling over. Bitterness against Mothmar itself, ceaselessly seeming to be working against her. But more than that—against the Celestials themselves. What kind of gods forced their devout to make such decisions? To take such actions in their name?

The cost was too great, the road too narrow. Solyana walked toward the prophecy with one foot on the path, and the other one questing for its own solid ground on which to stand. It was no wonder then, that her heart had grown cold.

"Hey, let me help you down."

Solyana blinked against the morning light to find Gamaliel, his hand gently extended toward her. She sat up and looked down at brown wiry fur. She was still astride Curry, who was kneeling on the ground.

Taking his proffered hand, Solyana slid off the side until she was pressed close to Gamaliel, his eyes searching her own. "How are you feeling?"

Solyana swallowed past the ache in her throat. "I'm okay." She forced herself to look around. "Where are we?"

"We rode all night until we could find some cover. Odie fell asleep as soon as the mammoths were settled. Jonas hasn't woken up since last night." He took a deep breath. "And Lone left to hunt."

Taking in her surroundings for the first time, Solyana realized they had found a forest that rested at the base of a small mountain. "Are we in danger?" She hadn't forgotten the harrowing incantation the tribe had begun, their bodies moving ever closer as they fled on the backs of their beasts.

"If Rahgah Voh and his tribe wanted to stop us, they would have. But we all agree, we don't want to cross paths with them again."

"I'm not sure we can avoid that," Solyana said while she untied her hair and squinted up at the sky. "I think we're all going to the same place." Though the cold never left, the sun warmed the tips of her nose and cheeks, bringing a semblance of relief.

"You know I won't let them harm you," Gamaliel said, his eyes suddenly intense. "Right?" He was standing a pace away, and a flame of longing burned in her belly as she stared at him: her best friend, her truest companion. He had protected her, guided her, and stood by her side from the beginning.

"I know you'll try." She took a step away from him, heat crawling up her neck in spite of winter's best efforts. "You may be able to keep me safe from people who mean to harm me, but you can't stop a prophecy, Gam. Some things are final; we can't change the outcome, no matter how much we may want to."

He stepped closer, closing the distance between them once more, his breath warm on her face. "I don't think you understand, Solyana." Her name was like honey from his lips, a salve to her soul. Had it always sounded so good? "Not a blizzard or a sea, not an avalanche or the prophecy itself could keep me from you. From Vestur to Takanah"—he raised an arm with each location, pointing in their directions—"from Endirinn to the rest of Mothmar—I go with you. I am yours, until the very end."

Solyana swallowed, the pressure of tears behind her eyes. "Until the very end?"

"And all that comes before it."

She leaned forward and kissed him. All doubts and questions disappeared as his arms circled her and pulled her tight to himself. Holding her steady with one hand, he wove his fingers into her hair with the other, lips moving with constancy, and then urgency.

Colors, warmth, and light filled every bit of Solyana, her heart blooming with something akin to joy. But even as they kissed, even as she breathed in the smell of musk and smoke she had come to know so well, the weight of her task, of her failure, threatened to pull her away. If he was so sure on following her, would he not be at more risk? If it came to it, would she be the cause of his death?

He stepped back, his face holding a small grin.

"I've been wanting to do that for a long time," he murmured, pressing his forehead into her own.

Solyana closed her eyes. "Me, too."

Something thrummed at the base of her skull.

She stumbled backward, hands gripping the back of her head.

"What happened! Oh, *häfa,* Solyana, I'm sorry. What's wrong?"

A screech rang out high above and Solyana felt her tether, her Tala tether, react like something alive. Shading her eyes with her hand, she spotted Halina making a slow descent. In the chaos of everything, she had completely forgotten about the bird.

The new tether inside of her wanted to latch onto the falcon. Fear and thrill flooded her in tandem.

"Gam, I don't know what kind of Tala I have, but I think I can tether to birds," she said, eyes on the falcon as Halina landed on a branch above them. "I can feel it."

Gamaliel's eyes grew wide as he looked from Solyana to the falcon above. "Solyana, after what we saw in Takanah, I would be wary of tethering to anything that could potentially house a human being."

"The people of Takanah *transformed*, Gamaliel. Remember when I first told you about Halina?"

Gamaliel nodded, hand rubbing the back of his neck at the memory of the second blizzard hitting the Valley, of trekking their way back to the Temple Celestial.

"We both agreed it could be Rhuth. I truly believe the night I'd been stranded on the Vatino Sea, after the storm had broken it, Rhuth used her Broad Tala to send creatures to save me. And yet..." Solyana's words began to stumble out, excitement building inside of her. "Rhuth remains in her bed in the Temple Celestial. She is not physically transforming, as the people of Takanah do. Jonas and I have been researching it, and there are accounts of similar connections to a Tala aptitude."

Gamaliel shook his head. "It's too risky. There's no telling what could happen if you tethered to a human, even by mistake."

"That's impossible, Gam." Solyana took his hand in her own. "People aren't animals. And besides, we've read every scroll Jonas can get his hands on. Such a thing has never been mentioned." She offered her arm up to Halina, and the falcon landed, flapping her wings before folding them to her sides. Her beak opened and head wagged side to side. Halina acted differently when Rhuth was latched with her tether.

"Ready?" Solyana murmured to the bird.

Halina bobbed her head and lifted her foot with the missing talon. If that hadn't been enough, she gave a curt screech, head turned to the side so her eye could focus on Solyana. She blinked.

Encouraging her tether forward, Solyana latched onto Halina and gasped.

Within half a second, Solyana was no longer in a dense forest of Greater Mothmar.

She could still smell the wet iron of snow and feel the chill of the wind on her cheeks, but all around her, she was staring at sleek walls, rising high and running long, every surface silver and metallic.

Crouched before her, wiry, naked, and wild, was her little sister.

"Rhuth!" Solyana launched herself at her, and the two of them embraced, crumpling together in a heap on the ground. "How is this possible? How are you—"

"Solyana." Rhuth pushed her away, her voice scratchy and panicked, not bothering to cover her bare body. "I don't have much time."

"What are you talking about?" Solyana scanned Rhuth's small frame, all jutting bones and pockets of shadow where soft skin and baby-fat used to be. "What's happened to you?"

"She's keeping me here!" Rhuth's eyes searched, jumping from one thing to the next. "In this Maze! I can't leave."

"Who's keeping you here?" Panic threated to overtake Solyana, her breathing coming fast. But her sister needed her. She took a deep breath, her hands gently grasping Rhuth around her frail shoulders, so emaciated, it was like holding a pile of sticks. "Tell me everything."

Rhuth's body trembled like a terrified mouse. "Priestess Avi is keeping me trapped. It has something to do with my Gift." Rhuth looked up as if she could see the priestess herself above them. But then her eyes, searching and frantic, fell back on Solyana's. "I can do things, things no other Tala can do. Halina and I are one, and not like she is, with her scary sabertooth tiger."

"So, that *was* her in Takanah!" Solyana's mind raced. "She came to save me?"

"She followed because I went to warn you, and she doesn't want me doing that—oh no!" Rhuth leaned back, listening for something that didn't come. Then she leaned in close, her voice a strained whisper, "I don't know why my Gift is different. I don't know what she wants from me!" Rhuth began to cry, tears tracking down her hollowed cheeks. "I think I'm figuring something out with Fera, though." She sniffed and wiped at her eyes. "I've begun to knock things over in my room. She always thinks it's her new Serviseer, but it's me."

Solyana caught a glimpse of her sister from before, playful and smart. But she shook her head. "You don't have Fera, Little Fyug."

"I know!" Rhuth shook her head and let out a wail that broke into sobs. "I don't know what's wrong with me." Her lips trembled and Solyana tried to embrace her, but Rhuth flinched and pulled away. "She's lied! About everything, Sol. The boy on the mountain? It's her brother! I don't know why she wants him, but I think they're planning do bad things together. You *cannot* free him."

"Rhuth." Solyana put a hand to her throat, the implications of her sister's words threatening to suffocate her. "It wasn't just Priestess Avi who sent me out; our people voted for this. I can't let them down. This is the only way to make it green again. To bring you back!"

"You're not listening!" Rhuth cried and Solyana scrambled back from her, something feral in the young girl's eyes. "The pieces of scroll! Halina brought them to you! Why can't you see?" Her eyes squeezed shut. "You're at the end of my tether, Solyana. After this, I won't be able to latch to Halina again. Doing it now hurts so bad." Rhuth moaned and rocked back and forth. "I've been waiting and waiting...but after this...I can't bring Halina back. I can't. I'll lose her either way." She cried, big choking sobs that left her gasping for air.

Solyana crept forward again, placing a hand on her sister's arm. "There are other Broad Tala in the villages! Why don't you bring Halina to—"

"She'll kill her!" Rhuth said, standing up. "I can't bring Halina back home; Avi is waiting to take her away!" Rhuth was searching above again, as if a hand would descend from the sky and grip her by the throat. "She wants my power! I would tell her—I would—but I don't know what it is!" Rhuth paced. "Please Solyana, turn back! She can't get to her brother, but *you* can. And she's willing to sacrifice you to get him. Please Sol, come home. Come home!"

Her mind thought back to what Orson had said.

There were others who had gone before.

What if this wasn't the first time Priestess Avi had sent someone to release her brother at the end of the light? What if this wasn't about white or green at all?

Solyana tipped her head into her hands, eyes searching the ground at her feet. There were only metal floors and walls, the empty sky above them stark and glaring—no deity to be found. She squeezed her eyes shut, unable to think clearly.

"Okay, Little Fyug." She looked her sister in the eye. If Rhuth was in danger, there was nothing to decide. "I'm coming home."

Then Solyana remembered—her sister's scar, the one Halina made the last day Rhuth had been awake—wasn't there. Rhuth's face was clean and clear. Was this really Rhuth? Or some kind of trick, conjured to stop her journey?

"Where's your scar, Rhuth?" Solyana tried to keep her voice level, but even she couldn't ignore the shake in it.

"What?" Rhuth stopped moving, hands dropping to her sides. "Solyana, we don't have much time. You need to come back!" She screamed the words at Solyana as if she wasn't mere paces from her.

Wary now, Solyana cleared her throat and stood cautiously, hands extended as if approaching a wild beast. "I need you to calm down." Solyana reached out and grabbed Rhuth's wrist, so tiny in Solyana's grip, her fingers wrapped all the way around.

Rhuth tore her arm away and launched to her feet. "Why don't you believe me?" She paced, two steps, turn, two steps again, hands tearing at her hair. "You're my sister! BELIEVE ME!"

"Rhuth!" Solyana reached for her again, but her little sister slapped her hand away, releasing an unnaturally loud scream that shoved Solyana back into the present. Her knees hit wet snow, Gamaliel at her side.

Halina took to the sky with a screech, becoming a black silhouette on the canvas of blue. Solyana's heart dropped to her gut as she watched the bird grow smaller against the sun.

"What was that?" Fear dripped from Gamaliel's words as his hands searched her face, her hands. "*Häfa,* Solyana you went blank! I didn't know what to do."

"Rhuth is in danger." Solyana's hands shook as she got to her feet. "I need to go home."

The sun was high in the sky when the rest of the team woke to find Solyana and Gamaliel discussing what had happened when she had tethered Halina. Dark circles beneath her eyes, Solyana recounted the events and information without restraint.

"I don't know," Lone said, pulling her knife from its holster in her mukluk. "You said your sister bore no remnant of the scar from when Halina cut her face." She began to toss the knife in her hand. "I believe you talked to someone you *think* is Rhuth. You went through a horrible experience yesterday, with the tribe and the transfer of—"

Gamaliel held up his hand as Solyana's entire body went rigid with the memory. "We don't need to discuss *that* right now."

"It could be a valid reason she's seeing hallucinations."

"It wasn't a hallucination." Solyana was adamant. "I saw my sister. She asked for help. And after what Orson said in Takanah, other people following the prophecy...I think we've been lied to." She pulled out a piece of parchment from the bottom of her bag, the torn scrap Halina had given to her the night before they'd left the Valley. "And Rhuth reminded me of this." She held up the dry and curling scrap.

"What does it say?" Lone crossed her arms.

"I read a bit after we left the Temple Celestial. With everything that's been going on, I forgot about it. But look..." Solyana spread the parchment flat on her leg before raising it to read.

"Vil has been telling me heinous things about my sister: that she has been part of the Taka Reu, and from the smilodon attack on our village, to the scroll going missing from Lóthkol, Pallah has been involved in all of it. He claims she'd even kept a smilodon cub for herself. I can't imagine anyone being so selfish."

"Vil? Pallah?" Lone shrugged. "I don't know anyone by those names."

"No," Solyana confessed, studying the torn scroll. "But we did see a smilodon in Takanah. It's not a common animal. And this scroll talks about this Pallah being someone's sister." Her mind also flitted to the stuffed smilodon in Priestess Avi's quarters, but she shoved it away.

Gamaliel twisted his lips. "I don't know if that's anything that relates to us."

Solyana ground her teeth and stuffed the parchment into the pocket of her parka.

"Priestess Avi wouldn't lie," Jonas piped up. "I've known her my whole life. She's the *priestess*! She communes with the Celestials every day."

Gamaliel and Solyana exchanged a look.

"I think it's time Solyana told you," Gamaliel said. "How the priestess can still use Heitt while living in a valley that hardly sees the sun."

Odie, Lone, and Jonas leveled their eyes at Solyana in unison; even Vinur tilted his head to the side, awaiting her answer.

There was no way to speak of Priestess Avi's actions without discrediting her. But what if Rhuth had been a test? What if the prophecy stood waiting to be fulfilled? What if sacrifice was part of what the Celestials required of their Chosen? The group had come so far and were so close to the end: Endirinn and the Norlos, the boy and the green. To turn back now would be to have endured so much for nothing. She would have little to show upon her return, no legacy to leave but failure.

Solyana considered Gamaliel's argument from days past. And as much as it pained her, he had been right. It would be better to fail in their journey with the truth than to succeed with lies. So, the truth was what she told.

"Before we left, Priestess Avi revealed she has more than one Gift. Yes, she has Heitt, but she also has Lakimi Fera."

Lone's mouth fell open, her own mother being the Healer of their land. Lakimi Fera, or manipulation of muscles, would have helped her work immensely.

Solyana pressed on. "She uses the Taka Reu and the Celestials simultaneously, in order to use multiple Gifts *and* continue using her Heitt, even when the Father of the Day hardly appears."

Jonas's eyes went wide.

"Who is this Priestess Avi?" Odie asked, hands clasped atop his belly. "Do her actions as an individual truly alter a path laid out by the Celestials themselves?"

"She's the ruling voice of the Temple Celestial," Lone said, eyes narrowed in thought. "I'm suspicious of this claim, her using the Taka Reu."

"You can say that again." Odie huffed.

Lone ran a hand through her shock of white-blonde hair. "We've come this far, and we do have the texts that support this mission." She took a moment to consider. "I vote we continue. And reevaluate when we find the end of the Norlos."

"I think this is ultimately Solyana's decision," Gamaliel said. "Rhuth is her sister."

"No." Solyana sighed. "Lone's right. We should vote. I can't, in good conscience, ask you all to follow me back home, not after we've come so far."

Lone's eyes bored into Solyana. "Is this how Priestess Avi expects you to obtain your three Gifts? Use both the Celestials and the Taka Reu?"

Solyana remained silent, unwilling to admit that much. And unwilling to concede the lengths to which she'd truly entertained the possibility. But the silence stretched too long, and like their journey, it seemed the only way to go was forward, one way or another.

"It was an option," she confessed.

"But not one Solyana is willing to employ," Gamaliel offered. "Even if she did know how to use it."

Solyana peered up at him, tension clawing at her gut. She dropped her gaze to her hands.

Lone crouched beside Solyana, elbows on knees. As private a conversation as they were going to have, under the circumstances. She spoke low. "Would you?"

"Of course not!" Solyana said out of habit. But it wasn't the complete truth. She couldn't bear to repeat the process forced by Rahgah Voh. What if obtaining Gifts with the Taka Reu was less dangerous?

"Well, what's the plan, folks?" Odie pulled out his waterskin and took a drink. "Are we voting?"

Gamaliel tried to catch Solyana's eyes, but she averted her gaze. "Yes," she said as she stood. "All in favor of going back home?" She raised her own hand, Gamaliel's following shortly after. "And all in favor of continuing to the end of the Norlos?"

Lone and Jonas raised their hands.

"I'm sorry, Sol," Jonas whispered. "But Priestess Avi wouldn't lie to us."

Solyana wasn't so sure anymore.

Everyone turned to Odie, who scratched at his beard. "If that priestess is using the Taka Reu, we shouldn't go to her. We can find new answers when we arrive in Endirinn. I vote for onward and upward."

He raised his hand.

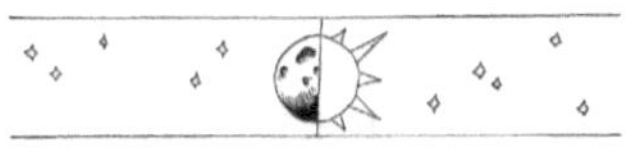

The group stayed the night beneath the trees, resting their bodies for the days of hard travel they knew were coming.

But Solyana couldn't sleep. Every time she closed her eyes, she saw Rhuth and heard her screams, her skin so cold beneath Solyana's touch. Was continuing to Endirinn betraying her family? Or would she doom them all the moment she turned back?

And then there was the problem with acquiring a third Gift. She could never subject anyone else to the veiled girl's fate. Jonas's research turned up nothing about the transfer of Gifts through the Taka Reu, and she didn't want to create suspicion by pressing him for more.

Alone, she walked through the trees, listening to the crunching of packed snow beneath each step.

Jonas and Lone lay by Björg. Gamaliel had left to hunt, and Odie kept watch by the fire. Even the Mother of the Night was hidden now behind dark, rolling clouds.

Alone and unwatched, Solyana crouched and removed her glove, letting her fingertips slide beneath the snow, pressing it into the cold ground beneath. She had one other option, and if this didn't work, she was at a loss. Perhaps she wasn't the Chosen One after all.

Squeezing her eyes shut, she imagined herself connecting to the Mother Below instead of the Celestials above. Did it matter how her fingers splayed, or how the rest of her body was aligned above it? Her paltry knowledge from Jonas's scrolls made her feel the fool.

A tingle fluttered near her heart.

Her mouth fell open as her Celestial tether slipped away, replaced by one blossoming in the center of her chest. It tugged her closer to the ground. The scar on her face burned with new ferocity, and Solyana hissed in pain, gritting her teeth.

Then she shook with abject horror as a thick, dark smoke slipped through the pockets of air in the snow, weaving through her fingers, seeking purchase as it climbed up her arm.

DAHVID THE DANGEROUS

PALLAH

PALLAH REMEMBERED THE SENSATION of falling: a blissful and painless duration before her body met the cold, hard floor. She wished she had died. She longed for it, lying in a broken heap, agony spilling into every sense. But death did not come.

The longer she lay prostrate and immobile on the ground, the deeper her rage burrowed. It boiled inside of her, growing stronger than despair. It was the rage that reorganized her mind, that reshaped her from victim to victor. If she couldn't end her misery inside of this *häfan* Maze, she would escape it. She had to.

When her nerves no longer felt like fire and her legs no longer quaked, she rose and wound her way back to the middle chamber. She had spent the last two years trying to find a way out. Now she wondered, if this entire time, it was the center which held the key to her release.

Her fingers trailed along the sleek walls, her feet stepping carefully over the chilly floor as she recounted the way. Finally, back at the center, she released a breath. Running a hand over her stomach, she could feel just how gaunt she'd become. Each individual rib jutted out, her hip bones doing much the same. Freya was allowing her to wither away to nothing. Rage flared once more, though it crested and fell like a single, tired wave.

So much time alone; so much time lost. She could not tether with the Celestials, nor with the Mother. She could not feel Tinloh, and Erval had left her. Would life be worth living when she left this *häfan* place? Would anything of what or whom she had known remain?

She was eighteen now. She didn't feel eighteen. Her body should have swelled into womanhood, but instead, malnutrition and whatever abuse she'd endured had stunted her. Perhaps her body here and her body out there were separate. She could only hope this skeletal form didn't reflect who she had truly become.

You've finally grown properly angry. Took you long enough.

"Erval?" Everything inside of Pallah filled. A voice! Someone was speaking to her! Maybe they could help her escape. No one had spoken to her in two years. Tears came so quickly, she didn't bother wiping them away. It was a relief to feel something other than the vile loathing that had taken up permanent residence inside her.

Who is Erval?

Pallah's heart sank, and fury slammed into her once more. This wasn't Erval's deep, silky voice. Its utterance was ragged and stunted, much like herself.

"Dahvid," she corrected herself, "what have you done to me?"

I've been hoping you would find this place. I've been waiting to speak with you.

"I've been here before; you didn't speak to me then." Pallah's chest heaved. There was no doubt in her mind; she wanted to murder this man. Unable to pace the tiny cube of a room, her fists clenched in time with her heartbeat.

Unfortunate timing. Freya doesn't think we should speak. I disagree. You see, Pallah, I've gained respect for you. Anyone who has the ability of Smilodon Tala deserves it. It is a difficult animal to wield, and even more difficult to gain its trust.

The blood drained from Pallah's face as Dahvid spoke of Tinloh. "What have you done with him?"

Do you know how long I have been searching for another smilodon, Pallah? I would never risk anything happening to him; he is precious. I'll admit, I had a few failed attempts before finding the family of smilodon tucked away in that mountain. The cub grew cold to me quickly, so I tried the mother. I was able to get further along with her. I didn't mean for her to get killed, of course. A regret I still harbor. But then, before I could establish a connection with this one, you tethered him...and he listened to you. A strength I have not seen in so long.

Pallah's eyes grew wide as her mind traced back to what felt like ages ago; her life before the dark. So, it had been Dahvid who had tethered to that mother smilodon. Dahvid who had sent her on Pallah's people.

"You let her kill four people," Pallah said, chilled with new terror.

An unfortunate turn of events. I was able to place the Maze but couldn't get her to follow instructions. She came for me with such fury; I couldn't quell it, so I redirected. She turned against the nearest settlement. I am truly sorry it was your home. It did pain me. I worried for my children and for my love. But based on your arrival here, I assume they're alive, they're safe.

Pallah's hands shook with rage. "And was it you who took control of Tinloh at the cabin? The rabbits?"

Indeed. He's a strong one, your cat.

Fuming, Pallah continued. "So, you would let Tinloh out of his cage, but not your own daughter?" A stone dropped in the pit of her being. Two fathers, and neither one could treat her with love.

Though I would like to claim you, as you have Smilodon Tala, Gifts aren't necessarily hereditary. And seeing you in the flesh has proved it. You are Bogdur's, through and through. The other two, however...they are mine.

Chin trembling, Pallah wanted nothing to do with this man, but she wanted to speak with *someone*, starving as she was for human contact. "Freya said I've been here for two years."

Yes.

"Why?" Pallah's hands groped the walls, formulating a plan. She began to shimmy up the wall.

Why? Oh, Pallah. I knew you would never relinquish your smilodon. And in case you hadn't noticed, I am quite weak physically. You would leave, and although my tether could reach Sodur, you would eventually learn to resist me completely. I couldn't have that. But I'm no monster. Why kill you when I can easily keep you here, with me?

Besides, there is so much to be learned. You see, although you began in the smilodon's Maze, you are now confined in your own. Sadly, I have but a week to accomplish my further goals. Perhaps if you work with me and build up some good will, I'll allow you to tether to Tinloh once again. How does that sound?

He had placed a Maze in her own mind. Pallah pressed her feet into the ledge and pushed herself up to the top yet again. He was insane, absolutely insane. How could he think this was a solution? She wanted to scream at him, denounce, curse, and threaten him. But she quieted her mind. To escape this prison, she needed to outsmart this man. So, for now, she remained silent.

You see, I had to build a Maze just for you. If you'd had access to Tinloh's mind, you would have had access to mine as well. He is the gate between us. But a gate swings both ways, doesn't it?

Pallah stood frozen. The implications of his story barely scratching the surface of her mind.

Please, don't be angry with me.

That was it. He wanted her validation, but why? Loyalty to her mother? Yes, she could use that.

"I suppose," she began haltingly, "if you truly intend to allow me time with Tinloh, I could learn to live here."

Don't patronize me, Pallah.

"I'm serious." She cleared her throat. "I see no other option. Your Maze is a masterpiece. Without you, I'm trapped here by myself."

Indeed. Pallah thought she heard a smile in his voice. *But you really can't know it's a masterpiece, can you? Not without seeing it.*

Pallah remained silent, unsure if it was a trick.

You should see it, at least for a time. It is a masterpiece; you're not wrong.

Silence fell and Pallah prayed, asking the Celestials, the Mother, whoever would listen to her, that he would give her light.

And then it came.

Too much light. Pallah scrambled and careened atop the wall, immediately regretting her request, like a dry, withered plant plunged into a river. She gripped the top edge, every muscle hauling herself back. She focused on her breath, counted to ten. Shaking with exertion, she summoned the bravery to crack her eyes open, just a tiny bit.

As her gaze roved back and forth, her heart sank. It was a circle, not a square, and so much more expansive than she'd originally thought. But with light, she had a chance. She could look down from the top, an advantage she wasn't ready to relinquish.

Beautiful, isn't it? Dahvid asked, his tone soft, gentle, hopeful.

"Truly." Pallah stood fully. "How did you manage it?" She began delicately shimmying around the top of the square, anxious the darkness would descend once again.

Well, I can't give away all my secrets. Though, if you prove to be more of an asset, perhaps you can work alongside me one day.

Pallah peered out over the landscape of metal walls, knowing she wouldn't be able to hear him anymore if she left the square in the center.

Well, it's getting late. I'm going to—

"Wait!" Pallah interrupted. Would the light disappear if he left her? And his voice was a comfort after so long in silence.

"Will you stay with me?" Pallah hated the desperation that leaked into her voice, feigned or not. "Until you fall asleep?"

I understand loneliness better than most. I have missed conversations with anyone other than Freya. She is a horrible woman.

It pained her to agree.

They chatted aimlessly for hours. And all the while, Pallah waited, mapping out the edges and the curves in her mind. She noticed, too, for the first time since entering the Maze, the look of her body. The hands that bore scars and scuffs from years of practicing with her hatchet showed only smooth flesh. Fingers running along foreign skin, she listened to her captor.

Dahvid spoke of his relationship with Freya, how she had taken him in after Phyllir had gone with Bogdur. And then, once the *Stasis* charm had failed, Freya had taken him on as her own responsibility.

There had been hope, in the beginning, that Dahvid would resume normal function. But after a year, and then two, Freya's care for him had begun to falter. She still spoke to him as if he were her son, but her lengthy absences to Takanah kept Dahvid without food or sanitation for several days at a time.

His voice faded, like the whisper of warm wind through White Wood in spring; air she hadn't felt in so long. It dissolved into nothingness, replaced by a gentle snore. Perfect.

Pallah sprang forward. Soon enough, the arches of her feet ached from the relentless demands on them for speed and accuracy. But she wouldn't let herself stop; she couldn't even slow. This was her chance, and she would not squander it.

Making it to the northern side—or what she was labeling north—she looked down the curving wall into...nothing. Determined, she continued along the top of the wall, circling the outside ring until she reached what she figured to be east. It took far longer than she'd thought.

She looked down again, fighting the vertigo that overcame her from her perch. She was so very high. There was nothing visible on that side either; no exit, no cracks in the walls. Everything was uniform. A choking sob escaped her throat. South or west? It had been hours now, scrambling over the top of the Maze. And Dahvid would only sleep for so long. How much further could she investigate? She had to pick a direction.

South. She scrambled along the twists and turns, using both hands and feet, like she was a smilodon herself. Panting, she made it to the other side and looked down.

But there was nothing.

Pallah bit into her fist, quelling the scream crawling up her throat. She stood atop the edge, peering down into the dark. Dahvid would surely wake soon. And he would take her light once again. The idea of the dark lurching up to consume her sent bolts of anxiety into every nerve. She looked to the west—what had to be her escape.

She could make it if she was on the ground; running without the danger of falling would be faster. She stood to her full height and began mapping the way to the western edge, repeating the 'lefts' and 'rights' in her mind. She did this four times before gripping the side of the ledge, her fingers pulsing with pain. She lowered herself as much as she was able, then dropped. Her ankles took the brunt of her fall, pain shooting up her legs like twin arrows.

Ignoring the pain, Pallah bolted down the corridors, repeating the directions in her mind again and again.

Left.

Right.

Straight and count three turns, left, right, then take the left.

Right.

Left.

Left.

Straight for two turns, left then take the right.

Right.

Straight.

Right.

Rounding the last corner, a breathless sob of relief released from her chest. She scoured the metal floor and the walls for a means of exit. Then she spotted it: a gap in the plating of the floor, so thin she would never have found it in the dark. It formed a square: a door. Was it that easy? She might have passed over it several times. Falling to her knees, her fingers scrambled to find a way to lift it. Panic shot through her heart as time was running out, desperately scraping her fingers into the gaps, nails breaking as she jammed her hands again and again. A memory jolted to the front of her mind, of the floorboard in Dahvid's room where she'd done this very same motion to steal a scroll. If only she had left it lie.

She sobbed uncontrollably, whole fingernails ripping away and blood coating her fingertips as she clawed at the floor, making it impossible to get a grip.

The Maze went dark.

Pallah froze, breath heaving. She had failed.

She closed her eyes in the dark, the tears rolling down her cheeks and falling to the floor, the last of her hope slipping away. She was stuck in this Maze, in a paralyzed body, in a shack in the middle of—Pallah's eyes shot open.

In.

She had been going about it all wrong.

Pallah centered herself in the middle of the square on the floor. Every muscle coiled, she jumped as high as she could, and let gravity hurl her weight into the door. It collapsed beneath her, pain slamming into her bones before her body fell through into nothing.

THE CAVE OF RED

SOLYANA

THE STENCH OF MAMMOTH and sweat was worse than usual. Solyana tucked her wind-chapped face further into her scarf, but it didn't help. Twelve days had passed since she had called upon the Taka Reu, and the Mother Below had answered. Terrified of doing anything further, she hadn't tried since. Instead, she had spent every waking moment with her nose buried in scrolls. She squinted up at the sky, the Father of the Day beating down upon them, ever-present. Solyana tucked her latest scroll into the bottom of her bag.

The party wove their way through a passage, a walled riverbed that grew ever narrower over the last few hours. They were forced to slow the mammoths to a stop as a massive ice cave loomed before them, the entrance smoothed over after centuries of wind polished it to glassy perfection.

Rubbing at her snow-encrusted eyes, she looked around from atop Curry. Gamaliel, with Vinur, Jonas, and Lone did the same from Björg's back. They were hemmed in. Tall walls of slick ice reaching skyward, the cave loomed before them; they would have to back out the entire way they came, and since no one had seen an alternative path on their way in...

"We go through?" Lone's voice echoed throughout the slim confines of the passage.

Gamaliel's doubtful expression turned to Jonas, who was tucked between his arms, the boy's nose in his knapsack. "Got a map, buddy?"

"Right here!" Jonas held up a small scroll triumphantly, opening it with difficulty with his mittens. "Endirinn is at the other end of this cave."

"How do we have a map to a place we've never been to before?" Lone asked from behind Gamaliel. "Is it from the archives beneath the Temple Celestial?"

"Yes...and no." Jonas said. "I've been working on it since we left."

"Jonas, you can't work on a map that you've—"

"I know!" Jonas interrupted with an eye roll. "But it just comes to me; it always has. As we walk, I see where we're supposed to go and what's up ahead. Like an image in my mind." He held the map out in front of him, squinting over his scarf. "And it's never been wrong."

Solyana remembered searching for Jonas when they had first left their valley and the small map Gamaliel had found on his bed. Jonas had guided them then, and she trusted him to guide them now. "If it's on the other side, we can go around it."

"What?" Lone sat up straighter. "We spent the entire day getting down this passage!"

"Yeah, we should be able to go through." Gamaliel nodded.

"I don't think it's a good idea," Jonas said.

Gamaliel sighed, his travel-weariness beginning to show. "Jonas, you can't possibly know."

"I just have a feeling! If we go into that cave, something bad will happen. Like the way I make maps. It's not a clear image, but..." He shook his head emphatically. "Can we please turn around?"

"I say we listen to Jonas." Solyana yawned. "Let's back up and go around."

"It will take days," Lone countered.

"If we're calculating correctly, we should have more than enough time before Skaer Sky and the lights disappear. And even then, we're so close," Solyana said, giving Lone an exasperated look. "Better to be safe. We can go around."

Lone crossed her arms. "I think we should vote."

"No vote," Odie spoke up, tugging at the reins. "There's no way Björg and Curry will make it through that cave."

Solyana opened her mouth to agree when something stopped her. A low rumble somewhere in the distance. Silence fell on the group as they craned their necks to look out of the passage.

The sky was dark, but too dark. With dusk approaching, Solyana had assumed it was an earlier night than usual. But this was different. The entire sky swirled as if being stirred by a celestial spoon, the white clouds turning gray and circling each other like prowling wolves.

Flashes of memory assaulted her—of ice and snow, of being trapped twice over, of the black waters of the Vatino pulling her under.

"I think there's a blizzard coming," Solyana mumbled. The wind picked up, ruffling mammoth and hood-fur alike.

Odie, beside her, went rigid. "How quickly? Do we have time to leave the pass?"

"*Holy Hekla*." Gamaliel's deep voice whipped past Solyana as his eyes found her own. "We need to get in there, now." Sitting on Björg, he and Lone could see more than the rest of them. The fear in Gamaliel's eyes told Solyana that this storm could end their journey here.

"Eyup!" Odie called, but his voice was lost to the wind. With the sudden roar of thunderous sound, Curry charged forward.

"Wait!" Gamaliel called as the clatter of millions of miniscule shards of ice separated the mammoths, the torrent advancing and enveloping them with such force that Lone fell from behind Gamaliel.

"Lone!" Solyana screamed from across the pass, only catching glimpses between snow drifts as her mammoth crossed into the cave. She turned in time to see Odie duck low, huddling into Curry's fur. Before she could do the same, her head smacked against the arch of the entryway and she fell back.

Head pounding, Solyana rolled to her side, clinging to the fur beneath her. The frosted glass of the cave sped past her vision, vertigo threatening to pull her under.

There was a sharp *crack* and Curry lurched as her weight broke through the ice of the cave. The mammoth's trumpet of fear mingled with a scream from Solyana's own mouth echoed between the frozen walls as the three tumbled into dark, into a blackness that swallowed them whole.

Curry was screaming.

Solyana's eyes flickered open, her surroundings slowly coming into focus. She feared something had happened to her eyes, as the cave, red-hued and sweltering, slowly became clear. Her tongue tasted ash, and her skin dripped sweat beneath her parka.

She rolled to her side and pushed herself up with a shaking arm. A few paces from her lay the source of the heat, which made Solyana's mouth drop open in disbelief. A pool of liquid fire bubbled and popped, dousing the room with its color.

Curry's screams grew, and Solyana gained the presence of mind to look for her. Squinting through the haze of steam, Solyana spotted the mammoth's flailing silhouette in the dark, far from where she lay. Her trunk searched and her lungs heaved shallow breaths. Beside Curry—no, under her—lay a still form.

Rocking to her feet, Solyana hobbled over to find Odie, his lower half trapped under Curry, eyes open and dull, chest still and silent. Solyana could only hope he had died a quick death, free of suffering. She knelt beside him, grasped the mammoth's wandering trunk, and tucked it around Odie's face, giving the animal an opportunity to say goodbye.

"Be with Lena now, Odie." Solyana folded his hands over his chest and pressed his eyes closed before humming the song of passing.

Turning her attention to Curry, Solyana called on her Heitt. She had done little with it since the day she had drawn upon the Taka Reu, but Solyana now turned her hope to the Celestials. But either due to her tampering with the Dark Gifts or the depth of the pit, the Celestials did not respond. She tried her Tala tether, but had the same result.

"*Häfa!*" She bit her fist, willing the tears building in front of her eyes to stay put. "I need to see how you're hurt, Curry girl. If I can heal you, maybe we can walk out of here together."

Curry's trunk and breathing slowed, her dark eyes blinking in what seemed to be resolution.

"Don't you dare give up, Curry." Solyana stood up, heeding her own advice. If the Celestials would not answer, she would find another way to save at least one life from dying for this cause. She patted Curry and stepped closer to the burning middle of the cave.

The red lake appeared alive as it oozed and rolled through narrow cracks in the cave walls, a flow like honey or burning mud. Jonas would probably know its name. Thinking of him made Solyana send a quick prayer to the Celestials for his wholeness and safety. But perhaps the Celestials were not the powers she ought to rely upon. If the scrolls she'd read could be believed, the Taka Reu was said to be a stronger, more potent source than the Celestials. And she had studied enough to know the reason for it. The core, the very earth itself, was so much closer to her than those above. And now? She was the closest she'd ever been. As if the Mother Below had orchestrated this very situation, her power calling out to Solyana.

Placing the Taka Reu, the Mother, in the forefront of her mind, she reached toward the pool of fire, hand outstretched and shaking.

A smoke rose from the ground, powdery like snow, soft like the fur of her bed back home. It floated up from crevices in the floor and coalesced around her hand, wrapping and coiling up her arm. Eyes widening and pulse racing, Solyana's free hand gripped her darkened one, which she could no longer control. Leaning back, she tried to rip the smoke away, but it puffed and reformed like a glove of black fog. Anxiety turned to terror, and her breathing grew shallow and panicked.

Curry began to trumpet, joining Solyana's cries, as the essence of the Taka Reu climbed across her chest, down her belly, extending over every limb, locking her in place.

A bubble of pure fire popped from the red mire of the lake, then began to churn and swirl, morphing into a form. Shaking with abject fear, Solyana could only watch as the heat of the growing form sent waves of sweat over her body.

The moving fire clarified into the image of an enormous man, his height towering above her. It locked its molten eyes on Solyana as she was held by the smoke, splayed like a hide ready for tanning. The giant's limbs dripped liquid fire as it brought itself closer, bending down to observe the girl before him. The heat became unbearable.

Solyana screamed, throaty and wild.

He blinked at her, slow and measured. "Who are you?" it asked with a spray of red liquid. "And why, pray tell, are you attempting to access my lava lake?"

Solyana's throat burned as if she had swallowed coal. She shook her head, but movement became more difficult as the smoke climbed up her neck and held her fast near her ears. Eyes rimmed with panic, she opened her mouth to speak, but nothing came out.

Her scar burned into being and the fire-man's white-hot eyes widened.

"You're the one they call Daughter of the Sun!" He grinned wickedly, each tooth a different shade of red. "Fancy meeting you here! But where are my manners? You'll forgive me. I offer my cordial salutations." He bowed slightly then stood straight once more. "And oh, the scandal!" He clicked his tongue. "Trying to access the Taka Reu. Sweet girl, you have no idea what you're doing."

"I'm trying to help her." The words barely scraped through Solyana's gritted teeth.

"Who?"

"The mammoth." Solyana flicked her eyes to Curry in the corner, the only thing she could move now. "Please, let me go."

"A mammoth?" Spark and lava rained as the form turned abruptly toward Curry, who was releasing stuttered squeals. "How did this happen?" He chuckled, shaking his head. "What a funny predicament you're in, Sun Daughter." He directed his burning gaze back to Solyana. "Oh, and that..." He motioned to the coiling smoke, now stretching over Solyana's mouth, continuing its climb up her face. "That's not me. It's you. The cost of trying to access the Taka Reu without beseeching the Mother."

Unable to move or speak, Solyana could only beg with her eyes.

"Beseech her," he repeated, and somehow, his eyes turned from pure flame to something like stone, hard and unmovable.

To give herself over to the Taka Reu, to relinquish her faith entirely, felt the ultimate betrayal. But what was betrayal to her own life? To the lives of all the others who had died because of this responsibility placed on her shoulders? All the suffering, the damage, all the deaths, would be for naught.

A tear slipped from her eye, evaporating in the heat of the cave. Solyana could see no other choice, no other action she could take to keep this smoke from swallowing her whole. The Celestials would forgive her. If she was the instrument of their prophecy, they would understand her willingness to do what was needed; she could only serve them if she survived.

With her mind focused on the Mother Below, she spoke to the earth directly, asking for mercy, asking for strength, asking for release.

The pressure in her chest expanded into her limbs and, within moments, the smoke retreated, leaving powdery trails on her parka. She shook herself free from the last of it, stepping away from the pool once more, sweat flowing over her sticky skin.

Curry continued screaming.

"There you go, Sun Daughter." The being held up a finger the size of Solyana's leg. "Or perhaps we should call you Earth Daughter?"

Pressure pounded in her mind. No! She was still the Daughter of the Sun! Fear welled in her throat as her eyes bored into the twin pits of fire glaring from the creature's face.

"I've been looking for you for a long while, Earth Daughter. Perhaps you have been hiding with my other lost one—WILL YOU STOP YOUR WAILING?" The being's outburst rocked the cave and Solyana fell to the ground from the shock. He towered over Curry, and, reaching a hand in her direction, a whip of lava wormed its way from the pool and wound around the mammoth's leg.

Curry thrashed and screamed, the rocks beneath her cracking against her mighty feet. Smoke rose from her fur as the coil of wet fire dragged her, slowly at first, then faster, with purpose. Her trumpeted screams choked and gurgled as she went over the lip of the lake and under, the lava enclosing itself around her massive form. Her trunk released a final wheeze, the last part of her to be consumed.

A bubble popped in her wake, spraying the ground, and Curry was gone.

Solyana clutched her knees close to herself, mouth agape. The being bent down, his face so close to hers, she thought her skin would melt.

"What are you?" she cried, shielding her face with her arms.

"An interested party." He gave a tilted grin. "Look, the mammoth wasn't making it out of here anyway, you knew that." He stood his full height and spotted Odie's body on the floor of the cave. "Oh, there were two of you. Pity. You're going to the boy, then?"

Solyana put her hands down, grateful for his distance. "How do you know this?"

"Let's just say you're a worthy investment. And I'm good with my resources."

"*Who* are you?"

The being stopped abruptly to stare at something past Solyana. She turned but saw nothing but the cave wall.

"Not a good time, Phineas," he said. "I'm in the middle of something." He blinked and turned his pitted eyes back on her. "What is your intention with this boy, then?"

"I aim to stop the boy on the mountain from tethering the lights of the Norlos. To end the anger of the Celestials." And in so doing, save Rhuth, her people, and her home, though she said none of those aloud.

The being crouched low, studying her, and his hand leaning against his leg tapped each finger in turn. "Well, she won't come out for him herself; I suppose you'll have to do."

"Who are you talking about?"

But he stood again, liquid fire sliding down his form. "And you've ended up in one of my caves. You should count yourself lucky."

"Lucky" was not the word she would have used. She looked back to the place where Curry had gone into the lava, and anger laced her next words. "Could you have healed her instead?"

"The mammoth?" the being arched an eyebrow. "Even if I had, there was no way she could have escaped this place. It was a mercy." He extended a finger from his fist that splashed liquid fire into the pool below. Solyana's eyes followed it to a dark crag in the wall, just big enough for her small form to fit through. "You'll leave through there. Follow the lava river until you arrive at the Cave of Crystals. It's a bit on the nose, I know. But I told Phineas he could name it, and..." The being shrugged his mighty shoulders. "He's not the most creative individual. After the cave, you'll hike the rest of the way. Hope you have good shoes; it's mostly uphill."

"Phineas? But, what's *your* name?" Solyana asked again, mind whirling with the task laid before her.

"We'll speak soon, Earth Daughter, and hopefully meet, in due time." He melted back into the pool, producing a wave that encroached on the ground around her feet.

Though she was all too ready to escape the cave and its overbearing heat, she couldn't leave Odie where he lay. Burnings were the appropriate burial in Mothmar, and she could give Odie a last courtesy.

The fire took quickly, a pyre in the deepest parts of the earth. Solyana watched, pulling her scarf up her nose though sweat was slick on her face. "No one else will die for me," she said to the pyre. "I promise, Odie. This path will take no more life."

Cobbling together what she could from the supplies Curry had carried, Solyana hoisted a bag onto her shoulder and squeezed through the crack in the far side of the cave.

OWNERSHIP

PALLAH

PALLAH HIT THE FLOOR with a crunch of stiff muscles and bones. Stretching her body, she took quick account of the workings of her limbs. They were nowhere near as wasted away as they had been in the Maze; her skin had revealed again its scrapes and scars. Adrenaline pumping, she scrambled, getting her bearings, trying to right herself as she looked wildly about the room.

Dahvid sat in his chair by the fireplace, glowing embers reflected in his shock-widened eyes, his mouth agape. The half of his face nearer the fireplace twitched. Horror filled Pallah at the sight of him: markedly ragged and worn, as if he had wasted away in the last two years, neglected in favor of Pallah's care.

He couldn't talk to her here, of course. He could only communicate directly into her mind when...had he been tethered to her? No, not tethered. He'd had access to her only through their shared relationship to Tinloh, the gate that swung both ways. The thought of it made her shake, the violation of such intimacy making her want to run and never look back. She'd had every intention to murder this man when she escaped, but now? Seeing him soiled in his chair, drool dripping steadily from his lips... Dark vines grew around Pallah's heart and squeezed. Death was an escape he didn't deserve.

He shifted his head, his eyes swinging around like an echo, like he was looking for something...someone—Tinloh. He must be looking for Tinloh. Eyes flying about the room, she didn't spot him. She had to get to her smilodon before Dahvid could use him against her.

Pallah! Erval's familiar voice spoke in her mind, and she ground her teeth. She'd thought she'd missed him, but feeling yet another presence intrude into her mind only sent a series of curses out of her mouth. *Häfa, child. What happened to you?*

"Shut up!" she roared. Flinging herself into the night, Pallah stumbled onto the snow-covered ground, frigid air blasting against her skin and scraping her tightening throat. Disoriented, she righted herself. It was winter. Two years of seasons had passed. She needed a minute—just a *häfan* minute—to gather her thoughts.

Something rustled in the woods and an owl hooted in the distance. Pallah crouched, readying herself to run. Dahvid wouldn't hesitate to use Tinloh against her, and if she tried to run back to Sodur now, she would surely die, either from cold or Tinloh's claws. She had to come up with another plan, and she needed something with which to defend herself.

Her feet tingled with the beginnings of numbness as she worked her way through the snow to the smithy. She swiped at the window with her tunic to peer inside, searching for anything she could use as a weapon. Her eyes landed on the sleek double-sided axe hanging in the back.

The door was locked. Pallah found a rock protruding from the snow and dug it out with her fingers. Her hands weren't damaged here as they had been in the Maze, and she was thankful. She would never go back to that *häfan* place.

A noise drew her attention back to Freya's cottage, the windchimes rustling a melody. She took a breath, forcing frigid air into her lungs and back out again. She needed to tether Tinloh before Dahvid could. Hefting the rock in her grip, she felt for her tether, something she hadn't done in two whole years. It was like regaining a lost limb. She used the Taka Reu, knowing the Mother of the Night would be hesitant to grant her power after too many times entreating the Mother Below.

The tether did nothing but flail and flop, finding nothing to hold onto. Tinloh must not be close. Or perhaps she'd lost her ability to recognize him. The thought pierced through her soul like a hot lance. Releasing her tether, she reared back, striking the lock with the stone. Beneath the echoing clang, something shifted behind her. Pallah turned, rock in hand, as a massive smilodon crept silently toward her, blending with the snow. His incisors glistened in the moonlight, his shoulder blades rising and falling with each stealthy step.

"*Häfa!*" Pallah began to jam harder on the lock, again and again. It held firm, and Pallah turned back. Tinloh—fully-grown, two-year-old Tinloh—stalked by the owlery, his eyes unwaveringly locked on Pallah. "Tinloh!" she screamed at him, tears coming to her cheeks, sobs wracking her chest. "Tinloh, it's me!" She tried her tether again, placing a hand on the side of the smithy. With him in her sights, it was easier. Her tether tried to latch, but the Maze Dahvid had set was like a fortress. She slammed into its side until finally she broke in, her tether racing through the halls.

You sneaky tik. Dahvid's voice crooned with malice.

Get out of my head, you häfan freak! Pallah spoke through her own tether.

I thought we were connecting. We are meant to do great things together, Pallah.

Then call off Tinloh!

Oh, Pallah. You've proven to be too much. Far too much. I could put you back into the Maze. And in a flash of terror, Pallah felt her soul being momentarily yanked from her body, the vision of the Maze coming before her eyes. Then she was back, panting, eyes wild. *But I think I'd rather see what my sweet kitten can do.*

Tinloh launched at her.

Pallah dove out of the way, disconnecting her tether and scrambling to her feet. The realization coming into focus: she may die here, and by her own beast.

Pallah skidded around the smithy, catching a glint of moonlight on another window. She threw her rock and it connected, shattering the glass. Tinloh tore behind her, silent but for the soft puffs of snow that came with each stride. Shoving a few jagged pieces out of the way, Pallah scrambled inside, barely registering glass shards slicing her skin.

Back to the wall beneath the window, Pallah slunk to the floor and listened to the low rumble of Tinloh's throat as he passed by outside. He had grown so much! Even running for her life, all she could think about was how much time she had lost with him. Bleeding, Pallah slipped on the floor as she tried to run to the back of the dusty room. She hoisted the double-headed axe from its pegs on the wall. For its size, she'd expected it to be heavier, but it leapt into her hands as light as a staff made of wood.

She turned it twice, getting a feel for it. She regretted not having searched the rooms for her hatchet before she'd come outside. Tinloh paced outside the window. Dahvid wasn't forcing him through; she was safe, for now.

Warm breath condensed in front of her, the white puffs disappearing as quickly as they appeared. She didn't want to hurt him, not Tinloh. But she needed to get back to Sodur.

Why would you go back? Erval whispered.

An image of her mother and her brother flashed before her.

"My mother, and Ahren," she whispered in turn.

It is unwise for you to return.

"I'm beholden to no one, Erval." Her hands tightened around the metal weapon. "Least of all to you."

Thinking of her family almost brought her to her knees. If it had truly been two years, they would also have grown. Vámae would be finishing her duties as a Serviseer, unless she had stayed to make it a career. Was Ahren still with Yuri? She didn't even know if her mother was alive, or if her father roamed free.

A meaty paw scraped through the broken window, questing in small swipes. Pallah released a yelp as she stepped back, holding the axe out in front of her. She needed to get into Tinloh's mind, but she couldn't do it effectively while Dahvid was tethered to him. She was too weak to contest him, and were he to trap her again, she wouldn't have the will to discover a new escape. Steeling herself, she refused to give this twisted man another second of her time.

She would cut off his connection at the source.

She would kill Dahvid.

Tinloh roared, a bellowing mighty sound that rattled Pallah's bones.

Move, Pallah.

Picking up the rock she had thrown, she brought it back to the window. Tinloh was pacing, making a trail in the snow. She glanced behind her to find another window on the other side.

Shifting her weight, she twirled the axe and heard a subtle click as both heads slipped into the staff. Interesting. Eyes closed, she took a deep breath, then threw the rock through the opposite window.

The diversion did its job, Tinloh launching around the small building toward the noise.

Pallah scrambled out, the snow swallowing the thumps of her feet on the ground. Her pulse in her ears, Pallah made a mad dash back to the house.

An owl screeched overhead, the only warning Pallah got before it swooped down, white as the moon, its claws slicing through her hair and into her scalp. She let out a shout as she fell to the ground, reaching up and tearing at the bird. She could feel blood seeping onto her forehead, making its way to her eyes. The snowy owl screeched and pumped its wings into the air before striking towards her once more. Pallah stood her ground, flinging the staff in a circle. The blades emerged, taking them both by surprise and cleaving the bird in two.

Feathers and meat flopped onto the snow. She twirled the staff again, and the blades slipped back into place. Pallah used it to stand and glanced over her shoulder. She nearly lost control of every bodily function at the sight of Tinloh, charging up the hill toward her at a full tilt, hardly hindered by slippery snow.

Faster than she thought possible for her weak legs, Pallah shot through the yard and crashed through the cottage door, locking it securely behind her. It hammered into her arm with a loud *crack* as Tinloh's heavy body crashed into it. Again and again, his bulk slammed into the door, Dahvid's tether whipping Tinloh into a frenzy strong enough to force self-harm if it meant reaching his prey.

"Dahvid!" Pallah screamed, her voice laced with rage. "Release him!" In four long strides, she was in the room, glaring at his stoic face carved by shadow. The fire had sunk down to embers, leaving the waxing moon to light the room. Dahvid would see her fury on full display, and his slack face only betrayed his fear with a slight widening of his eyes, his mouth a gaping hole.

The pounding escalated, claws raking the door under the animal's full weight; the wood began to crack and splinter.

Pallah pumped the staff once, ejecting the blades. He had to know she would do it. And she would...wouldn't she?

"You leave me no choice, Dahvid," Pallah said, bringing her fury into submission.

Something on Dahvid's face changed and Pallah knew he wanted to say something. Pallah stepped forward and pressed the sharp head of the axe to Dahvid's neck. Against her better judgment, she tethered Tinloh once more. The force of his obsessive focus slammed into her as she found her way into the Maze again, bracing her legs as physical pressure attempted to push her down.

You killed Ingrid! Dahvid whined, his eyes locked on hers.

Release him, Pallah responded through the tether.

I could trap you again, right now.

Pallah dug the axe head further, a line of blood coursing slowly down the man's neck. *But could you do it in time?*

Dahvid said nothing, his mind working hard to control the cat trying to break the threshold.

Mutinous tears blurred her vision.

The entire house shook with another strong thump, and Pallah whipped her head in the direction of the door.

Let him go, she gave Dahvid one final chance. Her heart hardened in her chest as she pulled the axe up, the angle of the swing set, the muscles in her arms flexed in readiness.

No. A mighty crash rang through the house, claws scrambling over wood.

Pallah screamed and untethered from the cat, from Dahvid's voice.

Tinloh slid into the room just behind her. He crouched, then sprang.

Pallah brought the blade down with all her strength, connecting with Dahvid's neck. He kept the same vacant stare as she followed through, shearing skin, muscle, and bone. His head rolled from his crumpling body, both coming to rest on the floor.

Tinloh crashed with him, like a puppet with severed strings. A paw swiped at Pallah's tunic, barely grazing her back. It knocked her forward, on top of Dahvid's headless corpse. Shaking, she pushed herself off, holding the axe close as she stared wide-eyed at the cat on the floor. He rose, shook his fur, and blinked. Was the Maze gone? Or would she have to find her way through it again?

Pallah wiped blood from her face and carefully reached her tether into Tinloh's mind. There was still a maze, but it was less solid, less foreboding. She knew the way quickly, having escaped it herself. And with no other tether fighting against her, she was able to make it through to the very center where she found Tinloh himself. She tethered him completely, and the entire world went quiet.

Pallah counted to ten.

He was hers once more. Damaged and traumatized, but hers. She sent him joy and peace, everything in her she could muster. Anything was better than what Dahvid had forced him to endure.

She asked him to sit, and he did. She knelt beside him, Dahvid's blood steadily covering the floor.

"Do you remember me, 'Loh?"

From a silky face of mottled-white fur, his glassy blue eyes found hers, and he sniffed the air. Pallah cupped his face in her hands. Her tether strong, something about his connection was new: relief.

"I am so sorry," she whispered.

Tinloh pushed his soft head against her hand and then up toward her face, leaning into her. Pallah fell back onto her haunches and grasped him around his neck, letting the tears come, sobbing as he tucked his head into her chest.

And there they sat for some time. Beast and girl, girl and beast. Grieving and rejoicing for the time lost, for the journey taken, for the pain caused.

PATH OF BETRAYAL

SOLYANA

E ACH STEP WAS BLISTERED agony as Solyana continued her trek through the winding rock, deep in the caves. The river of lava beside her continued its steady flow. And although she'd outpaced it at first, after several hours, its steady movement came to serve as a steady reminder of her own tiring slog.

With only the soft red glow of the lava beside her, she had little else to spur her on, save the need to find her friends. Whenever Solyana closed her eyes, she saw Lone being ripped from Björg's back, heard the cry from Gamaliel's lips, felt the jolt of Curry's fear as she charged into the cave.

Tempted to blame herself, she turned her thoughts to Priestess Avi instead. Rhuth had claimed the old woman had her own motivations for Solyana's journey out of their valley. And the scrap of parchment Halina had delivered, the smilodon? It couldn't be coincidence, but it wasn't conclusive either.

A moot point now. Whatever the motives that had led them into this mess, it was now Solyana's responsibility to get them out again.

A pounding ache kept a steady beat in her head, hunger gnawing at her insides, and although she still had a half-filled waterskin, her throat remained perpetually dry. As time passed, she thought about her connection to the Mother Below. Her eyes followed the lava, as if it were an extension of the deity herself. She couldn't help but think every path she had gone down since the beginning of this journey had led to death.

Every path she had taken with the Celestials.

But things could be different now.

They had to be.

For what kind of gods would demand their Chosen fulfill their will, without giving her the ability to succeed?

Well, she supposed, if she were choosing the wrong road now, at least she would be free of this cursed responsibility.

The Celestials could raise another. Perhaps one that wouldn't betray them as she had.

GOING BACK HOME

PALLAH

PALLAH CLEANED HERSELF UP and found her things, which had been stowed away in her old room. Dahvid's body remained where it had fallen. The first time she really took in the sight of it, fear and guilt nearly choked her. But each time she walked by, the events that took place there, and the reasons behind them, settled like sediment in her soul, not with guilt or fear, but with resolution. Tinloh was hers once more, and Pallah would do whatever was needed to protect him.

A growl rumbled from Tinloh's throat. Though he was out hunting, Pallah could feel his reverberations in her chest. Tethering him with energy from the Mother brought a stronger, more intimate connection. Tinloh sneezed and Pallah grinned. It had never been so clear with the Celestials. Pack on her back, hatchet strapped to her hip, staff in her hand, Pallah stepped out of the cabin and into the morning light. She drew up the hood of her cloak, stamping her mukluks over the cold ground, ready to leave.

Freya's hunched form, swathed in a heavy, colorful shawl, shuffled through the tree line, a tawny barn owl leading the way.

Pallah thought to run, but only for a moment. The old woman could not harm her, not now. She punched the staff out, the blades appearing with a scrape of metal against metal. She tugged on her tether, and by the time Freya stood a few paces from her, Tinloh was at Pallah's side.

"What have you done, child?" Freya's eyes were dark as her owl landed on her shoulder, its yellow eyes trained on Tinloh.

"What I needed to do," Pallah said. "And I have no need to do anything more." Pallah didn't seek to kill, though she couldn't deny this new tether she had with Tinloh laced the edges of her consciousness with something dark. Whatever it brought with it—a lust, a greed—she would have to be careful not to coax it to life too often.

"Dahvid." Freya's mouth went slack; the fingers wrapped around her walking stick twitched. She pushed past Pallah into the small house. "You *tik*!" Freya's voice came only slightly muffled from within the wooden walls. "You evil *tik*! *Häfa to Hekla!* What have you done? Curse that *häfan* mother of yours for ever sending you here! Curse you, and your *häfan* cat!"

Pallah left the woman sobbing in her hut, cursing Pallah's name and the day she was born. A twinge of guilt whispered into her soul, but one look at Tinloh silenced it. She would not harbor regret, nor would she coddle remorse. Pallah had no room for the past, only thoughts for what lay ahead.

With Tinloh at her side, Pallah stepped into the woods and set off for Sodur.

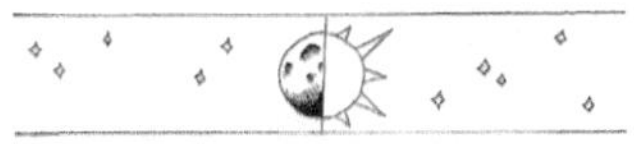

It was civil twilight two days later, the sun disappearing behind the mountains when Pallah eventually broke through Shadow Wood and into the clearing of Leif's cabin. Taking in the sight of it, Pallah's mind emptied of thought. The cabin where she had spent her final meal with Vil and her friends was now a charred shell of what it had been. A few hares bounded between the blackened, scattered logs, their inquisitive noses twitching.

Creeping around the remains, Pallah felt Tinloh's lust for the rabbits. When had Dahvid fed him last? She kept him close, unwilling to sully her name with the Taka Reu a second time. Her mind cycled with hundreds of hypotheses: perhaps the fire had been an accident, Rolf or Kristjan losing control of their Heitt; maybe Leif had stepped away from a cookfire, or—Pallah's heart stuttered as she thought of what Chief Olafur and his council would have done if they'd found the growing group of Taka Reu.

The destruction did not look fresh; there was no ash, and everything rang with cold as it whistled with wind. Chilled to the bone, Pallah pulled her cloak closer around her. She would find them; they would be on Eldfall.

Tinloh was impossible to hide now. Pallah was thankful to be trekking during a time of day when everyone would be inside, readying for sleep. Nevertheless, as she skirted the edge of Austur, she billowed out her cloak, attempting to obscure her sabertoothed cat, imploring him to keep low to the ground. They made quick work of the first village and were about to launch across the floating bridge of the Vatino when she spotted a few fishing boats coming in from a day's work.

Pallah redirected, plotting out a route. She would have to go around, into The Pines, then circle the northern tip of the Vatino before coming south into White Wood and scaling Eldfall. She bit her lip, thinking. She could wait for the fishermen to leave. But where?

Pallah kept her stride long and confident, Tinloh's muscled frame at her side, making her way to the Temple. Twilight in full bloom, the eastern side of the stone building fell into shadow, and she found an inlet between the towering parapets to hide.

Leaning against the wall, she pulled her pack off her back, placed her staff to the side, and took a few deep swallows from her water-skin. She had meant to lean the staff against the Temple, but when she'd let it go, it stood, vertical and without support, of its own accord. She raised her eyebrows and corked her waterskin.

A creak of hinges sounded to her left and Pallah lowered the skin, pressing her body into the stone. The parapet kept her hidden as voices breached the early evening.

"It's all I could get tonight." The whisperer was female and delicate. "They're watching me a lot more closely now. They've begun to notice my absences, and the missing scrolls."

"You're an angel! I told you you could do it." The voice was deep and masculine.

Pallah couldn't breathe. She didn't have to peek around the stone to know who the voices belonged to.

"Can you get away now?" the man spoke again.

"I don't know if—"

The girl's voice dropped away, replaced by the snuffling, wet patterns of lips on lips. Pallah's heart dropped from her chest.

"V, stop it!" the girl said with a breathy giggle.

"I don't want you down here when we begin." More kissing, a deep breath. "I want you beside me. If things get violent, I can protect you."

"I can protect myself. But..." The girl let out a sigh. "I'll try. Give me five minutes?"

"That's my girl."

Pallah did not move. She did not breathe. For five minutes, Tinloh pressed tight against her legs, she waited for one or both of them to walk around the stone structure and find her. They never did. Finally, the door creaked open again and Pallah heard the shuffling of feet over snow as Vámae and Vil walked down the path to the floating bridge of the Vatino, arm in arm.

THE CAVE OF CRYSTALS

SOLYANA

TRUDGING ALONG IN THE unfathomable heat, Solyana tried to tally the hours she'd lost in the caves. With no light other than the molten river to guide her, she continued in its hazy gloom for unknown hours--perhaps days. The Celestials were lost to her, or she to them; she wasn't quite sure.

You're much easier to spot, now that we've met.

Solyana stopped, arms and legs rigid in the sweltering passage. The voice had come from inside her head, and it sounded much like the lava being from before.

I'm not known for my patience, child. His voice was familiar and strange, ancient and new. *So, I assume you can walk and talk at the same time.*

"Will you at least tell me your name?" Solyana croaked.

I am Erval, and the pleasure is all mine, Miss...

"Solyana," she said, wondering if she were descending into insanity. Perhaps she had heat exhaustion. "Solyana Marusda."

What a lovely name.

Solyana kept walking.

Erval cleared his throat. *And where exactly do you hail from?*

She thought of the chief from Takanah and adjusted her answer. "Far southwest of here, there's a valley surrounded by mountains and hills too steep and icy to climb. Kana Ocean is to the west and Skrim Sea is due south. Eldfall Mountain hems us from the rest of the country."

Does it now? Hmm...what you describe sounds like a place I was told of long ago. Yet, when I searched for it, found nothing. Do you get many visitors?

What had Solyana to lose in talking to this man? She had nothing left, so she answered him. "None. And if anyone leaves, they don't return. We've had blizzards at the full moon, until recently, when they seemed to come for no reason at all. And they've grown to be more than blizzards. No one can travel without fear."

Any other weather phenomena?

"Well." Solyana stopped, uncorked her waterskin, and took a sip. "Yes, actually. Though, I suppose I never saw it as strange until leaving. Our valley is always shrouded in cloud. I only truly saw the sun once we'd left."

Erval was silent for a full minute as Solyana continued her trek forward. Had he left? "Erval?"

Have you ever met anyone by the name of Pallah?

Solyana's lips twisted in thought. There was something familiar about that name. She knew almost everyone in her valley, and Pallah wasn't one of them. "No." But she *had* seen that name somewhere before! Her fingers searched the pockets of her parka, digging around until her skin felt the dry chafe of parchment. Heart thudding in her chest, Solyana pulled it from its hiding spot and unfurled it. She squinted in the dim glow of the lava, trying to make out the words she had read before and had disregarded, forgotten.

...she has been part of the Taka Reu, and from the smilodon attack on our village, to the scroll going missing from Lóthkol; Pallah has been involved in all of it. He claims she'd even kept a smilodon cub for herself. I can't imagine anyone being so selfish.

Solyana lowered the torn scroll, her heat-addled brain making connections slower than she'd hoped.

Ah. Erval let out a chuff of laughter. *Pray tell, where did you find that tasty little journal entry?*

Solyana considered lying but couldn't find the strength to do so. "Back home," she said, the words barely sliding out of her mouth. "At the Temple Celestial." Her feet dragged over rock.

Hm, she wouldn't be working in a temple, surely. Not after all this time. Erval seemed to be speaking to himself. *But she could have adopted a new name, a new body, a new life... Oh, that clever girl. She's there, isn't she? It's the last place—she must be there!*

Dark laughter slithered smoothly through Solyana's inner ears.

Retribution, redemption, restoration... Erval sighed and its softness gave Solyana a picture of a man leaning back in a chair, crossing his arms behind his head. *All for that brother of hers. It's pathetic, really.*

The brother, the one Rhuth spoke of. No, no, it couldn't be true. Solyana wiped her head, dripping with sweat. Determined not to think on it, she refused to care who had truly sent her on this quest; her sole focus was surviving this part of it.

"How are you...talking to me?" She moved to change the subject.

Through a simple device called a finnevel. It amplifies my tether. Phineas made me a new one about a decade ago. You wear it like a spyglass, so I can walk around or even lay down. It's a marked improvement!

Solyana didn't have the energy or the understanding to fully comprehend what Erval was saying. There were several words she had never heard before. But the mention of his tether made her gut turn over. His tether to *what*?

But back to Pallah. Surely, you've met her. She's obsessed with her brother, getting him back. I had to hear about it, endlessly. I would've just got him for her, if it would have shut her up, but...that's just not how the Mother works, now, does she?

Solyana stopped walking, the truth staring her in the face. It didn't matter, she told herself. She didn't want to know. But Erval ambled on, oblivious or uncaring as to the affect the conversation was having on Solyana.

I should have seen it then, her obstinance, but I was a soft-hearted fool in those days. She used a charm, as some would call it. The more educated would call it a curse: Stasis. Does it protect someone that trusts you? Sure, but the catch! You see, no one thinks about the cost. The catch is, you don't get to decide where. Isn't that interesting? They simply get suspended forever in who-knows-where. And the person who spoke the curse doesn't even get to free their victim! No. They have to find a person bound by prophecy to do it.

"Prophecy..." Solyana heard herself say.

Indeed. Every Taka Reu curse is coupled with a prophecy, ready to break it. Funny, isn't it? It's almost as if the Celestials and the Taka Reu have to play by some sort of rules. Silly, really.

"How do you know all of this?"

Erval chuckled. *Oh child, I have lived far too long not to.*

Solyana licked her cracked lips. If this was the same man that had formed into the lava being, he had seen her connect to the Taka Reu. He had instructed her and proven himself to be knowing. Jonas hadn't been turning up anything definitive in his scrolls, perhaps it was time she asked someone else. "I was told I could use the Taka Reu and the Celestial's power in tandem. That I could borrow from Below what I couldn't find Above."

And who told you that?

"The priestess of my villages." Solyana took a breath, knowing once she said the woman's name, she wouldn't be able to ignore reality any longer. "Priestess Avi."

Erval fell silent, and Solyana continued walking, following the slow roll of the lava river beside her. If he would just deny it, if he could assure her the priestess wasn't the same person as this Pallah, then—

Avi. He made a clicking sound with his tongue.

Solyana halted, nausea turning in her gut.

Did this Avi give you anything? To prove to this 'light-tethering boy' you are who you say you are?

Fingers finding the hatchet still strapped to her hip, Solyana swallowed. "Yes."

And does this Priestess Avi have a penchant for beautiful things?

Solyana recalled the hallway on the second story of the Temple Celestial, with all its canvas paintings, plants, and cluttered trinkets. The woman's quarters and its beautiful furniture, stuffed creatures, and candles suspended above. "Yes," she admitted once more.

Listen to me carefully, Solyana. I have known this Priestess Avi for a long time, back when she went by the name of Pallah. She is a deceiver. A liar. And a murderer.

Knees beginning to shake, Solyana reached for the cave wall for support, her heart squeezing so tight in her chest, she thought she might faint. She took in some water and wiped her brow.

She has done many terrible things in her efforts to discover a more powerful source for her Gift. The Celestials were not enough, then the Taka Reu fell short, as well. She desires total control, and she's willing to use—or kill—anyone to get what she wants.

I was with her when she learned to tether the cloud and fog, I was with her when she learned to suppress others' Gifts. Are the Gifts in your home disappearing? Erval chuckled darkly and continued, leaving the question unanswered. *How do you think she has re-mained hidden from me all these years? My finnevel cannot find what I cannot feel. Even travelling, your valley is hidden to the eye of man. She has learned to conceal herself well, learned to deceive on a scale, I must say, surprises even me.*

Solyana couldn't breathe. Erval's words, coupled with the humid air of the cave, filled her lungs with lead. She pressed her back to the uneven wall, sliding down it until she was on the ground, trying and failing to steady her vision. "But the boy—he has been tethering the light for centuries. He angered the Celestials long ago!" Denial, she knew, but it was all she had.

Wake up! Stasis keeps a person in complete suspension. He's been asleep! This is all Pallah's doing. You really bought this 'boy who tethers light' story? How did she really convince you? What leverage does she have?

Every part of her shook. Rhuth had been telling the truth entirely. Whatever it was that had kept her sister's facial scar from appearing didn't matter. It was her Little Fyug, and Solyana had failed to listen. She began to cry, everything inside of her warring: one part surrendering, the other wanting to fight, go back, and destroy this woman who took so much from her, from her family, from her people.

Something of value, I see, Erval said soothingly. *Well, know that until she gets what she wants, she will not dispose of whomever it is. Pallah is patient, something I should have gleaned from her when I had the chance.*

"I should go back," Solyana said between gasps of hot air. "I need to get back to my sister!"

Ahh, well. In that case, she would just do to you what, I assume, she's done to the others.

Solyana waited, blinking against the heat, afraid of the answer to come.

Kill you, and wait for the next one marked to fulfill the same prophecy. It only takes a generation for most people to forget what has happened before. And if she's the priestess, she controls the scrolls. She controls history.

The implications of his speech stuck in Solyana's mind like the *aska* to her face. Had all of it been contrived? The scar itself a simple conjuring trick by the priestess's hand? Hopelessness threatened to pull her under. They had been so wrong, so deceived. But then...Solyana stood, pushing her legs faster than before.

"And what if I don't believe you?"

Have I not given enough evidence that I know this woman? Our goals are aligned in this, Solyana! You are here to fulfill a prophecy; I am here to find Pallah. Let us work together and I will help you along the way.

"I'm listening." The passageway grew more narrow, the flow of the river slowing.

You bring the boy on the mountain to me. Pallah will come out of hiding once she knows I have him. And I will make sure, whomever she has kept under lock and key is returned to you.

"You promise me?"

Cross my heart.

Solyana stuttered to a halt, the cave at a dead end. The river of lava beside her leveled off into a pool that seeped out in cracks running beneath the wall and into the earth below. Fear—no, anger—filled her. "And now you lead me here just to trap me?"

Have you listened to nothing I've said? We're a team! You must use the Taka Reu. I'll show you.

"I have nothing to use! I have Tala and Heitt." She began to pace. "And I haven't been in the sun for a long time."

Erval gave a light laugh. *You don't need the sun any longer. Use the ground beneath your feet. You are even closer to the Mother Below here. She will imbue you, fully and surely. Reach down.*

Solyana leaned down and opened her palms to the cave floor.

Good girl. Now your Heitt is strong enough to melt rock, just like this lava here beside you. The Cave of Crystals will be directly on the other side.

Solyana closed her eyes and dug deep.

Go ahead...light it up.

Deceived, betrayed, and sent on a journey that had never been meant to succeed, Solyana released her rage. A scream ripped through her throat, hands going from floor to cave wall. A blast of fire roared like twin pillars from her palms, obeying her every command and then more. The Taka Reu acted on its own, melting and destroying, riding her fury like it was born of it.

Erval laughed.

Solyana hardly heard him over the noise of the roaring flame and the pounding of blood in her ears. She was powerful, more powerful than she could have ever imagined to be. The feeling of pure control took over her senses as she watched a hole slowly appear in the rock, peeling open as if it had been made of parchment. Though her body should have burnt to ash, it stayed protected, kept safe by the Mother Below.

Closing her fists, Solyana stopped the fire and it obeyed, though reluctantly. It wanted more—*she* wanted more. But the hole was large enough to walk through, and her breath was coming in short gasps, her body suddenly exhausted.

I told you; we are a team.

Panting on the floor of the cave, Solyana saw powdery smoke slip back into the cracks of ground, as if it were being sucked away by something on the other side. But it didn't restrain her as it had before—it was merely present.

"If my people knew how powerful this was..." Solyana shook her head, her very core thrumming with life. "We would not be perishing as we have been."

Erval hummed his agreement. *Your people perish from blizzards contrived by Pallah, a woman bent on wielding ever more power, and only to serve herself. She's been knowingly sacrificing your people for generations, Solyana. But together, we have the means to stop her.*

This thought drove her to her feet, fully set on stealing this boy from the mountain and drawing the deceiver from her hole. Solyana slipped through the breach.

The cave was something of a cathedral, its crystalline walls spotted with sparkling clusters of luminescent purple rock. Solyana ran her fingers over the dim light and thought of Jonas. He would have loved this. She broke a piece of the rock from the wall, intent on showing him when they met again.

The cave's ceiling stretched high above her head, a set of stones ascending, looking too much like stairs to be coincidence. "Did you do this?" she asked Erval.

Do you think nature creates such things by itself? Follow these stairs and find the end of the light. You are growing weak. You must rest and regain your strength. I will speak with you again.

Solyana took the stairs, leaving behind the cave and its shimmering walls. She pushed on through the darkness, her hands along the rough rock, guiding her along the hewn path in front of her. Exhausted and alone, she steeled herself and continued ahead. It didn't matter *how* she made it to her destination, only that she did.

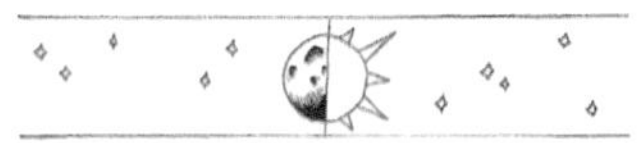

One foot in front of the other, light pricked in the distance, and Solyana stumbled her way up what became true steps. The light grew as she got closer, the air becoming cooler until fresh wind brushed her face with its chill. Her strength faded entirely as she crossed the threshold, collapsing into the sweet snow falling beneath a pale sun.

Shuffling noises and murmurs reached her, but she hadn't the strength to even lift her head. Through closing eyes, she saw a few mukluks approach before unconsciousness whisked her away.

THE REBELLION

PALLAH

P ALLAH WAITED PATIENTLY FOR Vámae and Vil to cross the Vatino Sea and disappear into White Wood before stepping out from the shadow of the Temple. Her axe-staff in her hand, Tinloh keeping time at her feet, Pallah stalked after them.

Ready to talk now? Erval whispered in her mind as she passed from the sea to the perimeter of Eldfall.

Pallah staggered against a birch tree, one of hundreds that made up White Wood, lining either side of the Vatino. "It's not a good time," she snapped at him, but her heart wasn't in it. In truth, she desired connection, she yearned for someone to see her. "Though I'm glad to hear your voice."

Thought I'd lost you. And even while Pallah's mind screamed that Erval was trespassing in her mind much like Dahvid, she didn't care.

He missed her. And that was enough.

She pushed herself from the tree and continued. "I killed someone, Erval." She didn't know why she said it, but the words hung in the air, and for a moment, she feared he would leave.

It gets easier.

Disconcerted or relieved, she couldn't decide, her feet following the familiar paths up the mountain on their own. "You've killed, too?"

Erval chuckled. *Yes, sweet child, I have.*

"Why?"

Why did you kill? he directed back at her.

"Because he was a threat to someone I love, and he always would be."

Ah, well. That's a noble enough reason.

"Was it the same for you?" A fresh wave of need pulsed through her mind. She had to know. "Did you kill to protect?"

Any death inflicted by my hand has had purpose. Whether to advance a cause or protect a legacy, there is reason. I do not kill needlessly.

"To protect a legacy?" Pallah looked down at the massive cat beside her, barely making a sound as he walked. "Not one you love?"

My heart holds little love for others, Pallah, Erval admitted, hesitation in his voice. *Little, but not nothing. You, however, have much potential. More than I've seen in some time.*

Heart thudding, Pallah wanted to believe him. But pulling tight the tether between her and Tinloh, she couldn't help but feel like a colt on spindly legs. Tinloh's mind was foreign to her, her tether brittle and stretched too thin. Her fingers curled in anger. Two years using Tala should have made her strong and experienced, but instead she was weak, struggling just to stand.

"I'm nowhere near where I should be."

I can help with that.

A rumble of voices rode along on the sharp wind that cut through her tunic. Pallah halted and crouched low, one hand on Tinloh's back. Peering up through the layers of trees and brush, she could barely make out the mass of forms on the plateau. Vil had accrued an *army*.

A crunch of snow snapped Pallah's eyes to the side as Issha stepped out from behind a tree. Pallah held her breath from the shadows. Though her tether to Tinloh was weak, she demanded he be still. He obeyed, but she could feel a growl rumble in his chest.

Issha's hair had grown; half of it was shaved while the other half had been braided close then formed a dark cloud that filtered the light of the moon. She cocked her head to the side and crouched to match Pallah.

"Is that you, Pallah?" Issha whispered.

Eyes wide, heart thudding in her chest, Pallah hesitated. There was no telling what had happened with this group over the last two years. The last correspondence she'd had from them had told her to stay away.

"If it is you, you shouldn't be here."

Pallah peeked over the side of the bush to find Issha staring straight at her. "It's good to see you, too."

Issha crouched low and jogged to Pallah's side, stopping short at the sight of Tinloh. She fell to her side in the snow. "*Häfa!* He's huge!"

Pallah grinned and reached over Tinloh's head to help Issha up.

"I see Vil wasted no time pouncing on my sister," Pallah bit as the group on the plateau spoke in garbled waves of sound.

"He's using her, like he uses everyone." Issha paused and peered back at the group.

"What do you mean? What happened?"

Issha's words came tumbling out of her mouth like a confession. "Things got bad after you left. With the council searching for you, they started sniffing around Sodur for more clues to your whereabouts. They found Leif's cabin and all the scrolls we had stolen, everything since the beginning. They burned it to the ground."

"Oh no." Pallah shook her head.

"Since then, Vil's goals shifted." Issha glanced at the group through the trees. "It went from freedom of religion to counter oppression. He wants to stamp the Temple out, overrun them." She shook her head. "By itself, that's not *so* bad. But he intends to do it with force, and take down anyone in his way. He claims it will please the Mother Below."

"He's starting a rebellion," Pallah whispered.

"Exactly. And the others ate it up. Even Karav; *especially* Karav. We'd always planned on making the Taka Reu accessible to all, but this? Forcing it down people's throats? That was never the plan."

"What do they plan on doing to the people in the Temple? My mother is in the infirmary there." Her heart hitched. "Right? Is she still alive?"

Issha nodded, placing a hand on Pallah's arm. "She's there, but she shouldn't be. At least, not tonight. Vil has said anyone present will be cut down. I don't know what to do; I don't know how to stop it."

Chills rushed over Pallah's limbs at Issha's words. Ahren would stand up for the Temple Celestial. He would protect their mother. He would get in their way. "Where is Ahren?"

"Vil!" someone erupted from the back of the cluster of people, their long strides beneath a dark cloak cutting a line through the gathered hoard. Pallah knew the voice, but couldn't believe her eyes. Her brother had grown; a boy no longer.

Pallah stood and Issha was beside her in sudden alarm. "I didn't know he was here, Pal, I promise!"

Pallah rushed from tree to bush until she was directly behind the mass of moonlit bodies, Tinloh keeping pace beside her.

"Oh, hello, Ahren." Vil stood atop a large boulder, flanked by Vámae and Karav, who were portraits of shock and arrogance. Vil spoke down his nose at Ahren's approach. "I've told you before and I'll tell you again: I don't know where Pallah is. She's probably dead."

Issha was at Pallah's side again, a hand on her shoulder in a plea to wait.

"Let me go to my brother!" Pallah hissed.

"Please, just listen." Issha's eyes held more fear than when the girl had stood before a manic grizzly.

"That's not why I'm here!" Ahren lowered the hood of his cloak and stepped into the circle of people gone silent. "You stole one sister from me, you won't take another. Vámae, we're leaving."

All heads turned to the girl on Vil's right, whose mouth opened and closed like a landed fish. "Ahren, you shouldn't be here."

"No, *you* shouldn't be here, Vámae. There is nothing for you here with these people. And it's time to stop fooling about."

"How do you know what we stand for?" Vil crossed his arms, a placating smile spreading over his face. His hair was shorter than it used to be, and his cornflower blue eyes flashed in the flames held high by the group before him. "I don't remember inviting you into our fold. Have you been snooping?" His eyes invited the hoard of people to join in his fun and they laughed, boisterous and echoing. It drifted into the valley below.

"Yes," Ahren admitted plainly.

Silence blanketed the mountainside like early morning snowfall.

Pallah's knuckles paled against her metal staff.

"I told the council what was brewing here on Eldfall." Ahren turned a slow circle, his face coming into view for the first time. His eyes held deep shadows, and his brows pulled together.

"Ahren, stop," Pallah whispered into the night. Issha shifted beside her, fingers curled, palms parallel to the ground.

"The scrolls going missing, Vámae's lengthy disappearances, the amount of people crossing the Vatino to hike up Eldfall..." He shook his head. "They know you're not all hunting. Now, they're willing to talk terms with you. But only"—Ahren raised a finger—"if Vámae comes down with me. If I come back alone, it's not going to go kindly."

Vil stepped off his boulder, arms swinging like a child. "And what if"—he leaned close, nose to nose with Ahren—"you don't come back at all?"

Pallah was through the hoard of people in less than five steps, Tinloh pressed close to her side, straining against his tether. Rotating the staff, its twin axe heads snapped into place. She stood beside Ahren.

"Back off," she bit, her chest heaving.

"Pallah!" The shake in Ahren's voice betrayed the boy he used to be, but Pallah kept her eyes on the snake before her. Vil glared, his eyes revealing nothing about her reappearance. He stayed where he was.

"I said back off!" Pallah used the tip of her staff to shove Vil, and he stumbled back, eyes wide and on the smilodon beside her. Now, with a gap formed between the two men, Pallah stepped into it.

"Here to join us, Pal?" Vil's eyes shifted to hers, his lips trying and failing to curve back into his sanguine smile. "I've missed you."

Vámae came to stand beside Vil, pulling his hand into her own, eyes scanning Pallah as if searching for imperfections. "Finally gracing us with your presence, Pallah?"

"He's using you, Vámae." Pallah shook her head. "And he just threatened Ahren!"

"Ahren is a child; he shouldn't even be here." Vámae tugged Vil closer to herself. "Vil was just trying to scare him"—she looked pointedly at their brother—"into going back home!"

"It's so sad to see what you've become," Pallah said pityingly.

Vámae's chin jerked upward. "Go back to wherever you've been hiding for the last two years. No one has missed you."

The injustice of it coursed heat through Pallah's veins, and Tinloh fought to break free of her hold. Eyes darting around for something to ground her, she spotted Karav, still standing on the boulder, arms crossed, braids falling on either side of her chest.

A memory flashed through Pallah's mind of the first time Karav had taught her about tethering. How she had allowed her tether to grow lax until Tinloh had filled Pallah's mind, and she had felt the cub's warmth and happiness. Karav had warned her then, such was the path to the cat slaying Pallah in her sleep.

Or slaying someone else.

Perhaps it was time to let Tinloh lead.

Ahren tugged on her arm, pulling her back to the present. "We should go," he told Pallah. "I'll protect you."

"No," Vil commanded, extricating himself from Vámae's hold. He breathed in, a rolling smoke seeping through the ground at his feet. It climbed his body, filling his eyes with darkness. "Neither of you are getting off this mountain."

He crossed his arms as Kristjan, Rolf, and Leif came level with him, their eyes filled with the same pooling black.

Vil pointed. "Take them."

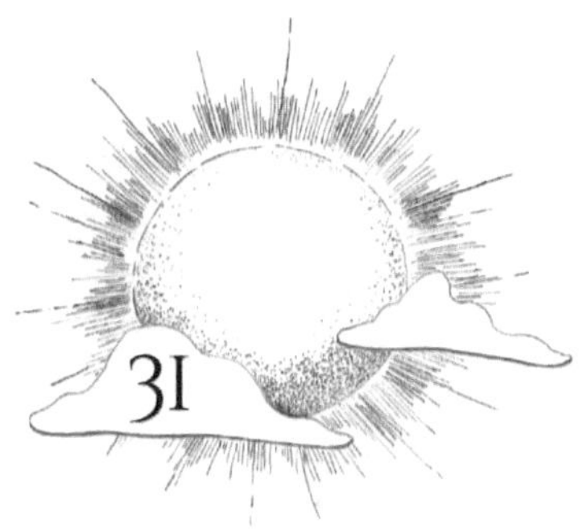

THE CITY OF ENDIRINN

SOLYANA

SOLYANA WOKE WITH A start, her breath coming out in a burst as she launched herself upright. Her head pounded against the back of her eyes as they squinted against the morning light. Where was she?

In bed. She looked around her. The most comfortable bed she'd ever been in, plush and pillowed. Flowers and greenery were strewn about her in a concentric pattern, as if she were their source. Her fingers at her temple, she felt something crowning her head. Pulling it free from the loose curls of sweet-smelling hair around her face, she produced a metal crown. It appeared to be delicately woven by a Malmur Fera, the emblems of the Gifts coupled at the center. The wire twisted like branches and leaves.

She placed it on a small table next to her bed, eyes wide in wonder at her surroundings. Wooden planks lined the walls, and great panes of glass on the ceiling welcomed the sun's rays. There was one window swathed in a gauzy fabric, dimming the incandescence to a comfortable glow.

Bones creaking as she moved, Solyana swung her legs off the side of the bed and stood. Someone had changed her clothes. Looking down her body, arms outstretched, she examined the white, airy tunic. The hem kissed the floor and the sleeves hid her fingertips, the edges elegantly embroidered.

Padding to the window cloudy with condensation, she wiped it away evenly with a swipe of her arm.

She gasped.

A thriving city lay before her, lit by a midday sun. Throngs of people traded and bartered in the square. A group of bards strummed their instruments on a street corner, drawing a gaggle of children that danced and twirled.

Her eyes searched the grounds as fear began its clawing way into her heart. This wasn't Takanah, was it? But no, she took a breath to steady herself. Wherever she was, it was lit by the Father of the Day, burning and bright. Deep inside, she felt a belonging, a peace. The grounds of the courtyard before her held no wayward creatures, there were no warriors with painted eyes.

A group of colorfully swathed youths passed below her window, their long white-blonde hair wrapping them like scarves to stay the cold. Solyana blinked, recognizing the members of Rahgah Voh's tribe. The fear returned. They had ceased to believe she was the Celestial's Chosen, though could she blame them? She shook her head to herself, her fingers finding the ends of her wavy hair. She had done what needed doing. And she would fulfill their beloved prophecy. She would bring the green.

Her eyes returned to the festive grounds, so unlike her desolate home under constant cloud. This place was larger by far, and sprawling. Snow was evenly piled out of the roadways, clear and clean for customer, cattle, and cart. This city had no blizzards of destruction brought on by a mad priestess. This city was not home.

Then she spotted a head moving amongst the others, confidently striding into the building beneath her. All worry slid from her mind as Gamaliel opened the door below and slipped inside.

Solyana's eyes burned as she turned from the window, a smile wide on her face. Racing across the room, she flung the door open, stopping short before crashing into a small woman in a gray Serviseer uniform.

"Oh dear!" The gray-haired woman jumped but recovered with a soft smile. "We are so glad to see you awake and well, Daughter of the Sun."

Her thoughts only for Gamaliel, Solyana wanted nothing more than to extricate herself from this woman's presence. "Thank you," she said quickly, "but I'm sorry, I really need to—" She tried to step around the woman. The Serviseer barred her path.

"I know you must have many questions," she said, folding her hands in front of her tunic. "And we will answer them, in time. But for now, we ask that you remain in your room."

Solyana blinked, her focus narrowing on the woman in front of her. "Excuse me?" Her heart thudded in her chest.

"There are many things to do, and in such a short time. Now that you're awake, we will start the purification process tomorrow."

"You can't keep bringing that dog in here," came a distant voice from the floor below.

Solyana strained to see around the Serviseer, but the woman was undeterred. "Do you have everything to your liking?" she asked.

"He's a wolf." Gamaliel's low timbre drifted up from below.

"Yes." Solyana nodded quickly. "Everything is wonderful, but I need to—"

Vinur crashed up the stairs, sped past the Serviseer, and launched into Solyana's arms.

"Vinur!" Solyana tried to recover her balance as he licked her face, his claws scratching at her white tunic. "Hi, boy! Calm down! I'm okay!" She grinned, burying her face into his fur.

"You're okay." Gamaliel's voice came only seconds before he was drawing her from Vinur's greeting and into his arms. He lifted and spun her once before setting her back down. "You're okay!" As if finally believing the words he had been repeating to himself for some time. Gamaliel began to cry. He tipped his head into her shoulder, hands gripping her upper arms.

"Oh, Gam." Solyana pulled her arms from his hold and hugged him around the neck, hoping the ferocity in her embrace conveyed what her face could not. For even in this moment of intimacy, she could never tell her best friend all that had transpired in the caves. He must never know of Erval, of the Taka Reu, of the smokey substance that had nearly consumed her.

For now, she was simply grateful he was alive and well, and that he was here with her.

He pulled away, holding her at arm's length, and Solyana drank him in, every aspect of his face, his golden-brown eyes and the sweetness in them. Something unnamed blossomed inside, a feeling she wished would sweep her away and cocoon her against the outside world.

"We searched for days. But I knew the Celestials wouldn't let me lose you, not after bringing us through so much." He rubbed his thumb along her jaw, hand cupping the back of her head. "And when I found you there, lying in the snow…" He took a shuddering breath.

Closer to him—that's all she wanted to be. She pressed her hands to either side of his face. He'd found time to shave, and she pressed the backs of her fingers to his face. "I'm here now." She tipped her face to his and he leaned in.

"Ahem!" The Serviseer's arms were crossed, fingers tapping impatiently on her upper arm. "Stop that!" She gave each of them a soft thwack on the arm. "She is to be purified!" She whispered it, as though it were a secret.

Gamaliel righted himself, a blush creeping over his cheeks. "Purified?" he asked.

"You have come to fulfill the prophecy, have you not?"

"Yes." Solyana closed her eyes, wishing she could just be a girl of sixteen for a few seconds longer.

"Well then, you will ascend in nine days, after a period of purification. We have several candidates waiting to give you their Gift. It appears you only lack Fera."

Cold dread seeped through Solyana, as if she had fallen into Vatino Sea. "I need no other Gift," she said, feeling Gamaliel's eyes on her.

The Serviseer looked back and forth between them before settling with a knowing smile. "Seer Brotnur has assured us he detected only Heitt and Tala."

Blinking back disbelief, Solyana stared at the woman. "A Seer?"

"Why, yes." The woman gave a smug grin and tilt of her chin. "He is the last."

"*Was*," Gamaliel said excitedly. "Was the last."

The woman faltered. "Yes, well. There are rumors, of course. The boy you brought apparently carries Seer blood as well." She waved the news away with a flick of her hand.

Solyana had to stifle a cry. "Jonas?"

"Yes!" Gamaliel gave her another squeeze. "He's having the time of his life here. I'll explain later."

"Regardless," the woman continued crisply, "you will stay put, Solyana. Your friends are well cared for here in Endirinn."

"You said her purification starts tomorrow. Can't she see the city today?" Gamaliel asked, though Solyana could sense he was not truly asking; he would get her out one way or another.

The woman twisted her thin lips. "We have a great influx of people coming into Endirinn tonight and tomorrow. Many peoples of Mothmar will be present for Skaer Sky, the conclusion of the annual Norlos, and witness the Daughter of the Sun's ascension," she motioned toward Solyana. "We need to be vigilant, as there are many different adherents to many...different," she emphasized, "beliefs."

Gamaliel's chest puffed out marginally and his back straightened. "She'll be safe with me. No harm will come to her."

The old woman rolled disparaging eyes. "Be back here by the time the Norlos appears," she grumbled as she shuffled away.

Gamaliel took Solyana by the hand and headed toward the stairs.

"Wait! Where are my things?" Solyana asked over her shoulder.

"We've laundered them. They're hanging in your room," said the Serviseer halfway down the hall.

Solyana took a minute to change, leaving the circlet behind. She didn't need to draw any more attention than she already had.

Gamaliel practically tugged her from the building, babbling the entire way. He was happy. And for the moment, his happiness was enough to lift them both.

PHYLLIR THE FRAIL

PALLAH

"I ssha!" Pallah roared as she kept her axe-staff raised. She would not allow Tinloh full control, not when Ahren was so close.

Leif held a butcher's cleaver in his hand, his eyes dark as pitch, his face holding nothing of the tender man she used to know. Flames burst to life in the palms of Kristjan and Rolf, veins on their arms bulging, expressions ugly and unrecognizable.

The group of Taka Reu surrounding Pallah, Ahren, and Tinloh pressed closer, weapons drawn.

Vil's hands filled with ropes of water, his Vatin Fera on display. "Issha's not—" His jaw slackened, and his arms dropped to his sides. Water sloshed to the ground, wetting the snow around him.

"Go, Pallah!" Issha stood at the back of the group, hand outstretched toward Vil.

Everyone seemed frozen in place as Issha's Fera brought their ever-charismatic leader to his knees. Pallah grasped Ahren's hand and tugged him away, pushing and shoving distracted bodies until they were free and stumbling headlong down Eldfall Mountain.

"What about Vámae?" Ahren cried from beside Pallah.

"She's chosen her path!" Pallah kept her tether tight on Tinloh, still thin and brittle after his time with Dahvid. A spear whistled past her shoulder and embedded into the snow before her. Pallah tripped, sprawling out, hitting hidden rocks in the snow.

"Pallah!" Ahren was at her side, pulling her up.

Pallah blinked, something like vertigo affecting her, surroundings suddenly muffled and pulling far away. Something was trying to push her tether off; *that* snapped her to clarity. Issha stumbled to her side, chest heaving. She pulled the spear from the ground and tossed it to Ahren, who held it awkwardly.

"I think Karav is trying to get Tinloh!" Pallah said, picking up her speed again. "We need to get out of range!" It came again as they scrambled down Eldfall, the nudge and the pull of another tether as they sped over the well-worn trails. She risked a look back into White Wood to see Karav leading a group of four, only recognizable by her braids whipping out behind her like reins in unseen hands.

If Karav wanted Tinloh, she'd have to fight harder than that. Pallah relaxed her tether, allowing Tinloh his head. Immediately, the lust for blood that had been a flutter in the back of Pallah's mind grew to a pounding roar.

A scream ripped through the air behind them, and the iron of blood tasted on her tongue. She kept going, leaving Tinloh to his prey. The edge of White Wood came into view, the Vatino Sea just beyond. Pallah, Issha, and Ahren kept their pace down Eldfall, the growing distance between them and the Taka Reu pulling Pallah up short. She couldn't get too far from Tinloh; the tether would snap.

Tripping and falling against a birch tree at the very edge of White Wood, Pallah turned to look for her smilodon only to find a man, eyes black as the night, a scythe raised high. Pallah matched it with her double axe, blocking the curved blade, the tip almost piercing her eye.

Releasing a hand from the scythe's haft, the man's gnarled fingers grasped at the air before Pallah and tightened into a fist. Immediately, Pallah dropped to her knees, barely holding her double-headed axe aloft. The man was Lakimi Fera, and Pallah could feel her muscles responding to his touch.

Eyes wide, panic crawling in her gut like spiders, Pallah's back and sides cramped with such ferocity she cried out in pain. Pulling her tether back to herself, Pallah brought Tinloh's attention to her attacker, commanding he seek the man's life. Body shaking, Pallah's resolve began to weaken as her arms grew strained against the scythe.

Get up, girl! Erval's casual tone had been exchanged with alarm. *Fight!*

Her muscles weren't working, obeying a different master. Pallah pulled her tether back to herself as fast as she could, though Tinloh had yet to come into view. Ahren and Issha were gone, somewhere down at the Vatino, wondering where she was. The cries of the Taka Reu grew closer, and Pallah thought her heart would explode in her chest.

"I got this one!" the man called over her shoulder. "Get the other two before they hit the Valley!"

The man turned back to her, eyes steeped in darkness, lips curling to reveal yellowed teeth. Then he was lurching forward, body tumbling atop Pallah as Tinloh's muscled frame pounced on him from behind, massive incisors puncturing the flesh between the man's neck and shoulders.

He screamed, and Pallah scrambled out from underneath him as the man's tether to her muscles released. With a mighty shake of his head, Tinloh ripped away from the man, leaving him writhing in the blood-spattered snow.

Finish him, Erval rumbled. *Do it! Before he strikes you down!*

Pallah raised her staff, the more moral part of her screaming to stop, pleading for her to turn back—but, no. That part of her had been left in the Maze. That part of her had been stripped away, first by Bogdur, and then by Dahvid. The man wailing beneath her lifted axe could thank her fathers for their work.

She pulled down the haft, bringing it down in one swift motion. His screams died in his throat as his body jerked in final resignation. Pallah pulled her axe away and couldn't take her eyes from the blood that dripped down the sharp edge.

Now, listen to me carefully. Reach deep and touch his chest. Pallah! Pay attention and do what I tell you!

"What?" she cried as Tinloh lunged in front of her, taking down another man mere moments from piercing her through with his sword.

Say these words, Pallah! Es tekbinn lifid, giofin bin arin, takanar.

"Es—what?" Pallah's mind couldn't keep up with what was happening. Tinloh dragged the man to the side of the path.

Take his Gift! Repeat the words, the essence of the Taka Reu. Say it with me. He repeated the phrases again, pausing for Pallah to say it with him.

Es tekbinn

"Es tekbinn." Pallah pressed a palm to the man's chest.

Lifid, giofin bin arin.

"Lifid, giofin bin arin." She connected to the Mother Below.

Takanar.

"Takanar!" A grainy smoke, like snakes of sand from an ocean of ink, wove over his body and between Pallah's fingers. It swirled around her hand, forming a glove, before rushing up her arm and into her nose, her mouth, her eyes. Every orifice was blocked with its tendrils; she couldn't see, couldn't hear, couldn't breathe. *Häfa!*

And then it was gone, or had been completely consumed, she couldn't tell. But deep inside came the thrum of something new.

The crackle of branches and crunching of snow brought her eyes up to the rest of the group storming toward her. She raised her double axe as an arrow whistled past. Another thwacked against one of the axe heads and ricocheted into the snow. Tinloh tirelessly launched himself toward them, taking down two more men, his teeth sinking deep into their flesh. Pallah stumbled to the bridge.

Pumping her axe, the heads slid back inside with a satisfying click. She secured it to her back in the holster she'd fashioned at Freya's. Ahren and Issha would have already made it across the Vatino, hopefully moments from warning the Valley of the Taka Reu's intentions. Pallah just had to stay out of sight long enough to finish what needed to be done: find their mother, retrieve Ahren, and finally get out for good. Bogdur flitted at the back of her mind. Did she have time to take care of him too?

I told you. It gets easier.

It was, if she was being honest. The guilt that had gripped her after Dahvid was distant now, and she held none for the man in White Wood. The thought of taking Bogdur down held no pain either—only exhilaration.

She charged across the bridge at full speed, glancing back to see the mass of people breaking the tree line.

The bells of the Temple began to ring, heavy and dolorous clangs through the night.

In the village ahead, people clambered from their homes and ran to the Temple. Pallah, standing at the sea, pulled her staff from the strap at her back, axe heads protruding with the motion. The blades shone in the moonlight, streaked with black blood. The entire force of the Taka Reu scrambled across the floating bridge, elemental Gifts at their fingertips, beasts at their sides.

From the courtyard before Pallah, a group of men emerged. Holding simple weapons aloft, they marched across the snow to where Pallah stood, panting and planning her next move.

"It's as the boy says!" one cried, his meaty fist raised over the moonlit grounds. "The Taka Reu rebels against our land!"

"We take down their leader!" another cried, fire blooming in his palms as he stepped forward to block Pallah's path.

Raising her hands high, Pallah shook her head. "No! I'm not with them! I came to warn you!"

But Tinloh's tether faltered, so lax it had become, as control of it slid between girl and beast. Pallah only had time to cry out before he was taking down one of the men, everything in her cat lit with fury.

Screams erupted as the Taka Reu burst out behind her. Pallah whipped around to parry the blow of a sword. It slid along the length of the staff, dropping off the end, before pivoting back to connect with an axe head as Pallah turned, catching the sword between axe and metal pole.

She spun away as a villager came in with a pitchfork. "Taka Reu scum!" he cried.

Pallah ran.

Tearing away from the Vatino Sea, Pallah left her valley to fend for themselves. Each crunch of snow beneath her feet accompanied the sounds of hatchets flying, loosed arrows whistling, beasts growling, and the screams of the dying.

The infirmary was in a wing of the Temple Celestial, and Pallah ran straight for it, her path unobstructed. The terrified villagers who remained in the streets gave her a wide berth. Her double headed axe and the smilodon loping beside her proved to be strong deterrents to those less brave.

Throwing open the doors to the Temple Celestial, she passed by the large mirror in the foyer from where she'd spoken to Erval for the first time. She commanded Tinloh to stay put there, hoping he would listen.

Look at yourself, Pallah.

Pallah stopped short at the mirror, finding a warrior where a girl used to be.

You have the eyes of the Mother.

And she noticed it then. Her eyes—*häfa*—her eyes were pitch black, consumed with the Mother herself. She stared for a moment more as her breaths became measured, and the darkness dissipated, her gray-green irises coming back into view.

"Is that normal?" she asked the man in her mind.

No, Pallah. It's extraordinary.

Passing a few terrified Temple Serviseers huddled in the corner, Pallah strode confidently through the halls before shoving the door open to the infirmary. It smelled of medicinal alcohol and moth-balls, pungent even over the stench of blood Pallah knew drenched her clothes. It was dark, but a single candle on a wooden table illuminated the bed holding the form of a woman. Blanket tucked beneath the woman's arms and around her chest, Pallah could see the skeletal face of her mother.

"Mama—" The word choked out of her, and emotion rose up in visceral purity. "Oh, Mama."

If Phyllir had been gaunt before, she was but bone now. Her face was sunken, her skin almost translucent. Guilt plunged deep into Pallah. She had left her, right when her mother had needed Pallah most.

Her eyes went to her mother's ankle, poking out from under the covers. She could wrap her hand around the bones and tendons and her fingers would overlap. Tears fell down Pallah's cheeks and she wiped them with the back of her hand, pulling the blanket over her mother's foot and looking up to find her mother's eyes on her.

Pallah gasped.

"Pallah," Phyllir said, her voice wet, ragged. "You've come back to me."

"Yes, Mama. I'm here. I'm home." Though Pallah wasn't home. She had no home.

"Thank the Celestials." Hands shaking, Phyllir reached out for Pallah's, and they clasped them together, the younger steadying the older, their shadows dancing in the light of the lone candle.

"I found Freya, Mama. Like you asked. She told me everything."

A low hum vibrated from Phyllir's feeble frame. "So, you know then—you know why..."

Pallah blinked. She had known long ago. Bogdur had hated her since she was but a babe. But seeing her mother like this, the why seemed less important. Darkness unfurled in her belly.

"I know," Pallah said past gritted teeth.

The hand gripped in Pallah's grew slack and fell to the bedspread.

"I'm going, Pallah," Phyllir croaked.

"Going? Where—"

"Take care of your siblings. Take them somewhere he won't find you."

"Mama, you're coming with us. I'm not leaving you here."

But Phyllir shook her head and closed her eyes, sinking further into her pillow. "I have been done with this life for some time, Pal. The snap only hastened what Bogdur had been doing for years. The Healer says I have been holding on for your return." She cracked one eye open, the lines at its edge wrinkling in a half smile. "She was right."

"No!" Like a child, a tantrum rolled to the surface. Her mother could not leave her now! "Mama, I have too much to tell you!" But her desire to reveal the atrocities that had happened within Freya's cabin dried up on her tongue. If her mother was truly dying, Pallah wouldn't sully the one man she'd loved, the one man Pallah believed had been good to the woman lying before her.

"Oh, dear girl, let me hear your tale."

"I met Dahvid." Pallah's voice broke in its low whisper, the single candle casting a soft glow over her mother's face. Pallah sat on a stool near her mother's bed and recounted, not of the evil the man had done, but what he had proclaimed himself to be in that scroll. Nothing about the Maze, nothing about his paralysis or cruelty. No, she told of the before. His words from when they met, his love for her, his affection for the children who he knew were his own, and even for the one who wasn't.

Phyllir smiled, broad and serene. And that alone, was worth it.

"And we happened to have the same Gift, Mama," Pallah whispered at the end of her tale, watching her mother's chest rise and fall.

One eye cracked open, her mother peering through thinning lashes. Breath rattling in her chest, lips puckered, Phyllir's voice pushed past her frailty. "Pallah, I-I love..."

Eyes wide and brimming, Pallah watched as her mother breathed her last.

There, and then gone.

Tears spilling over, the darkness that had found a home in Pallah's belly climbed its way up her throat. She had escaped hell itself, only to find more hell waiting for her: her mother, refusing death until she heard the sound of her daughter's voice. A voice filled with kind lies of the man that had locked Pallah in the dark.

This, all of this, because of a man named Bogdur.

She leaned down and planted a kiss on her mother's forehead.

Then she was out the door, Tinloh on her heels, running through the Temple Celestial, heading straight for Sodur.

EARTH DAUGHTER

SOLYANA

"N o, no, no. That's not how it happened—at all!" Lone emphasized the last two words with two slaps of her palm to the wooden table.

Jonas giggled so hard, he fell off the bench.

"I'm just telling it how I saw it!" Gamaliel shrugged.

"Wait, so Björg sat on you?" Solyana asked, cupping the steaming mug of lavender tea in her hands. It wasn't saxifrage, but it would do. They sat in the darkened corner of a tavern in the city of Endirinn. Comprised of mountain people whose trade lay in goats and ore, the city rose in a semicircle, sprawling around the base of Mount Endirinn, the mountain where the Norlos was said to end or begin, depending on the tale.

A lutist with true red hair played near the bar, singing tunes the quartet had never heard before, melodies untouched by their valley, so far southwest of this place. After touring the city and checking on Björg at the stables, their last stop before the tavern had been the infirmary. It was there they had recovered Lone. They'd assisted her over the cobblestone streets and into the music-filled building where they now sat drinking tea.

Lone shook her head, a lock of her white-blonde hair falling over her eyes. "Björg didn't sit on me, he stepped on me. Big difference." She took a swig from her mug and wiped her mouth with the back of her hand. "Actually, if he had sat on me, I probably wouldn't have been left with this." She stuck her leg out to the side, revealing a clipped pant leg where her left foot used to be.

"I'm really sorry, Lone. I can't imagine." Solyana shook her head, unsure of what to say. Yet another loss for which she blamed herself. "How long until it's healed, do you think?"

"A Heitt and Lakimi Fera fixed me up quite well. It's mostly phantom itchiness now. They're crafting some kind of hardware for me, so I'll be able to walk, good as new."

"I still feel sick thinking about it," Gamaliel admitted, bringing his tea below his nose and taking a whiff.

"You should've closed your eyes, like me." Jonas said.

"Should have, indeed." Gamaliel gave Lone a one-sided smile and held aloft his steaming mug. "To Lone, who successfully cut off her own leg in the middle of a whiteout. The toughest of us all!"

"To Lone!" The group clinked their mugs together before settling into a cozy silence. Solyana surveyed the faces of her friends, of the people surrounding their table, and for this space in time, she felt whole, complete.

You'll have to leave them.

Solyana coughed into her drink, tea dribbling out and onto the table.

"Too hot?" Gamaliel asked, passing her a cloth napkin.

"Yeah." Solyana took it from him and wiped up her mess, her mind on high alert.

They worship the Celestials, don't they? They will never accept you, now that you've practiced the Taka Reu.

Dread pooled in Solyana's gut at the thought. She couldn't speak to Erval in this busy tavern, so he continued uncontested.

It's a perilous road from here. And though I do promise to return your sister to you, I cannot guarantee the same for your friends.

The clink and clatter of mugs, the laughter of patrons, the sweeping melody of the lute—all deadened to a dull din. Together again, it was too easy to bury the memories of the last few days spent apart. Solyana's friends had fought for their lives without her—*because* of her. And she refused to be the cause of more loss, not for the ones she loved most.

Jonas poked her shoulder, clarity returning to Solyana's mind as the room snapped back into focus. "And I figured out why I didn't die when I gave you my Gift!" Jonas said, waving a scroll he had materialized from somewhere on his person. "It's because I already had two!"

Gamaliel rolled his eyes. "Yes, Jonas, we've all heard. You're a—"

"I'm a Seer!" Jonas finished, elbowing him in the ribs. "And now that I've met Seer Brotnur, so many things make sense!" His arms flung out wide as if trying to embrace all mysteries now come to light. "Why I'm so good at making maps, why I seem to know what's going to happen before it does, how I was so sure that Solyana was the answer to this prophecy—"

"And he's super humble, too," Lone said into her mug, a grin on her face.

"I am very humble…" Jonas nodded sagely. "You're right."

There was a chorus of laughter to Jonas's confused expression, though he simply shrugged and opened the scroll again.

"Sounds like you guys were able to manage just fine without me." Solyana smiled softly. "I mean—" She cleared her throat, setting her mug on the table. "Between the blizzard, saving Björg from the pack of wolves, and Lone's injury, I'd say you guys make a great team."

"We do make a good team," Gamaliel said. "*All* of us." His soft eyes met hers from across the table. She smiled but looked quickly away.

"And *I* finished this map for you!" Jonas rolled the scroll back onto itself and handed it over. Solyana took it with a grin and tucked it into her parka. "For when we go up the mountain."

Gamaliel turned back to Solyana, his face turning somber. "What happened to Odie and Curry? To you?"

Solyana flinched as images returned unbidden: Odie's lifeless eyes, the massive being rising from the lava pool, his whip of fire snaking out and dragging Curry under, his voice now inside her head. She decided to remain tight-lipped about the encounter, half-hoping to forget about it completely.

"A few paces into the cave, we fell through the ice. I woke up at the bottom of a cave, and Odie—" She let out an unsteady breath. "He died on impact."

Gamaliel reached across to hold her hand. Lone gasped and Jonas's eyes instantly filled with tears. "It was fast; he didn't suffer. I gave him a burning."

The group was silent with the weight of the news. "And Curry?" Jonas whispered.

"Curry, she—" Solyana stumbled between words, between half-truths. "I had to leave Curry down there. She couldn't walk."

Silence blanketed the table before Jonas piped up.

"And you survived," he said between gulps of tea, his eyes wide, his tone reverent. "Truly, the Chosen One."

Solyana smiled at him sadly. "You're a Seer. I think if any of us is chosen, it's you." She pinched him softly on the cheek, which grew red and warm at her touch.

"You honored them as best you could." Lone gave her a stiff nod. "Odie knew the risks; he told us he was ready to see his daughter Lena again."

"His and Curry's sacrifice brought Solyana here safely," Gamaliel agreed before taking another sip of his tea. "To Odie!"

"To Odie!" Lone and Jonas chimed in, mugs raised.

"And Curry!" Jonas said. "Eyup!"

"Eyup!" the group responded.

Solyana raised her mug, and they drank to the two who had died in the caverns, deep beneath the ice. She squeezed her eyes shut, the image of Curry's trunk slipping beneath lava ripples fresh in her mind.

The tavern was beginning to fill, the chill of night drawing travelers come for Skaer Sky to warm up with drink and song. And Solyana wanted nothing more than to leave. It was growing late, and she knew the Serviseers would be expecting her back at the temple soon. Her friends were laughing and teasing as they made friends with the people beside them. Jonas danced to the lutists songs.

Missing her family and longing for home, Solyana left the table, intent on finding some solace in sleep.

The air was cool and crisp, and Solyana's breath created clouds of warmth in front of her as she exited the tavern. With Endirinn being so close to the mountain, the Norlos shone brighter than Solyana had ever seen it.

The people of Endirinn kept their grounds clean of snow, something Solyana's valley could never accomplish with the constant threat of blizzards. Blizzards, Erval had told her, originating from the woman she knew as Priestess Avi, and he knew as Pallah. Seized with a sudden need to warn her family, Solyana scanned the street. A large city like this would surely have a falconry or owlery fit for carrier birds.

The wind wound its way down the streets, disturbing a large wooden sign bearing Halina's likeness. A man stepped away from the door, a bushy brown beard covering his lips so entirely, the words he spoke were nearly swallowed as well.

"Just locked up, girl. We'll be open tomorrow." He squinted with cordial pleasantness.

"Oh." Solyana wrapped her arms around herself. "I was hoping to send a message, but I'm not going to be available tomorrow. Could I—"

"Oh! It's you!" The man's eyebrows disappeared into his hairline. "You're the Sun Daughter!" Bowing three times in succession, he fumbled with his keys, flung open the door, and ushered her inside. "Of course, I am so sorry. So sorry!"

"It's really okay," Solyana said, feeling the scar on her face.

"And don't you even think about payment! We here in Endirinn have been waiting for you for some time. It's an honor." He hadn't brought his body up from his numerous bows since meeting her eyes outside the shop, and it made her uneasy.

Solyana helped herself to parchment and a charcoal pencil. She sat at a small table, the pencil hovering over the parchment. What would she say? How could she say it?

The man disappeared into a backroom, presumably where he kept the birds. He returned with a small spotted owl on his arm and continued sneaking furtive glances at Solyana. She didn't want to keep him, so she scribbled the first thing that came to mind.

Priestess Avi has deceived us all, Rhuth needs to be freed from her care. The blizzards come by her word. She uses the Taka—

Solyana stopped, pencil hovering over the parchment. Who was she to warn of the priestess using Dark Gifts when she herself had become acquainted with their ways? And what proof did she have of the priestess's deception other than the words of her sister, communicated over such a distance while trapped in darlöh? No one would believe it. Tapping the pencil, she chewed her lip. She extracted a new scrap of parchment and tried again.

We are here at Endirinn, and I am to be purified tomorrow. I miss and love you all dearly. I will bring the green soon, I promise it. No matter what it takes.

Gamaliel, Lone, and Jonas are safe and well.

Love,

Solyana Marusda

She rolled it up and handed it to the man. He grinned again with an upward shift of his beard. Shuffling to the other side of the room, he grabbed a bit of leather and used it to tie the message to the owl's bare leg.

"She's been sleeping all day, so she'll get there quickly. To what city is she going?"

"A village called Vestur," Solyana said. "In the valley, west of Eldfall."

The man shook his head. "My apologies, I haven't heard of that. Would it help to look at a map?" He motioned toward the wall nearest the door, and Solyana walked to it, eyes widening at what was her first glimpse of the entirety of Mothmar. A land mass surrounded by sea and ocean, the map held scattered towns, cities, and villages. She traced a finger over the width of it, branching down from where they'd come. She found Takanah, then moved her finger to the left.

There was nothing there. Nothing but trees until the land disappeared into Kana Ocean.

"But there's a sea right here." She pointed to the spot where the Vatino Sea lay. "And Eldfall Mountain." She noticed Hasta Mountains were labeled, but Eldfall was nowhere to be found.

"This map is pretty old," the man admitted as he scratched his beard. "Most cartographers halted their journeys once the cold descended, centuries ago." He shrugged. "I'm sorry, girl. I can't send my birds without a destination."

Shoulders drooping, Solyana nodded and held out her hand. "I'll take the scroll then, please." She tucked it into her tunic.

A numbness threatened to overtake Solyana as she stepped into the cold street. She looked up at the Norlos glistening above and wondered if Erval had been right. Perhaps she should leave without her friends, and sooner rather than later. Even with only two Gifts, perhaps the Mother would help her gain the third, once she finally made it to the end of the Norlos.

"What if I found you tonight?" Solyana asked the boy on the mountain, so far away.

The sooner the better. Erval, not the boy, responded.

"But I'm supposed to be purified."

Erval scoffed. *Tradition.*

Solyana's thoughts, once again, landed on the words Orson had spoken back in Takanah. Many had come before her, seeking to fulfill the prophecy. Perhaps it *was* tradition, one that had been going on for long before she was ever born.

A scraping sounded from down the street, and Solyana snapped to attention, suddenly aware of how dark it had become. Hair prickling on her arms, Solyana walked in the direction of the temple...or at least she thought it was this way. Lanterns began winking out as the people of Endirinn began to turn in for the evening. But the Norlos was bright enough to guide her, and she used it to lead her northward to the temple. Neck craned toward the lights above her, her feet skittered over cobblestones, her mukluks soft and quiet.

Another scuff sounded up ahead, and Solyana's heart jumped in her chest, breath catching in her throat. A group of four shadowed figures lounged at the end of the street. They leaned against the side of a building, chatting to each other. Solyana tried to slow her heart. Nothing unusual about a few people passing the night outdoors.

Finding a small alley, she turned off the main road. She was trying to wind her way back around when a man stepped before her. He was silent, but Solyana felt his intent, a wolf come for his prey.

"Let me pass," her voice squeaked out, devoid of any reason to make him obey.

He stepped forward, and goosebumps rolled over Solyana's flesh. Running would only spur on a chase, so she stood tall instead.

"You're the one they call, Sun Daughter?" the man asked, only his eyes visible as most of his face lay hidden beneath a dark scarf.

"Y-yes," she said, turning her face so he could see her scar.

The man caught her chin in his rough and calloused hands and peered down at her scar. Three more figures and a wolverine stepped from the shadows. Solyana's entire body began to quake as she heard Erval's voice weasel its way back into her mind.

Connect to the Mother, Solyana. Stop wasting time!

"Orson requests your return." The man spoke low in her ear, roughly grabbing her by the upper arm and tugging her away from any remaining light. "He's been missing his little arctic fox."

What began as a scream became a garbled, wet groan against the man's hand as he clamped it tight over her mouth. The four formed a tight circle around her, keeping her hidden from those still making their way home on the streets.

Solyana's feet stumbled and caught on the cobblestones as she was rushed and tugged along. Crying out and straining against her captors, Erval's voice rolled through her mind.

She's at your call, Earth Daughter.

There was no way she was going back to Takanah, to that dark and twisted city with its dark and twisted chief.

Solyana buckled her knees. The men hesitated, caught off guard as she slumped to the ground. "Too much ale for this one," they chuckled as a villager scuttled by. Then he whispered to Solyana, "If you don't walk, we'll carry you!"

Solyana splayed her hands over the cobblestones, beseeching the Mother Below.

The Mother awoke.

That's it! Yes!

It was easy, too easy.

Fire burst from her like a fountain, palms extended toward her captors. They scrambled and jumped away. A piece of jagged rock cut through her flame, catching her across the jaw. Her fire faltered and faded as she realized one of them, a Stein Fera, was hurtling stones.

She turned and ran, slipping over the smooth cobblestones of the street, the sound of nails scraping behind her until rows of razor sharp teeth dug into her calf, bringing her to the ground. The wolverine was on her, so she switched her tether to Tala, attempting a connection to the beast, even as she kicked at it with her other foot.

Whatever connection the other Tala had was too strong, and Solyana brought the flame once more, shooting it at the animal in one large ball of fire. It flew backward, the taste of burning hair and flesh sour on Solyana's tongue.

She closed her fists, intent on running again. Defending herself was one thing; killing was entirely another.

But two steps away, the men surrounded her once again, their scarves pulled down to reveal tattooed and malevolent faces. "What Chief Orson wants, he gets, girl." Then one of the men began to transform, the darkness of the Taka Reu enveloping him into something large, bearing claws and teeth.

Take him down, Solyana! You've been playing nice for too long.

Mouth agape and stricken with horror as she stared at the mountain lion that was once a man, Solyana could only imagine what her future held. Surely, this was not the same Taka Reu. Surely, this was some perversion of the thing that could enable her to save her people. Solyana wasn't like Orson or these men; she was different. She would never allow such warped misuse of her power.

She closed her eyes.

A thump and a skitter of claws broke through the chaos. Solyana's eyes flew open to see black, brown, and white fur mix together in a flurry of teeth. Vinur! He had launched himself at the mountain lion, distracting it enough to stop the men before her. Behind Solyana, Gamaliel rushed into the fray with a staff in hand.

Throwing knives with birchwood handles whipped past Solyana in quick succession, burying themselves in the flesh of her attackers. They dropped, one by one, as the mountain lion bounded off without his companions. Only the man with the wolverine remained, his eyes wide and black as night.

Pahlak and Rorhan, the brother and sister from Rahgah Voh's tribe, ran to stand beside Solyana, hands gripping more knives, their expressions taut with determination.

"Leave now, or we'll finish the job," Gamaliel snarled, placing a hand on Solyana's shoulder.

"There's still nine days," the man growled before hobbling into the shadows.

The siblings retrieved their knives from the men on the ground whose mouths were quiet, and bodies were still. Solyana's eyes seemed to avoid them of their own accord. She found Gamaliel instead. "You came just in time," she said. "And with these two?" She motioned to Pahlak and Rorhan.

Gamaliel helped her to her feet. "They found us in the tavern. Turns out Pahlak does know a bit of our language and they don't seem to agree with how their tribe treated you after everything happened. They stand with us; with *you*."

"We are letting him go?" Pahlak asked as she ambled over, sheathing her knife.

"No sense shedding more blood in this city," Gamaliel said. "The Serviseer did warn us of people being against your path, Solyana."

"It wasn't anyone from here," Solyana said, her hair falling around her face. "They were Orson's men."

"Orson?" Gamaliel's brows lowered. "They followed us all the way here?"

Rorhan grunted and said something in ancient Mothmari. Pahlak nodded, crossing her arms. She stood before Solyana, her head coming just below Solyana's nose. "Rorhan wants to follow that man, and I agree. He's a danger to everyone else here. It is a pleasure to help you, Sun Daughter." She gave Solyana a quick bow, motioned for her brother to join her, and the two jogged into the shadows, promising to return if they were needed.

"*Stars to heaven!*" The Serviseer snapped her fingers as several gray-clad women surrounded Solyana.

She and Gamaliel had walked back to the temple, Vinur at their side. It had been a silent trek, though Solyana's mind had been anything but. It was clear to her, more than ever, if she wanted to keep her friends safe, she would need to go alone.

Frenzied hands and worried brows fussed over her appearance. The lead Serviseer fluttered like a flustered bird. "I told you to return by the time the Norlos appeared. It's been hours!"

"She was attacked," Gamaliel said, low and careful. "Your city harbors more danger than safety."

"Why do you think I told you to bring her back before dark?" the woman snapped, eyes meeting Gamaliel's before swinging to Solyana, scanning her for injury. She clucked her tongue. "I told you, girl. There are many who may wish you harm, even more that doubt your ascension. You see now the heresy that strangles the people of this world?"

Solyana shook her head, unsure of what to say, unsure of what she believed. Her connection to the Celestials was in jeopardy; perhaps she could fix it when this was all over. Her connection to the Taka Reu, however, was stronger than ever. The response from the Mother seemed so easy, yet it still took immense control to keep her world from burning to the ground. The whole ordeal was exhausting.

"I just want to sleep," she whispered as the hands of the women in gray fussed over every inch of her, searching for injury. "Please!" They pulled away, their eyes flicking from her to the lead Serviseer.

The woman gave a slow nod, her gray hair unmoving in a tight bun at the base of her neck. "Yes, sleep. Best forget about what happened this evening." She peered through her brows at Gamaliel.

"You, get to where you need to go. We'll look after her, as is our duty."

"He can stay." Solyana held fast to Gamaliel's hand. "I would feel safer if he were near."

The Serviseer glanced between the two of them, lips pursed. "Fine, he can sleep in the room adjacent." She jabbed a finger at each of them in turn. "Stay out of each other's rooms. Purification starts *tomorrow*."

They agreed.

IT GETS EASIER

PALLAH

OODED CLOAK PULLED UP to hide her face, Pallah marched confidently through Sodur, all prior fear overshadowed by her singular need to rid the world of Bogdur. Every point when her life had turned for the worse, each time she could have risen and was knocked back down—it was all the result of Bogdur: his biting words in the back of her mind, his disgust, his anger, and his manipulation.

With her smilodon at her side, they moved as one, weaving between burning houses, dodging the running and screaming villagers. Pallah only struck out at those who actively opposed her. Axe heads and claws cleared her path of any aggressive impediments.

It did get easier.

Standing before the door of her home, chest heaving, she pushed it open, a long creak announcing her arrival. A lantern sat on a newly-crafted table; the previous one had been demolished the last time she'd been here. A man sat at the table, head bowed. He chuckled through his nose as Pallah entered the room.

"Throwing a temper tantrum, are we?" Bogdur's oily voice filled Pallah with so much hate, she had to tighten Tinloh's tether to keep him from mauling the man outright. "Welcome home, Pallah." His eyes came up to meet her own but quickly shifted to Tinloh instead. He stiffened.

"I know everything, Bogdur." She said it carefully as she slowly stalked into the room.

"And what would that be, you little *tik*?" The word crawled from a loathing sneer, but Pallah hardly blinked.

"Mother never loved you." Pallah enjoyed the flash of expression that darkened Bogdur's face before she continued. "She has always loved Dahvid. You know she tried to leave with him, twice." Pallah paced across the kitchen floor, counting on her fingers. "First, after Ahren was born. And the second time was only a few years ago; you thought she was going to the temple in Takanah."

Bogdur shifted. So, he didn't know about that one.

The corner of Pallah's mouth twitched upward. "She was going to leave with him."

"But she didn't," Bogdur said, eyes still on the sabertooth tiger. "She came home. She stayed with *me*."

"It had nothing to do with you. She only returned because the *Stasis* charm Dahvid had used failed. Mother stayed for *us*, not for you! You were the remains, the leftovers, the gristle on the bones you toss to the dogs."

Bogdur stood suddenly and Pallah pumped her staff, axe heads flashing into place. Tinloh crouched beside her, a low growl in his throat.

"No, Pallah." Bogdur's lips tipped into a malicious grin. "That was *you*. We had a perfectly healthy daughter in your sister, and your brother was a worthy addition, too. But you? You've always been unnecessary, and far more trouble that you've ever been worth."

Pallah counted to ten as he spoke, her mind fuming with new fury.

"An extra mouth to feed." Bogdur advanced toward her, step by step. "Additional weight on our patience, with your worthless, idle hands that could never contribute a single thing of value!"

Pallah rushed him. Pressing one side of the axe to his neck, she backed him into the wall. "You *häfan* bastard!" She wanted to cut him. Yet something inside of her bucked against her rage. Was it duty to blood? Or a need for approval from a man that had always kept it just out of reach? "You think me a Rána? I have full control over this smilodon. I'm more powerful a Tala than you have ever been with Fera!"

"Oh, that's right." The pale column of Bogdur's neck bobbed under the blade as he swallowed and licked his lips, chin raised high. "Did you two chat about it? Did he try to take your beast from you like he tried to take my wife?" Pallah's hand shook, and though she didn't intend to, she told him with her eyes.

His countenance changed, seemingly forgetting about the curved blade streaked with other people's blood poised beneath his jaw. "What did you do, girl?"

Pallah's answer hid in her throat.

Bogdur laughed. "Oh, Celestials be praised! He finally gets what he's deserved. Well done, child. You have more spine than I ever gave you credit for."

Pallah blinked, almost fooled for a moment by his backhanded compliment.

"I'm proud of you, Pallah. You've managed to do the one thing I couldn't. You defended what was yours. Maybe you are worthy, after all. A daughter I can claim, in spite of all the *häfan* whispers."

His words snaked into her ears and her resolve began to crumble. The noise of the battle rang from outside. Pallah turned toward it, numb as she wiped her face.

You aren't alone, Pallah. Let me help you.

"Erval?" Pallah asked aloud, stepping away from Bogdur, the axe dropped limply to her side.

Bogdur released a breath, rubbing his neck and eyeing her from against the wall. He began to sidle away, one hand grasping for something behind him.

See this through! We'll end his sick existence together. It's long past time he be put down.

A flicker of fast movement caught her attention and Pallah jerked her gaze upward to find Bogdur careening forward, something shiny held high in his hand.

"Erval!" Pallah backpedaled away from Bogdur.

No, you don't, you bastard!

And Erval tethered through her, latching onto Bogdur himself. Vertigo slammed into Pallah and she dropped to the floor. Tinloh paced anxiously as Pallah looked up, her mouth dropping open. Bogdur was lifting from the floor, his wiry gray hair, tunic and trousers floating as if he were suspended in water. His eyes held pure shock, his mouth gaping open in horror.

"You demon girl! What are you doing? What are you—"

But his words were cut off as Erval, through Pallah, shoved the man against the far wall of the small home. The cabinets shuddered, plates and bowls clacking together inside.

Tinloh nudged Pallah as she watched her father press deeper into the wall, the wooden boards he'd constructed years ago cracking behind him, branching out like spiderwebs. His breath grew labored, and Pallah stood, leaning against Tinloh to keep from falling.

She raised a hand toward her father, feeling Erval's tether, supple yet strong, reaching through her and into the man before her. Her chest constricted and she felt everything powerful, everything wild, come under her control.

That's my girl.

Pallah squeezed her hand shut.

Bogdur, unable to even release a final cry, slumped. Blood seeped through every orifice of his face as his body slid to the floor, leaving a crimson streak on the wall behind him. He collapsed onto the floor, a broken corpse that would be left to rot.

It gets easier.

She didn't know what she had expected to feel, but a numbness descended on her, wrapping Pallah in its warmth. She would waste nothing more on Bogdur, not a tear, not even a glance.

"Thank you, Erval."

The pleasure was mine. Now, come find me.

"One more thing." Pallah twirled her axe, hooked it to her back, and threw her hood over her features. "'Loh, to me!"

Pallah and Tinloh sped into the night, intent on finding her people, for she had so few left. The vertigo had dissipated, but Erval's tether still wound through her, giving speed to her step and malice to her intentions.

Use it as you will, he told her darkly.

Villagers began to recognize the girl striding amongst the carnage. Pallah lifted her hands, sending out the tether to latch onto those unwise enough to raise weapons against her. One by one, like a wave crashing over Sodur, Pallah allowed Erval's Gift to destroy all opposition in her path. Bodies flew, crashing into buildings, snapping under pressure, launching wholly into the air for gravity to finish them; screams were the only sounds around her, screams and loud thumps deadened by snow.

With every tether, she and Erval used his Gift in tandem. She could only assume it was some kind of body Tala, though far stronger than she had ever witnessed before. Something deep inside begged her to stop, but the strength of the Mother Below consumed her, and she had no true willingness to concede. She only touched those who opposed her, leaving those who steered clear alone. She gave Tinloh his head, tired of exhibiting so much control over him, over herself. She gave him room to make his own decisions—and my, he was hungry. He branched off, a beast doing what beasts do. She would regret none of the blood he shed.

Spotting them in the moonlight, Pallah found the figures she was looking for huddled near the Vatino Sea. Though she had expected only two, instead there were four: two standing, and two on the ground. Her heart began to race as her feet scrambled over the crimson-spattered snow, every surface holding the stains of war.

A wail cut the air, heavy with grief. Running to the scene, Pallah found Vámae clutching a body. Fear and regret squeezed the breath from her lungs. Ahren? Was she too late? All of this, only to lose her brother?

But as she got closer, she realized it was not Ahren who lay on the ground, eyes lifeless and dull.

It was Vil.

Pallah's hands shook and she went to her knees. She moved to touch her sister, to comfort her. They had both loved this man, manipulative though he was.

"Get off me!" Vámae shoved Pallah away, scrambling back on all fours. Her face was smeared in dark blood, her hair matted and tangled. "How *dare* you show your face again. This is all your fault!"

"I never meant for any of this to happen! It was never supposed to happen!" Pallah began, hands extended. But her twin's face only vacillated between hatred and fear. Issha crouched to stay near Vil's body. Ahren backed away, keeping up with Vámae.

"Can't you see this was all Vil and his people?" Pallah explained. "They brought this on all of us!"

Vámae was shaking her head, her full lips trembling with fury. "You blame the man dead not even five minutes? You're a monster, Pallah!"

Shouts rang out from the other side of the Temple Celestial. The fighting had died down as few were left alive to do it. But Pallah knew if either side got ahold of her, she wouldn't see the morning.

She had to leave, again.

Voice shaking, Pallah licked dry lips. "I have somewhere we can go. It's—" Erval spoke through her lips as if they were his own, "North. A city called Thonethren."

He released her, and Pallah blinked, continuing. "It's not safe for us here."

The shouts grew louder and Pallah stood, ready to flee into the night. But where was Tinloh? She tugged on his tether and turned to find him loping back to meet her, his eyes bright with curiosity, incisors stained with blood.

A flash of heat threw Pallah to the ground as a ball of flame blew past her and slammed directly into Tinloh. His legs buckled, head hitting the ground, and his body flipped twice the wrong way over his neck until he lay still in the snow.

35

NO KIN

SOLYANA

S OLYANA AND GAMALIEL EMBRACED in the hall of the temple before the Serviseer ushered Solyana back through her
doorway. The woman glanced between them, tutting to herself
about the 'frivolities of youth.'

Back in Solyana's room, littered with beautiful greenery, welcoming and warm, she couldn't help the shiver that ran down her
spine as she climbed beneath the fur covers. Her chill came, not
from cold, but from the recollection of the events in the dark alley.
If Orson was sending men far and wide to bring Solyana back,
then what had become of Maral and her children? Her friend from
Takanah had led a rebellion in the wake of Solyana's escape from
the city. Had she succeeded, and now Orson was scrambling for
any last hope? Or had she failed, and now he hungered for revenge?

As Solyana lay in the dark, her mind continued to anxiously
hum, refusing to find peace enough to sleep. After an hour of

grinding her teeth against her persistent worries, she finally flung the covers away and stood, fists clenched in frustration. She padded to the small vanity in the corner. The mirror revealed a haggard, thin woman, someone she almost didn't recognize. A sheen of sweat covered her forehead, and Solyana wondered if perhaps she was falling ill. It wouldn't surprise her, given the harsh conditions she'd endured, the stress she was under. For a predestined event, it seemed every circumstance and person they'd encountered, including her own body, was intent on keeping her from the mountain, from the boy tethering light. Maybe it was a sign she was doing something—or perhaps everything—wrong.

A soft knock sounded at her door.

Solyana turned from the mirror, hope blooming in her chest. Gamaliel? She couldn't deny the flutter and thrill that wound its way through her belly and up her neck. She didn't want to be alone, not tonight.

A floorboard creaked under her toes as she made her way to the door, and she winced; waking a Serviseer would bring nothing good. The last thing she wanted was an embarrassing lecture which would be hard to deny with a boy in her room.

She opened the door. "I was ho—"

A hand pressed solidly to her mouth and another on the back of her neck as wild eyes walked her backward into her room. The man closed the door with his foot, the latch only giving a soft *click*. Eyes wide in fear, Solyana took in her captor's near-white hair, wrapped around his neck like a scarf, and his once-colorful cloak turned inside out to reveal dark animal hide.

One of the men of the Ancient Mothmari tribe, the man whom she'd rejected after the first Gift had been given, the man whom she had kept from perishing at her hand, was now in her room.

Nostrils flaring, Solyana smelled his sour sweat and the dirt beneath his nails. His ice-blue eyes were determined, a thread of fear shining beneath them. Heitt, she needed to use her Heitt. Solyana tried, but something was wrong; her body refused, frozen in place as if her muscles had turned to ice. The man released her mouth and neck and stepped back. He was only a bit taller than Solyana herself, but with his Gift of Lakimi Fera, he was not weak. She had never met another with this Gift, other than Priestess Avi, and even then, she couldn't begin to assume the implications of manipulating muscle.

Even her eyes were locked in place, staring in horror at the man before her. Silent as midnight snowfall, the man, his lips set in a thin white line, pressed the blade of a small knife into his palm, drawing a line of red. He walked to the fire, squeezing a few drops of blood into the flames.

"Syna oku merki," he rasped as the fire sizzled.

Solyana could only whine with the breath his invisible grip allowed as her scar erupted on her face. Belying his confidence, the man trembled, sweat thick across his brow. He unwrapped the hair from his neck to reveal a smooth face: a youth, though nowhere near as young as the one who had given her Tala. He took her head in his hands once more. One clammy hand rested on her neck, the other rose to her face, slick with blood.

"You take Fera." The hand on her neck squeezed, willing her to act.

Fighting beneath his Gift, Solyana managed to force out a single "No," though the effort was agony.

He blinked at her, his upper lip dotted with perspiration and early sprouts of blonde hair.

"You'll...die," Solyana growled out the words, feeling a sliver of control coming back as his confidence waned.

"It is honor," he said.

"No," she choked. She wanted none of this; she never had. If she could turn back time, she would have defied Priestess Avi. She would have stayed in her valley, cared for her sister, or better yet, rescued her from whatever place the priestess held her captive. She refused to be responsible for the end of another life.

The man hesitated. In his lapse, Solyana reached out to the Mother, the connection forming with comfortable ease. Twin flames sparked to life in her palms.

The voice rolled through her mind like a passing breeze. *Yes, dear girl. Show him your power.*

No, she defied the voice. She wouldn't harm him.

His eyes grew wide, lips twitching, and he gave a partial bow as if he couldn't decide whether to submit or regain control. If his true intent were to please the Celestials, Solyana would utilize this weakness. His hold on her was marginal now; she strained to cross her arms before her.

"You dishonor me! And you dishonor the Celestials by coming into my room!"

"Dishonor?" The man stumbled back as if struck. "No, honor only!" He crossed an arm over his chest and beat a fist above his heart.

"You—" Solyana closed her left hand to snuff out the flame and pointed to him. "Give me—" She pointed to herself. "Choice." She spoke clearly, truthfully. "I do not want Lakimi Fera."

The man released his hold on her immediately, fear burrowing in his eyes. "You have choice, yes!" He threw himself to the ground, his knees cracking on the wooden floor. "Choose me!"

Solyana hoped his racket would bring Gamaliel, the Serviseer, the priest, anyone, but her door remained silent. "You must let me sleep," she spoke soothingly, as if he were a feral animal in danger of striking.

The man nodded, prostrate, nose to the ground. "Yes, I come. You need three Gifts. I come next day."

He scrambled to his feet, gave one more bow, and extricated himself, a smear of his blood on the floor all that remained of his intrusion.

Solyana let out a shaky breath and fell to her knees. She *did* need three Gifts. What consequences would she incur if she attempted to reach the boy with only two? Whatever it was, it had to be better than the payment required with the giving of Gifts.

The Mother Below welcomes all.

"Leave me be," Solyana rasped.

Gamaliel and Vinur burst into her room; the former, shirtless, loose pants low on his hips, eyes wide with panic as he twirled his staff in his hands.

"Are you okay? The guards posted outside your door were knocked out. I called for the Serviseer." His eyes searched the room. Vinur began licking the blood off the floor and when Gamaliel noticed, he knelt to inspect it. "What happened?"

Solyana recounted the entire exchange, leaving out her connection to the Mother Below, and the voice that seemed to accompany it.

"Will you stay?" she asked at the story's conclusion, feeling small and irrevocably desolate after enduring two attacks in one night. "Please?"

"Of course." Gamaliel rested his staff against the foot of her bed and Vinur laid down beside it. "Let me just"—he chuckled to himself—"go get a shirt."

Solyana had insisted he use the other half of her overly large bed, but, ever the gentleman, he refused and curled up with a blanket by the fire.

"What happens after tonight?" Gamaliel's voice came soft and low from the floor.

Solyana stared at the ceiling, at the shadows cast by the fire. Though her bed was warm, and a fire crackled at the hearth, the chill in her bones would not dissipate. She would give anything for Gamaliel to climb in next to her, but the last thing she wanted was to initiate more complications into what was already so entangled and uncertain. What *would* happen after today? It would be foolish to make any promises she couldn't keep.

"I don't know, Gamaliel."

"Don't give me that." He shuffled in his blankets. "You always do that, Sol. I can hear your mind working from here, holding all your thoughts captive. You have so much more to say but you never do." He was silent for a beat. "Why?"

A thread of longing pierced her heart, knowing she could never be completely honest with him. Even if he suspected or accused her of using the Taka Reu, she would never admit it. But she could be open about other things.

Solyana took a breath. "I don't know if I'm coming back." The fire popped. "I'm afraid I'm going to go up this mountain, and that will be it. I'll become the core of future fireside stories, some whispered myth, an empty legend. I've always wanted to be more than I am. Being born a Rána…" She raised her hand, turning it over to look at it against the wood-grained ceiling. "You can't understand it unless you've been one. Growing up in a Gifted family, wanting to be something—anything, really. Only to become something, but again, unlike anyone else." She took a breath and dropped her hand to the pillow. "I have no kin, not really. I am alone in my task, and even more in my being."

Gamaliel was silent.

"I don't have—"

Her blanket lifted and Gamaliel slipped beneath it. Her back to him, he wordlessly lay behind her, bringing nothing but his presence.

"Is this okay?" Gamaliel's voice was quiet.

Solyana slowly slid backward until she was pressed against his chest. "Yes."

"And this?" He tucked his arm beneath her head, so it was pulled close against his shoulder, his legs tucking up to fit neatly behind her curled body.

"Yes."

"Do you want me here?" He wrapped his other arm around her tight and snug, like they were two parts of one whole, as if every hollow of him was satisfied with her alone to fill.

"Yes."

"You're not alone Solyana, not tonight." He tucked his face into her hair, and every part of her calmed to the rhythm of his breath.

It was there they fell asleep.

DON'T LOOK

PALLAH

PALLAH WAITED FOR HIM to get up.

Wind blew the fur on his back.

Tinloh did not move.

Pallah's tether slithered back to her, her heart broken, half of it lying in the snow a few paces beyond.

"I saved us. It won't hurt us." Vámae's breathy voice came from behind Pallah, and she turned slowly to find her twin over Vil's body once more, speaking to the dead. "I'll save you, Vil. You're safe. This nightmare is almost over." She pulled Vil's head into her arms and rocked back and forth before her eyes locked with Pallah's. "Get out of here, before I—"

But Vámae's words were cut short as Pallah found her hand clutching the familiar wooden handle of her hatchet, the blade sunk deep into her sister's chest. Dark blood bloomed beneath her grip. Vámae's wide blue eyes blinked against the night, a sputtering cough shaking her chest and her twin connected to it. Catching Pallah in her gaze, lips parted to speak, nothing but a groan escaped. Then Vámae slumped, sprawled atop Vil. Beautiful, even to the end.

"Was that you?" Pallah's mouth moved but she hardly heard her own words. "Erval, was that you or me?"

There was no answer.

Issha, mouth agape and eyes wide, held tight to a shaking Ahren. "Don't turn around," she spoke unwaveringly in his ear, hand pressed to the back of his head as she kept him in an embrace. "Don't look."

Pallah barely heard the exchange, mind focused on the next step, for she wasn't quite done. Not yet. She pressed a sticky hand to her sister's back and connected with the Mother Below, whispering the words Erval had taught her. Rising from the core, the powdery smoke wound its way up and shot into all of her, feeding her the Gift her sister once bore.

Eyes surely black as night, Pallah went to Tinloh. She placed a hand to him, letting her fingers trace his features one last time.

"They're coming!" Issha's shout rode the wind and Pallah's head snapped up as she caught sight of the group marching around the Temple.

Running back to her brother, she saw the fear on his face, the horror in his eyes, and she knew: she could not bring him to Erval. He wasn't like them; he was too pure. She would save him, though. She would keep him from harm. His eyes squeezed shut as she pressed a hand to his cheek.

"You saved me." She drew his head down and pressed her forehead to his. "And now it's my turn to save you."

Issha ran a few paces before them, her hands outstretched as she waited for the group to launch an attack.

"Did you—did you kill—"

"Ahren," Pallah interrupted, and her brother's eyes opened. "She was with Vil. And Vil was attacking our people."

"But she—"

"You trust me, right?"

His mouth opened and closed. He nodded.

Pallah drew Ahren into an embrace, wind whipping at them from off the Vatino Sea. Pallah recited the words she had read in the scroll so long ago. Words that had stuck with her, for they had broken the man that had kept her captive. But they would not break Pallah. Because her brother trusted her, fully and truly.

Smoke, thick and dark, eddied around them as they stood affixed. Issha fought for time, while Pallah held her brother tight, until there was nothing more to hold, until his entire being faded away with the smoke. The darkness gathered itself and fell back into the earth below.

The group was on them now, and Issha was shouting something, grabbing at Pallah who stood, staring at the place her brother had been.

He was somewhere safe now. Somewhere sure.

"—to leave!" Issha's voice finally broke through.

Whirling, Pallah motioned to her sister. "Grab Vámae!"

"But she's—"

"Just do it!"

Issha cradled Vámae's body in her arms and took off behind the Temple, Pallah close behind.

A volley of arrows and even a spear rushed past them as they ran, but Pallah still chanced a look back, taking one final glimpse at her smilodon in the snow.

We'll find you another. Now, come north.

They took off into the night, and Pallah was sure, more than she was of anything else, that she would never go back to that valley again.

THE FOUR WEIGHTS

SOLYANA

THERE WAS THE WEIGHT of the thick fur blanket, the weight of Gamaliel's arm draped across her middle, and the weight of the world outside. His body wrapped hers, tight and secure, as if they shared the same premonition. As if he could hear the unceasing drum that beat in her mind: she would leave, she would leave, she would leave him.

The time had finally come; she would fulfill her duty to the prophecy and to Mothmar. She would ascend Mount Endirinn, and she would do so alone.

The threats on her life, the bloodied man in her room, her friends losing so much for the sake of this *häfan* prophecy...was it all worth it? What really waited for her atop the peak? She was beginning to doubt it was a boy at all. Perhaps she would find nothing but a mirror, a reflection of herself, twisted and bent beneath all that had been asked of her, beneath all she had done. A sacrifice, a tribute to the Celestials to sate their appetites and quell the unnatural cold.

Solyana would not lead her friends to see such a thing—no, she could not.

With painful slowness, Solyana extricated herself from Gamaliel's grasp, feeling hollow even as she leaned down to kiss his hair. "Until the very end," she whispered. What could they have been, had she not been bound to such destiny? They could never know.

Vinur's head popped up at the sound of her feet on the floor. Solyana went to him, petting his ears and pressing her forehead to his. She stayed there a moment, breathing in his wolf scent, thanking him in her mind. He licked her, his pink tongue sweeping across the better part of her face. She chuckled, wiping herself dry.

"Go to sleep," she whispered. Vinur sneezed, then turned back to the fire.

On their tour of Endirinn the day before, Gamaliel had shown her where Björg was being stabled and where their supplies were kept. Solyana traced her way back, the cobalt blue of the sky before dawn keeping her hidden as she crept along roads and alleys.

After gathering a knapsack of what she would need, Solyana stood at the northern border of town, regarding the steep, snow-filled path to Mount Endirinn. Björg waited for her there; she had used her Tala to guide him, slowly and quietly, to the city's edge.

Solyana climbed him with a pang of loss, remembering Curry. At the time, she hadn't known she could tether to Curry, and guilt gnawed at her for letting her die in such a horrible way, untethered and alone. If something happened to Björg, she wouldn't make that same mistake. She wouldn't leave him to face the end alone.

Solyana scanned the mountain. There was no true path flat enough to permit a mammoth all the way up; he would only be able to go so far. How would Odie have felt, knowing she would have to leave Björg, knowing the giant mammoth would wander the mountain on his own, her tether snapping once their space grew too far apart? She could only hope she would catch up with him again, if she came back down at all.

Wind cascaded down the mountain and blew past her from her perch atop her mammoth. Her fingers were already numb inside her sealskin gloves, and it would only grow colder. While Eldfall was a slow incline, full of switchbacks and paths to the top, Endirinn was uncharted and wild. She remembered the scroll Jonas had given her back in the tavern. She reached into her parka and found it, encouraging Björg forward as she unrolled the crisp parchment.

"Oh Jonas, you always pull through." It was a map of Mount Endirinn—hand drawn in striking detail. The mountain held several points where it came to winding peaks, pillars of rock that rose straight and true. Without Jonas's color-coded suggested paths for travel, she could have wandered for months over this mountain. She looked at his key: the preferred route outlined in red, a secondary in blue, and most dangerous in black—"steer clear," he would say.

The sun kissed Solyana's cheeks as it peeked over the trees in the east. She took a breath and urged Björg up the forested mountainside.

Seer blood running in his veins or not, Jonas's homemade map had Solyana thinking she was foolish to trust a child with such a weighty job. It *was* Mount Endirinn right? Solyana turned the map on its head and back again with a frustrated sigh.

Björg snorted and came to a halt. They had steadily ascended for most of the day, the sun tipping ever westward, the Norlos mere hours from making its appearance.

She slid from his back and took a few gulps of water from her waterskin. Her mammoth rooted around in some brush. She hadn't had much time to use her Tala since acquiring it, and she took a moment to explore it now.

It was as people described, an almost tangible rope extending between human and beast, though without any visible evidence. She was using it through the Taka Reu, of course, as her connection to the Celestials seemed to have dissolved entirely. The chasm of loss that lay hollow inside accused her. How could she so easily reject the Celestials and depart from the heartbeat of her people? She ought to mourn the severance of her connection to them all.

But to such thoughts, she steeled herself. The Celestials had simply given her an alternate route, a deeper tool to wield, to succeed on the path set. She even had a mentor, someone knowledgeable she could trust. Nothing like the false priestess in their valley.

"Erval?" she asked, if only to stave off the loneliness.

But even after a few minutes, where he was usually attentive, there was nothing but silence.

"Erval, can you help me?" she tried again, a pit of despair sinking in her stomach.

No words came.

Erval had promised to be with her, hadn't he? The warmth of a single tear traced down Solyana's cheek as it escaped through frost-laced lashes. Had this all been for nothing? The study, the danger, the death, the journey as a whole—all for what?

She asked Björg to kneel, and he did. She climbed onto his back, and he stood, raising her up to the darkening sky. The Children of the Sky were barely recognizable, but if she squinted, she could see them—stars scattered across the night.

"We are all but children of the earth, aren't we?" she asked the ether, desperate for a response. "We like to think we have a special connection to the Celestials. But how can something so far away be more sufficient than the ground we can touch right beneath us?" Her bitter filled words were simply lobbed into the sky before dissipating into the wind.

Björg's trunk wound its way to Solyana's foot and wrapped it in something like a hug.

Solyana, savior of her people, sobbed atop the mammoth as dusk fell on the side of Mount Endirinn.

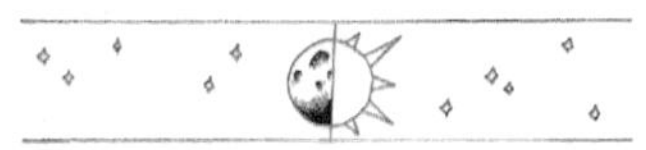

Björg was beginning to wane; Solyana could feel it in her tether. The mammoth's once-driven steps turned sluggish. And judging by the sheer wall of ice ahead of her, it was time to let him go.

It had been a few hours since the sun dipped completely out of view, and the Norlos had bloomed across the sky. Never had Solyana been so close; never had the lights looked so brilliant. It kept her way clear, though she still doubted where she was going. All she could do was go up.

Before her rose a wide waterfall, caught in icy stasis. Solyana slid a gloved hand over the rippling whites and blues, gauging its thickness. She had climbed her fair share of ice walls back home in her valley. Though walking over ice was filled with constant worry, ice picking, on the other hand, was something at which she had grown competent. Peering up the length of it, she could only hope what she was searching for was at the top.

Her lungs had grown strained and taught, her head pounded, and her eyelashes were caked with snow. It hadn't stormed, not since she'd sought shelter in the treacherous cave that took Odie and Curry, but something brewed in the dark clouds that slowly rolled toward her from the west.

Dismounting from Björg, Solyana hoisted her pack further up her shoulders and stood in front of him, letting his dark, knowing eyes take the measure of her.

"Thank you, Björg." She pressed a hand to his trunk. He snuffled as he drew it up around her shoulders, pulling her close to himself. Solyana snuggled into his soft hug. "You have been good to me." There was sorrow in his tether. "I'm so sorry about Curry. I did try. I tried to help her."

The beast gave a final squeeze, and Solyana stepped out from beneath the weight of his trunk.

"Go home, Björg. Don't wait for me." She gave a sad smile. "Find Gamaliel."

The mammoth and girl parted ways, the former down the mountain, the latter toward the wall she was to climb. She gathered the supplies she would need from her bag: rope, anchors, ice picks, and shoe picks. Weaving the thick rope into a harness, she pulled it on over her woolen pants, keeping the bulk of it coiled over her shoulder. She stretched the shoe picks over her mukluks and strapped them tightly. Finally, raising an ice pick in each hand, she took a breath. She struck, pounding the point of her ice pick deep, making a firm hold, then kicking and swinging, began her ascent.

Memories of ice climbing with Papa came into her mind. Her father, holding the rope below her, keeping her weight aloft with his own body on the ground.

"Pound that anchor in, Sol!" he had called up to her.

Solyana, alone on Mount Endirinn, flipped her ice pick around to bang her next anchor into the ice.

"Good!" he'd shouted up to her, always so exuberant when teaching his daughters. "Now, keep going!"

"Keep going," Solyana told herself.

"And what's the one thing we're *not* going to do?" Papa's instruction rang in her ears.

"Don't look down," she'd whispered, breathless.

"Don't look down." She didn't have to look to know he was beaming. "One hold at a time, Sol." His voice had grown distant. "You've got this!"

"I've got this," Solyana repeated. She would make Papa proud.

Ice chips flew off the wall as she ascended, anchors keeping her rope secure. She'd brought fewer of them than she'd have liked; she had to ration them. But rotation after rotation, she continued upward until she was far above the trees. She resisted the urge to peer down, instead looking up to find the lip of the wall appearing within cloud. The Norlos illuminated the mountain as if it were a green-stained day.

Pressing upward, Solyana saw a flash of lightning shoot across the sky. Up on this wall, with metal picks in her hands and on her feet, fear drove her faster.

Forgoing her anchors, Solyana climbed ever higher, her arms and legs burning and shaking as she stamped her way up the wall, hand and foot, hand and foot, over and over. Sweat snaked down her back as the wind picked up, threatening to pluck her from the mountainside.

Solyana paused for a moment, clinging to her half-buried picks. With shaking fingers, she hammered an anchor, trading time for safety in case this *häfan* storm succeeded in lashing the mountain before she reached the lip. She peered behind her, balancing one foot against the wall.

Solyana watched the clouds like the waves of Kana Ocean, rolling and unstoppable, heading straight for her.

Heart thudding in her chest, Solyana climbed faster than before, settling for one solid kick for each foot instead of two, one swing of her pick to lock in her climb. The storm picked up and small shards of ice began to pelt her back. The lip of the wall was so close, she would need only four or five more reaches before she would eclipse it.

She lifted her left arm, stretching as far as her muscles would go, urging them to move faster. The blanket she had tied in a roll at the base of her knapsack came loose and flapped like a sail. It flailed in the wind and yanked her off balance, tearing her grip away in one quick tug.

Solyana's body dropped like a stone.

With a stifled grunt, she swung her left arm back, her ice pick digging a gash down the wall. She swung towards the ice with a strong kick, her toe-pick looking for purchase but finding none as a spray of chips flurried away. The anchor she had buried caught her, jolting her to a halt, straining against the sudden force. Her knapsack broke free and she watched it fall, taking longer to hit the ground than she wanted to accept. She hung there taking quick breaths, swinging languidly, her shoulder screaming for relief.

She looked back up, no other choice but to gather her strength and regain the distance she'd lost. She kicked her right foot back into the wall, swinging until her next kick held fast. She launched her ice pick, bringing herself flush to the ice once more. She had to stop to catch her breath. Exhausted, she tucked her head against her arm and squeezed her eyes shut. Solyana breathed hard into her ice-encrusted parka, taking one sure step at a time.

"There will come one," she spoke to herself, "who will bring green."

She inhaled, and lifted.

"One who must follow the path of the sky."

She exhaled, and lifted.

"One who is all light."

Inhale, and rise.

"To stand to the one who is all dark."

Exhale, and rise.

"And that person…" Solyana opened her eyes. "Is *me*."

It had to be.

She looked back at the clouds. The bulk of the storm had yet to reach her. She could beat it.

She took to the wall with renewed vigor. Calling, not on the Mother Below, not on the Celestials above, but on those who brought her here. Those who had sacrificed for her, those who had stood with her, from her first steps to the soles of her feet reaching the top of this mountain.

"Papa, Mama, Fridmey, Rhuth!" She sank her picks into the ice and rose again. "Gamaliel, Lone, Jonas, Odie!" She repeated their names again and again, keeping the anthem in time with the pound of each hand and each foot.

She reached the lip. And with a final swing of her leg, Solyana dug her ice pick up and over the side of the wall, pulling and scrambling over the top gracelessly, the storm rushing up with a roar of ice and wind. She rolled to her back as the storm broke overhead, the prelude of razor-sharp rain and ice promising only moments until the full blizzard. Solyana got to her knees, peering through the fur of her hood, her eyes shielded in its shadow.

There was something up ahead, blurred by the fierce waves of snow that buffeted her. A ravine? She crawled her way there but found herself stymied by the harness around her waist. She swung at it with the ice pick, fresh snow already collecting rapidly on the ground around her. She aimed at her target, driven by panic, striking over and over until the rope finally snapped. Free of its grasp, she crawled her way to the side and strained her eyes to see through the thickening elements.

The storm crashed down in full. Solyana, seeking to find shelter any place she could find it, slid over the side of the ravine like an upended turtle. Desperately trying to turn over or slow her rapid descent, she attempted to bury her ice pick into the ground, but nothing stuck. Her pick pinged off rocks and frozen soil, ricocheting back at her. If not for the leather strap securing the pick to her wrist, she would have lost it.

She began to slow as the ground beneath her turned from slick ice to something that made no sound as it brushed beneath her parka. Turning over, she smelled its sweetness, its warmth and softness tickling the side of her face.

Solyana looked up to the light streaming from the Father of the Day. But...it had been night, just before. Solyana blinked, a strange awareness dawning that she wasn't where she thought she was. Here, the night and the clouds were gone, as if the storm had never been. The ground beneath her was...grass? She pulled off a glove to touch it. Yes, grass. Just as Jonas had drawn it. Had she done it? Had she fixed it so quickly? As she rose to her feet, she found herself entirely surrounded: a meadow of grass, flowers, and trees—so beautiful, all of them.

She turned, finding birds, butterflies, and in the middle of the meadow—

A boy.

Solyana staggered toward him, his face serene and...frozen in the sun. His expression bore something of fear, of grief, of terror. He stood, arms outstretched as if in an embrace, though he did not move. He didn't even appear to be breathing. On closer inspection, Solyana's eyes grew wide as she saw his face and hands were spattered in blood. Pulling down her hood, lowering her scarf, and removing her gloves, she stepped close enough to see the blue of his eyes. As blue as the sky above her now.

She reached up to brush his hair from his face.

He grabbed her wrist, inhaling a sharp panicked gasp. "Pall—" He released her and stumbled backward. "Who—who are you?" His eyes, red-rimmed and desperate, sought out answers in Solyana's gray-blue ones.

Solyana reached for him, opening her palm in the customary Mothmari greeting. He looked from her hand to her face, and finally grasped her arm in return. They shook once, then held their grip, eyes finding each other as years and time coalesced, as prophecy and curse came to fruition.

"Hi, Ahren. I'm Solyana."

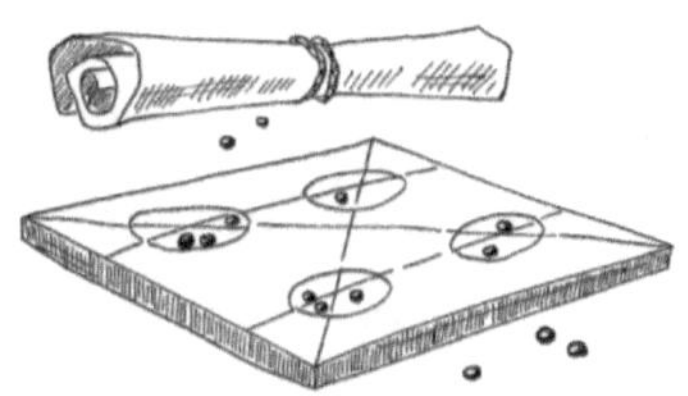

THE SEER, THE SCRIBE
TWO MONTHS LATER

J ONAS COULDN'T TEAR HIS eyes from the windows as they rattled and whistled with frigid wind. He sipped his tea, keeping his vigil, waiting for a shadow to pass to reveal his wandering brother. Lone had told Jonas the long treks across the mountain were Gamaliel's way of grieving. But Jonas didn't understand what there was to grieve. He fingered the necklace given to him, a simple leather strap holding an amethyst crystal. He had no doubt in his mind Solyana would return—she had to.

Seer Brotnur tapped the table with a knobby knuckle, drawing Jonas's eyes back to the game of Stökk. The old Seer had captured two of his stones, but in doing so, left himself open to attack.

Jonas peered across the table at the wizened old man. "You did that on purpose," he ventured. But he wasn't about to turn down a free point. Focusing on the board of crossed lines and circles, he slid a pebble across two planes to knock into Brotnur's piece.

Collecting the stones in hand, Jonas caught the old man grinning. "Stop trying to make me feel better," Jonas chided. "I know he's coming back."

The Seer gave a low hum of agreement, and it suppressed the fear fluttering in Jonas's belly. They had grown close over the last two months, the Seer and Jonas. He had been learning much about his Gift of Sight, though never from Brotnur's own mouth. The old man had adopted a vow of silence, as the Seers of ancient Mothmar were rumored to undertake. And while he was unable to offer his own words of wisdom, Brotnur allowed Jonas to read any scroll the boy could get his hands on.

A rush of cold air chased a small wolf into the room, melting Jonas's fears. A figure covered in frost and snow stamped his feet by the door before slamming it shut, making the whole house shudder.

"Vinur! Gam!" Jonas scrambled from his seat and scurried to his brother's side, Vinur bouncing at his heels. "Want the next game? I think I'm going to win this round, so it'll be you and me!"

But Gamaliel said nothing as he peeled off layers and hung them by the door.

"Don't let me win, though." Jonas cast a look back at Brotnur and rolled his eyes. "Like *some* people."

Turning back to Gamaliel, Jonas finally caught his face in the firelight and fell silent, shoulders drooping. It was one of those days.

"She'll come back, Gam." Jonas placed a reassuring hand on his brother's arm.

"I don't understand," Gamaliel whispered as he gazed at his hands covered in scrapes, scabs, and a few fresh cuts. "I've touched every part of that *häfan* mountain, with only this to show for it." He held up a small scroll and a brown woolen blanket. "This proves she hadn't been planning on going alone. She wrote about going to purification. About going back to her family! And yet I find no trace of *her*!" He threw the items down with such fury it knocked Jonas off-balance. Gamaliel swung his fist into the wall. Something cracked, and Jonas was unsure if it was the house or Gamaliel's hand.

"You're scaring him!" Lone reprimanded as she appeared from a back room. Jonas ran to her, ashamed of the tears pricking his eyes. He wasn't a kid anymore; he shouldn't be crying. But Gamaliel's behavior over the last two months had dredged up unwanted memories, sadness that had been trapped deep down, reminders of his parents.

"He's fine," Gamaliel bit back, rubbing his knuckles.

Lone shifted her weight, her metal leg creaking at the joint. "Maybe, but you're clearly not."

"I don't want to hear it, Lone. This isn't about me."

"You're right, it's *not*." Lone pushed Jonas behind her and took a step forward, folding her arms.

Gamaliel's head rose slowly to meet Lone's eyes. "I don't see you crawling all over this gods-forsaken mountain. What have *you* done to help?"

"By being present, Gamaliel." She tipped her head toward Jonas. "It's not easy for me either."

Jonas exchanged a glance with Seer Brotnur, who took a delicate sip of his tea.

"Maybe she has to show her mastery of the three Gifts," Jonas suggested. "Or battle that boy on the mountain."

"But she never got a third Gift!" Gamaliel vented and Vinur let out a howl. "She *häfan* left before she could get it! Don't any of you understand? The world is no different than it was two months ago! Something's gone wrong! And now we're left here with nothing to do but twiddle our thumbs and—what? Just wait? Just hope?"

"Gamaliel," Lone soothed. "You should sit down."

"She's gone!" Gamaliel turned on her. Vinur circled him, nudging his legs and his hands. "She's gone, and I didn't...I couldn't..." He slumped to the floor, his face in his hands, shoulders shaking with sobs he had held for too long.

Lone hobbled to him, still clumsy on her new leg. She gracelessly sat beside him, head tucked in the crook of his neck. They held each other, and Jonas watched, feeling like an intruder. It's not that he wasn't sad—he missed Solyana—but he knew she was coming back. He didn't know how he knew, but he did. This faith, which angered Gamaliel, felt only natural to Jonas. It could be no other way.

Seer Brotnur came to his feet and shuffled to the hook on the wall that held his parka. Jonas helped him into it. He had grown in the last two months and no longer needed to stand on his tip-toes to do it. Silently, they wove around Gamaliel and Lone, then pulled on their mukluks and headed into the night.

Seer Brotnur lived south of the Temple, near Endirinn's main square. Jonas, Lone, and Gamaliel had found a place to stay, tucked far from the main road in the northwestern district. In spite of the distance, the Seer and his protégé often paid visits to each other, especially on nights when Gamaliel was out late, searching. Jonas loved the Seer for that. In exchange, Jonas always offered to walk the old man home.

Before the door slammed shut, Vinur shot out and Jonas grinned.

"Thanks, buddy." He gave him a pat, thankful for the company Vinur would provide on the long and lonely walk back.

The wind and snow were picking up and Jonas ushered the Seer along, not wanting to get caught in a storm. The streets were empty, the people nestled safely in their homes, turning in for the evening.

"Ah!" the Seer croaked as he stumbled.

"Seer Brotnur!" Jonas grabbed for the man but missed, and the Seer fell to the cobblestone street, wind and snow swirling heavier around them. "Are you alright?" He knelt beside him, trying to get a look at the man.

Seer Brotnur's head snapped upward, eyes directed at the sky. Arms extending wide, he unwittingly smacked Jonas in the face, sending him backwards into the snow dusted street.

Jonas peered through the thickening onslaught of snow as Seer Brotnur's voice boomed into the night.

"In five centuries—"

Jonas gasped. A prophecy!

He scoured the interior pockets of his parka, pulling free a loose scrap of parchment and a charcoal pencil.

"An uprising of darkness will consume the hearts of men. Desiring what is impossible to attain, they will capture the very souls of their kin."

He scribbled madly, taking note of each detail, excitement burning through his body, feeling no cold in spite of the gathering snow. Jonas himself was recording the first prophecy that had been spoken in centuries.

"Trapped, many will die at their hands, unknown to the one fore-told. This continual dark will bring the cold."

Jonas blinked. Wait a minute...

"But when all hope seems lost, and the world knows nothing but white, there will come one who will bring green." Pencil quivering, Jonas's mouth gaped open. This wasn't a new prophecy; it was *the* prophecy. The one that started their journey, the one that set them on their quest to save the world from the cold. *"One who must follow the paths of the sky. One who is all light, to stand to the one who is all dark, of which there will be two."*

It was *more*. Jonas continued his scribbling, writing down the familiar words of the prophecy he had heard his entire life. The prophecy his parents had died for. The prophecy that sent him across all of Mothmar, leading him to this very moment.

"One who possesses the three as one, who will save us all through the antithesis of darkness. Unaided by this world's gifts, filled with the one—the way that connects one to all, three in one. You will know this one by the mark, known by the one who brings the white."

With a groan Seer Brotnur crumpled to the ground, his head hitting the cobblestones, the sound of it made Jonas flinch. He ran to his mentor, eyes wide in panic, heart thumping like a herd of mammoths. But his Seer lay still, his soul having found safe harbor with the Celestials.

Jonas held up the parchment, eyes scanning the words once more. *"Unaided by this world's gifts..."* Jonas said to no one. Vinur whimpered and nudged the body of the man before them. "She was never supposed to get all three Gifts."

Jonas's eyes shifted over the parchment, pathways of under-standing connecting through his mind, theories falling into place, solidifying as reality. "There's another Gift. A final, better one." The thought should have rung with heresy, but instead it filled him with surety; it rang with truth.

He leaned over and squeezed the hand of his mentor, tears of both sorrow and joy trickling down his face.

Scrambling to his feet, parchment held high in the air, Jonas, Seer-in-Training, raced back to his small home in Endirinn with news that would change the world.

SON
OF THE
STARS
A MOTHMAR NOVEL
BOOK THREE
AMANDA AULER

THE MACHINE

E RVAL'S RING-LADEN HAND RELEASED the ball toward the far side of the room at speed. *Rat-tat-pop!* It hit the stone of the basement wall and the ground near Phineas's feet before returning to Erval.

His old steward yelped, and a tool clattered to the floor. "Sire!"

Erval chuckled. "Just making sure you're awake, Phin."

The man grumbled, retrieved the tool, and continued his work.

It was finally ready. The machine he had spent so long working on, honing, and tuning. The device that would give him access to every beating heart, soul, and breath. Well, almost.

Erval squinted at his steward, whose hands worried over the gears and tubing at the back of the intricate contraption. Phineas had made promise after promise over the years, yet there was always something keeping it from working as it should. Erval recalled the first person he had ever positioned in the throne-like chair, other than himself, of course. She had been so young yet so stuffed with others' years. He had thought her preparations sufficient.

He was wrong. Strapped to the chair, she'd had no way to escape as the device sucked her dry until she was but skin stretched across cracked bones. Erval had been able to tether to hundreds in just those few moments, an all-consuming power like nothing he'd experienced before—at least until the girl expired and his tether snapped. Leaving Erval chasing that rush of power ever since.

He knew it truly then: he could not be the one to secure himself to the device. Not only because of the danger it would present to his body, but more importantly, how fast it would diminish the souls he had accrued. So much time and effort spent, shoring up years for generations. To lose them in one fell swoop would not only be foolish but pointless. How would he be able to use his Taka Reu if he himself were the conduit? What a waste that would be.

But now... Erval studied his steward, calculating the amount of years stored in Phineas's stout body. Success would be guaranteed, but at what cost? Phineas was the closest Erval had to a confidant, something resembling a partner. And then there was Phineas's aversion to performing the Taking. Ever since the first time in the cells of Thonethren, Erval had known his steward hadn't been cut from the same shrewd cloth as he.

No, there was only one other person that could don the helm and imbue enough energy into the machine before him.

Pallah.

He ground his teeth and threw the ball again.

Rat-tat-pop! Back to his hand it flew.

"I found out where she's been hiding, you know," he told Phineas, and the tinkerer stilled. "All these years later." Erval wouldn't need to elaborate, Phineas knew of whom he spoke.

"Did you?"

Erval pulled the finnevel from his breast pocket, so convenient-ly small he usually carried it on his person. The device fit over his eye, a monocle of power. It amplified his tether far and wide until it could reach even the most obscure places on the map.

"Perhaps..." The steward held up a hand then seemed to think better of it.

Erval rolled his eyes, halfway to securing the device. "Prob-lem?"

"Just...would you not kill her if you connected now? A straight connection to an adult has always proved fatal."

"I was able to connect to Solyana," he said with a shrug.

"Yes, but you had appeared to her in a physical form before latching onto her mind. Even if it was as a giant trapped in magma, it kept her alive."

Erval pursed his lips. He was tempted to reveal to his steward he had honed his Mann Tala to such a razor-edged point, adults no longer perished at the sound of his voice. Not all of them, anyway.

"Solyana had still been young," Phineas added, pushing his spectacles up the bridge of his nose. "I just wouldn't want you to kill Pallah, after all this time."

A laugh escaped Erval, so forceful he dropped his ball. "That would be hilarious."

"Quite." Phineas gave him a sideways look.

"Don't you worry your little head, Phin. If she's put in this much work to stay hidden from me, she's probably drinking the tea anyway."

"Right, sire."

"I'm sure there's a child around that cloaked valley, though." He fitted the finnevel over his eye and extended the metal arm behind one ear. "One that dislikes the taste of the tea. I'll just pay them a little visit is all." He relaxed into his chair with a sigh.

"You'd be showing your hand." Phineas didn't look at him, his eyes trained on his work. "She would know it's you."

"Well, that's the point, isn't it?" Erval's mouth curved into a languid smile. "Why should I waste any more time trying to track her down when one connection to some unsuspecting brat will convince her to come to me?"

Now Phineas turned to him, his eyebrows lifting in confusion. How could a man be so equally genius and daft at once?

"I'll spell it out for you, then." Erval pushed the finnevel up to his hairline, retrieved the ball at his feet, and began tossing it between his hands. "I cannot tether to her, as she's hidden herself so well. However, I've tethered in that valley before; I know where it is on the map. The news of my voice peppering thoughts would surely not escape her notice. Then she will come to me. It will be to kill me, but nevertheless..."

Phineas's mouth straightened to a grim line. "To kill you?"

"To finish the botched job she did so long ago, yes." A cold smile. "She's right to hide. She knows I'd make her life a living nightmare, even from this distance."

"Wouldn't she just keep running? It's been almost two centuries, and the tactic has served her."

"She won't run. Not if I tell her I have her brother."

The steward's eyes bulged from behind his spectacles. "You do?"

"Keep up with me, Phin! We just discussed Solyana, and you know she never returned from the mountain. Pallah's brother is a lost cause." He grinned wickedly. "However, she doesn't have to know that."

Erval waited on a laugh or at least a smirk from his steward—but none came. In fact, it looked as if the man was…sweating? Erval shook his head.

"What Pallah doesn't know won't hurt her—but it will hurry her."

Phineas wiped his hands on a small oily rag that hung from his apron. The torch protruding from the wall flickered, casting the small man a much larger shadow. "Brilliant, sire," he said quietly.

"Oh, don't flatter me." Erval rolled his eyes. "Are you quite finished?"

"I believe so. But until I have a suitable test subject, I won't know if—"

"Then what are you waiting for? Grab someone and test it out."

"Who do you—"

"The guard outside the door, a man from the cells, a woman off the street—do you think I care, Phineas? Do you think I lie awake at night feeling remorse or languishing in regret for the souls I have Taken and used?"

Phineas seemed to shrink into his skin.

"Grow up or get out. I have had enough of your sniveling." He turned and exited the dank basement, leaving his steward alone. He had felt discontentment from the man for years now, though he tried his best to ignore it. It was as if he purposefully wielded incompetence, as if he weaponized mediocrity.

He lowered the finnevel back over one eye as he ascended the staircase. Though the small device could be used just about any-where, the connections it made occurred far more easily when he was in the observatory. High above spires and roofs, the device did its job with an efficiency lost in the basement of the castle.

His boots clacked as he went, heralding his arrival and sending his guards scurrying like rats to attention.

He had toyed with the idea of a new steward over the years, with how much trouble Phineas seemed to enjoy injecting into his life. Sometimes the man's small rebellions were welcomed; it's not like Erval wanted zero resistance on his chosen paths—where was the game in that? But the persistent perspiring and quiet conflicts were beginning to truly grate. Erval considered. If he were to use The Taking on Phineas himself... He couldn't help the chill that shook him with pleasure—he would truly live forever. What was Phineas's lifespan up to now? Four hundred years? Five?

Erval's hair slid across his brow as he shook his head, dispelling the thought. He had, at some point, come to associate his own humanity with the rotund tinkerer. The steward reminded him where he'd come from, how long it had taken him to get here, and where he still intended to go. Doing away with him so quickly would be...irreverent.

Though, if the man continued to be so obstinate, not out of the question.

He wound his way through the stone hallways and corridors until he found himself at the highest point of his domain. Beneath the convex glass ceiling, plants trailed from hanging pots above a large map of Mothmar lain flat on a table. The sun streamed through the room, and Erval reveled in the warmth after having been underground for some time.

He cracked his neck side to side, and with the finnevel still fitted to his face, he settled into a high back chair that overlooked all of Thonethren. He focused his vision, closing one eye, the other staring straight into Kjarn's Eye.

Color, shape, and a vast stretch of land flashed before his vision as Erval covered distance like a falcon; over rolling hills and snow-sprinkled treetops his mind's eye flew. He searched, farther and farther south, until he found nothing but a land of fog and distorted reality. As if nothing were present—an empty void.

"Clever girl," he whispered to himself. "Hiding behind your masks. With all you told me of that place, I never counted on you returning to it. Though, I'll concede. Going back to the place of your birth, only to conquer it—we are more alike than you think."

His tether, amplified by the finnevel, failed to find whatever Pallah had created. What had she used? What Gift had she manipulated to make such a fortress? Then Erval felt him. A small boy, no more than four years of age, just at the edge of the barrier. Perhaps wandering without his mother? Erval grinned to himself and dove in, connecting to the boy's mind, to his soul.

There was a spark, a jolt, and Erval saw through the boy's very own eyes. "Hello there, son."

The boy's head whipped side to side, searching for the voice.

He was alone. Perfect.

"Listen close, boy. I have a message for you."

Continue in *Son of the Stars*, the third and final book of **The Mothmar Trilogy!**

A Letter to the Reader

If you made it this far it means you've read not one, but two of my books. How can I ever thank you? I am beyond grateful for your kindness. And yes, I know this book ends in much the same *cliffhangery* way as the first. Don't fret, all is answered in book three, *Son of the Stars*.

If you'd like to keep up to date on any future projects or events, please sign up for my newsletter. And if you could rate and review *Children of the Earth* on Amazon and Goodreads, it would help get this book in the right hands!

Your eyes be upward,
Amanda Auler

Review
Here!

Newsletter
Sign Up

ACKNOWLEDGEMENTS

To The Creator above, may my writing be a testament to your goodness and glory, a reflection of your work in me.

To my husband, until the very end and all that comes before it. Nothing can keep me from you.

To my children, you are my inspiration, my hope, and my world.

To Tim, Lisa, John, and Karen, the best grandparents to my sons, and my most outspoken and loving supporters. I could not have done this without you.

To Addison, Moriah, Stacey, Emily, Emma, Angela, and Kayla, without your early input and help, this book would be half of what it is. Thank you for lending your time and your wisdom.

To all my wonderful friends on Instagram, you've truly made my time on that app well worth it. Your encouragement, kindness, and support speaks life into my soul.

To Eva, thank you for transforming into whatever editor I need at the time, even if you say you're bad at it. Finding you was the best thing that's happened to my writing career. Truly.

To Nem, Timea, Sarah, and Rebecca, your art elevated this book to a whole new level. Thank you for pouring your heart into it!

To everyone who supported me on Kickstarter, this book is beautiful because of you. (Find your names on the following page.)

And finally, to my ARC readers and Street Team, thank you for being people I can entrust my book to and for writing such amazing reviews. I am in your debt.

Kickstarter Acknowledgments

Abigail Hobbs
Addison Horner
Adelina Milano
Alaina Piscioneri
Alecia
Alex Brazle
Alex & Emma Clark
Alicia Nichols
Alyssa Pressley
Angela Morse
Angela Riesberg
Angelica Meade
Anna Fetterhoff
Anna Layton
Ashley Cook
Ashley Sills
Bill Schmitt and Family
Bina
Bradey Hesse
Brenna Greenfield
Brittany Mack
Brooke Katz
Callum Paff
Carl Hicks
Céline Vangelabbeek
Charles Elbert Norton III
Christi
Christine Morrison
Christopher Clayton
Claire Von Almay
Corinne Sprenger
Cortney Cortopassi
Courtney Easters
Craig Smith
Dakota Houston
Dalessi Markham
Dallas
Danielle Bullen
Elizabeth Evans
Ellen Pilcher
Ellie Tran
Emily Blackburn
Emily Jacobson
Emma Sture
Evelyn Gerber

Fiona Johnston
Gerald P. McDaniel
Hannah Bihn
Hannah Pennington
Ian Pendleton
IndifferentMaw
Irinel Finco
Isabel Kishi
Jake and Rachel Swink
Jake Booher
Janet Dray
Jason
Jen Woodrum
Jennifer Hoffer
Jeremiah Daniel Sater
John & Karen Auler
Jon Jackson
Jordynn Allen
Josie Livengood
Josie Young
Kaleb & Ashley Dekker
Karna Hoffman
Kate Foster
Kayla Ann
Kelly Strangfeld
Kimberly Werntz
Laura S.
Lauren Martin
Lauren McCoy
Laurie Phillips
Lissette Buckley
Liz DuRoss
Madeleine Jensen
Maud Lelarge
Maelys Antoine Dominique
Maggie Martinescu
Mallory Wanless
Mary Galat
Marybeth Martin
Meagan
Megan Astell
Megan Iffland
Melanie Stockman
Michelle Forman

Michelle Piper
Mike McCue
Molly Killian
Mom & Dad Swink
Morgan Cameron
Moriah
Nathan and Sam Walsh
Nicole McNaughton
Nirkatze
Olivia Reiff
Paige Searcy
Paige Wright
Patrick Coffey
Phil & Elisabeth Drake
Rachel Barrow
Rachel Carter
Rachel Hansen
Rachel and Amaryllis Hikida
Rachel Nalevanko
Rachel Vance
Rachelle Yutzy
RC McKinney
Rebecca Thompson
R.J. Lavender
Ryan H.
Sara Rainbolt
Sarah Ann Cools
Sarah Denk
Sarah Grimaldi
Sarah
Scott Casey
Shanon Brown
Sister Elli Saltyprose
Stephanie Crachiolo
Stephanie Meredith
Stephanie Wokan-Sallis
Tammy Rhyne
Tenko Nikolov
Theresa Ortiz
Tyler Mullis
Victoria Clemm
Victoria Dixon
Vivian Montez
Yvonne Coyle
Zach Grizzell

ABOUT THE AUTHOR

Amanda Auler lives in Sanford, North Carolina with her husband and four growing boys. Though Amanda writes for every audience, her roots in Christianity shine through her work as she explores themes of redemption, forgiveness, and grace. When she's not writing you can find her baking cookies, drinking too much coffee, and staying up past her bedtime to watch anime with her husband.

Amanda's Links